'Baldacci is still peerless'
Sunday Times

'Top book! Thrill a minute, page-turning stuff'
Sun

'One of the world's biggest-selling thriller writers,
Baldacci needs no introduction . . . Brilliant plotting,
heart-grabbing action and characters to die for'
Daily Mail

King
and
Maxwell

David Baldacci is a worldwide bestselling novelist. With his books published in over 45 different languages and in more than 80 countries, and with over 110 million copies in print, he is one of the world's favourite storytellers. David is also the co-founder, along with his wife, of the Wish You Well Foundation, a non-profit organization, dedicated to eliminating illiteracy across America. Still a resident of his native Virginia, he invites you to visit him at www.DavidBaldacci.com, and his foundation at www.WishYouWellFoundation.org, and to look into its programme to spread books across America at www.FeedingBodyandMind.com.

DAVID BALDACCI

King
and
Maxwell

PAN BOOKS

First published 2013 by Grand Central Publishing, USA

First published in the UK 2013 by Macmillan

This edition published 2014 by Pan Books
an imprint of Pan Macmillan, a division of Macmillan Publishers Limited
Pan Macmillan, 20 New Wharf Road, London N1 9RR
Basingstoke and Oxford
Associated companies throughout the world
www.panmacmillan.com

ISBN 978-1-4472-6505-4

1 3 5 7 9 8 6 4 2

A CIP catalogue record for this book is available from the British Library.

Typeset by Ellipsis Digital Limited, Glasgow
Printed and bound by CPI Group (UK) Ltd, Croydon, CR0 4YY

King
and
Maxwell

1

Forty-eight hundred pounds.

That was roughly how much the cargo in the crate weighed. It was off-loaded from the tractor-trailer by forklift and placed in the back of the smaller box truck. The rear door was closed and secured with two different locks, one a key, the other a combo. Each lock was rated to be tamper-proof. The reality was, given time, any lock could be beaten and any door broken through.

The man climbed into the driver's seat of the truck, closed the door, locked it, started the engine, revved the motor, cranked the AC, and adjusted his seat. He had a long way to drive and not much time to get there. And it was hot as hell. Maybe hotter. Waves of visible heat shimmered, distorting the landscape. He didn't focus on that, because he might just start puking.

He would have preferred an armed escort. Perhaps an Abrams tank for good measure, but that was not in the budget or the mission plan. The ground was rocky and, in the distance, mountainous. The roads had more potholes than asphalt. He had guns and plenty of ammo. But he was only one man with only one trigger finger.

He no longer wore the uniform. He had taken it off for the last time about an hour ago. He fingered his "new" clothes. They were worn and not overly clean. He pulled out his map and spread it out on the front seat as the tractor-trailer pulled away.

He was now alone in the middle of nowhere in a country that was still largely entrenched in the ninth century.

As he stared out the windshield at the imposing terrain, he briefly thought about how he had ended up here. Back then it had seemed brave, even heroic. Right now he felt like the world's biggest idiot for accepting a mission that held such a low chance of survival.

The reality was he was here. He was alone. He had a job to do and he had better get to it. And if he died, well, his mortal worries were over and he would have at least one person to mourn him.

In addition to the map, he had GPS. However, it was spotty out here, as though the satellites above didn't know there was actually a country down here that required folks getting from point A to point B. Hence the old-fashioned paper version on the front seat.

He put the truck in drive and thought about what was in the crate. It was more than two tons of very special cargo. Without it he was certainly a dead man.

Even with it, he might be a dead man, but his odds were far better by having it.

As he passed over the rough road, he calculated he had twenty hours' hard driving ahead of him. There were no highways here. The pace would be plodding and bumpy. And there might even be folks shooting at him.

There also would be people waiting for him at the end. The cargo would be transferred, and he would be transferred along with it. Communications had been made. Promises given. Alliances formed. Now it was just up to him to talk a good game and the others to keep their word.

That had all sounded good in the endless meetings with people in shirts and ties and with their smartphones jangling nonstop. Out here alone with nothing around him except the bleakest landscape one could imagine, it all sounded delusional.

But he was still a soldier so he soldiered on.

He worked his way toward the mountains in the distance. He carried not one piece of personal information on him. Yet he did have papers that should allow him safe passage through the area.

Should, not would.

If he was stopped, he would have to talk his way out of it if the papers were deemed insufficient. If they asked to see what was in the truck, he had to refuse. If they insisted, he had a little metal box with a black matte finish. It had a switch on the side and one red button on top. When he engaged the switch and pushed down the button, everything would still be okay. If his finger came off the button while the device was still engaged, he and everything else within twenty square meters would disappear.

He drove for twelve straight hours and saw not a single living person. He glimpsed a camel and a donkey wandering around. He saw a dead snake. He observed a rotted human body, its carcass being reduced to bone by vultures. He was surprised there was only one dead body. Normally there would have been a lot more. This country had seen its share of slaughter. Every so often another country tried to invade it. They quickly won the war and then lost everything else and went home with their tanks tucked between their legs.

During the dozen hours, he saw the sun set and then rise again. He was heading east so he was driving right into it. He lowered the visor on the truck and kept going. He played CD after CD of rock music, blasting the truck cab. He listened to Meat Loaf's "Paradise by the Dashboard Light" twenty times in a row, as loud as his ears could stand. He smiled every time the baseball announcer's voice came on. It was a little bit of home out here.

Despite Meat Loaf screaming at him, his eyelids still drooped and he kept jolting back awake after his truck had strayed across the road. Luckily there was no other traffic. There weren't many people who would want to live around here. Foreboding would be one way to describe it. Insanely dangerous would be another, more accurate one.

Thirteen hours into the trip he grew so tired that he decided to pull off the road to take a quick nap. He had made good progress and had a little time to spare. But as he was about to stop he looked down the road and saw what was coming. His weariness vanished. His nap would have to wait.

The open-bed truck was speeding directly at him. The truck was driving squarely in the center of the road, blocking passage in either direction.

Two men sat in front, three stood in the bed, all holding subguns. They were the Welcome Wagon, Afghan-style.

He pulled partially off the road, rolled down the window, let the heat waves push in, and waited. He turned off the CD player, and Meat Loaf's baritone vanished. These men would not appreciate the rocker's prodigious pipes or lustful lyrics.

The smaller truck stopped beside his. While two of the turbaned men with subguns pointed their weapons at him, the man in the truck's passenger seat climbed out and walked to the cab door of the other vehicle. He also wore a turban; the bands of sweat soaked into the material spoke of the prolonged intensity of the heat.

The driver looked at the man as he approached.

He reached for the sheaf of papers on the front seat. They sat next to his fully loaded Glock with one round already in the chamber. He hoped he didn't have to use it, because a pistol against a subgun would only have one outcome—his death.

"Papers?" the man said in Pashto.

He handed them through. They were appropriately signed and distinctively sealed by each of the tribal chieftains who controlled these stretches of land. He was counting on it that they would be honored. He was encouraged by the fact that in this part of the world, not abiding by a chieftain's orders often resulted in the death of those who disobeyed. And death here was nearly always brutal and almost never immediate. They liked for you to feel yourself die, as they said around here.

The turbaned man was drenched in sweat, his eyes red and his clothes as dirty as his face. He read through the papers, blinking rapidly when he saw the august signatories.

He looked up at the driver and appraised him keenly, then he handed back the papers. The man's gaze went to the back of the truck, his look a curious one. The driver's hand closed around the small black box and he pressed the switch on the side, engaging it. The man spoke again in Pashto. The driver shook his head and said that opening the truck was not possible. It was locked and he did not have a key or the combo required.

The man pointed to his gun and said that that was his key.

The driver's finger pressed down on the red button. If they shot him, his finger would release and this "idiot switch" feature would detonate the explosives and kill them all.

He said in Pashto, "The tribal leaders were clear. The cargo could not be revealed until its final destination. Very clear," he added for emphasis. "If you have a problem, you need to take it up with them."

The man considered this and slid his hand down to his holstered sidearm.

The driver tried to keep his breathing normal and his limbs from twitching, but being seconds from getting blown into oblivion did certain physiological things to the body that he could not control.

Five tense seconds passed during which it was not clear if the turban would stand down or not.

The man finally withdrew, climbed back into the truck, and said something to the driver. Moments later the truck sped off, kicking up a cloud of dust behind its rear wheels.

The driver disengaged the detonator and waited until they were nearly out of sight before putting the truck back in gear. He drove off slowly at first, and then punched the gas. His weariness was gone.

He didn't need the music anymore. He lowered the AC because he suddenly felt rather cold. He followed his directions, keeping to the exact route. It did not pay to stray out here. He scanned the horizon for any other pickup trucks with armed men coming his way, but saw none. He hoped that word had been communicated along the route that the cargo truck was to be given safe passage.

Nearly eight hours later he arrived at his final destination. The dusk was starting to gather and the wind was picking up. The sky was streaked with clouds, and the rain looked to be a few minutes from bucketing down.

When he arrived here, he had expected one precise thing to happen.

It didn't.

2

The first thing to go wrong was his running out of gas as he pulled through the stone building's open overhead door. He had extra fuel tanks, but apparently someone had miscalculated.

The second thing to go wrong was the gun being shoved in his face.

This was no turban toting a subgun. It was a white man like him with a .357 pistol, its hammer already pulled back.

"Is there a problem?" the driver said.

"Not for us," said the man, who was heavyset and jowly and looked closer to forty than thirty.

"Us?" He looked around and saw other white guys creeping out of the shadows. They were all armed, and every gun they had was pointing at him.

This many white faces here stuck out like a planet going out of its orbit.

"This is not part of the plan," the driver said.

The other man held out a cred pack. "There's been a change in plan."

The driver studied the ID card and badge. It showed

that the man's name was Tim Simons and identified him as being an agent with the CIA. He said, "If we're on the same side, why the gun in my face?"

"In this part of the world I've learned not to trust anybody. Out, now!"

The driver slung his fully loaded knapsack over his shoulder and stepped down onto the dirt floor holding two things.

One was his Glock, which was useless with so many guns centered on him.

The second item was the black box. That was entirely useful. In fact, it was the only real bargaining chip he had. He engaged the detonator and pressed down the button.

He held it up to Simons.

"Fail-safe," he said. "Red button gets released, we all get vaporized. Truck is wired all the way around with cakes of Semtex. Enough to make this just a hole in the ground."

"Bullshit," countered Simons.

"Guess you weren't entirely wired in on the op."

"I think I was."

"Then think again. Look under the wheel wells."

Simons nodded at a colleague, who drew a flashlight and ducked under the truck's right rear wheel well.

He backed out and turned. His expression said it all.

The armed men looked back at the driver. Their superior numbers had just been rendered irrelevant.

He knew it, but he also knew this advantage was precarious. A game of chicken could only have, at best, one winner. But it could likely also have two losers. And he was running out of time. He could sense this in the fingers gliding to triggers, in the backward steps the men were trying to make surreptitiously. He could read their minds in every movement.

Get out of the Semtex's explosive radius and either let him detonate and kill himself or take him out with a kill shot and hopefully save the cargo. Either way they would live, which would be their primary objective. There would be other cargo to hijack, but they could not conjure additional lives.

"Unless you can run a lot faster than Usain Bolt, you'll never get outside the blast zone in time," he said. He held the box higher. "And we'll have an eternity to think about our sins."

Simons said, "We want what's in the truck. You give us that, you go free."

"I'm not sure how that would work."

Simons nervously eyed the box. "There're two pickup trucks parked in the far corner over there. Both are fully fueled with extra cans in the back and each has a GPS. They were our rides getting here, but you take one of them. Your choice."

The driver eyed the black truck. Next to it was a green pickup.

"And where exactly do I take it?" he asked.

"I'm assuming out of this shithole."

11

"I have a job to do."

"That job has changed."

"Why don't we just end this?" He started to lessen the pressure on the button.

"Wait," said Simons. "Wait." He held up his hand.

"I'm waiting."

"Just take a truck and get out of here. Your cargo is not worth dying for, is it?"

"Maybe it is."

"You've got a family back in the States."

"How do you know that?"

"I just do. And I have to believe you want to get back to them."

"And how do I explain losing the cargo?"

"You won't have to, trust me," replied Simons.

"That's the problem, I don't trust you."

"Then we're all going to die right here. It's that simple."

The driver eyed the pickup trucks. He didn't believe anything he had been told. But he desperately wanted to get out of this alive, if only to make things right later.

Simons said, "Look, we're obviously not the Taliban. Hell, I'm from Nebraska. My creds are the real deal. We're on the same side here, okay? Why else would I be here?"

The driver finally said, "So you want me to just withdraw quietly from the field?"

"That was my offer."

"How do you propose doing this?"

"First thing, don't release the button," advised Simons.

"Then don't pull your triggers." He edged toward the pickup trucks. The men parted to allow him passage.

"I'll be taking the green truck," he said abruptly. He saw Simons give a nearly imperceptible flinch, which was good. He'd made the right decision. The black truck was obviously booby-trapped.

He reached the green truck and eyed the ignition. The keys were in there. There was also a GPS mounted on the dash.

Simons called out, "What's the range on the detonator?"

"I'll keep that to myself."

He threw his knapsack on the front seat, climbed into the truck, and started the engine. He eyed the gas gauge. Full. He kept his free hand ready with the detonator.

Simons said, "How can we trust you not to detonate when you're well away?"

"It's a question of range," he replied.

"Which you haven't told us."

"So you just have to trust me, Nebraska. Just like I have to trust you that this truck isn't wired to blow up as soon as I'm out of here. Or maybe it was the other one that was."

He pushed the gas pedal to the floor and the truck

roared out of the stone building. He expected shots to be fired at him. None came.

He imagined they believed that would lead to their deaths when he released the button in retaliation.

When he was far enough away, he looked at the black box. If the guys back there were CIA, there was a lot more going on here than he cared to think about right now. But he wanted to see it through. And the only way to do that was to let this play out. And stay alive.

He disengaged the detonator and tossed it on the front seat.

Now he just had to get the hell out of here.

He hoped that was possible. Most people came to this part of the world simply to kill or be killed.

3

Sean King drove while Michelle Maxwell rode shot-gun.

This was the reverse of what the pair normally did. She usually drove the car, like she was piloting a ride at Daytona. And Sean hung on for dear life and mumbled his prayers, but without much confidence that they would be answered.

There was a good reason for his driving tonight, and for the last twenty-one nights. Michelle was simply not herself, at least not yet. She was getting there, only more slowly than she wanted.

He looked at her. "How you doing?"

She stared straight ahead. "I am armed. So you ask me that one more time and I *will* shoot you, Sean."

"I'm just concerned, okay?"

"I know that, Sean. And I appreciate it. But I've been out of rehab for three weeks. I think I'm good to go. And that's what your concern can do: *Go*."

"Your injuries were life threatening, Michelle. You almost didn't make it. You nearly bled out. Trust me, I was there for every second of it. So three weeks out of rehab after something like that is actually not very long."

Michelle touched her lower back and then her upper thigh. There were scars there. There would always be scars there. The memory of how she had come by these injuries was as vivid as the initial knife thrust into her back. It had been done by someone she thought was an ally.

Yet she was alive. And Sean *had* been with her every step of the way. Only now his hovering was starting to annoy her.

"I know. But it was two full months of rehab. And I'm a fast healer. You of all people should understand that by now."

"It was just close, Michelle. Way too close."

"How many times have I almost lost you?" she said, shooting him a glance. "It's part of what we do. It comes with the territory. If we want safe, we have to get into another line of work."

Sean looked out through the windshield as the rain continued bucketing down. The night was cold, gloomy, the clouds shifty as a coyote. They were driving through a particularly lonely area of northern Virginia on their way back from meeting with a former client, Edgar Roy. They had saved him from a death sentence. He had been as suitably appreciative as any high-functioning autistic savant with severely limited social skills could be.

"Edgar looked good," said Michelle.

"He looked really good considering the alternative of lethal injection," replied Sean, who seemed relieved by the change in topic.

Sean took a turn too fast on the rain-slicked, curvy road and Michelle grabbed her armrest for support.

"Slow it down," she warned.

He feigned astonishment. "Words I never thought I would hear leave your mouth."

"I drive fast because I know how to."

"I've got the injuries and therapy bills to prove otherwise," he shot back.

She gave him a scowl. "So, what now, since we've finished all the work on Edgar Roy's matter?"

"We continue our careers as private investigators. Both Peter Bunting and the U.S. government were very generous with their payments to us, but we're socking that away to either retire on or spend on a rainy day."

Michelle looked to the stormy sky. "Rainy day? Then let's go buy a boat. We might need it to get home."

Sean would have said something back, but he was suddenly preoccupied.

"Damn!"

He cut the wheel hard to the left and the Land Cruiser spun sideways across the slick roadway.

"Turn into it," advised Michelle calmly.

Sean turned into the spin and quickly regained control of the vehicle. He applied the brakes and brought them to a stop on the shoulder.

"What the hell was that?" he snapped.

"You mean *who* was that," answered Michelle.

She opened the door and leaned out into the rain.

"Michelle, wait," said Sean.

"Point the lights to the right. Quick!"

She slammed the door shut, and Sean drove the vehicle back onto the road.

"Hit your brights," she told him.

He did so. The lights swelled in intensity, letting them see farther in front of them with as much clarity as the darkness and rain would allow.

"There," said Michelle, pointing to the right. "Go, go."

Sean hit the gas and the Land Cruiser sped forward.

The person running down the right shoulder of the road looked back only once. But it was enough.

"It's a kid," said Sean in amazement.

"It's a teenager," corrected Michelle.

"Well, he was almost a dead teenager," added Sean sternly.

"Sean, he's got a gun."

Sean leaned closer to the windshield and saw the weapon in the boy's right hand. "This does not look good," he said.

"He looks terrified."

"He's running in the middle of a thunderstorm with a metal object in his hand. He should be scared. And on top of that I almost hit him and then he wouldn't be scared, just dead."

"Get closer."

"What?"

"Get closer."

"Why would I do that? He's got a gun, Michelle."

"We have guns too. Just get closer."

He sped up while Michelle rolled down the window.

A spear of lightning lit the sky with a billion-candlepower burst of energy followed by a crack of thunder so loud it sounded like a skyscraper imploding.

"Hey," Michelle yelled at the boy. "Hey!"

The teen looked back again, his face whitewashed in the glare of the headlights.

"What happened?" yelled Michelle. "Are you okay?"

The boy's answer was to point the gun at them. But he didn't fire. He left the road and cut across a field, his feet slipping and sliding over the wet grass.

"I'm calling the cops," said Sean.

"Just wait," she replied. "Stop the truck."

Sean slowed the Land Cruiser and pulled to a stop a few feet later.

Michelle hopped out of the vehicle.

"What the hell are you doing?" Sean cried out.

"He's obviously in trouble. I'm going to find out why."

"Did it occur to you that he might be in trouble because he just shot somebody and is running from the scene of the crime?"

"Don't think so."

He looked at her incredulously. "You don't think so? Based on what?"

"I'll be back."

"What? Michelle, wait."

He made a grab for her arm, but missed.

The next instant she was sprinting across the field. In a few seconds she was soaked to the skin in the driving rain.

Sean slapped his palm against the steering wheel in disbelief. He yelled at the window. "Do you *have* a death wish?" But Michelle was long since out of earshot.

He calmed, studied the lay of the land for a few moments, and sped off, hanging a right at the next intersection and punching the gas so hard the rear of the truck spun out. He righted it and drove off, cursing his partner loudly with every turn of the wheel.

4

Michelle had chased many things in her life. As a track star and later Olympic rower, she had constantly pitted herself against others in races. As a cop in Tennessee she had run down her share of felons fleeing the scenes of their crimes. As a Secret Service agent she had been fleet of foot next to limos carrying important leaders.

Tonight, though, she was competing against a long-legged teenager with the boundless energy and fresh knees of youth who had a substantial head start and was running as if the devil were on his heels. And her feet kept slipping with every stride over the wet terrain.

"Wait," she called out as she caught a glimpse of him before he changed direction and disappeared down a path through some trees.

He didn't wait. He simply sped up.

Michelle, despite her protestations to Sean, was not 100 percent. Her back hurt. Her leg hurt. Her lungs were burning. And it didn't help that the wind and rain were blinding her.

She raced down the path and just in case drew her gun. She always felt better with her Sig in hand. She redoubled her efforts, fought through the pain and fatigue that were coursing through her, and markedly closed the gap between them. A lightning strike followed by a crack of thunder momentarily distracted her. A tree on the side of the path, punished by stiff winds, started to topple; she found an extra burst of speed and flashed past it. The shallow-rooted tree slammed into the dirt about ten feet behind her but its thick branches missed her by only a few inches. Any of them could have crushed her skull.

That had been close.

The teen had fallen when the tree crashed, yet now he was up and running once more. But the gap between them was narrower.

Calling on reserves she wasn't sure she possessed anymore, she propelled herself forward as if she had been shot out of a mortar. She leapt and hit him in the back of the legs. He sprawled forward into the dirt while Michelle pitched sideways and then rose, her lungs burning, her breath coming in gulps. She bent over but kept her gaze on him, her gun ready, because she could see he still had his, although one glance confirmed that she didn't have to worry about him firing it.

He turned over, his butt in the dirt, his knees bent to his chest.

"Who the hell are you? Why are you chasing me?"

"Why are you running around with a gun in the middle of a storm?" she countered.

He looked very young, maybe fifteen. His auburn hair was plastered to his freckled face.

"Just leave me alone," he cried out.

He rose and Michelle straightened. They were barely three feet apart. At five foot ten Michelle was at least three inches taller than he was, although his long legs and size twelve feet promised that he would probably zip right through the six-foot mark before he was done growing.

"What's your name?" she asked.

He started to back up. "Just please leave me alone."

"I'm trying to help you. My partner and I almost hit you back there."

"Your partner?"

Michelle decided a lie was better than the truth right now. "I'm a cop."

"A cop?" He looked at her suspiciously. "Let me see some ID."

She put her hand inside her jacket and withdrew her PI license. In the dark she hoped it would look legit enough. She flashed it.

"Now will you tell me what this is about? Maybe I can help you."

He looked down, his thin chest rising and falling quickly with each of his uneven breaths.

"Nobody can help me."

"That's a big statement to make. Things can't be that bad."

His lips started trembling. "Look, I…I need to get back home."

"Is that where you ran away from?"

He nodded.

"And where you got the gun?"

"It belonged to my dad."

Michelle pulled her wet hair out of her eyes. "We can give you a ride there. Just tell us where it is."

"No, I'll walk."

"That's not a good idea. Not in a storm like this. You might get hit by a car or have a tree fall on you, both of which have already almost happened. What's your name?"

He said nothing.

She said, "My name is Michelle. Michelle Maxwell."

"Are you really a cop?"

"I used to be one. After that I was a Secret Service agent."

"For real?" Now he sounded like a teenager. An awed teenager.

"Yep. I'm a private investigator now. But I still act like a cop sometimes. Now what's your name?"

"Tyler, Tyler Wingo," he said.

"Okay, Tyler Wingo, that's a good start. Now let's go to my car and…" She glanced behind him but had no time to say anything.

Sean grabbed Tyler from behind, knocked the pistol from his grip, kicked it away, and twirled him around.

Staggered, Tyler started to run off again, but Sean clamped a hand around his wrist. At six-two and over two hundred pounds, he had the size to keep the kid from going anywhere.

"Let me go!" yelled Tyler.

"Sean, it's okay," said Michelle. "Let him go."

Sean reluctantly released his grip, then bent down and picked up the gun. He looked at it. "What the hell is this?"

"A German Mauser," said Tyler, scowling up at him.

"Without a trigger," pointed out Michelle. "Saw that in the headlights. Makes it a little hard to use as a weapon unless you throw it at somebody."

"Right," said Sean.

"Tyler was just going to tell me where he lives so we can drive him there," said Michelle.

"Tyler?" said Sean.

"Tyler Wingo," said Tyler sulkily. "And you better not have damaged my dad's gun. It's a collectible."

Sean slipped the gun into his waistband. "Which made it pretty dumb to run around in the rain with it," he pointed out.

Tyler looked at Michelle. "Can you just give me a lift home?"

"Yes," she said. "And maybe on the way you can tell us what happened."

"I already told you, there's nothing you can do."

"You're right, there is absolutely nothing we can do if you don't tell us anything," replied Michelle.

"Can we go get in the truck?" said Sean. "Or the only place we'll be going is a hospital where they can treat us for pneumonia. Unless the lightning kills us first," he added as another bolt precipitated a deafening crack of thunder.

They got back to the Land Cruiser where Sean had parked it off the road. There were some blankets in the back cargo area. Michelle grabbed three of these and handed one to Tyler, who draped it around his shoulders. She handed another to Sean and wrapped the last around herself.

"Thanks," Tyler mumbled.

He climbed into the back while Michelle sat next to him. Sean drove.

"Where to?" he asked.

Tyler told him.

"Directions from here?" said Sean. "I'm not familiar with this area."

Tyler gave him turn-by-turn directions until he hung a left down a street where there were a few older homes located at the end of a cul-de-sac.

"Which house?" asked Sean.

Tyler pointed to one on the right. It was ablaze in light.

Michelle and Sean exchanged a glance. Parked in the driveway of the house was a dull green Ford with U.S. Army plates. As they turned into the drive a woman and two uniformed Army officers came outside on the covered porch.

"Why are they here?" she asked Tyler.

"To tell me my dad was killed in Afghanistan," said Tyler.

5

The woman rushed toward them in the rain as Sean, Michelle, and Tyler climbed out of the truck. She slipped on one of the cement steps, but quickly righted herself and raced across the small patch of soggy lawn. Smoky air rose from her mouth with each breath.

"Tyler," she called out. She was short, about five-three and petite, yet she wrapped Tyler in an embrace that threatened to squeeze the life out of him.

"Thank God you're all right," she said. "Thank God."

Both Sean and Michelle observed that Tyler was expressionless during all this. Then he quickly pushed her away.

"Just stop," he said. "You don't have to pretend anymore. He's gone."

She stood there, drenched with rain, mascara running down her face. Then she slapped him. "Damn you, Tyler Wingo, you scared me to death."

Michelle stepped in front of her. "Okay, that won't help anything."

"Who are you?" demanded the woman, looking up at Michelle.

Sean said, "Just a couple of people who happened on your son and brought him safely home. That's all. We'll be going now."

The soldiers on the porch were dressed in their Class A uniforms and carried dour expressions. One was a case notification officer whose thankless job it was to tell survivors that their family member was dead. The other was a chaplain whose task it was to help the survivors get through this most difficult of times.

Michelle put one arm on Tyler's shoulder. "You okay?"

He dumbly nodded, his gaze on the two men on the porch. He looked as though they were aliens here to snatch him.

Michelle took a card from her jacket and handed it to him. "You need anything, give us a call, okay?"

Tyler said nothing but slipped the card into his jeans and headed to the porch.

The woman said, "I didn't mean to slap him. I was just so worried. Thank you for bringing him back."

Sean held out his hand. "I'm Sean King. This is Michelle Maxwell. We're very sorry for your loss. Things like this are never easy, especially on the kids."

"It's not easy on any of us," said the woman. "I'm Jean Wingo, by the way. Tyler is my stepson."

Sean started to pull out the German Mauser, but Michelle froze him with a glance. She said, "Again, we're really sorry, Mrs. Wingo. Tyler seems like a good kid. Anything we can do to help, just let us know."

"Thank you, but the Army will be there for us. They have a family care program the soldiers were telling us about. They'll be in touch tomorrow."

"That's good," said Sean. "I'm sure they'll be a big comfort to you now."

"How long had Tyler been gone?" Michelle asked.

Jean said, "He ran out of here about two hours ago. I had no idea where he'd gone. I was so worried."

"I see," said Michelle with a frown as she glanced up at Tyler, who was standing on the porch looking down at them. The two soldiers were trying to speak to him, but it was clear he wasn't listening to them.

"Again, we're very sorry," said Sean. He turned to Michelle. "You ready to go? I'm sure the Army and the Wingos have a lot to go over."

Michelle nodded, but her gaze stayed on Tyler. She held up one of her business cards as a reminder to him. Then she and Sean climbed into the Land Cruiser and drove off.

Michelle watched in the rearview mirror as the Wingos and the soldiers slowly walked back inside the house. As Sean sped up, Michelle eased gingerly back into the seat. He noted her discomfort.

"Little sore? You only have yourself to blame. Chasing a kid in a thunderstorm. You probably pulled every muscle you have. I know my knees are killing me and I didn't run half as far or hard as you did."

"KIA," said Michelle.

"Killed in action, right," replied Sean. "It sucks. One U.S. soldier dead is one too many in my book."

"Tyler and his stepmom don't seem to get along."

"Just because she slapped him? He'd run off. And like she said, she was worried sick. She overreacted. They're going through the worst stress a family will ever have to endure, Michelle. You have to cut her some slack."

"Right, she was worried sick. Yet Tyler was gone for two hours and she wasn't even wet until she came down to slap him. If it were my kid I would've run down the street after him. It's not like he took a car. He was on foot. She couldn't go after him? What, was she afraid of a little rain?"

Sean started to say something but then stopped. He finally said, "I don't know. The soldiers weren't wet either. But maybe it's not their job to go chasing after a kid. We weren't there. We don't know how it went down. Maybe she went after him in the car."

"She still would've been wet. They didn't have a garage. Not even a carport. And remember what Tyler said? After he pushed her away he said she could stop pretending now that his dad was gone. Stop pretending what? That she cared about Tyler's dad?"

"Maybe, maybe not. But it's none of our business."

"And why would Tyler take his dad's collectible gun, of all things?"

"What part of 'none of our business' did you fail to grasp?"

31

"I don't like things that don't make sense."

"Look, we don't know anything about him. Maybe the gun meant something to Tyler. Maybe the kid was so crushed finding out his dad was dead that he just grabbed the first thing he saw of his and took off. And why are we even talking about this? He's back home where he belongs." Sean glanced down at his waistband. "Crap, I've still got the gun. I was going to give it back until you gave me the evil eye. And why exactly did you do that?"

"Because it gives us an excuse to go back there, preferably tomorrow."

"Go back? Why?" he exclaimed.

"I want to find out more."

"We found the kid and brought him home. Our work is done."

"You're not the least bit curious?"

"No. Why would I be?"

"I saw how he looked at his stepmom. I heard what he said. There was no love there."

"That's life. All families are dysfunctional. It's only a question of degrees. But it doesn't make me want to jump into the middle of the traumatic situation they're going through. Right now they need family and friends to support them."

"We could be Tyler's friend."

"Look, why the hell are you doing this?"

"Doing what?"

"Inserting yourself in the lives of people we don't even know?"

"Don't we do that all the time as part of our work?"

"Yes, our *work*. Not something like this. It's not a case, so don't treat it like one. No one has hired us, Michelle. So we move on."

"I feel like I know Tyler, or at least what he's going through."

"How can you? Your dad is still alive—" Sean broke off.

Michelle's father *was* still alive, but her mother wasn't. She'd been murdered. And Michelle had initially suspected her father of committing the crime. And that had eventually led to her coming to grips with a memory from childhood that had eaten at her like a cancer throughout her adult life.

A psychologist friend of Sean's had subsequently gotten through to her and had done some investigation into her past. With his help, coupled with some traumatic moments at the home where she'd grown up, Michelle had finally righted herself. But none of it had been easy. And he never wanted her to go through something like that again.

The knife wounds had healed. The emotional scars she had suffered would remain just that. The weight of each one was immense. He didn't know how many she could carry around before being crushed.

Sean tapped on the steering wheel to the beat of the rain on the truck's roof. He glanced at Michelle.

She was staring off, seemingly lost. And a part of him felt like he was losing her again, when he had just gotten her back.

"We can at least return the gun," said Sean quietly. He wiped wet hair out of his face. "Let's do it tomorrow, hopefully when it's not raining."

"Thanks," said Michelle, without looking at him.

They drove to Michelle's apartment, where Sean had left his car, a Lexus convertible hardtop. In the covered garage they climbed out of the truck. Sean passed the keys over to her.

"You going to be okay tonight?" he asked.

"A soak in the tub and I'll be fine. You should ice your knees."

"Sucks getting old."

"You're not old."

"But I'm getting close." He fiddled with his own keys. "Even though it's cold you should go sculling tomorrow on the Potomac. That always makes you feel better."

"Sean, stop worrying. I'm not going nuts again."

"You *never* went nuts," he said emphatically.

"But I got close," she replied, paraphrasing his earlier statement.

"You want some company tonight?" he asked, giving her a sideways glance.

"Not tonight. But thanks for the offer."

"I'm sure this Tyler Wingo thing is nothing."

"You're probably right."

"But we'll take the gun back and see what we see."

"Thanks for humoring me."

"I'm not humoring you. I'm being diplomatic."

"Then thanks for being diplomatic."

She walked toward the elevator that would take her up into the building.

Sean watched her until she was safely inside the elevator car. He needn't have bothered. He had watched her take out five guys at the same time without breaking much of a sweat.

Still, he watched her. Still, he worried about her. He guessed that's what being a partner was all about.

He walked to his car, climbed in, and drove off, at a slow, safe speed.

6

Sam Wingo stared down at the map.

First, he'd lost his cargo and nearly his life. Second, the pickup truck he'd taken had run out of fuel halfway across Afghanistan, not where one would want to come up empty on petrol.

His options from that point had been limited. To the north were three of the Stan countries, to the west was Iran, and to the east and south was Pakistan. Not a clear winner among them as an escape route. Being an American in one of the Stans was probably preferable to being an American in Iran or even Pakistan. But Wingo knew where he eventually wanted to get to: India. Yet going through one of the Stans and hooking around to India through China was not going to cut it for him. It was just too far.

After he'd run out of fuel he had waylaid a man with a spare camel. He'd paid him far more in local currency than he had probably ever seen. Then Wingo had ridden the beast over some of the roughest terrain in the country, with the sun beating down on him, turning any bit of exposed skin red and dry.

He arrived on the outskirts of Kabul in the morning hours. He finally had cell reception. He had turned off his phone on the trip to conserve his battery. The camel did not come equipped with a 110V outlet.

He phoned his superior, Colonel Leon South.

"What in the hell happened out there?" said South.

"I was hoping you could tell me," said Wingo.

"Where are you?"

"I got ambushed out there. A dozen to one."

"Where are you, Sam?"

It was bothering Wingo that the man had asked that same question twice.

Wingo said, "Where are *you*?"

"This is beyond a disaster," snapped South.

"There was nothing I could do. Like I said, it was a dozen to one. And the leader had a cred pack that said CIA. It looked real enough, but I still didn't buy their story."

"Bullshit."

"Tim Simons. He said he was from Nebraska. Check it out."

"I'm not checking out anything until you come in."

"There was nothing I could do, sir."

"You had a fail-safe, Wingo. But since you're talking to me I guess you didn't deploy it when you were under strict orders to do just that if things went wrong. If you had doubts about who they were, why are you still alive?"

"The cred pack said CIA. Even if I was skeptical, I didn't want to risk blowing up our own guys."

"I don't give a shit if the cred pack said Jesus Christ. Do you realize what you've done?"

"Yeah, it had occurred to me."

"Where is the truck?"

"I don't know."

"And the cargo?"

"With the truck, last time I checked."

"This is not good, Wingo, not good at all."

"Yeah, that had occurred to me too."

"If you did something with the cargo—" began South.

Wingo cut him off. "If I had stolen it, do you think I'd be wasting time calling you?"

"If you wanted to cover your ass, you would."

"With that cargo, why would I need to do that?"

"Couldn't tell you. I don't think like a criminal or a traitor."

"Of which I'm neither."

"That's good to hear. No fallout then. But you really need to come in."

"Not until I know more."

"We recruited you especially for this mission. We laid all the groundwork, spent God knows how much time and money, took more risks than we ever should have, and now it's all gone to hell. And you're right in the middle of it. I knew we never should have just sent out one guy. Temptation was too great."

"I was never tempted."

"Yeah, some guys just strolled along in the middle of freakin' Afghanistan and in the mother of all coincidences took it from you."

"I was supposed to be met by freedom fighters, not the CIA."

"They were *not* the CIA," yelled South.

"You know that for sure?" Wingo snapped.

He could hear South breathing heavily, but the colonel did not answer him.

"They were there. They knew what was in the truck. Their cred pack looked legit. This guy Simons said the plan had changed."

"The plan had not changed. I would have known if it had."

"I am not making this shit up, sir. It happened."

South didn't say anything for a few moments. "Okay, give me a description of this guy. And anybody else with him."

Wingo did so. It was easy enough. He had been trained to remember details like that. And the truth was, when someone shoved a gun in your face, you did remember what he looked like, because it might be the last face you ever saw.

"I'll see what I can find out, Wingo. But your staying out there has already confirmed your guilt to a lot of folks here that matter."

"What happened to the people I was supposed to meet?"

"They were at the rendezvous spot."

"No they weren't."

"Let me be more specific. They were found in shallow graves behind the building that was the rendezvous spot."

Wingo drew a quick breath. "Then the CIA must've killed them."

"Or maybe you did."

"Sir—"

"Did you kill them?" South roared.

"No," snapped Wingo. "If those guys weren't CIA and the plan hasn't changed, then they were wired into the whole thing. Which means we have a damn leak somewhere."

"Look, Wingo, your part in this is done. You need to come in, give your debriefing, and we'll go from there."

"I need to make this right," said Wingo.

"What you need to do is come in, soldier."

"Why, so you can stick me in some prison somewhere? It sounds like you're pretty well convinced of my guilt."

"It doesn't really matter if you're guilty or not. You royally screwed up your mission and disobeyed direct orders. Any way you cut it you're ending up in the stockade for a long time."

At these words Wingo rested his head against the stone wall of the old building he was standing next to. His heart sank right down to the Afghan dirt.

Military prison for the rest of my life?

"I need you to contact my son and tell him I'm all right," said Wingo. "I don't want him to worry."

Wingo heard South clear his throat. "That's not possible," said South.

"Why not? He was told I was MIA. Just tell him I've been found. I don't want him to worry about me."

"He doesn't think you're MIA." South paused. "He was told you were KIA."

Wingo didn't say anything for five beats. "What the hell are you talking about?" he said in a deadly whisper.

"The chances were very high you would not come back alive, Wingo."

"I'm not dead yet."

"It's done. It can't be undone without doing huge damage to the mission. Even more damage," he added.

"I can't believe this. My son thinks I'm dead? What idiot authorized that?" Wingo barked.

"You have no one to blame but yourself. We thought you were dead. You didn't report in."

"I couldn't report in. I had no way to report in until just now."

"Well, you have a lot more to worry about than that, soldier," South said. "Are you still in country? I can send a chopper or a Humvee depending on where you are."

"I'm not in country," lied Wingo, his head still spinning.

South spoke slowly and with great deliberation. "Tell me exactly where you are and I will send people to pick you up."

"I don't think so, sir."

"Wingo!"

"Next time I call I would appreciate some real answers, instead of bullshit. And if anything happens to my son, anything, because of this, I will hold you personally responsible."

"Wingo!"

But Wingo had already clicked off. And then he turned off his phone. He'd already disabled the GPS chip in it. He knew that South had been stationed in Kabul, so the good colonel was probably within fifteen minutes by car from him. But Wingo was not hanging around Kabul. Or Afghanistan.

He started walking. It was clear from what South had said and what he had left unspoken that Wingo was being set up as the fall guy on this.

But what felt like a dozen AR-15 rounds penetrating his body was the thought of Tyler believing his dad was dead.

He tightened his knapsack strap and picked up his pace. Inside the knapsack was everything he had. But South knew about the IDs he'd been given, which meant he couldn't use them or the next thing he'd be facing was a court-martial. He had to get out of Afghanistan, through Pakistan and into India. He could lose himself in New Delhi or Mumbai and then figure out a new course of action. It would also give him time to change his appearance and construct a new ID, because he wasn't planning on staying in India. His ultimate destination was home. He was going to make this right somehow.

He looked down at his phone and turned it on. Should he call his son? He hesitated, trying to think through what such an action might do. Finally, he compromised with himself. He thumbed in a carefully worded email and hit send.

Then he hurried off.

Thousands of miles away Tyler Wingo's phone buzzed. And a hand reached for the phone.

And nothing would ever be the same again.

7

The oars cut cleanly through the murky water.

The rains had passed and the sky was cloudless. The winds that had beaten off the storm system had come up from the warmer southwest, but it was still cold enough to see your breath.

Michelle worked the oars with a polished motion built up over many years of piloting narrow vessels with barely a foot-deep draft through water. She didn't have to think about what she was doing. She just had to pull and recoil, pull and recoil, moving in a precise straight line because getting off-course cost precious seconds. Every muscle in her body was engaged at some point, particularly the core and the lower body where a person's real strength was housed. She would take oblique mass and corded thighs over tank-top beach muscle.

The Potomac was empty of boats except for a police vessel that was slowly chugging its way south toward Memorial Bridge. Michelle was heading the other way, following a route to the old boathouses that hugged the shore near Georgetown.

Perched on the hood of his Lexus, Sean watched his partner methodically make her way back to her starting point. He was glad to see that she had taken his advice and put her shell in the water even if it was cold outside. She was at peace there, he knew, one of the few places she was likely to find it. He only took his gaze off her once, when a mass of gulls started swirling in the air, pivoting, dropping, and then swooping upward.

That was real freedom, thought Sean. Must be nice.

He settled his gaze back on his partner. They had been intimate on one occasion and never again after that. He had thought about the reasons behind this. They were many and varied. The sex had been great. The morning after had been confused, as though they had both been culpable in stepping over a sacred boundary and had nearly ruined a perfectly good partnership by doing so.

She pulled up at the ramp to one of the boathouses painted yellow and green. Sean pushed himself off the Lexus's hood and came forward to help her. She wore a dark blue one-piece wet suit with booties that allowed free range of motion and protected her against the chill. It revealed not an ounce of fat on her tall body. But it also showcased how thin she was.

Together they tied the shell to the top of her Land Cruiser, and Michelle angled her oars through the truck's back window. They were long enough to reach into the front seats.

Sean gazed inside her car. It was full of trash, most of which should have been tossed a long time ago.

She noted him staring and said, "Don't go there. I'll clean it out at some point."

"Right. When you can no longer reach the steering wheel?"

"That's very funny, Sean. And you always claim not to be a morning person."

Sean snagged two coffees from his car and handed her one. She took a sip.

"You looked good out there," he said.

"BS I can do without."

"What do you mean?"

She stretched out her shoulder until she was rewarded with a pop. "I'm slower than I've ever been. I couldn't make a high school team right now."

"We all get old."

"Not all of us. Not Tyler's dad."

Sean drank his coffee and looked off toward the water. "We're officially pulling out of Afghanistan. But we still have casualties. Dying for what?"

"You could ask that question in just about every war."

"I didn't see the trigger was missing from the Mauser," he admitted, glancing at her.

"I probably had a better angle than you did. He was on my side of the road. If we'd been in England, you would've spotted it instead of me."

"You still lie really well."

"Comes in handy in our line of work."

"I know I said we needed to get back on casework, but maybe I was wrong. Maybe, instead, we should take some of the money and go somewhere."

Michelle stared at him quizzically. She leaned against the hood of her truck and said, "Why the sudden change in plan?"

"I'm a spontaneous person."

"Your idea of spontaneity is going with eighty-nine octane over full premium."

"You never really got any downtime, Michelle. It was hospital, surgeries, rehab. That was hard work. You need a break. We both need a break."

"And our rainy-day fund?"

"Frankly, we've got enough money to get away for a while and have plenty left over. I vote for someplace warm and sandy where they line the drinks up for you all loaded with limes and salt. You can see me in my swimsuit and you can wear a bikini."

"Why? To better show off my scars?" she said harshly.

Sean's face fell. "You know I didn't mean it like that."

Her features softened. "I know," she said quietly.

"Besides, I've got some of my own," he said. "And you've seen them all," he added, smiling.

"One of them is actually sort of cute."

"So will you at least think about us getting away for a little R and R?"

"That actually might be nice."

"And Tyler Wingo?"

"I guess I was trying to insert myself where I don't belong. Maybe we can just mail him back the gun."

"Now you're talking. I can check into travel arrangements and we can nail this whole thing down in a couple of days. You ever been to New Zealand?"

"No."

"I went there on a trip when I was guarding the VP. Let me tell you, the word *paradise* does not cut it. And it's their summer season now."

Her phone buzzed. She looked at the screen.

"Just hold that thought. Hello? Yes, this is Michelle Maxwell."

She listened and then said, "Okay, I understand." She was silent for about a minute as she listened some more, then said, "We can make that. Give me the address."

She saw Sean giving her the high sign not to commit but ignored it. She clicked off and slipped the phone back into her waterproof fanny pack.

"Who was that?" asked Sean.

"Tyler Wingo."

"Does he want his gun that bad?"

"No. He didn't mention the gun."

"What then?"

"He wants to hire us."

Sean gaped at her. "Hire us? For what?"

"To find out what happened to his dad."

"We know what happened to his dad. He was killed in action while serving in the Army in Afghanistan. And we are not going to Afghanistan to confirm his death, if that's what he's asking us to do. The military can do that perfectly fine without our help. And you just said yourself that you were inserting yourself where you didn't belong. We were going to jump on a plane to New Zealand."

"But that was before he called. Tyler wants to meet."

Sean let out a long sigh. "Meet where, at his house?"

"No, he wants to keep this between him and us for now. He didn't mention anyone specifically but it was easy to tell that he doesn't want his stepmother to know."

"First of all, he's a minor and he can't hire us because he can't legally enter into a service agreement with us. It would be unenforceable by us."

She gave him a disappointed look. "That's just legal mumbo jumbo. You're not an attorney anymore."

"Once an attorney always an attorney. And it's not just mumbo jumbo. It's how we get paid."

"I'm sure he'll pay us."

"I'm glad you're confident. But I'm also not going to take money from a grieving teenager when there is no investigative work for us to do. His dad is KIA. It's a moot point. The Pentagon is really good at identifying remains. And soldiers carry dog tags and they keep DNA samples now and everything. If they say he's dead, then he's dead."

"I don't know if Tyler is disputing that his father is dead. He has another reason he wants to hire us."

"What?"

"He wants to know *how* he died."

"Didn't the Army tell him and his stepmom? That's part of what they do when they notify next of kin."

"Apparently, Tyler was not satisfied with their explanation."

"This is crazy, Michelle. The kid is obviously not thinking clearly."

"It might be crazy," she agreed. "But there's something to be said for helping grieving teenagers get through a really bad situation."

"And you think we can do that?"

"We've done it lots of times before for lots of different people, some even younger than Tyler."

"That's true," said Sean halfheartedly. "So if not at his home, where does he want to meet?"

"At his high school."

"His high school? He just found out his dad was killed yesterday and he went to school today?"

"Yeah, I thought that was odd too. But then again, if he and his stepmother don't get along, he might not want to be there with her. And maybe he thinks if he sticks to his routine, he won't have to think too much about his dad never coming back."

"I guess everybody handles grief differently," said Sean.

"I guess they do. And he's just a kid."

"Exactly when does he want to meet?"

"He gets out at three fifteen. He has swim practice starting at four thirty. He can meet with us in between."

Sean chuckled.

Michelle pulled her car keys from her fanny pack. "What's so funny?"

"Oh, I was just afraid we were going to have to do a confidential client meeting on the playground during recess."

"He's in high school, not kindergarten. And they don't do recess anymore."

"My apologies. But I just don't see this going anywhere."

"At the very least we can return his gun, although it's probably not a good idea to pass him a weapon while he's on school grounds. Maybe we can meet him someplace else."

"Which high school?" he asked. She told him.

"We drove past there last night. There's a strip mall across the street with a Panera café. Call him back and tell him we'll meet him there."

"I won't call. I'll just text. That's what kids do these days."

"However you want to do it."

"You're not into this case, are you?" she asked.

"There is no case," he replied.

"There might be a case," she corrected. "Depending on what we find out."

"You're just not letting this go, are you?"

"I really don't know why this has gotten ahold of me. But it has. And I have to do it. Okay?"

"Fine. In for a dime, in for a dollar."

"Now you sound really old."

"Our new 'client' is barely past puberty. Of course I feel old."

She nudged his shoulder with her hand. "Thanks for indulging me."

"What I live for," he replied. "But you have to promise me, if there is nothing to this case, and I can tell you right now that there isn't, you will drop it and we go on vacation. I want your word."

"You have my word. If there is nothing to the case, we go to New Zealand and I'll wear a bikini. But you have to wear a Speedo."

He said, "That would not do wonders for New Zealand's tourism business."

But what he was really thinking was, *I'm just thrilled that I'm not grieving about losing you.*

8

Tyler met them at the Panera café across from the high school. He was dressed in the school's uniform of khaki pants, a black polo shirt with the school's official insignia on it, and black shoes.

"You drink coffee?" Michelle asked him as they walked together into the Panera.

"I'll just get some water," said Tyler.

"You don't get enough in the pool?" asked Sean in a joking manner.

Tyler didn't seem to hear him. He just trudged on.

Sean and Michelle purchased coffees while Tyler bought his own bottle of water, declining their offer to purchase it for him. They sat at a table near the back. The only other people in the café were students with laptops and two moms with young kids in strollers. One pretty brunette about Tyler's age waved at him. He self-consciously waved back before turning to Sean and Michelle.

"I want to hire you guys."

Sean sat back and folded his arms over his chest. "So Michelle told me. Why?"

"I already told her," replied Tyler. "To find out about my dad."

"And you're saying the Army didn't tell you how he died?"

"No, they said he was shot."

"Okay. It happened in Afghanistan, right?"

"That's what they said."

"And you don't believe that?" asked Sean.

"I guess I do. I mean, I don't know."

Sean said, "Okay, so we're not in Afghanistan, Tyler. We have no realistic way to get to Afghanistan in order to look over the Army's shoulder on this. No jurisdiction. No resources. Zip."

Tyler swallowed a mouthful of water and took his time responding. "But you're private investigators. Don't you guys have ways of finding stuff out? I mean, that's sort of the point of what you do, right?"

"Yes, it is," said Michelle, leaning in closer. She glanced once at Sean and said to Tyler, "First things first. What's your dad's name?"

"Samuel, but everybody calls him Sam."

"What exactly did the Army tell you about your dad?"

"They said he was with his squad in Kandahar. He was out on patrol at night and someone shot him."

"That someone being the Taliban, al-Qaeda, an Afghan soldier turned traitor?" prompted Sean.

"They said they didn't know. Whoever shot him got away, they said, but they're looking for the person."

Sean nodded slowly. "Unfortunately, that happens on a battlefield, Tyler. I'm sure the Army will do all it can to find out who killed your dad and make sure they're punished."

"When do his remains arrive at Dover Air Force Base?" asked Michelle.

Tyler shook his head. "They didn't talk about that."

Michelle frowned. "But all the bodies of slain servicemen come through Dover. The Army normally allows the family members to go up there when the remains arrive. And then you can have the burial take place at Arlington National Cemetery. All soldiers killed in combat get that honor."

Sean stared at her strangely. "How do you know all that?"

"I did some quick research last night."

Sean scowled and said in a low voice, "Before or after your relaxing bath?"

Tyler was shaking his head. "They didn't say anything about Dover."

Sean said, "Well, maybe those details come later. Your mom—"

Tyler glanced sharply at him.

Sean continued, "Sorry, your *stepmom* said that the Army was sending more people. Maybe they have that information. Have you talked to her about it?"

"No. I leave early for school. She's always still in bed," he added reproachfully.

Sean looked at him closely. "I'm surprised you made

it to school today, Tyler. Must've been tough after last night."

He shrugged and mumbled something that was too low for either Sean or Michelle to hear.

Sean said, "Well, maybe you should give your step-mom a buzz and find out. Go ahead and do it while we're here."

Instead of calling, Tyler thumbed in a text and sent it off.

Sean glanced at Michelle. A tiny smile crept across her face. She mouthed the words, *I told you so.*

"She's not going to answer, at least not for a while," said Tyler.

"She doesn't keep her phone with her?" asked Michelle.

"Oh, she does. But the text was from me so it's not a priority."

Michelle and Sean exchanged another glance.

"Okay, cutting to the chase. Do we have the evil stepmother syndrome going on here?" asked Sean.

Tyler's face turned nearly as red as his hair. "I'm not saying she's evil. She just doesn't have a clue. She's a lot younger than my dad. I don't know why he even married her."

"What happened to your mom?" asked Michelle gently.

Tyler fiddled with the label on his water bottle, peeling it off and piling the scraps of paper on the table in front of him.

"She got sick and died. Four years ago."

"I'm sorry," said Michelle.

"How long ago did your dad remarry?" asked Sean.

"What does that matter?" Tyler blurted out. "I just want to find out what happened to him. This other stuff is just crap. It has nothing to do with anything."

He had raised his voice, and the pretty brunette glanced over with a worried look.

Tyler caught her eye, looked embarrassed, and stared down at the paper pile in front of him.

Michelle put a hand on his shoulder. "I know this is really hard, Tyler. I lost a parent unexpectedly too. But the more we know about things, the more ideas we can come up with. That's why we're asking these questions that don't seem important right now. On a case, you don't know what will end up being important or not. You can see that, right?"

Tyler licked his chapped lips and took another swig of water. "They got married about a year ago. They didn't have a wedding. They went to a judge or something. My dad didn't even tell me until it was over. I didn't even really know her. And they hadn't been seeing each other very long. And she's like fifteen years younger than him. It was weird."

"I can see why that might make things awkward," commented Sean.

"Yeah," said Tyler. "Like real awkward."

Michelle said, "Was your dad career Army?"

Tyler shook his head. "He was in the Army for a

long time, then he went into the reserves. Then he got called up. He'd been over there twice before on deployment when he was regular Army. Then he came back home. I thought he was going to stay home for good but he had to go back again as a reservist."

Sean took out a small notebook and started jotting some things down. Michelle gave him a grateful look.

"How old was your father?" he asked.

"Forty-five."

"Tough to make a transition back into combat at that age."

"I guess, for some guys. But my dad is really jacked. He ran and lifted weights and he knows karate too. He's like a triple black belt. And he would swim with me. It got to the point where he couldn't really keep up with me, but he was tons better than most guys his age. He even did some triathlons."

Sean said, "I doubt I could do one lap in the pool. Sounds like your dad was really an iron man."

"Yeah, he *is*." Tyler bit his lower lip and his eyes glimmered.

Sean asked quickly, "What did he do before he was called up?"

"Um, he worked at a company called DTI in Reston. He was a salesman. Nothing real exciting."

"What was your dad's position in the Army?"

"He's a sergeant."

"You're sure?"

Tyler drew out an envelope from his backpack. "I

wrote some stuff down. His unit, when he deployed, stuff like that."

He handed it to Michelle. She said, smiling, "Very perceptive of you. I wish all our clients were as prepared as you."

"So will you guys look into it for me? I don't know how much you charge, but I can pay you. I got money in an account my dad set up for me. And I worked my butt off during the summer as a lifeguard. Saved up nearly a thousand dollars."

"That's great, Tyler," said Michelle. "We can go into those details later."

"So you just want to know more about his death?" asked Sean.

"Well, yeah."

"The thing is, Tyler, the Army will give you all of that. You don't need us. And I don't want to take your money to find out information you're going to get for free."

Tyler rubbed at his eyes and didn't answer.

Sean sipped his coffee and waited, choosing not to break the silence. He gave a knowing look to Michelle and inclined his head at Tyler.

Michelle touched Tyler's arm. "Is there something else? Something you haven't told us that's troubling you?"

Tyler started to say something but then shrugged and looked at his watch. "I need to get going. We take a bus to the pool where we practice. I can't be late."

"What do you swim?" asked Michelle.

"Fifty free and the two hundred medley. I'm not that good. I mean, there are guys on the team a lot better than me." He added, "Do you swim?"

Michelle said, "I prefer to keep just above the water and dry."

"So…you guys will work for me?" said Tyler hesitantly.

Sean started to say something but Michelle said, "We'll make inquiries, report back, and go from there, okay?"

"Yeah, okay," said Tyler, sounding a little disappointed.

He got up and walked out in a slouch, his backpack dangling off one shoulder.

Sean looked at Michelle. "Something is off here."

"Glad you're finally coming around to that," she said.

"I mean, the kid was a shambles last night. Running around in a storm with a gun half out of his mind. And then he goes to school and sits here talking to us about his father's death like it's a business transaction. Where was the emotion? Where were the tears?"

"Girls cry a lot more easily than boys, Sean."

"Not girls like you."

"I have four older brothers. I was never officially a girl." She paused and stared after Tyler. "But I get what you mean."

"So what inquiries are you planning?" he asked.

"Got any contacts at the Pentagon?"

"Couple."

Michelle held up the envelope. "Well, let's take a look at these notes and then see what we can do."

"And if all we can do is confirm what the Army has already told him?"

"Then that will have to be enough. But I don't think it'll play out like that."

"Why not?"

"That kid is holding something back, Sean. Something that is scaring him."

"Soldiers die all the time, Michelle. And their next of kin get notified. It's standard procedure."

"Well, this might just prove to be the exception to the standard. But there's something else," she said.

"What?"

"You referred to his dad in the past tense. Tyler answered but he spoke about his dad in the present tense. As though he were still alive."

"Wishful thinking maybe?"

"He didn't strike me as the type."

Sean sighed. "Okay. We'll do what we can. But just remember our deal about New Zealand."

"Don't worry. I ordered your Speedo online this morning."

9

The next day Sean put down the phone and stared at his desk. He was alone in the Spartan offices of King and Maxwell, Private Investigation. Michelle's desk abutted his. His desktop was pristine. Everything in its place and items lined up precisely. He looked across at Michelle's desk and frowned. It looked like someone had dumped a box of junk on it and then rifled through, spreading the debris around even more.

"I really don't know how she finds anything," he muttered darkly.

"Having another OCD fantasy about my desk?"

He looked up at the doorway. Michelle stood there holding two coffees, a folded newspaper under her arm.

"I'm that easy to read?" he asked innocently.

"We'll be finishing each other's sentences before long," she replied. "And we're not even married."

"In some ways we're more married than married people," he shot back.

She handed him one of the coffees, laid the newspaper on her desk, and sat down across from him. "So did you reach your contacts at the Pentagon?"

Sean nodded. "Just got off with one, in fact."

"And?"

Sean leaned back in his chair and studied the computer screen in front of him.

"And what I thought was straightforward is turning out not to be."

Michelle sipped her coffee and fought back a shiver. The forecast called for a chilly rain or even possibly snow. And the sky looked like it would deliver on that forecast any minute.

"Meaning what?"

"I emailed him the name Sam Wingo along with the particulars that Tyler gave us about his squad, rank, and so forth. I figured I'd give my contact some time to look into it and that when I called he'd have all the answers."

"But he didn't?"

"No. In fact, he had no answers."

"Did he say why?"

"He put it off on notification of next of kin, privacy policies, and things like that. Only I told him the next of kin had been notified."

"What did he say to that?"

"Only that he could not go into it further."

"Could not or would not?"

"Does it matter?"

"Did he confirm that Sam Wingo was dead at least?"

"No, he didn't."

"Okay, that's officially weird."

"It could just be that they're reluctant to release information about a KIA, Michelle. It's a pretty sensitive situation. They don't want to be accused of giving out the information to just anybody."

Michelle picked up the newspaper and opened it to a page in the front section.

"I'm not sure that's a valid excuse. Have a look."

She handed the paper over to Sean, who glanced down it. It was a photo page of casualties in the Middle East wars.

She said, "Fourth row, fifth photo over."

Sean looked there and read, "Samuel Wingo, age forty-five, sergeant first class, part of a battalion out of the Eighty-Second Division from Fort Bragg. Killed by small-arms fire in the Kandahar province."

"Pretty much everything Tyler told us," noted Michelle.

"Meaning everything they told him," said Sean.

"So you're having doubts too?"

"Don't read too much into this. It could still be nothing."

"They printed his picture, his name, and his rank in the paper along with the fact that he's dead. So how confidential can it be? They wouldn't even confirm to you that he's dead, but all the readers of the *Washington Post* know that he is? How exactly does that make sense?"

"At one level maybe it doesn't," he said. "But keep in mind that they've had thousands of casualties over there. My contact might not have even known that was printed in the paper today. The Pentagon is a pretty big organism."

"Okay, but I know that Tyler was holding something back from us."

"So how do you want to proceed?"

"We told Tyler we would check into it and report back. We checked into it and now we're reporting back."

"We have nothing to report, Michelle. Unless you count abject failure."

"We have to get him to open up. Maybe it'll be better if I go alone."

"To his house? With the wicked stepmother there? She might not let you in."

Michelle held up her phone. "I'll text him and arrange to meet him at the same place before swim practice."

"You're really going out on a limb with this, Michelle."

"He's a kid who lost his dad. He needs help, Sean."

"I'm not saying don't do it. Just be careful."

"I don't consider Tyler Wingo dangerous."

"I'm not necessarily talking about him."

She glanced out the window. "They're calling for snow today."

"Great, Washington drivers have a hard enough time driving in the sunshine."

"While I'm with Tyler, why don't you try another angle on the Pentagon?"

"I'll see what I can do. But those guys usually close ranks pretty fast."

He shot a reproachful glance at her messy desk. "Come on, Michelle? Can't you do something about that crap? Even a symbolic gesture would be appreciated."

She smiled brightly, picked up a single piece of paper amid the mounds of it, and dropped it into the trash can next to her desk. "Feel better?"

"It's a start."

Later that afternoon Michelle pulled into the parking lot next to the Panera, cut her engine, and stared across the street at the high school where Tyler was a student. It was a relatively new school, but was still probably bursting at the seams with students. The Washington area just couldn't seem to keep up with the population growth.

She slipped the page out of her jacket. It was the *Washington Post* article with Sam Wingo's picture. He was a good-looking man, she thought. Ruggedly handsome, strong features, intense eyes, his face stamped with the years. He looked a little like Sean, she realized. By comparison most of the other faces of the dead on the page were tragically young. They had barely had a chance to live their lives, and now there were no more chances left to them.

She checked her watch. At three sixteen on the dot she saw Tyler Wingo emerge from a door at the school and start to walk in her direction. The chilly rain had turned into light snow. In deference to the weather Tyler wore a hoodie.

She climbed out of her truck when Tyler passed by.

"Hey," she said.

He turned and spotted her. "Where's your partner?"

"Following up some other leads."

They walked into the Panera together. The place was busier than last time. Michelle figured that it would start to fill up even more since the school had let out. It really was a gold mine, having a coffee shop with a pretty full food menu located across from a high school and perpetually hungry teens.

This time they both got bottles of water. Michelle added a muffin.

"Haven't really eaten today," she explained.

They took seats at a table in the rear. Michelle opened her bottle, took a drink, and then attacked her muffin.

"So what did you find out?" Tyler asked.

"You saw the newspaper today?"

"No."

"Sorry, I guess teenagers don't read print media anymore. Anyway, your dad's picture was in it."

She pulled out the page and slid it across to him. "Just for positive ID."

Tyler glanced down at the page and then looked away. "That's him."

"Small-arms fire with his unit in Kandahar," said Michelle.

"Yeah."

"Hi, Tyler."

They both glanced up. It was the same pretty brunette from yesterday. She looked from Michelle back to Tyler and then down at the page.

"I'm really sorry about your dad," she said.

She was barely five-two, with soft brown eyes.

"Thanks," said Tyler, not meeting her gaze.

"Michelle Maxwell," said Michelle, putting out her hand.

The girl took it. "I'm Kathleen Burnett, but I go by Kathy."

"Are you in class with Tyler?"

"Yes, she is," interjected Tyler. "We were just meeting on some stuff, Kathy," he added in obvious embarrassment. "About my dad."

"Oh, I'm sorry, Tyler. I'll talk to you later."

She hurried off. Michelle watched her go.

"She's really cute."

"I guess."

"You're friends?"

"We're in some classes together."

"She was here yesterday before us even though you came over right after school ended. How come?"

"She's really smart. Skipped a grade and everything. And she doesn't have a last-period class. She gets out early."

"Nice to be smart. But she also seems to care about you."

Tyler was now staring at the page of photos.

Michelle folded it up and slipped it back into her pocket.

"Does she care about you, Tyler?"

He shrugged. "I don't know, why?"

"It's good to have people who care, that's all. Especially during times like this."

"So what did you find out?"

"Nothing more than you saw in the newspaper. The Pentagon apparently does not want to talk about your dad. I wonder why?"

"I guess they have their reasons." He hesitated. "So how much do I owe you?"

Michelle gazed blankly at him. "Why do I detect finality with that question?"

Tyler looked up. "What?"

"You just hired us and now it sounds like you want to fire us."

"I'm not firing you."

"Okay, that's good to know. I came here to ask you something so let me just get to it." She leaned in closer. "What aren't you telling us?"

"You asked me that before."

"And you didn't answer me. And just so you know,

I'm the sort of person that when I don't get an answer, I keep asking until I do."

"I've told you everything."

"Your voice says you have, but your face says otherwise. I was a Secret Service agent. We read faces like nobody else, Tyler."

He immediately looked away from her.

She sat back, folded her arms over her chest. "Okay. Is that how it's going to be?"

Tyler stared down at his hands.

"You could have saved me a trip here, you know. I do have other things to work on," said Michelle.

He let out a long breath. "I'm sorry. It's just—I mean, I guess I was just being stupid. My dad's dead. Nothing you could do will bring him back, right?"

"No, Tyler, there's nothing we can do about that," said Michelle quietly.

"And I was thinking about things last night. And…and I guess—" He faltered here and looked so miserable that Michelle's heart went out to him.

"Tyler, if you want us to stand down, I'm okay with that. It's your decision. Don't beat yourself up over it. You have enough to deal with as it is."

"I…I guess that's what I want. I mean, for you to, like, you know, stand down, like you said."

"You're sure?"

He nodded. "So, how much do I owe? I brought some cash with me."

"Consultations are free, so you can keep your wallet in your pocket."

"You sure?"

"Are you?" she said curtly.

He wouldn't look at her. "I gotta go now."

"Right, swim practice."

He rose.

Michelle said, "Oh, we need to bring your dad's gun back to you. I didn't want to do it here because having a gun on school grounds would be pretty bad. We can drop it by your house tonight. You going to be home?"

Tyler looked nervously at her. "Um, I'm not sure. I might have stuff tonight."

"No problem. We can just drop it off with your stepmom. That okay with you?"

Tyler turned and fled. He looked back twice at Michelle before he even got to the front door, and the distance in between was not that great.

Michelle sat there for a bit wondering one thing.

Who had gotten to Tyler Wingo?

10

The snow was coming down harder when Michelle stepped out of the Panera.

As a Secret Service agent she had spent years dissecting the physical world into discrete grids as part of her security matrix, looking for danger in all the right places. Though she had been out of the Service for a while now, that instinct still rode with her. It probably would forever. And right now her antennae were quivering.

The parking lot was half full, which still constituted a great many cars because the lot was a large one. Yet there was only one vehicle that drew her attention. She stared across at it.

Government plates, one silhouette inside, motor off, and the driver had been there awhile because the sedan was covered in snow. And no one had gotten out of the car, because there were no footprints in the snow around it. This was a strip mall where one made quick stops, in and out and on one's way. Yet this driver had pulled in, cut the engine, and sat there in the freezing cold waiting for something.

Or someone. *Maybe me.*

She walked to her truck, climbed in, and started it up. Without appearing to do so she was watching the government sedan. The silhouette had not moved. She was considering whether she had been wrong in her deductions when the situation status abruptly changed.

The silhouette transformed into a man with wide shoulders and military-cropped hair, wearing a long, dark overcoat and regulation black shoes. His military rank rode on the sleeves of the overcoat in the form of pinned-on bars.

Bars, not stars. But then again, Michelle hadn't expected them to send out a general to grapple with her.

When the man drew close, she rolled down her window. "You must've been cold sitting in the car all that time. Want to jump in and get warm?"

In response he showed her his credentials.

"Captain Aubrey Jones, military police," Michelle read off the ID card. "What can I do for you?"

Jones said, "You were meeting with Tyler Wingo?"

"If you say so."

"Why?"

"That's confidential."

"I understand that you're a private investigator?"

"Again, if you say so. But if I am and if I was meeting with him, you can understand why I can't reveal confidences."

"Wingo is a minor. He can't be your client."

"On the contrary, yes he can," replied Michelle.

"Why would he need a PI?"

"Could be lots of reasons. Why does it matter to you?"

"He just lost his father."

"I'm well aware of that."

"He's vulnerable and scared and the Army does not want to see him taken advantage of. Did you ask for money from him?"

"So you think I'm shaking down a grieving teenager for cash?"

"Are you?"

"Yeah, that's how I make my living. I look up dead soldiers in the newspaper and then arrange to meet with their crushed kids so I can get rich one dollar bill at a time." She paused. "How likely does that sound?"

"We know that you were formerly with the Secret Service but were asked to leave."

"Actually, I was offered full reinstatement but chose to voluntarily resign instead. And that's ancient history."

"You and your partner have been involved in some high-level cases. Serial killers, CIA, national security."

"Stop, you'll make me blush."

Jones drew closer and leaned in so that his head and shoulders nearly filled the window. "We are politely asking that you stay away from the Wingos. They're going through a lot right now. They don't need this sort of distraction."

"So how were you made aware of our involvement?" asked Michelle.

"The Army has lots of resources."

"Do you do this for all the families that have lost service members?"

"No, just for the ones who have people like you trying to mess with their lives at a particularly tragic point. Fortunately, not that many stoop so low."

"That's your opinion, and for the record it's the wrong one," Michelle said firmly.

"His father was KIA. He was notified of that fact. I don't know what he asked you to do, but whatever it was, you shouldn't have accepted. In my book you're just taking advantage of a heartbroken boy. Maybe you're doing it to make a few bucks, or scoring some points somehow with someone. Maybe you're doing it because you feel sorry for him. I don't know and I don't really care. But what I do care about is that you leave this family alone so they can grieve properly and get through this in one piece." He paused and said, "Did I deliver the message clearly, Ms. Maxwell?"

"Crystal clear, Captain Jones."

He spun on his heel and walked back to his sedan. Ten seconds later he was gone.

Michelle sat in her truck tapping the steering wheel with her fingers as she thought this through. Military police watching. Military police delivering a message. Stay away from the Wingos. They must have already talked to Tyler. Perhaps they were monitoring his phone, saw the meeting set up, and went directly to him. That could explain his sudden decision to have her and Sean stand down.

She called Sean and told him what had just happened.

"What do you think?" he said.

"Jones sounded legit, but maybe all they told him was what he needed to know to deliver the message loud and clear."

"Well, coupled with the stone wall I got at the Pentagon I'm coming down on the side of this starting to look really suspicious. The question now is what do we do about it?"

"We still have the German Mauser to take back."

"Michelle, they'll be watching the Wingos' house. They see us pull up, the next visit we get will not be from an MP delivering a polite if tough message."

"It's not like they're going to waterboard us, Sean."

"There are worse things than waterboarding."

"Name one."

"Maiming? Death?"

"Come on, this is our government we're talking about. And I can't leave it like this. And I don't think you can either. Tyler is holding something back. I really believe he needs our help, but he's been warned off too. I doubt even the Army can afford to have its personnel wait in snowy parking lots to dress down somebody they think might be taking advantage of a slain service member's family."

"I know. Something is off, way off."

"But you're right about the Army fence around the Wingos now. We go there, it won't be pleasant. So what other angle can we attack this thing from?"

"Well, if we can't get to Tyler right now, we can dig into his dad's background. Tyler said he worked at a company called DTI in Reston. We can start there."

"But if we go there, the Army will probably find out."

"We don't have to go there. There's this thing called the Internet. It has lots of information you can access from a computer. Maybe you've heard of it?"

"Okay, you go tap your little keys. I'm going to do some real detective work."

Michelle was staring back up at the Panera.

He said, "Like what? I don't want you to go off half-cocked. Finesse is needed here. Not the Charge of the Light Brigade. And didn't they get wiped out to a man?"

"*Man* being the operative word. If they had been led by a woman, that slaughter never would have happened."

"So what are you going to do?"

"Talk to one teenager about another teenager. Female-to-female."

Michelle clicked off, climbed back out into the snow, and headed into the Panera once more. She was going to find out how much Kathy Burnett really cared about Tyler Wingo.

11

"Hi, Kathy."

Kathy Burnett looked up from her computer to find Michelle staring down at her. She was holding a cup of coffee and a tray on which sat a bowl of soup and a roll.

"Oh, hi."

"Mind if I join you?"

Kathy glanced around. "I thought you and Tyler had gone."

"He did. To swim practice. And I was thinking of leaving but I thought I'd see what the snow was going to do. And then I decided a cup of coffee and a bowl of soup were calling my name."

Michelle sat down across from her and took a few seconds to situate her coffee and her soup while Kathy pulled her laptop and backpack out of the way.

"Thanks," said Michelle. She took a spoonful of soup and smiled. "Not many things better than soup on a cold, snowy day."

"I guess not," said Kathy, smiling awkwardly.

Michelle looked at her computer. "I hope I'm not interrupting homework."

"No, it's okay. This stuff isn't due for another week. I'm just trying to get a jump on it." She closed her laptop and looked questioningly at Michelle. "So you were meeting with Tyler about his dad?"

Michelle dipped a chunk of bread into the soup and took a bite. She nodded, swallowed, and said, "It's really tragic. Nothing worse for a kid than losing a parent, especially like that."

"Are you with the Army?"

"No. I wasn't helping Tyler with that. Just some other things. He said you two were in a few classes together. He also said you were really smart and had skipped a grade."

"He said that?" Kathy asked as a smile spread across her face.

Michelle took a sip of coffee and nodded slowly. "Yes he did."

"He's a straight-A student too, really smart. But he doesn't brag about it like some of the other people do. He's, well, he's just sort of quiet."

"I take it you two are good friends?"

"We've known each other since elementary school."

"Friends are important right now for Tyler. I'm sure you can see that."

"Yeah, I guess so," she said somberly.

"Did you know his dad?"

"He and Tyler have been to our house for dinner

David Baldacci

quite a few times. And he picked me and Tyler up from school a few times. He was always really nice. I knew he'd been deployed overseas. My mom was over there two years ago. She's back now and I hope she never has to leave again."

"Your mom in the Army too?"

"Air Force. She's a pilot."

"That's pretty cool, Kathy."

"I'm really proud of her. She can fly anything. I've been up with her in a Cessna. She did some things that made my stomach do flip-flops but it never fazed her."

"I'm sure." Michelle took another swallow of soup. "I guess everyone at school knows about Tyler's dad?"

"They made an announcement today. Everybody was so sad. But I think Tyler was really embarrassed by it."

"So if you've known Tyler since elementary school, I guess you knew his mom?"

Kathy nodded. "I did. That was tragic too."

"Yeah. Considering how old Tyler was when she died, she must've been very young."

"She was."

"Did she die of cancer?"

Kathy looked startled. "Is that what Tyler told you?"

"No, he didn't say. But judging by your look, I'm guessing that's not what she died of."

"Look, if Tyler didn't tell you I don't think I should. He must have had a reason."

"Well, frankly, I don't think Tyler is thinking all that clearly right now. So she didn't die from an illness?"

"Well, I guess you could call it an illness."

"I'm not following," said Michelle.

"Mental illness. Depression." Kathy paused. "Mrs. Wingo killed herself."

Michelle took another spoonful of soup. She wasn't particularly hungry, but she also wanted a few beats of time to digest this and decide how best to proceed.

"My God," she finally said. "His mom killed herself and now his dad dies in combat."

"I know," said Kathy, her voice starting to tremble. "I feel so bad for him."

"But at least he has his stepmom," Michelle threw out.

Kathy frowned. "I'm not sure how good that is for Tyler."

Michelle nodded thoughtfully. "He never came out and said, but I could tell he doesn't really get along with her."

"Why should he?" Kathy said, her voice rising. "I mean, Mr. Wingo goes off and gets married to a woman a lot younger than he was and they hadn't even known each other that long. Tyler didn't know her at all really. And did he tell you they got married by a judge? There wasn't even a wedding. They just showed up at the house one day and they were married. Tyler was so upset."

"And his dad never explained to him why he did that?"

"Not that Tyler ever told me." Kathy stopped and stared at Michelle. "You never said what you were helping Tyler with."

Michelle took out a business card and slid it across to Kathy. She looked down at it and her eyes widened.

"What does Tyler need with a detective?"

"Answers. That's why most people hire detectives."

"Answers to what?"

"I'm not sure he knows yet, Kathy. Tyler told me that his dad was in the reserves now but he'd been in the regular Army as well."

"I remember when I was in second grade Mr. Wingo came to our class and spoke about serving our country. He was in uniform then. He told my mom about it and she came in and spoke to us too."

"So your parents knew him well?"

"My mom knew him pretty well because of the military connection. And like I said, they came over for dinner quite a few times after Tyler's mom died. And we'd bring care packages over. And Tyler sometimes stayed with us. He's a good cook. He even taught my mom a few dishes to make."

"You live near each other?"

"Not in the same neighborhood. But it's only about five minutes by car." She brightened. "Tyler has his permit but he gets his real license soon. He was talking about us driving to school together sometimes."

"He's a year older than you?"

"That's right. I'll be sixteen next month. He turns seventeen in May."

"He ever talk to you about something troubling him?"

"I haven't really spoken to him since his dad died, if that's what you mean."

"Before that, was everything okay with him?"

"Seemed to be. I mean, he and his stepmom didn't get along."

"How about his dad? Anger still there over his dad getting remarried?"

"There was. But I think Tyler had finally just accepted it. He loved his dad. He wouldn't stay mad at him long."

"But now with him gone?"

"Yeah, now it's just him and his stepmom. Not good."

"He have any other relatives in the area?"

"Not that he ever talked about."

"Would you mind giving me a call if anything occurs to you that might help me help Tyler?"

"Like what?"

"Hard to say at this point. But you might know it when you see it."

"He's not in any trouble, is he?"

"Any reason why he should be?" asked Michelle.

"No. He's a really good person."

"That's what I think too. And that's why I want to help him, if I can."

Kathy slipped the card into her coat pocket. "Maybe you'll hear from me."

Michelle said, "Fair enough."

12

Michelle met Sean later that evening at a bar in Georgetown. They sat at a table near the window and over beers tried to reconcile what they each had learned about the Wingo case.

"Any blowback from the Pentagon?" asked Michelle.

"Nothing like you got," he answered. "But that's not to say tomorrow won't bring something. Suffice it to say I don't think any of my other contacts there will be returning my calls anytime soon."

Michelle took a sip of her beer and leaned back in her chair. The snow had stopped falling and the temperature had risen to a level sufficient to melt what had already accumulated. "So if we can't go to see Tyler or his stepmother and the Pentagon is a stone wall, that leaves the dad's employer, DTI. You said you were going to do a web search on them."

"I did. They're a government contractor."

"Every other company located here is a government contractor. What sector are they in?"

"Providing translator services for the military."

"I hear that's pretty lucrative."

"It certainly can be. But it only goes as far as our engagement over there. They specialize in the Middle East, so if the military pulls out they might be hurting."

"And was Wingo a salesman, like Tyler said?"

"I never got a chance to actually ask a human being that question." He drank some of his beer. "I think we've hit a dead end, Michelle."

She inserted her finger in the long neck of her beer and swung it back and forth over the table. "I don't like to admit defeat."

"And you think I do?"

"You're a miracle worker, Sean. You know everybody. Are you telling me you can't think of some other angle to hit this with?"

"I'm actually trying to decide whether this is worth it or not."

"I thought we were past that analysis?"

"Maybe *you* were."

"I might have an in through his friend Kathy Burnett. I laid the groundwork with her already."

"And you don't feel bad involving an innocent young girl in all this?"

"If I knew what 'all this' was, maybe I would feel bad. Chicken and the egg."

"I still don't like it."

"I didn't ask her to spy on Tyler, Sean. I just asked her to contact me if she thought she had any information that might help him."

"I'm not sure she's in the best position to make that decision."

"Then I can tell her to stand down, if it'll make you happy."

The two sat there staring stonily across at each other.

Sean said, "Look, I'm not wussing out. I'm just not sure what we can accomplish."

"Well, considering we've accomplished nothing so far it wouldn't take much to move the bar up."

"I can see we're not going to reach common ground on this."

"I'm being as reasonable as I possibly can be."

"Really? Because I'm not seeing that."

She eyed him severely. "What's that supposed to mean?"

He hunched forward. "You barely know this Wingo kid and it's like he's suddenly your little brother and all his problems are your problems. How is that reasonable?"

Michelle set her beer down and pointed her gaze out the window.

Sean said, "You want to tell me what's really going on here, Michelle?"

"You think it's wrong of me to want to help this kid?"

"I'm not saying it's right or wrong. I'm just saying it's…it's a little off."

She turned to him. "I know what it's like to be a

kid and scared, Sean. Him running through that storm, I saw the terror in his eyes." She looked off. "And the gun," she added quietly. "That could have been me running with that gun."

"It *wasn't* you running with that gun, Michelle," he said firmly.

She didn't appear to have heard him. "The only thing is he couldn't fire his. I did."

"That was a long, long time ago. And you were what, six?"

"Six or sixteen, what does it matter? It happened."

"You know it's not that simple," said Sean.

"It took a whole lot of shrink work and time in a psych hospital and going back to the old homestead to even remember it. And even then I can't fully understand it. And because I can't fully understand it, it scares the hell out of me."

"So you're relating your experience as a kid to Tyler's situation now?"

"Maybe I am. Is that wrong?"

"I don't know if it is or not. But why put yourself through this? It's too much."

"I wish I had an answer for you about that. I don't. Life isn't nearly as simple or perfect as we would like it to be."

"Okay."

Michelle shook her head, as though clearing away perilous thoughts. "Look, you've always been there for me. Always. I have no right to involve you in something you don't want to be part of. It's not fair."

"Actually, you have every right. Yeah, I've been there for you. But you've also been there for me. And saved my life more than a few times."

Sean finished his beer and drummed the table with his fingers. "I have one more contact who might be able to help us."

"But you said they'd close ranks on this."

"My contact doesn't exactly conform to strict military protocols."

"Who is it?"

Sean hesitated and then said, "My ex-wife."

Michelle gaped at him. "Your ex?"

"You knew I was married before."

"Yeah, but you never talk about her."

"Well, I don't like talking about her because there's a very compelling reason she's my ex-wife. And I'm not into self-flagellation."

"I didn't know she was in the military."

"Dana's not. Her current husband is. She got remarried about eight years ago. He's a newly minted two-star stationed at the Pentagon. Major General Curtis Brown."

"I've heard that name."

"He's a sometimes spokesperson for the Pentagon. He looks like a general. Tall, handsome, and ramrod-straight. Combat vet. Yet I'm very surprised he's survived Dana. She's a real piece of work."

"Did you go to the wedding?"

"What do you think? The only reason I knew was because I could finally stop paying alimony."

"Did you ever meet General Brown?"

Sean shook his head. "If I did I'd wish him luck. Dana's not exactly low-maintenance."

"It doesn't sound like she's someone you can call up and ask a favor of."

"I can do anything if the motivation is right."

"Meaning what?"

"Meaning that if you wanted me to, I would call up Dana and see what she could do for us. She might hang up on me. She might tell me to go to hell and then hang up on me. But it's the only path I can see right now. So, you tell me. Is Tyler Wingo worth it?"

"That's not exactly fair, Sean. You're putting me on the spot here."

"No, I'm just stating the reality of the situation."

Michelle sighed and gazed down at her empty beer bottle. "Maybe one phone call to her?"

"Consider it done."

"So you know how to reach her?"

"I have ways, yes. If not, I can always hire a good private investigator."

She gave him a playful smirk. "You know, you've met my brothers and my father, but I've never met your family."

"My sisters are in Ohio. They never come here and I haven't come up with a good reason to go there. My parents are in Florida leading the good life in retirement."

"Do you talk to them much?"

"Hardly ever. When I got drummed out of the Secret Service, well, let's just say they didn't really see a need to support me."

"Funny family."

"Look who's talking!" he said sharply.

She pursed her lips and said, "I'm sorry I'm so screwed up."

"It's actually one of your most endearing qualities."

"Let's never find out what it would be like not to have each other."

"I'm always on your six," he said.

"I know," she said quietly.

Sean gazed off, his mouth edging downward.

"I didn't die, Sean. I'm still here," she said, obviously reading his look.

"But you don't realize how close you came to not being here," he replied, turning his gaze to her.

"I actually *do* know. I could see it in your face when I finally woke up. And don't forget that I've stood over your hospital bed and wondered the very same thing."

He looked away again. "I guess it's what we signed up for."

"Never doubted that for a second. Now let's focus on Tyler Wingo."

"I'll get my ex on it."

"I think I need to be doing something too."

"Michelle, we've been warned off. At least you have."

"We have a gun to return, Sean."

"So you want to go to their house?"

"We don't have to be that direct, do we?"

He considered this. "No. You have an idea?"

"I think I have an idea," she replied. "But it'll be better if I go alone."

13

Tyler Wingo cut through the water as fast as he could. He was at swim practice at a local aquatic facility that his school used. The facility had multiple pools, but since this one was the largest the adult members also used it. Tyler touched the tile wall and came up for air. He slipped his goggles off, cleared them of condensation, and put them back on.

In the lane next to him a female swimmer wearing a swim cap and goggles was just about ready to push off. Tyler grinned and timed it so he pushed off at the same time. He was feeling the need to rip through the water like a dolphin. And it didn't hurt that the woman was tall and lean and attractive, at least the glimpse he had gotten of her. Despite all his troubles, he was sixteen with hormones about ready to explode and he suddenly felt the urge to show off.

As he cut through the water he wondered how far ahead of her he would be at the end. He contemplated what he might do when she broke the surface of the water and saw him already there. Could he come up with something clever? In reality, he was terribly shy and would be unlikely to muster the courage to say anything. But still, she would at least see him.

Then as he looked to his right the only thing visible were her long feet. Stunned, he redoubled his efforts, swimming as he never had before. He gave it every ounce of stamina he had—and still she was actually pulling away from him.

When he touched the wall and stood, she was leaning on the lane divider rope. Her cap was off, her goggles on her forehead. And she was staring directly at him.

"Wow. What a coincidence seeing you here," said Michelle.

"You're not even breathing hard," said Tyler, who was gasping. "I thought you said you didn't swim?" he added in a hurt tone.

"I said I preferred keeping above it and dry. I didn't say I couldn't swim."

"You're really fast for your age."

"I'll take that as a mixed compliment."

Tyler looked around. "Where's your partner?"

"He doesn't like the water nearly as much as I do."

"I know it's not a coincidence you're here. What do you want? I'd thought we had, you know, finished stuff."

"I still have your dad's Mauser."

"Oh, crap, that's right."

"It's in my bag. I can give it to you after I finish up here."

"Hey, Tyler!"

They looked over to see Tyler's coach, an older man in dungarees and a sweatshirt with a whistle around his neck, staring at them.

"Yeah, Coach?"

"Since this is swim practice do you think you can tear yourself away from the nice lady to actually *practice your swimming*?"

Tyler turned red. "Okay, Coach. Sure."

"I'll be waiting in the lobby," said Michelle. "How do you get home usually?"

"A friend."

"I'll take you."

"I don't think that's a good idea."

"I think it's a great idea, Tyler. I think you need to think things through on your own. Not just do what people are telling you to do. I'll be in the lobby. It's up to you if you go with me or not. I'll give you the Mauser either way. I put it in a canvas bag so no one can see it."

Michelle slipped her goggles back on, turned, and kicked off to do more laps.

Admiring her athleticism, Tyler watched her cut through the pool lane. Then he dropped back into the water and started swimming to the other side, though his strokes weren't nearly as clean.

When he came out of the locker room about an hour later Michelle was waiting for him in the lobby, a canvas bag in one hand and a knapsack over her shoulder. She had on a knitted cap with her damp hair bundled under it, jeans, a North Face jacket, and a long muffler wrapped around her neck.

Tyler's hair was slicked back and his jeans hung low; his sneakers had no laces and he wore his high school hoodie. He crossed the lobby to her.

She held up the canvas bag. "Here it is. You riding with me or taking your usual way home?"

Tyler looked around at the other team members passing by. He nodded to some and knuckle-smacked one boy who lustily eyed Michelle and then grinned at Tyler and mouthed the word, *Sweet.*

The boy said in a normal voice, "See you tomorrow, Ty."

After he passed by, Michelle said, "You go by Ty?"

"Just to some of the guys," Tyler said absently.

"So what's it going to be?"

"Can we stop for some hot chocolate? The water was freezing."

She handed him the canvas bag with the Mauser.

At a nearby Starbucks, Michelle bought Tyler a hot chocolate and herself a latte. They got back into her Land Cruiser. Tyler stared around at all the mess on the seat and the floorboard.

Michelle scooped the junk off the seat and tossed it into the back.

He peered into the backseat, where the piles of junk were even more pronounced.

"Is that a shotgun back there?" he asked, his eyes wide.

"Yeah, but it's not loaded. I've been meaning to clean my truck out for like two years."

"It might take you that long," muttered Tyler as he stared at the piles.

"I get enough crap from my partner about my untidiness, thank you very much."

"So what do you want?" he asked.

"I think you know."

"I don't."

"A military policeman was waiting for me outside Panera after we met. He read me the riot act about trying to shake you down for money."

"I didn't know about that."

"But someone did come and talk to you, right?"

Tyler sipped his hot chocolate and didn't answer right away. He stared up at the sky.

"Looks like more snow is on the way," noted Michelle as she glanced over at him. He seemed so conflicted that her empathy for him suddenly swelled.

Are my maternal instincts finally kicking in? How scary is that?

More miles passed in silence.

"We'll be home soon," prompted Michelle.

Tyler kept staring out the window. "They told me not to talk to you."

"Who is 'they'?"

"The Army."

"So guys in uniform?"

Tyler glanced at her. "They weren't wearing uniforms. They had on suits."

"So how do you know they were from the Army?"

"Because they were there to talk about my dad. He was in the Army. Who else would they be?"

"Did they show you some ID?"

"Yeah, but they flashed them so fast I couldn't see what they said. Besides, I wasn't really focused on that."

"Was your stepmom there?" Tyler nodded. "So what else did they tell you?"

"That you were probably trying to take advantage of me. That you couldn't find out anything they hadn't already told me."

"About your dad's death, you mean?"

"Yes."

"And what did you say to that?" she asked.

"I…I didn't say much," Tyler admitted.

"What else did they say?"

"That you could cause trouble for us. That it might mess up our getting stuff from the Army—you know, like benefits."

Michelle sighed, but then looked angry. "So they really laid a guilt trip on you. Talk about taking advantage of someone."

"I don't want to mess things up for my dad, Michelle."

"Trust me, neither do we. Are you going up to Dover to get your dad's remains?"

Tyler shook his head.

"Why not?"

"Because of what else they said."

"Which was?"

"I don't want to talk about it."

"Come on, Tyler. You chose to ride home with me. You must *want* to talk to me."

Another mile went by without either of them breaking the silence.

"They said there wasn't enough left of my dad to put in a coffin," he finally said.

Michelle jerked the wheel and the truck did a little wobble across the lane before she righted it. "What! I thought he was shot?"

"He was. Only a mortar hit right at the spot where he had gone down. It…it sort of blew him to pieces."

Now Tyler put his sleeve up to his face and quietly wept into his arm.

Michelle pulled the Land Cruiser off onto a side road, put it in park, and handed him some tissues from her console. He took them without looking at her. She wanted to lean over and hold him, but decided that might be unwelcome and more than a little awkward under the circumstances.

So she simply sat there staring straight ahead and watched shimmers of heat vapor lift off the hood of her truck and disappear into the darkness.

"Thanks."

She turned to Tyler and accepted the crumpled

pieces of now wet tissues. She tossed them into the backseat.

"Why didn't they tell you that before?" asked Michelle. "Why wait until now?"

"I don't know," said Tyler softly.

"What did Jean say to all this?"

"Not much. She just took it all in and then started crying so hard the men in suits got up and left."

"Very compassionate of them to drop the hammer and then flee the scene. What did you do?"

"I went up to my room and locked the door."

Michelle reached out an arm and lightly touched him on the shoulder.

He glanced over at her. She read apprehension on his features.

"Tyler, why were you so determined to hire Sean and me? Your father was dead. Nothing would change that. Any other details would be hard to come by since his death happened in Afghanistan. It's not like Sean and I can fly there and start investigating."

He shrugged but said nothing.

"There has to be something, Tyler. You're a smart young man. You don't strike me as the type to just jump into a decision without thinking it through."

When he still said nothing, Michelle asked, "Will you be driving Kathy to school next year?"

He glanced at her in surprise. "Kathy? How did you know about that?"

"I spoke to her at Panera. She really likes you. And she's worried about you."

"I was thinking about maybe driving her to school. Sometimes," he added.

"I think she'd like that."

Michelle grew quiet and waited. Nothing might come out of the next few seconds. Then again, everything might come out of the next few seconds. She surreptitiously crossed her fingers wishing for the latter.

"The thing is, it was the date the guys gave me."

"What date and what guys?"

"The Army guys who came the first night to tell me about my dad."

"Okay. What about the date?"

"He died the day before they came to tell us."

"All right. Sometimes it takes that long to confirm everything. They don't want to get it wrong."

"Yeah, I know that."

He stopped talking but Michelle said nothing. She sensed he was about to drop a bombshell.

"See, the thing is, my dad sent me an email."

Michelle shot him a glance. "*When* did he send you the email?"

"After he was dead."

14

Sean watched her enter the restaurant. She was thinner and healthier looking than the last time he'd seen her. Her hair and makeup were immaculate. She was dressed in a hip fashion that belied her actual age. The fishnet stockings and stilettos made her long legs even longer and sexier. The skirt was a little too short for Sean's taste, and the neckline revealed a bit too much. Several men at other tables gaped at her, earning the instant wrath of their wives or dates.

Sean had to admit his ex was even more put together than when they were married, and still a very lovely woman.

On the outside.

He rose when she walked over. When she attempted a hug, he instead quickly put out his hand for her to shake. She looked amused and shook it. They sat. She hooked her coat over the back of her chair.

"I was very surprised to hear from you, Sean."

"I guess I surprised myself, Dana."

She leaned forward, eyeing him closely.

"Let me guess, you want some of the alimony back?"

He managed a chuckle. "Little late for that. Statute of limitations has expired."

"Lucky me."

"Plus, what grounds would I have?"

"Don't look to me to tell you." She ran her eye over him. "You've kept yourself in shape."

"So have you."

"You like the new hair color? Blonde never seems to go out of style so I made the switch, permanently."

"Very becoming."

"Very understated compliment, thanks."

"How is the general?"

"Piling up the air miles and working longer hours than I would like."

"Nature of the beast. You want a drink?"

"Your memory is failing if you even have to ask."

Sean motioned for the waitress, who came and took their drink orders.

Sean ordered a Bombay Sapphire and tonic; Dana, Johnnie Walker Black solo on the rocks.

"That'll put hair on your chest," said Sean after the waitress left.

"Would you like to see for yourself?"

He sat back. "Ever the flirt."

"Nothing wrong with that. It brings me joy."

"But you go home to the general every night, of course."

"I would, except he's not there most nights. The

military is like bigamy on a massive scale. Curtis is married to me *and* the DoD."

"So why did you marry him?"

"Because he comes from a prominent family and has a trust fund that helps support us. We live in a beautiful home complete with a housekeeper. I drive an SL550 Roadster. I travel where I want when I want. We're invited to great parties and I get to meet the most interesting and influential people. And he loves me."

"I note that you put the love part at the end."

"I like to prioritize."

"I can see that."

"So what have you been doing with yourself? Still a private detective with what's-her-name?"

"Her name would be Michelle Maxwell."

"Right. I read about some case you were involved in recently. She almost got killed, didn't she?"

"She's very much alive and fully healed."

"What a relief," she said casually.

Sean gritted his teeth and said nothing.

When their drinks came he took a sip of his. She took a longer pull of hers.

"I thought you would go for the Gold Label. It's even more expensive," he said.

She put her glass down and licked her lips. "At a base level I'm a simple girl. I have my desires, and not all of them are expensive. In fact, some of the best are free."

"Nothing is really free."

"Well, you found that out, didn't you?"

"That I did. You screwed around on me and ended up with half my money and alimony for more years than I care to count. Doesn't seem fair, does it?"

"The fact is, we never should have divorced, Sean. You were just overly sensitive."

His features darkened. "About your sleeping with other men while I was out of town working? I wouldn't call it overly sensitive. I'd just call it appropriately pissed."

"You were gone. I was bored. What exactly did you expect? You know my sex drive has always been insatiable. It's math, one and one gets you to two. Anything less than that just doesn't work."

An older man at the table next to theirs who had been lasciviously eyeing Dana nearly choked on a mouthful of pork.

"Did you ever consider getting a pet?" asked Sean.

"No. And for the record I don't have a pet now."

"So what the general doesn't know won't hurt him?"

She shrugged, took a sip of her drink, and said, "Can we get down to why you called?"

"I need a favor."

She looked suitably surprised. "Then your foreplay was quite underwhelming. Care to try again?"

He leaned forward. "I've got a client, a very young client who just lost his dad in Afghanistan."

"I assume the father was military?"

"Yes."

"So you really want the favor from Curtis, not me."

"In a roundabout way, yes."

"What do you mean roundabout?"

Sean took another drink of his gin and tonic. "It's sensitive."

"I thought these things were pretty straightforward. Soldiers die, the Army notifies the next of kin. They go to Dover to see the flag-draped coffins and then they bury the dead at Arlington, if that's their wish."

"Very clinical of you."

"In all the time I've been married to Curtis we've been at war. I've seen this film play out a lot. I hate it that we're losing young men and women over there every damn day. It has aged Curtis like you wouldn't believe. Years ago, while we were dating and he didn't have a single star on his shoulder, he was a field commander over there. He was in combat. He was badly wounded. He very nearly came home in a coffin. I sat next to his hospital bed at Walter Reed for over a month wondering if he was going to make it."

"I'm sorry, I didn't know that."

"I may not be the perfect wife, but I do care about him. We have a good life together." She looked away. "And the fact is I haven't, well—" She paused and glanced down for a moment before staring directly at him. "The fact is I've been completely faithful to Curtis. I just wait at home like a good wife until he comes back, whenever that might be. And even though he's technically stationed at the Pentagon he goes to the Middle East on a regular basis and I wait here holding my breath and praying he gets back in one piece. I'm not sure why I go for the guys who carry guns and get shot at."

Sean gave her a puzzled look. "Then why are you all dressed up like you're going to walk down a Victoria's Secret runway? And why all the 'insatiable' talk?"

She pursed her lips. "Because I haven't seen you in a long time and I thought it was the act you wanted to see."

"How could you possibly think that, Dana?"

"Because I know you would never believe that I've changed so why should I even bother trying to convince you? The old Dana was just easier and not nearly as soul searching. And today has been a long day and I guess I just couldn't muster the energy."

"As crazy as that sounds, it actually makes sense."

"Oh goody." She pulled her coat on, covering her chest. "I'm freezing. I should have worn a sweater, and these stilettos are killing my feet." She kicked them off and rubbed one foot against the other. "And these stockings look a lot better than they feel. It's like being a tuna caught in a net."

He smiled. "Why do I feel like I'm talking to an entirely different person?"

"Do you not realize that I know how much I hurt you?"

"I guess I never thought about it. Your actions spoke quite loudly."

"I was selfish and stupid. We could have had kids."

"We could have had lots of things, Dana."

"I'm too old for that now."

"You're not that old. Women your age have kids all the time."

"Curtis is set in his ways. And I'm not sure I have the energy to run after toddlers, Sean."

"We all make choices."

She finished her drink. "Can we order some food? And then we can talk more about *your* kid who needs my roundabout help."

Later, when their plates were cleared and the coffees had been brought, Dana said, "Okay, talk to me."

"His name is Tyler Wingo."

Sean went on to tell her most but not all of what had transpired.

He was about to add something else when his phone buzzed. He looked down at the text he had just gotten from Michelle.

In it she had recounted what Tyler had told her on the drive home about his father.

Dana watched his face and said, "Developments?"

"Could be. Now they're telling him that his father was first shot and then hit by a mortar. There are no remains left to bring home."

"They always bring the remains home, Sean, trust me on that. If a mortar shell did hit him, the coffin will be closed and sealed. But the Army is really good about identifying the dead. I know from Curtis that the Pentagon is borderline fanatical about that."

"I'm sure they are. It's just curious they didn't tell him the first time."

"It could be as simple as they didn't want to tell the son or the wife something that disturbing when they were already delivering such devastating news. They have protocols for this but each situation is different. You said Tyler was running through the rain with his father's old collectible gun. It could be the Army reps deemed it unwise to tell him about the condition of his father's body at that time since he was so clearly upset. They wouldn't have wanted to risk traumatizing him and his mother further."

"Stepmother," he corrected. "But that does make sense. So why the stone wall at the Pentagon?"

"Confidentiality. They take it seriously there, particularly about combat deaths."

"Tyler seemed like he was holding something back, though. Something that only he knew but didn't want to tell."

"Something about his father?"

From Michelle's text Sean knew exactly what he had been holding back. His father had sent him a message after he was supposedly killed. He debated whether to tell Dana this, but then decided against it. She was married to a general, after all, and owed him far more allegiance than she owed Sean.

"I don't know. Michelle seemed to think so, and she has good instincts."

Dana drank her coffee and appraised him keenly. "So are you two a couple as well as business partners?"

"What's it to you?"

"I'll take that as a yes. I've seen her picture, read up on her. Quite a beauty. Quite an overachiever. I mean, an Olympian who can shoot straight? What a combination."

"Why did you read up on her? And before it seemed you could barely remember her name."

"Just a game we girls play. I'm sure she's a ball of fire between the sheets."

"Now, there's the Dana I know."

"I never said I had changed completely. What exactly do you want me to do about Tyler Wingo?"

"I would appreciate whatever you could find out."

"I'm not a spy. I do some work with wounded soldiers and their families and I'm involved in many of the organizations that generals' spouses typically are. But I don't have the security clearances or computer skills to get into the Pentagon's inner rings or hack into databases."

"Don't underestimate your skills, Dana."

"What do you mean?"

Sean ran his eyes over her. "I was thinking more along the lines of pillow talk."

She smiled. "Okay, now *that* I can do. Curtis is a

stickler for protocols, but any man can be manipulated given the right…inducements."

He smiled. "Like riding a bike." His expression quickly turned serious. "But let's be clear. Just try to work it into a conversation with the general and see what comes of it. I don't want you to go out on a limb or take unnecessary chances. That would not be good."

"You're making this seem dangerous," she scoffed.

"It potentially is very dangerous."

She stared across the table at him. "You're giving me your steely Secret Service stare."

"Surprised you remember what it looks like after all these years."

"There were many things that were unforgettable about you, Sean. That just happens to be one of them."

"If you do decide to help us and anything weird happens you call me." He slid his card across to her.

"Okay, you're officially scaring me," she said in a mirthful tone, although her troubled look clearly said otherwise.

"Good," said Sean.

15

Michelle dropped Tyler off about three blocks from his house. She watched him walk away and then slowly followed him to make sure he arrived safely. She didn't see any Pentagon cars lurking like feral cats in an alley, ready to pounce on unsuspecting prey. But that didn't mean they weren't there.

She drove off with one thought nagging her.

Tyler had refused to tell her what his father had written him in the email. She had asked nicely and then less politely when her frustration got the better of her. Yet the more she tried, the more Tyler had dug his heels in. They had not parted on the best of terms. She had promised him she would keep digging. He had been largely unresponsive to her on this point.

He had walked away, head down, feet shuffling, looking very much like a young man who had lost everything of value in his life.

She was annoyed and empathetic at the same time, and the disparate emotions were making her feel a bit dizzy.

She had texted Sean all of this information and

wondered how his meeting with Dana was going. It had surprised her at first when Sean had started talking his ex-wife. Michelle learned shortly after the two of them met that Sean had once been married. Yet Dana's name had never once come up since then. It was as if she had disappeared from the earth, and it was a little jolting to discover that this was not the case, and that Sean would be meeting with her.

She wasn't feeling jealousy, really, just apprehension. Yet maybe at some level they were the same thing. She also wondered if Dana would actually consent to use her husband's status in the military to help the man who had divorced her.

As she was driving back to her apartment her phone buzzed. It was Sean. She arranged to meet with him at their office.

"How did it go with Dana?" she asked.

"Not what I expected," he replied.

Michelle put the phone away not quite knowing how to take that statement.

The offices of King and Maxwell were on the second floor of an unremarkable low-rise building in Fairfax. The views were limited, the building not overly clean, but the rent was cheap, or as cheap as it got around here.

He was already waiting for her when she opened the door and came in. They only had the one large room. The benefit of a secretary was not in their budget—nor was it necessary, Michelle felt. They did quite well on their own; adding a third person to the mix might destroy that delicate balance.

She sat across from him at her still-messy desk. He was seated in his chair, his feet up on his desk.

"So how was it unexpected?" she asked, looking at him pointedly.

He stopped staring at the ceiling and focused on her. "I felt like a priest witnessing a confession."

"A catharsis for the soul by your ex?"

"I think she really loves her husband."

"That's refreshing. Will she help us?"

"Yes. But I told her to be careful."

"Does she know about the email?"

"I didn't think that would be productive. I told her about the mortar shell part. She had a reasonable explanation for why they wouldn't have told the family about that the first night."

"What do you really think she can do?"

"I have no idea. I don't know what we can do actually." He lifted his feet off the desk and sat up in his chair. "So he wouldn't tell you what the email said?"

"No. And believe me I tried. Maybe too hard in retrospect."

"Do you believe him?"

Michelle looked surprised. "Why would he lie about something like that?"

"I'm just mentioning it as a possibility. Since we

don't have independent verification of it, I can't really treat it as fact yet."

"Yes, I believe him."

Sean nodded absently. "We really need to see that email. It could tell us lots of things."

"You'd think the Army would be monitoring things like that. Emails from soldiers in the battlefield coming back, they have to be under surveillance."

"No, they don't. At least not typically. You can use your government email or even a Gmail account to send and receive messages."

"Even so, maybe Wingo was treated differently?"

"I don't know. But maybe Sam Wingo figured out a way around that and got a message to his son that only he knows about."

She said, "Or maybe there was a technical snafu somehow. Maybe the email got delayed and it was sent before Sam was killed but Tyler only received it afterward."

"Did the email have a time stamp showing when it was sent?" asked Sean.

"I suppose it did. I didn't actually see it."

"Right. But someone else with access to Wingo's computer could have sent it from his father's email account *after* Wingo officially died."

"I asked Tyler about that. He was adamant that only his dad could have sent it."

"Based on what?"

"He wouldn't say. And why would someone write

such an email in the first place making it seem like it was from Sam Wingo? Pretty cruel trick to play on a kid."

"We really need to know why Tyler believes his dad wrote it."

"Sean, he flat-out refused to tell me."

"It's tough having an uncooperative client."

"Do we ever get any other kind?" she shot back. "Our last one initially refused to talk to us at all."

"Edgar Roy. That's right, he did." Sean swiveled around in his chair and then swung it back around to face her. "I wonder if Edgar could get access to that email?"

"How?"

"Do we have Tyler's email address?"

"I can get it from his friend Kathy. I don't think kids email much anymore. Or use Facebook. They don't talk on the phone either. They text or Tumblr or whatever the hell else they do."

"You sound really old," Sean pointed out.

"Compared with that age I'm ancient. I'm Maggie Smith in *Downton Abbey* wondering where the horse and carriage is when the Model T drives up."

"So get the email from Kathy and we'll give it to Edgar. If he can sit in front of this huge wall of screens with data flowing in from around the world and make sense of it, I think he can probably hack a teenager's email."

"So how did you leave it with Dana?"

"She would see what she could find out. I told her to be careful. It might be dangerous."

Michelle straightened out a paper clip on her desk. Without looking up she said, "So how was it seeing your ex after all this time?"

"I felt lucky."

She glanced up frowning. "Lucky?"

"Yeah, lucky that I escaped with my sanity and manhood intact."

"Think you'll ever take the plunge again?"

"I don't know. You've never taken it."

"I'm a lot younger than you," she said, smiling.

"Yes you are."

"But we've both been aged by life's events," she added, her smile fading.

He leaned forward, resting his elbows on his desktop. "Yes we have. Regrets?"

"Wouldn't have missed a minute of it. Well, maybe the minutes that hurt like a bitch."

"I wonder if Jean Wingo knows about the email?" asked Sean.

"If I had to guess, I would guess not. They don't seem to be two people who share much of anything except a house." Michelle added, "But if Sam Wingo is alive, why is the Army saying he was shot and killed?"

Sean said, "And then mortared. Which gets them around the pesky detail of remains that can be identified by family members."

"I was thinking the same thing, actually," said Michelle.

"So again, why? Because the Army has to be in on the subterfuge. They would certainly know if the man was alive or dead, as would members of his unit."

"Pity we can't get to them and ask them," said Michelle.

"I guess it would behoove us to find out when his unit's coming back stateside."

"Do you think Dana could wheedle that out of her hubby?"

Sean nodded. "Soldiers are made of strong stuff. But Dana has a way of making men talk."

"Really?" said Michelle, but her features were clearly annoyed.

Sean didn't see this warning sign. He gazed at the ceiling, a smile playing off his lips. "She came into the restaurant dressed in a miniskirt, fishnets, and stilettos, with her cleavage spilling out and this really hip blonde hairdo. I have to admit, she looked great. I thought every guy in the restaurant was going to fall out of his chair. One old guy almost choked when she talked about being sexually insatiable."

"*Every* guy?" said Michelle, a definite hard edge to her words.

Sean looked at her, suddenly taken aback. "No, of course not every guy."

"Sexually insatiable? How the hell did that come up in the conversation?"

Sean sputtered, "We were just…I mean, we were just talking…about what went wrong between us, and I—"

Michelle rose. "I'm beat. I'm going to bed. See you in the morning."

She headed for the door.

"Michelle, you're being silly," he called after her.

"Great, Sean, just what a woman wants to hear."

She slammed the door behind her.

16

When Michelle came out of her apartment the next morning it was early, the sun barely up.

Yet there he was.

Sean was standing next to his Lexus, two cups of coffee in hand. He was shivering with the chill in the air.

"Why are you here?" she asked.

"To beg forgiveness for being a total ass last night." He held up the coffee. "It's not much, but it is hot. I timed your appearance just right. You are definitely not one to linger in bed."

She stared at him for a few uncomfortable seconds, then walked over and snagged the Styrofoam cup.

"I *am* sorry," he said quietly.

"You have nothing to be sorry about. We're business partners. What you fantasize about in your spare time is entirely up to you."

"I don't fantasize about her. Don't forget, I only looked her up because you asked me to."

Michelle's anger faded with this statement. She took a drink of her coffee and just stared at the pavement.

"Look, Michelle, Dana is happily married. I know it sounds incredible, but she really cares for her general. She went on and on about him."

"And you?"

"I'm really happy she loves the general."

They eyed each other.

"I guess I get that," said Michelle.

"Trust me, my years with Dana were some of the worst of my life. I do not have enough time left to go back down that road, even if I wanted to, which I don't."

Michelle sipped her coffee. "Okay, what now? We're waiting on Dana and Kathy. We really can't approach Tyler at this point."

Michelle's phone dinged. She looked at the screen and then held it up for Sean to see. "We just got Tyler's email address from Kathy."

"Then our next stop is Edgar Roy."

"At his farm?" she asked.

"No, I checked. He's working in D.C. the rest of this week."

"Bunting Enterprises?"

"Satellite office thereof," replied Sean.

"Can we see him there? Isn't it classified and fire-walled with attack dogs ready to eat trespassers?"

"I'm sure it is. But we can call and arrange to meet with him outside the Emerald City. I'll tell him to bring his laptop. And his big brain."

Sean started to get in on the driver's side of his Lexus.

Michelle said, "I'll drive."

"But—" Sean started to protest. Michelle was already climbing into her truck, however.

Sean opened the passenger door to the Land Cruiser and a pile of junk fell out onto the pavement. He jumped when a half-empty carton of orange juice spilled on his shoes.

"Just throw it in the backseat," advised Michelle.

"How about I just put it all in that trash can over there?" he said angrily.

"But it's not all trash."

"If it looks like trash and smells like trash…?"

"In the backseat, Sean. Thanks."

Sean glared for a moment at the pile of stuff and then proceeded to hurl it into the backseat with velocity. Finished, he slammed the door shut.

"Feel better?" she asked.

"No, not really," he said between gritted teeth as he stared straight ahead. "I have orange juice in my socks."

"Then your feet will never get a cold."

Sean called Edgar on the drive over. He did not keep normal hours and had been at work for some time already.

When they reached the office building a block over from K Street, they both saw him at the same time. Edgar Roy was hard to miss. He was six foot nine, which was extremely tall on any surface other than an NBA court. He was also exceedingly thin, which made him seem even taller. He was carrying a laptop computer under one arm.

They pulled to the curb and Sean rolled down the window.

"Hey, Edgar."

Edgar glanced over at him. Partially obscured behind the thick glasses was a pair of eyes that fronted one of the premier minds in the country, if not the world. Edgar Roy was America's most invaluable intelligence analyst. The amount of material his mind was able to burrow through to find small nuggets of intelligence gold was truly unprecedented.

Yet right now all Sean was hoping was that he could hack a teenage boy's email.

Sean and Michelle hopped out of the truck and approached. Both tall, they still had to stare nearly straight up to come close to an eyeball-to-eyeball with Edgar.

Edgar nodded at both of them and then turned his gaze fully to Michelle.

"I didn't say this the last time we met but I'm glad you're doing so well, Ms. Maxwell."

Michelle had tried and failed to get him to call her by her first name.

"Thanks, Edgar. But I should be doing the thanking. You're the one who saved my life. And we appreciate your taking the time to meet with us. It won't take long."

Sean said, "I've got an email account here that I'm

hoping you can hack into. We need to see some of the most recent flow."

Edgar looked at the email address. Sean knew that he had instantly memorized it. He sat down with his laptop on a nearby bench, opened it, and started hitting keys.

"You don't have to do it now, Edgar," said Sean. "When you get a break from whatever it is you do in there, you can work on it, not sit out here in the cold. And then—"

"Here," said Edgar.

He had turned the laptop around so that they could see the screen. On it were Tyler Wingo's email postings.

"How did you do that so fast?" asked an amazed Sean.

"I'm not sure you would understand," said Edgar politely.

"You're right there," said Michelle. She sat down next to Edgar while Sean perched on the other side of the bench. They ran their eyes down the screen. There weren't many emails.

"I don't see it," said Sean. "He might have deleted it. That means we're SOL."

"Highly doubtful," said Edgar. "There are ways to fry drives. Unless you do, simple deletions mean nothing."

Edgar hit some more keys, and a new list of posts appeared. "He also deleted it from his trash, but there was another cache it was copied to that wasn't so apparent. Easy enough if you know where to look."

"I'm glad you know where to look," said Sean.

"There," said Michelle, pointing at the third email from the top. "It's from Sam Wingo."

Sean and Michelle read it and then looked at each other. Sean said, "I don't see anything in that message that Tyler wouldn't want us or anyone else to know. It's pretty short, and it's just his dad talking about school and Tyler's swimming."

"Maybe that's why he merely deleted it and didn't truly erase it," suggested Edgar.

"Did he reply to the email?" asked Sean.

Edgar hit some more keys but finally shook his head. "No."

Michelle said, "Sean, look at the time stamp. It was sent after they told him his father was dead. Just like Tyler said."

Sean ran his eye over the message again and an idea occurred to him.

"It might be in code, Edgar. Think you can help us out?"

"Right." Edgar ran his eye over the message, his pupils flicking back and forth at speed. His lips were moving but no words were coming out.

He opened another screen and typed the letters *IASPFM*.

He said, "I ran it through the typical hundred or so initial possibilities. Looks to be an every seventh word, initial letter substitution cipher. Low security value point, but it's so old and seldom used that it could have some worth. Useless against a real cyber strike, of course. And any legitimate code breaker would have had no trouble with it. But it is a bit more sophisticated since it spells out an acronym and not actual words, meaning it's a double-layer encryption."

"But what does the acronym mean?" asked Michelle.

"Ordinary web shorthand," said Edgar, sounding surprised. "Initial letter based with straightforward extrapolation intended. I thought you would know."

"I missed that class," said Michelle.

"Me too," added Sean quickly. "Along with all math and science courses."

"It means 'I am sorry, please forgive me,'" said Edgar.

Sean and Michelle exchanged a glance.

"Does that help?" asked Edgar.

"It certainly doesn't hurt," said Sean.

17

Sean and Michelle had just returned to their office when the phone rang.

It was Peter Bunting, head of a large defense contracting firm and Edgar Roy's employer.

And the man was a little upset.

Sean actually held the phone away from his ear as Bunting's screams poured out.

"Who exactly are we talking about, Mr. Bunting?" Sean asked when the man stopped to take a breath.

Bunting said something and Sean nodded. "Okay, we will look into this. And I'm sorry."

Bunting yelled something and hung up.

Sean turned to Michelle.

"What was that all about?"

"DoD just came and yanked Edgar Roy from his office."

"What? Why?" exclaimed Michelle.

"Cause and effect apparently."

"Meaning we were the cause?"

Sean nodded. "Because of the timing Bunting can't think of any other reason he would've been snatched, and I tend to agree with him. Edgar told him of our meeting." He added, "Bunting's a little mad right now."

"I could hear. What did he say right before he hung up?"

"Something about damaging my testicles, although he used a less polite term."

Michelle plopped into her desk chair and glanced at the door. "Should we be prepared for invasion too?"

"Edgar Roy is employed by a government contractor and thus technically works for the government. He did us a favor on government time. They may be able to ding him a little for that but there's no way they'll keep him locked up somewhere. He's too valuable an asset."

"Which doesn't really answer my question. *We're* not that valuable. So they wouldn't have a problem locking us up and throwing away the key."

"We're also not employed by the government. And there's the little issue of habeas corpus. That still means something in this country."

"Yeah, but we got a government genius to hack a private account for us. Isn't that illegal?"

"We also have the permission of the account holder to investigate. Tyler did hire us."

"And he also fired us," Michelle reminded him.

"A technicality only."

"So you say."

"I *am* a lawyer."

"And lawyers are full of bullshit. In fact, they charge more for that."

"If they break our doors down, I think we'll have enough of a defense to escape any real trouble."

Michelle feigned a smile. "Five years in prison versus ten, what a relief."

"I tend to believe that the email came from Sam Wingo. Which means the Army is lying its collective ass off."

Michelle said, "But what was he sorry for and why did he want his son's forgiveness?"

"For lying to him? For getting into this mess and causing Tyler to suffer?" suggested Sean.

"Okay, but that leaves us with hunches and not a lot of paths to follow them up."

"We have Tyler. We have Kathy. We have Dana. And we have DTI," noted Sean.

"Let's go with the low-hanging fruit first."

"Dana?" said Sean.

"I was thinking Kathy."

"You want to split up?"

"I'll take Dana. You take Kathy."

"You're kidding, right?" he said.

"Am I?" she said, staring at him.

"Kathy doesn't know me. And it might be a little awkward for me to be meeting a high school girl."

"Okay, let's partner up on both then. I've always wanted to meet your ex."

"Always?"

"Always since yesterday."

"She might not know anything yet. It hasn't been very long."

"From what you said, she can be very persuasive, particularly with her choice in clothes."

"Why don't you text Kathy first? If she's found something out we can meet her. I'll text Dana."

"And DTI?"

"I'd love to hit those folks, but DoD has to be watching them."

"Is there any law against us asking questions? People don't have to answer."

"Sometimes people make up their own laws. By the time it's all figured out we're eligible for Social Security."

Michelle said, "It would help if we knew the names of some of Sam Wingo's co-workers there."

"Well, from what I could find out the actual office where Wingo worked isn't that big. Maybe twenty people. I bet they all knew each other. At least somewhat."

"Do we wait outside and see who looks promising when they leave work?"

"Maybe. But that will be after we meet with Kathy, if she has anything. Text her now."

Michelle did.

Five minutes went by.

"Maybe she cut us off too," said Michelle as she stared at her phone.

"Give it time."

Another minute went by, and then a text popped up on Michelle's phone.

"She talked to Tyler. She'll meet us at the same café."

"You should get a Panera card," advised Sean.

Michelle frowned. "This thing is looking stranger by the minute. I don't want to end up back in a CIA cell that no one knows about."

Sean laced his fingers behind his head and leaned back in his chair. "Frankly, I'm more worried about Tyler and his stepmom than I am about us."

Michelle shot him a glance. "Why?"

"Tyler got that email. Edgar hacked it and figured it out. Who's to say a third party won't do the same?"

"So they know the father communicated with the son?"

"After he supposedly died."

"And Tyler knows that because he told me that. Do you think he might tell anyone else?"

"I sincerely doubt he'll confide anything to his stepmom Jean."

"Kathy said she'd talked to him. Maybe he told her."

"I hope they talked without using their phones or computers."

Michelle nodded in understanding. "The Pentagon would have all of that locked down. The thing is, kids these days don't seem to actually *talk* to each other anymore. They just text each other."

"Well, for their sakes I hope they broke that rule this time."

"Sean, why would the Army say a soldier is dead if he really isn't?"

"I guess I can think of a few reasons, but none that make any sense at all."

"And Dad wanted his son's forgiveness. For pretending to be dead? For putting him through all of that horror?"

"Maybe. And now Tyler believes that his father is alive," Sean pointed out.

"Part of me hopes he is. Because if he isn't and Tyler finds out the truth?"

Sean nodded in understanding. "He'll have lost his dad. Twice."

18

"How is Tyler doing?" asked Michelle.

She and Sean were sitting across from Kathy Burnett at the Panera.

"Not that good. He's really moody and doesn't want to talk."

"But you said he did talk to you?" noted Sean.

Kathy fiddled with the paper cover from the straw for her soda.

"A little."

"Face-to-face?" asked Michelle. "Meaning not over your phones?"

"No, he drove over to my house earlier today. We talked in my backyard."

"What did he tell you?" asked Michelle.

"Is Tyler in some sort of trouble?" Kathy blurted out.

"No," said Sean. "Does he think he is?"

"I know he's worried."

"Just tell us what he said and maybe we can make some sense out of it," advised Michelle.

"And you're really wanting to help him, right?"

"He came to *us*, Kathy," replied Michelle quite truthfully. "He hired us to look into this for him. Since he's our client, our only interest is what's best for him."

Sean nodded in agreement and then they both eyed the teenage girl.

"He told me there's something weird with his dad's death."

"Weird how?"

"The Army is saying that he's dead, but Tyler thinks there's more to it."

"Based on what?" asked Michelle, though she knew the answer.

"He wouldn't say. But he did tell me that the Army is jerking him around. Changing the story on how his dad died. They were supposed to go up to Dover to see his dad's coffin come in. But then they said there was a delay."

"Did they tell him for how long?" asked Sean.

"If they did he didn't tell me. He was really upset about that."

"Did he mention any emails he might have gotten from anyone?" asked Sean quietly.

Kathy shot him a glance. "Emails? From who?"

"I don't know. I'm just asking. Trying to feel out the situation."

She looked suspiciously at both of them. "If Tyler hired you, why aren't you asking *him* these questions?"

Sean and Michelle exchanged a glance.

Sean said, "It's a little complicated, Kathy."

Michelle added, "We wanted to get some information from a friend of his, to gauge how he's doing, what he's talking about. We know he's really upset and maybe not thinking too clearly. But what you've said so far is consistent with what Tyler has already told us."

Kathy nodded, apparently satisfied with the explanation. "He did tell me that he doesn't trust the Army."

"I can understand that," said Sean. "How are things with him and his stepmom?"

"Tyler didn't mention her. He never really talks about her actually. I know they live in the same house, but that's about it. I don't think there's much interaction at all."

"When did his dad go into the Army reserves?"

"About a year or so ago."

When Kathy again seemed to be growing suspicious from all the questions, Sean quickly said, "How about your mom? How much longer will she be in?"

"She has two more years to go to get her full pension. Then she gets it right away, so she can enjoy it before she's, you know, really, really old, like fifty."

Sean exchanged a glance with Michelle.

"Perish the thought she should have to wait until she's *that* old," said Sean dryly.

"Foot in the grave," added a smiling Michelle.

"I wonder if Sam Wingo pulled his full twenty?" said Sean.

Kathy said, "I don't think so. Tyler said his dad went

135

into the Army after he turned twenty-five. The paper
said he was forty-five when he was killed. That means
he's not old enough to have served twenty years if he
left the Army a year ago."

Michelle said, "Okay, but then he apparently left the
Army only one year short of a full pension. Why do
that after busting your hump for nineteen years?"

"Maybe he got a better job that would pay him a
lot more money," said Kathy.

"Could be," said Sean, who sounded far from convinced.

"Have you seen any sign of more money in the
Wingo household?" asked Michelle. "I mean, they
haven't moved, right? But what about a new car, computers, renovation to the house?"

"No, nothing like that. And Tyler never mentioned
anything. Their house is nice but it's, you know, like
just a regular house."

"So if not money, why else would he have left?"
wondered Sean. He glanced at Kathy. "Did Tyler ever
talk to you about what his dad did at work? DTI?"

"He just said he was in sales. You know, he'd meet
with clients and stuff and sell things."

"DTI specializes in foreign translators for the country of Afghanistan primarily," said Michelle. "You
wouldn't think you'd need a big sales force to push
that product."

Kathy shrugged. "My mom says it takes forever to
sell stuff to the government because of all the rules

and red tape. But when you do sell something you can make a lot of money. But you have to know people, she told me."

"Which would make sense to use an Army vet to sell things to the Army," said Michelle, looking at Sean.

He nodded slowly. "Kathy, can you think of anything else that might help us?"

She started to shake her head no, but then stopped. "Well, Tyler did say one thing. It might not be important, especially since his dad is dead."

"What?" asked Michelle.

"He and his dad had this code language they used that only the two of them could understand. They'd use it in emails when his dad was deployed."

Michelle asked, "Why would they use a code?"

"The military's not supposed to monitor personal emails but lots of people think they do. And I think it meant a lot to Tyler that he and his dad had this special code. I did something similar when my mom was over there."

Sean said, "Did he tell you what the code was?"

"No." Kathy drew a long breath. "I don't understand why all this is happening to him but I know it's not his fault."

"No, it's not," agreed Michelle.

Kathy checked her watch. "I have to get going. My mom is expecting me."

"Do you need a lift?" asked Michelle.

"No, the bus picks up right outside."

"We can take you," said Sean. Kathy looked at him warily and he added, "And you're very smart not to accept rides from people you don't really know."

Kathy gave him a shy smile, collected her bag, and started to walk off.

"I hope you can help Tyler," she said.

"We *will* help him," replied Michelle.

After she left Sean turned to Michelle. He said, "Okay, we learned a lot, but not much that was actually helpful."

"What's bugging me is why leave the Army one year short of getting your full pension? I mean, who does that?"

"Well, whoever does it has to have an awfully good reason. And with Wingo it can't be because of disciplinary problems," observed Sean.

"Right. He was in the reserves and they sent him back over there so it wasn't like he'd screwed up or gotten a bad-conduct discharge."

She looked over at the doorway and stiffened.

"Okay, this is about to get a little dicey."

Sean looked at the door.

Two men in military uniforms were standing there. They spotted Sean and Michelle and started walking toward them. And both men were armed.

19

"Would you two like some coffee?" asked Sean as the uniforms stopped in front of their table. "It's cold out there. Almost as cold as it's gotten in here."

"Sean King and Michelle Maxwell?" asked one of them.

"The military knows all," said Sean pleasantly.

"Could you please step outside?" said the same uniform. His stripes and insignia showed him to be a sergeant in the military police.

"I think we're just fine right here, actually," said Michelle.

"Could you step outside?" said the uniform again.

"Why?" asked Sean.

"We need to talk to you."

"Which is something you can do right here." He motioned to two empty seats at the table.

"We would prefer if this took place outside."

"Then we have a difference of opinion. But since you're military police and neither of us is in the military, I'm not seeing how you get us outside against our wishes when we are breaking no laws that would allow you to execute a citizen's arrest."

"You the lawyer?" said the other uniform. "You sound like one," he added when Sean nodded.

The sergeant laid a hand on top of his sidearm.

"That would be a career-ending mistake, Sergeant," said Sean. "And neither you nor I would want that."

"Then I guess we do this the harder way."

"What way would that be?" asked Michelle warily.

The sergeant slipped his phone out and sent a text.

Five seconds later the door to the Panera burst open and in walked three men in suits.

"Sean King and Michelle Maxwell?" said the lead man.

"Who wants to know?" replied Sean.

Three Homeland Security badges were shoved in their faces.

"Let's go," barked the lead agent.

As Sean and Michelle were yanked from their seats, the sergeant said, with a smile, "*That's* the harder way."

The forty-minute ride in an SUV with blacked-out windows landed them at a facility in Loudoun County, Virginia, that was surrounded by large stands of trees. They were hustled through the front doors, taken past security after their weapons were confiscated, and led down a hallway.

Sean said, for the umpteenth futile time, "What the

hell is this about?" And for the umpteenth time he received not a single answer.

They were taken to a small, bare conference room and told to sit. The door was closed and locked behind them.

Sean looked around the space.

Michelle said, "DHS? Why are they involved? Isn't the DoD enough of an eight-hundred-pound gorilla?"

Sean put a finger to his lips and pointed to a small listening device poking out above the molding next to the ceiling.

A few minutes later the door opened and a man entered. He was about Sean's height, around fifty, still trim, with thick legs that stretched his pants to near capacity. He wore no jacket. Against his white dress shirt was a shoulder holster with no pistol in it.

He was holding a file. He sat across from them and read from the file for so long that Sean was about to say something when the other man looked up.

"Interesting stuff," said the man. "I'm Jeff McKinney, by the way. DHS Special Agent Jeff McKinney to be precise."

"And I'm an especially pissed-off private citizen," replied Sean.

"Make that two," said Michelle.

McKinney sat back. "Coffee, water, tea?"

"Answers and apologies would do just fine," answered Sean. "With the apologies preferably up front."

"Apologize for what? Doing our job?"

Sean shook his head. "Not gonna cut it, McKinney. I don't think Homeland's job is to jerk law-abiding citizens out of their chairs at a public place without telling them why or reading them their rights. So we've technically been kidnapped. Unless you've added felonies to your official duties, you've got a massive lawsuit coming your way. I'll want to spell your name right. Is it M-c or M-a-c?"

McKinney smiled and tapped the file. "Let's talk Tyler Wingo."

Sean leaned forward. "Let's talk you letting us the hell out of here."

"But I haven't asked my questions," McKinney said pleasantly.

"You can direct them to my lawyer. I'm going to call him right now."

"You don't need a lawyer. You haven't been arrested."

"We have been detained against our will. Same thing in my book. But if we haven't been arrested, then you have no power to hold us." He started to rise.

"National security trumps a lot of what's in the Constitution, Mr. King. So please sit back down. I don't want to resort to restraints, but I will if I have to."

"You're only digging your hole deeper."

"I think we both want the same thing. What's good for Tyler Wingo."

Sean sat back down while Michelle warily watched both men.

"Well, if you're working with the Army I seriously doubt that."

"What do you have against the Army? They're good people."

Sean leaned back in his chair and seemed to make up his mind. "Okay, ask your questions."

"What's your connection with Tyler Wingo?"

"Confidential. Unless he's waived it."

"He's not old enough to be your client."

"While it's true we couldn't enforce a contract against Tyler because he has not yet reached the age of majority, we accord all clients, regardless of age, the same professional courtesy of maintaining confidentialities."

"Then this conversation will be very short."

"What I was hoping for, actually," said Sean.

McKinney opened the file, pulled a piece of paper from it, and slid it across to Sean. He looked down at it while Michelle read over his shoulder.

"As you can see, Tyler Wingo has waived any confidentiality rights he might have. So you can answer my question. What is your relationship with him?"

Sean pushed the paper away. "How much did you have to threaten to get him to sign that?"

"We don't threaten kids, Mr. King. He signed it because he wanted to. Now, what is your relationship?"

"He retained us to investigate his father's death."

"His father was KIA in Afghanistan. He and his stepmother were duly informed of this. There is nothing you can add to that. It's not like you can fly into Afghanistan and start poking around. It's a war zone and a military zone and you would have no jurisdiction whatsoever as your PI license does not extend to international domains. I checked."

Sean said nothing to this.

"So were you trying to take advantage of the boy? Did he pay you money? Did you ask for a retainer?"

"We haven't gotten a cent from Tyler."

"You mean not yet? But you would have billed him, right?"

"Have you really checked us out?" asked Michelle. "I'm assuming you have. So you have to know that we're legit. We don't run around like ambulance chasers trying to get money out of grieving teenagers. We found Tyler running down the street in the middle of a storm. He was upset. We took him back home. He contacted me and said he wanted us to look into his father's death. We told him there wasn't much we could do."

"And so why didn't it end right there?" interjected McKinney.

"Because he was insistent. We really didn't want to take the case," said Sean. "But at the same time, if he was going to pursue it, I would rather it be people like us than others who might take advantage of him."

"What more did you possibly think you could learn

about his father's death? It occurred in Kandahar in combat, for God's sake."

Michelle said, "On the surface it seemed like nothing. His father was dead. Small-arms fire. Coffin was supposed to arrive at Dover." She paused and looked at Sean. "But then things started getting a little squirrelly."

"Squirrelly how?" asked McKinney.

"For starters, now the Army is telling him that his father was also hit by a mortar shell and there is really nothing left of the body. So no Dover."

"So what?" asked McKinney. "Combat is not neat and tidy. The man is still dead. He's certainly not the first casualty, nor will he be the last unfortunately."

"Right," said Sean. "So why is the Army and now DHS so interested? You said this was a national security issue. How?"

"You really think I can answer that?"

"Well, if it is a national security issue then you've just as good as told us this situation is different, because most soldiers who get killed in combat are not normally at the epicenter of a DHS matter. You can't have it both ways, Agent McKinney."

"On the contrary, I can have it any way I want. What I'm telling you is to back off and stay away from Tyler Wingo."

"So the kid is not going to be told the truth?"

"His father is dead. That's all he needs to know. Now let him grieve properly."

"But *is* his father really dead?" asked Michelle. The

statement drew a warning glance from Sean that she ignored.

"What the hell do you mean by that?" snapped McKinney.

Michelle leaned forward and went eye-to-eye with him. "Well, national security claims are so often accompanied by bullshit that I was just wondering. Are you guys going back to the daily color updates anytime soon? What was orange for again, imminent annihilation or perilous peril? I could never keep them straight."

"Do you know how miserable I can make your life?" said McKinney, pointing a finger at her.

"Pretty miserable," replied Sean as he hooked Michelle's arm. "We'll be going now unless you have any more questions or objections."

McKinney glared at Michelle. "I do not want to see you again. If I do, it will not be pleasant for you. That's a promise and I always keep my word."

"Is that it?" asked Sean.

McKinney leaned forward. "This is your last warning. You're at the edge of the cliff. Don't take the next step."

A minute later Sean and Michelle were being escorted out of the building.

They were dropped off at the Panera. The black SUV roared away, leaving them staring at each other in the parking lot.

Michelle folded her arms over her chest and leaned against her Land Cruiser.

"I am officially and majorly pissed off," she exclaimed.

Sean wearily rubbed his temples. "Why did you think it was smart to let him know we doubt Sam Wingo is dead?"

"Because I was *unofficially* pissed off back then and he was acting like such a smug bastard. I lost control."

"You need to *control* your emotions better, Michelle, or we're going to get our asses handed to us. This is DHS and DoD we're facing. Together they are the one-ton gorilla that stomps on anyone it wants to."

She pushed off from the truck. "How can we leave this alone now? There is something going on, Sean. You know it and I know it."

"I'm not disputing that. The question is how do we keep going and stay out of jail at the same time."

"We haven't done anything wrong."

"Do you think they need a real reason to stick us away somewhere? He as good as told us that. National security, Michelle. Like McKinney said, it trumps the Constitution. Hell, they might even send us to Gitmo. No one would ever find us."

"Well, I'm not giving up."

"I didn't say anything about giving up. I just meant we had to do it smart."

"So what's the plan?"

"Oh, don't worry. When I think of one you'll be the first to know."

20

Tyler Wingo sat on his bed in his room and studied the piece of paper. He'd written down the message he'd received from his father before deleting it. Not that he could ever forget it. But he'd written it down because that made it seem more real than if it was just in his head.

His father's message was both straightforward and puzzling.

I am sorry. Please forgive me.

Sorry for what, Dad? What do you want me to forgive you for? Dying? But you can't be dead. You aren't *dead.*

Tyler folded the paper twice and slipped it into the front pocket of his jeans. He lay back on his bed and gazed around his room. Every surface carried memories of his father, from the sports and music posters on the walls, to the baseball glove and football gathering dust on a shelf, to the framed photo of the two of them at a swim meet where his father had been a timer.

Tyler snaked a hand inside his T-shirt and pulled out the pair of official dog tags his father had had made for him. He rubbed the flat metal between his fingers and wondered where his dad might be right now. Did he have his dog tags? Was he safe? Was the email sent after he was supposedly dead really from him? Or was it somehow a big mistake? He knew his father had written it, because it had been in their special code.

He rolled over onto his stomach and stared at the raindrops on his window. It had been a gloomy day and now a cold overcast night and thus a perfect match for what he was feeling. He had always thought that he would know if his dad had been injured over there. He thought he would just feel it. But then again he thought he would be able to tell that about his mom. And he and his dad had found her on the floor of her bathroom with a bullet in her head and the gun beside her. Her suicide note had been neatly folded and on the counter next to the sink. Its contents had been terse.

I can't do this anymore. I'm sorry. I'll miss you.

He shook his head to rid himself of the image of this final message from her. But it was always there, just in the back of his mind, ready to poke out when he least expected it. It could drive the smile off his face in a split second or drown a laugh in his throat.

He rose and walked over to his desk, an old-style military metal model that his father had gotten when the Army had cleaned out some surplus inventory during the expansion of Fort Belvoir in Alexandria.

He sat down, slid open the top drawer, and pulled the photo out.

He traced the faces of his father, his mom, and him. They had been at the Army 5K that he had run with his dad. They were happy, all smiles; the sun was shining and they were celebrating with ice cream cones after the run. Hugs, smiles, and ice cream barely five years ago. Then less than a year later everything had changed. No, everything had collapsed. His life became something else entirely. It was as though this room, this photo even, didn't belong to him. As though it were telling the history of someone else, because Tyler really no longer recognized the person that used to be him.

First, his mom dying. And then his dad marrying a woman Tyler didn't really even know. And now his dad was gone. In a way each of the people in that photo, his dad, his mom, and even him, was truly gone.

"Tyler?"

He didn't move. He just sat there staring at the photo.

Jean slipped into the room and perched on the edge of his bed.

"Tyler?" she said again but barely above a whisper.

He still didn't move.

"Can you at least look at me?"

He finally looked at her blankly.

She said, "You didn't eat your dinner."

"Wasn't hungry."

"You swim miles at practice. How can you not be starving?"

"Just not."

He turned back to the photo.

"They told me about those people."

He glanced at her sharply. "What people?"

"The man and woman who brought you home that night. I don't remember their names."

"Sean King and Michelle Maxwell."

"Right. Anyway, they won't be bothering you anymore."

"They *weren't* bothering me. I hired them."

"To do what exactly?"

"You wouldn't understand."

"Try me."

"No, I'm not going to *try* you."

"Your father is dead, Tyler. We can't change that."

"That's right, we can't."

"So why hire those people?"

"Like I said, you wouldn't understand."

She stood. "Don't you think I miss him too?"

"I don't know, Jean. Do you?"

"How can you possibly say that? I loved him."

"If you say so."

"Why do you have to be this way to me?"

He spun around in his chair. "Because I don't really know you. It's like I'm living with a stranger."

"I've been your stepmother for nearly a year."

"Okay, but that doesn't mean I know you. We've never spoken more than a few words to each other. I wasn't invited to see you get married. I didn't even know you two were getting married. Don't you think that's weird? I'm his only kid."

"Your father wanted it that way."

Tyler rose, his face flushed. "No," he snapped. "My dad would not have wanted it that way. He would have wanted me to be a part of it."

"He was afraid you'd be upset that he was remarrying."

"And his solution was to just bring you home one day and tell me you're my stepmom? How does that make sense?"

"Regardless, honey, we have to try to get along. We're all that's left for each other."

Tyler looked like he might be sick. "We don't have each other, Jean. We've never had each other. I'm an orphan now. I don't have anybody."

There was an awkward silence and then Jean said, "The Army is sending some care volunteers here tomorrow."

"Care volunteers? What for?"

"To help us. They can run errands. Take you to school. Help with meals. I've got a lot on my plate right now. A lot of things to cope with."

"Well, you can take me off your coping list. I don't need any help. And I can get myself to school."

"Tyler, you can't just shut everyone out."

"I'm going to find out what really happened to my dad. And I've got people who will help me. I'm going to find the truth, Jean." He added with a shout, "I will."

He jumped up and rushed down the stairs.

She started to go after him but then stopped. She walked to his desk, gazed down at the photo of the three Wingos, and then slipped a phone from her jeans pocket.

She thumbed in a text message and sent it off. It was only four words, but they actually said quite a lot.

We have a problem.

Tyler grabbed a set of car keys off the hook next to the fridge, went out the side door, and climbed into his father's pickup truck. Every scent was his dad's. There was a gun rack in the back window and an American flag sticker on the lower right-hand corner of the windshield. A pair of miniature plastic army boots dangled on a chain hung from the rearview mirror.

The two floor mats read, I Am Army Strong.

Tyler started the truck, popped it into reverse, and backed out of the driveway. He glanced at the clock on the dash. Nearly eight p.m. He stopped at the curb and thumbed in a text. He waited. A few seconds later he got a reply. He hit the gas and sped down the road.

Five minutes later he pulled up in front of Kathy Burnett's house. She was waiting for him on the sidewalk. She climbed into the truck and shut the door firmly behind her.

He looked at her. "What did you tell your parents?"

"That I was going to see Linda down the street. She'll cover for me."

He nodded and drove off.

"What did you want to talk about?" asked Kathy.

Tyler didn't answer her right away. "Stuff," he said at last.

"What kind of stuff? About your dad, you mean?"

He nodded.

"Tyler, what's really going on?"

He glanced at her and slowed down. "What do you mean?"

"I'm talking about those two detectives you hired? Why did you need them?"

"Stuff about my dad, I told you."

"But your dad was killed in combat. The Army told you that. I'm a military brat like you. We all understand that could happen. There's no mystery about it."

"Well, there might be some mystery here," he replied.

"Like what?"

"I hired these detectives because I didn't think the Army was telling me the truth about my dad."

"I know you were upset about what they told you. But why in the world would you think they'd lie about that?"

"Because at first they told me he was shot. Then they said he was blown up and that there was nothing left of him and there was no need to go to Dover. I'm not really sure how the Army could have gotten that so wrong."

"Well, maybe they did. Mistakes happen, even in the military. The stories my mom could tell you."

"Yeah, well, they shouldn't make mistakes about stuff like this," Tyler replied, his voice sounding hoarse.

Kathy put a hand on his shoulder. "No, you're right, they shouldn't."

"But then some more men from the Army came to see us. And also guys in suits who they said were with another agency, only I don't know which one."

"Why did they come to see you?"

"To tell me to fire King and Maxwell."

"Why?"

"I don't think they wanted them digging around into my dad's case." He looked over at Kathy. "Something is going on here that's really weird."

"Like what?"

He pulled the truck off to the side of the road and put it in park. He turned to her. "I got an email from my dad."

"When?"

"After he died."

Kathy stared at him, her face growing pale. "How could that be?"

"It was date-stamped. They told me when my dad was supposed to have been killed. The email was sent days after that."

"Maybe somebody else sent it."

"Couldn't have. It was in the code only my dad and I would know how to read."

Kathy looked out the window and shivered. "This is really creepy, Tyler." She glanced back at him. "Do you...do you really think your dad might be alive?"

Tyler didn't answer right away. He was afraid that if he said what he believed, it would not come true. "Yeah, I do."

"But your dad was a sergeant in the reserves. Nothing against him but why would this be such a big deal for the Army? It wasn't like he was a general."

"I think my dad was a bigger deal than people knew."

"What do you mean?"

"He left the Army right before his twenty years was up. Who does that? He blew his pension."

"That lady detective said the same thing."

"You met with Michelle?" he said, surprised.

"And Sean. Earlier today. They knew we were friends."

"So that means they're still working the case," he said thoughtfully.

"The Army might not like that, Tyler."

"I don't give a crap what the Army doesn't like. This is my dad we're talking about. If he's not dead, I want to know where he is. I want him to come back home. I'm not letting this drop."

"I guess if it were my mom, I wouldn't let it go either."

"You can't tell anybody about this."

"I won't. I promise."

He stared at her intently and then turned the truck around and drove her back home.

When Tyler got back to his house, his stepmother wasn't there and her car was gone. He went up to his bedroom and studied his cell phone. He started to make a call on it but then stopped. What if they had his phone under surveillance?

He ran back downstairs, climbed into the truck, and drove off again.

There was a payphone, one of the last in the area, at a 7-Eleven about two miles from his house. He dropped in the coins and dialed the number.

Michelle answered on the second ring.

Tyler said, "I want to hire you again."

"You sure?" said Michelle.

"Very sure," replied Tyler.

"Good, because we were never really off the case."

21

Sam Wingo had finally dozed off on the bus on which he was a passenger, but he was nearly lifted out of his seat when the vehicle struck a particularly large pothole. He looked out the window into the gathering dawn. The terrain was bleak and would grow bleaker still. He might as well have been on the moon.

He turned to the person sitting next to him. She was an old woman dressed in traditional Muslim garb. A crate of vegetables was in her lap. She was softly snoring. She was obviously more used to the rough roads than he was.

Years ago he had traveled from Turkey into Iran for some clandestine work with a team of soldiers. They had made their crossing at the foot of Mount Ararat where Noah, according to the Scriptures, had completed his voyage on the Ark. The trip from Istanbul to Tehran could normally be made overland in three days. But Wingo's team had not been able to avail itself of ordinary modes of transportation, nor could the men make the border crossing at a legitimate site because they would have been arrested on the spot. Thus a three-day journey had taken a week.

Six hours after the team had arrived at its destination in Iran, three terrorists who had escaped American justice were dead. Wingo and his team had gotten out of the country a lot faster than they had taken to get in. The exit plan had been carefully constructed and still they had barely made it, with Iranian security forces right on their heels.

His journey now wasn't carefully constructed. He was flying by the seat of his pants. His odds of success, he knew, were abysmal. And yet he didn't care. He was going to make this work because he was going to get back to his son.

From Kabul to Peshawar in Pakistan normally took about ten hours' driving, with a border crossing in between. Buses were slower and relatively cheap. Taxis were faster but they cost more. Wingo didn't really care about money; the difference of a few euros was not important. The problem was getting across the border. And while he had originally been given papers that would have allowed him to do that, he couldn't use them now. He couldn't trust anyone, not even, it seemed, his own government.

While the road between Kabul and Jalalabad was not the best, major portions of it had been resurfaced recently. However, the route was considered one of the most dangerous in the world because of the numerous traffic accidents, many of them fatal. And the driver of

Wingo's bus seemed determined to add to that count. He drove with barely concealed ferocity, both cursing and swerving with regularity and pushing the bus forward with bursts of stomach-lurching acceleration, followed by abrupt braking that threw passengers around like pinballs. Sometimes it seemed like the creaky bus would simply flip over.

Wingo gazed around for at least the twentieth time at his fellow passengers, who didn't seem to care about the maniacal driver. They appeared to be typical Afghans or Pakistanis making their way back and forth across the two countries. Wingo was the only Westerner on board, which alone made him stand out. He had tried to lessen this some by darkening his face and covering himself with a hoodie and glasses. And he had grown a full beard since being deployed.

The largest city in between Kabul and the Pakistani border was Jalalabad, which was the second-largest city in eastern Afghanistan and also the capital of the Nangarhar province. Despite being considered one of the most beautiful of all Afghan cities, with its prime location at the confluence of the Kabul and Kunar Rivers, it was not considered safe for Westerners because the political climate was too unstable. This was so despite the presence of the largest American base in Afghanistan, Forward Operating Base Fenty adjacent to the Jalalabad Airport.

Wingo knew that the mujahideen had taken the city in the early 1990s after expelling the Soviets.

Commencing at that point and continuing until the present virtually every Afghan man had at least one automatic weapon, many of them Russian-made AK-47s. The Taliban had taken control of the city after the expulsion of the Soviets before being defeated by the United States and driven from power in retaliation for 9/11. Wingo also knew the Taliban was desperate to take over Afghanistan once more. And Jalalabad's proximity to the Pakistani border made it a prime goal for the insurgents' efforts to reclaim the country; hence the current instability.

The road ended at the border. Travelers crossed over on foot and then were picked up by buses or taxis for their onward journey—unless it was lunchtime, when the border was closed. Yet there was another complication involved for Wingo. This part of Pakistan was not controlled by the government.

This was Khyber Pakhtunkhwa, formerly the North West Frontier Territory, and the area was under the rigid rule of local tribes. Foreign travelers had to obtain permission to pass through here, which followed the legendary Khyber Pass between the two countries. The trip would be made by taxi, and in the taxi with you there would be a solider. The permission was free. The taxi ride and accompanying soldier were not. All in all, the price was astonishingly cheap by Western standards. But then again, what was your life worth?

Wingo could not cross at the border. He had no

permission and no papers he could use, and he was in no position to ask for permission, free or not. Thus he was getting off at Jalalabad. He was the only one who did. The bus would continue on and reach the border before it closed at lunchtime. His crossing, if it came, would be at night.

He had a contact in the city, though, and he intended to exploit that contact to the fullest. Because of the heavy American presence here he had to be careful. There would be watchful eyes everywhere, both Americans and locals. And right now neither side was his ally. He was fluent in Pashto, which was the primary language spoken in the country. He was also conversant in Dari, the second most popular language here. But he could not speak either one in a native dialect; virtually no American could. He would simply keep his mouth closed for the most part.

He had arranged to meet his contact later in a room in a hotel that was as far from the airport as he could manage. He got to the hotel early so he could see if anything was amiss. He had to trust his contact to a certain degree, but he trusted no one fully.

It was early in the morning, but the temperature was already nearing sixty. In the heat of the day it would soar into the eighties this time of year. Still, Wingo had endured far worse; a thermometer even close to triple digits was not a particular hardship.

He waited in the hall outside the room, keeping to the shadows. Through a window in the corridor he could see planes lifting off from the airport. They used to be all military aircraft, but the Americans had released the airport back to the Afghans, and commercial flights had started up soon thereafter. Wingo wished he could have climbed aboard such a flight. The trip in the air to New Delhi would have taken only about ninety minutes. On land the nearly thousand-kilometer distance would take him far longer. But traveling by plane, particularly in this region, involved lots of security checkpoints and required specific documents, none of which he had. So he was grounded, for now.

He continued to wait in the shadows until he heard someone coming. When the man approached the door, Wingo was next to him in an instant, one hand around the butt of his pistol. The two men entered the room, and Wingo locked it behind them.

The man was a Pashtun whom Wingo had met three years ago. It was a mission that had ended successfully and allowed the Pashtun to rise higher in his official organization. The men had become as friendly as they possibly could under the circumstances. His name was Adeel, and right now he was Wingo's last and only hope for getting out of the country.

Adeel sat on the rickety bed and looked up at him.

"I understand that it is bad," he said solemnly.

"What have you heard?" asked Wingo.

"Your name over official communication channels. The comments were not flattering."

"What are they saying?"

"A botched mission and missing assets."

"Where do they think I am?"

"No one seems to know. I doubt they think you are in Jalalabad."

"I don't want to be here long. I need to get across the border, unofficially. I have to think my photo will be in the border guards' hands. And though I look a bit different now, it's not enough."

"Can you tell me what happened?" asked Adeel.

"A mission did go to hell, Adeel. But I was set up. By who, I don't know right now. But I can't trust my own guys, that's how bad it is."

Adeel nodded. "Do you trust me?"

"It's the only reason you're sitting here."

Adeel lifted a packet of papers from his jacket. "This will get you through to New Delhi. That is all I can promise."

"You get me to India, I can make it the rest of the way back to the States."

Adeel looked surprised. "You will go back there even though you do not trust your own people?"

Wingo took the documents, examined them, came away satisfied, and thrust them into the inner pocket of his duffel. "I have a son back there who thinks I'm dead."

Adeel nodded. "I have four sons. They often think that their father is dead. I understand. And now I know that you are innocent. Guilty men do not return to their homes."

"So you didn't believe in my innocence from the start?"

Adeel shrugged. "This part of the world is not known for its trust in anything or anyone."

"I have to make this right, Adeel."

Adeel rose and said, "Then may Allah be with you, my friend."

That night Wingo made the crossing into Pakistan at Torkham, along a route devised by Adeel, while two uniformed guards, cash bribes in their pockets, looked the other way.

Wingo was out of the fire and now into the frying pan—Afghanistan swapped for Pakistan. His next destination was the city of Peshawar, about sixty miles distant through the switchbacks of the Khyber Pass. He was traveling by private taxi, with a member of the Khyber Rifles sitting next to him as a guard. The journey would take the better part of two hours. Without the local guard, Wingo would be going nowhere. This protection was costing him all of two euros while the taxi was setting him back about four times that. He considered it money well spent. With Adeel's help he had avoided going through immigration control at the border. Traveling from Afghanistan into Pakistan was a bit more rigorous and chaotic than going the other way.

He looked out the window of the taxi as they

traveled along the pass. This was the same route taken by the likes of Alexander the Great and Genghis Khan on their way to violently annex large parts of the known world. The pass had been largely closed during the Soviet occupation, and it was still shut down sometimes to foreigners. Wingo noted the blazing lights of drug smugglers' massive estates, which dotted the stark, denuded hills, complete with anti-aircraft guns. There would always be money in drugs, he knew, but that wasn't his concern right now.

The guard never once looked at him, perhaps on orders from Adeel. Wingo was fine with that. He was not a chatty person and never said with ten words what he could say with only one, or better yet simply a glance.

After Peshawar would come the capital city of Islamabad. From there he would make his crossing into northern India with the documents provided him by Adeel. Then it was a straight shot south to New Delhi. And from there a long-haul flight home with one connection in Doha, provided he could get a fake passport in India. Total flight time to go halfway around the world, about twenty hours. It had taken him far longer than that to go only two hundred miles.

Yet he had a lot farther to go to catch his ride on a jumbo jet to the States.

When he glanced behind him and saw the other vehicle closing in, Wingo suddenly realized that he might not even make it to Peshawar.

22

Wingo's first thought was that this had been a total setup, with the guard next to him fully in on the conspiracy. When the shot came through the window and blew through the back of the guard's head, Wingo didn't think that anymore.

He screamed at the driver in Pashto to basically put the gas pedal through the floorboard if he wanted to keep living. The taxi surged ahead even as shots pinged off the car.

As the dead guard slumped against him, Wingo grabbed the man's AR-15. He aimed it through the blown-out window, waited for the other car to edge closer, and then pulled the trigger. There were three men in the other car, but he was aiming for only one of them.

Wingo fired and the other driver's blood exploded against the windshield. The vehicle veered off to the side, slammed against a solid road barrier, caught fire, overturned, and a few seconds later exploded.

Wingo turned back around and looked at his driver. "Shit."

He felt the cab drift. He leapt over the front seat and settled next to the driver. He was an older man who would not age one day more. A bullet to the back of his head, probably a ricochet, had seen to that.

Wingo took control of the steering wheel, then stretched his leg out and hit the brakes. He guided the car over to the side. Luckily there were no other vehicles on this stretch of road. He lifted both bodies out of the vehicle, pushed them over the barrier, and watched as they rolled down the dirt slope and settled at the bottom on a pile of boulders. He did not have time to give them a proper burial. He simply muttered a prayer.

Then he glanced over at the flaming car. His first impulse was to run over and find out who they were and why they were after him. But the flame ball increased as the gas in the tank was burned off. He quickly realized there would be nothing useful left. Just blackened corpses, bone, and twisted metal.

He drove off with no guard and no driver and his clothes covered in the guard's blood. He had a destroyed rear window, a blood-splattered interior, and no guarantee that he had not been betrayed. If they did know where he was, another car would be sent after him. Or they might simply be waiting up ahead for him. And "up ahead" was formidable enough as it was, and it didn't involve men with guns.

Wingo had read Rudyard Kipling, who had described the Khyber Pass as a "sword cut through the mountains." This was an apt description, he felt, only unlike a sword blade the road was far from straight. The area here could have been the landscape on another planet that did not allow for human life. It was beyond bleak, beyond foreboding. No trees grew here. No animals made their homes here. No humans really lived here. It was simply here so one could go from one country to another as fast as possible, with "fast" being a relative term.

The pass was largely shut down in the late fall and winter. The grade was too steep and the climate too dangerous during those times. And Wingo was perilously close to "those times." He could feel the winds coursing through the mountains settling under his car and lifting it slightly. The pass was essentially a series of switchbacks connected by short distances of straight roads and tunnels through the Hindu Kush Mountain Range. It could be nauseating to drive even at slow speeds.

Wingo was not driving slowly. He was channeling his inner Formula One driver. The wind was blowing in through the shattered window and making his teeth chatter despite his having the heat cranked.

As he raced along, in his mind he was sorting through the possible scenarios and his counter for each one. He checked his watch and calculated how much farther it was to Peshawar. Then he debated whether he needed to even go there. Peshawar was a large city, with more than two and a half million residents spread over nearly five hundred square miles. That was good in that it was easier to hide among so many people. But it was bad in that you had many more eyes that might be spying on you, and the authorities would be only minutes away no matter where you were.

He decided to head directly to the Indian border. The documents that he had been given by Adeel should be sufficient to get him across. However, if Adeel had betrayed him, tipping off the men in the destroyed car, these documents were useless.

Wingo had to make a judgment call. Trust Adeel or not?

Normally, the answer would be an easy one for Wingo. You couldn't trust anyone. But he had looked the man in the eye. He had heard his words for himself. He decided that he trusted Adeel. The men in the car coming after them might have simply been criminals looking to rob or kidnap an American and hold him for ransom. That was not unusual in these parts.

Once through the pass he pulled off the road and changed into fresh clothes from his knapsack, burying the bloody ones. He drove into a small town late that night and left the shattered and bloodied taxi on a side street. He took a room in a local hotel where the manager accepted cash and asked no questions. The next morning he arranged for the rental of a motorbike using the document that Adeel had provided. He rode off on the bike. His next goal was to make the Indian border. Pakistan's national highway system was a good one, and the kilometers flew past. He stopped to eat and refuel. As he neared the border, he slowed.

This would be the real test of Adeel's loyalty. Or betrayal.

Wingo had been through this border before. The crossing was right down the middle of the village of Wagah. It had been split in half when demarcation took place in 1947, creating the country of Pakistan from land that had formerly been part of India. Wagah had perhaps the most elaborate border closing ceremony in the world. It took place right before sunset each day and involved the Indian and Pakistan border guards putting on an elaborate dance of exaggerated marching and high stepping with feet routinely reaching above heads. Crowds gathered, music was played, and the opposing guards would confront each other with aggressive posturing and grim faces, like two roosters about to duel.

Wingo didn't care about the performance. He simply wanted to hit the crossing shortly before the performance was to begin, because the crowds would have gathered and the guards would be focusing more on their upcoming performances than on border scrutiny. He timed it well, because he was the last person to cross the border before it was closed. When he reached Indian soil he looked back only once as the music started, the guards marching out to do their dancing battle. No one would remember the sole American on the motorbike who was so eager to leave Pakistan.

23

"I see what you mean," said Michelle to Sean as she watched the lady walking toward them.

They were sitting in a food court at a local mall. It was late afternoon so there were few patrons at the court. They were at a table as far away as possible from the other diners eating there.

Approaching from one end of the food court was Dana Brown. She was dressed down from the last time Sean had seen her, but her black tights and long white shirt rode well on her curvy and buxom figure.

"Pretty complete package, at least on the surface," noted Michelle, staring at the approaching woman.

"Yeah," said Sean. "But just keep any and all thoughts like that to yourself. We're here for information, and to get that we have to play nice."

"I always play nice."

He glanced at her, shook his head, and looked back at his ex as she arrived at their table. They rose and Sean said, "Michelle Maxwell, Dana Brown."

The two women exchanged tight, polite smiles and a quick handshake. They all sat and Sean said, "I'm assuming you have something for us since you called to meet?"

Dana kept her gaze on Michelle for a second longer and then turned to Sean.

"It was harder than I thought."

"Did you think it would be easy?" remarked Michelle.

"Since I was dealing with my husband, yes, actually. I'm sure you know how easily a man can be manipulated if a woman merely addresses his basic needs." She glanced demurely at Sean. "Pillow talk, like you said."

Michelle shot a glance at Sean and said, "I'm sure." She added, "But it sounds like addressing basic needs wasn't enough here."

Dana smiled and sat back. "That's why you have a Plan B, which I did. I won't go into great detail about how I accomplished it. I'm assuming you simply want the results." She turned to Sean. "This Wingo situation is being treated very seriously at the Pentagon."

"But how did you broach it with him?" asked Sean. "Like I said, I didn't want you to go out on a limb."

"I told him I was worried about him. He hasn't been eating; he's been moody. I knew something was up. So I just flat out asked him what was wrong and I wouldn't take national security BS for an answer. I was his wife and I trumped that. And if he couldn't trust me we had big problems."

"And what did he tell you?" asked Sean.

Dana looked down, her features not nearly as

confident. "I know this might sound somewhat surprising for me to say at this point, but I do feel guilty about doing this, Sean. He told me certain things in the strictest confidence, and I guess I'm having some doubts."

"He will never find out you told us, Dana. I promise you that. I don't care if they subpoena us and we have to commit perjury and go to prison. Your name will never come out from us."

He glanced at Michelle, who nodded. "You have my word too, Dana. As you know, we're former Secret Service agents, with emphasis on the 'secret.' We're just trying to help a kid who's trying to find out the truth about his dad."

Dana took a deep breath and leaned in closer. "Sam Wingo wasn't really in the reserves. He was still regular Army, but he left a year before his pension technically would have kicked in."

"Why?" asked Sean.

"To establish himself as a civilian. To take a job with a company."

"And to get married to a woman he hardly knew?" said Sean.

"Curtis didn't come out and say that, but I suspect that was also true."

"A lot of subterfuge. With what goal in mind?" asked Michelle.

"Something happened in Afghanistan. Wingo was on a top-secret mission to deliver something to someone. Only it never got there."

"What was it?"

"Curtis drew the line there and wouldn't tell me. And he might not even know. Okay, he's a two-star but there are lots of two-stars and they seem to have built a wall around this, at least the most important elements."

"And Sam Wingo?"

"Can't be located."

"Do they suspect that he might have pulled off some sort of a double cross?" asked Michelle.

"Curtis seemed to think he was a good man. But since he hasn't come in, things aren't looking too positive for him." She looked at Sean. "What do you know about it?"

Sean and Michelle exchanged glances.

He said, "Since you've been frank with us, I'll be frank with you. Tyler thinks his dad is alive."

"Well, according to Curtis it seems the Pentagon thinks he is too. The KIA stuff might have just been made up to cover the situation."

"While they look for Wingo?" noted Michelle.

She nodded. "And with the DoD after him I doubt the man can remain at large much longer." She glanced sharply at Sean. "But why does Tyler think his dad is still alive? He certainly isn't privy to the inner workings at the DoD."

Sean hesitated. "If I tell you, will you tell your husband?"

"Realistically I can't tell Curtis anything without

revealing all of this. And I'm afraid doing so would wreck my marriage. So, no, your secret is safe with me."

"Sam Wingo sent Tyler an email. Apparently after he was supposed to have died."

"What did it say?"

"'Please forgive me. I am sorry.'"

"Was that a confession of wrongdoing?"

Michelle said, "Or an apology for the military telling his son he was KIA."

"I guess if I had a child and that had happened, I would feel the need to apologize too," Dana said. She tapped the Formica tabletop with her fingernails. "What will you do now?"

Sean said, "What you've told us certainly helps answer some questions we've had. But it doesn't get us any closer to Wingo and the actual truth."

"I suppose you were right telling me to be afraid," said Dana. "This all sounds highly clandestine and not for the average citizen to know about."

"It is," said Michelle. She glanced to the left and stiffened just a fraction. Her Secret Service training had just aided her once more.

She picked up her cup of coffee and said in a low voice, "Three bogies, six nine and twelve, armed and with comm packs. And while they look legit, something is telling me they're not."

Sean didn't look in that direction. He simply stared over at Dana.

He said, "Dana, I want you to listen to me very carefully and then do exactly as I say."

His tone startled her, but she quickly regained her composure.

"I'm listening," she said a little breathlessly.

"There is a mall police substation right down that hall and to the left. Two policemen are stationed there. I want you to get up and go there. Don't hurry. Don't look around. Just walk normally. When you get there, tell them that you saw three men with guns in the food court and you were scared. They will call in backup and will go to investigate. You will proceed to your car by the shortest route possible and drive straight to the Pentagon. Is Curtis there?"

She slowly nodded.

"Okay, you will call him on the way and tell him that something has you concerned. You need to speak to him."

Dana frowned. "And what about you?"

"We'll be fine."

"That's what you always told me when you were with the Secret Service."

"Sean," hissed Michelle. "They're almost here."

"Just do it, Dana. Do it now."

Dana smiled, rose, and said, "See you next time. Take care." She turned and walked away and toward the police substation that was just around the corner.

Sean rose, and Michelle did, too. But they turned the other way, to face the three men heading toward them. Sean and Michelle split up, one heading right and the other left, which meant their opponents had to watch two targets instead of one.

Sean knew that if they were the authorities, creds would have come out by now. They hadn't. He searched each of the men's faces. His conclusion: military. But if so, where were the creds?

They could be former military.

They were within five feet of each other. In his periphery Sean saw Michelle's hand drift to her waist. His own hand rose nearer the gun in his shoulder holster. He would prefer to do this outside; although the food court was sparsely inhabited right now, there was still the potential for a lot of collateral damage.

The man directly in front of Sean stopped and said, "We need you to come with us. And the woman who was just with you too. Get on your phone and call her back here."

"And who might be asking?"

"All will be explained once you accompany us outside."

"Don't think so. My mother always told me to never go anywhere with strangers."

"You don't have a choice."

Michelle called out, "There are always choices."

Sean was about to say something when a voice yelled, "Freeze!"

The three men in front of Sean could see who was

calling out. When their hands reached for their guns Sean knew it was the mall police behind him.

Michelle had already darted forward and kicked the gun out of the man's hand directly in front of her. Then she laid him out with a blow to his throat. He dropped to the floor, gasping for air.

The man in the middle pulled his weapon and opened fire at the approaching police. One of the cops dropped dead to the floor. The other threw himself over a fast-food counter. Sean leapt forward, grabbed the gun hand of the man who had spoken to him, and wrestled with him over the weapon.

The surviving policeman shouted, "Drop your weapons."

All that got him was more shots fired at him. He ducked back down as all the civilians in the vicinity ran away screaming.

"Call in backup," Sean yelled at the cop.

Michelle had dipped low, used one arm as a pivot point, swung her long legs around, and clipped the feet out from under the middle shooter. He went down hard but kept his gun. He pointed it upward at her, but she was no longer there. She slid on her back, feet-first at him, ramming one of her heels into the side of his face. He yelled and grabbed her ankle. She rolled up and came down on top of his head with her right elbow. The back of his head smacked the hard floor, knocking him out. She rose in time to see Sean whirling at her after being thrown off by the man he had been fighting.

The man grabbed a second gun from a backup holster, aimed, but did not fire.

This was because Sean had turned and shot him in the chest with the gun he had ripped from the man's grip. The man fell to the floor.

Sean and Michelle turned in time to see the man she had first fought with lining up his sights on the second policeman as he tried to climb back over the fast-food counter.

Michelle pulled her gun and shot him in the side of his head right as he fired. He dropped back to the floor, dead. But his round had clipped the cop in the arm and he fell to the floor bleeding.

Michelle slid over to the dead shooter and searched his pockets.

"Nothing," she called out. "No wallet. No ID."

Sean ran over to the downed cop, ripped open his shirtsleeve, and examined the wound.

"Round went in and out. You're going to be okay," said Sean. He fashioned a tourniquet from the torn sleeve. "You called in backup?"

The cop nodded, pain hardening his features. "What the hell is going on?"

"I wish I could tell you."

Michelle knelt near him. "Is he okay?"

"He will be. Can't say the same for his partner."

An instant later they heard an ominous sound

behind them: a gun slide being racked back. They turned. The man in the middle had regained consciousness and had his gun pointed at them.

"No!" a voice shouted.

In disbelief Sean watched as Dana darted toward the man and hit him with her purse. "Dana, no!" shouted Sean.

The man turned and shot Dana in the chest. She stood frozen for a moment and then dropped to the floor.

Sean lined up his shot and put a bullet right into the man's brain.

He lowered his weapon and stared down at Dana on the floor, the blood pouring from her wound.

Sean ran toward her. "Dana!"

24

When Sean had reached Dana he used every procedure he had learned from his Secret Service days to stop the bleeding. But she had still lost a lot of blood, perhaps too much. Then she stopped breathing and Sean performed CPR on her, and finally her lungs expanded and her heart restarted. The paramedics arrived, took over, and stabilized her. Sean rode over in the ambulance while Michelle followed in her truck.

Sean and Michelle were now in the waiting room at the hospital. They had been interrogated by both local Virginia police and federal authorities. They told some but not all of what they knew. It was fortunate that witnesses to the events at the mall had uniformly reported that the three dead men were the aggressors and that Sean and Michelle's actions had been in self-defense, and had actually saved the life of one of the police officers.

That still did not buy them many points, particularly with the Feds.

A despondent Michelle looked up when she heard

the door to the waiting room open. She hoped it was a doctor with good news. But her features grew even more depressed when she saw who it was.

Agent McKinney from Homeland Security stood there.

"What part of 'stay out of it' didn't you get?" he barked.

"We were just at the mall having coffee," said Sean wearily. "If there's a law against that, I must've missed it."

McKinney plopped into a chair across from them. "You know exactly what I'm talking about. The woman who was shot? She just happened to be the wife of an Army two-star *and* your ex?"

"I was meeting with Dana, yes," Sean said stiffly. "She was helping us out on something."

McKinney snapped, "On the Wingo something? The something I told you to stay the hell away from?"

"I don't remember you being appointed to tell us which cases we could or couldn't take," said Sean sharply.

"Oh, I'm exactly that person. So you got her to help. How? Getting info from her hubby? Did you really stoop that low? Because it looks like you might have killed her in the process."

Sean said nothing to this, because McKinney was actually right. He had used Dana and she'd been shot and might not live. All because of him. What had seemed like a fairly innocuous way to get some helpful information now seemed like the most insane idea he'd ever had. And the most selfish.

They heard a noise at the door and looked up. General Curtis Brown stood there in full uniform, red-eyed, his lean face sagging with despair. He had obviously heard this exchange.

"Sean King?"

Sean rose, his face pale. "Yes? How's Dana?"

In answer Brown lunged and slammed a fist into Sean's face, knocking him over a chair and onto the floor.

Michelle instantly put herself between the general and Sean.

"Back off!" she snapped.

"I'm going to kill you," screamed Brown, and he tried to lunge past Michelle to get to Sean. She gripped his wrist and twisted it sideways and ripped his arm behind his back. He gasped, bent over in pain, and then with a massive effort broke free. When he took a swing at her, Michelle ducked and neatly clipped Brown's legs out from under him. He fell heavily to the floor. She put a boot on his back.

"Stay down," ordered Michelle.

When Brown tried to rise again, Michelle kicked him to put him back down.

"Stop, Michelle, just stop."

Sean had gotten to his feet. His face was cut and bruised and already swelling. Brown rose, too.

Sean stood in front of him. "You want to take

another swing, go ahead. I deserve it. Go ahead." He grabbed the general's hand and made a fist with it. "Go ahead," he shouted.

But Brown backed away, obviously confused by Sean's outburst. He sat heavily in a chair, put his face in his hands, and silently wept.

McKinney stood, flashed his ID although Brown wasn't even looking at him, and said, "General, I'm with DHS. My sincerest apologies for what happened to your wife. Please rest assured that I will do all I can to make sure *everyone* responsible for this horrendous state of affairs is held fully accountable."

He glared at Sean when he spoke this last part.

Sean stood there, his face bloody and puffy. He looked at no one other than Brown.

The door to the waiting room opened. The surgeon appeared, still in his operating room scrubs.

"General Brown?"

Brown looked up, his eyes wet with tears. "Yes," he said shakily.

The surgeon moved over to him and spoke in a low voice, but one that Sean and Michelle could still hear.

"Your wife is out of surgery. She did well. Now, the bullet did quite a bit of damage and she's still not out of the woods, but I'm hoping for a fairly complete recovery." He added, "It was a miracle she didn't bleed out. Whoever stopped the blood loss right after she was shot saved her life."

Michelle glanced encouragingly at Sean, but he was now staring at the floor.

"Would you like to see her?" the surgeon asked Brown. "She's not conscious of course, but—"

Brown quickly said, "Yes, please." He followed the surgeon out of the room without a backward glance at any of them.

Sean sat down while Michelle grabbed some tissues out of a box on a table, wet them at the water fountain outside the door, and used them to clean Sean's face. He neither stopped her nor assisted her. It was as though he didn't even know she was doing it.

McKinney sat down across from them. "Damn, he really cleaned your clock. Can't blame him, though." He added snidely, "Good thing you had your partner here to defend you or else you might be in the hospital too."

Michelle snapped, "Sean didn't exactly fight back, did he? And just for the record the person who stopped her bleeding out is this guy," she added, pointing at Sean.

"But she never would have been shot in the first place if not for him."

"Actually, he was the one who told her to get the police and then go to her car and drive to the Pentagon. If she had listened to him, none of this would have happened."

"No, if he hadn't gotten her mixed up in this none of it would have happened."

"He's right, Michelle," said Sean. He pushed her hand away from his face and stood. He looked down at McKinney. "You're right."

"Glad we agree on something. Now let's get down to it."

"To what exactly?" said Michelle since Sean did not appear to be listening.

"To what exactly you two are involved in."

"We already told you that, Agent McKinney," said Michelle in exasperation. "This all started with Sam Wingo disappearing and then coming back from the dead."

"Back from the dead?" said McKinney.

Sean looked down at him. "Why were you called in on this to shake us down? Who made the call?"

"I'm not going to answer that."

"Well, you should at least try to answer it for yourself. Any IDs on the dead guys?"

"Part of an ongoing investigation and thus not any of your business."

"They looked like military but they had no ID," said Sean.

"Military like Wingo?" asked McKinney curiously.

"Who wasn't really in the reserves at all."

"How do you know that?"

"That's confidential and I keep confidences. So, did some higher-ups at the Pentagon sic you on us?"

"That is no concern of yours."

"Oh, it's very much a matter of concern for me.

Those men were going to kill us, Agent McKinney. And they almost did kill someone I care about. I always take things like that very personally."

McKinney grabbed Sean's arm. "If you keep this up, I will have your ass arrested."

Sean pulled McKinney's hand off. "And if you keep stomping on my constitutional rights I will have a field day with you and DHS both in court and in the press."

Sean rubbed a trickle of blood off his face and started for the door.

Michelle glanced at McKinney. "You really are a piece of work."

McKinney ignored this and said, "Hey, King. What's next for you? Getting the kid shot?"

Sean kept walking.

Michelle followed and slammed the door behind her.

25

Sean sat in the truck, Michelle next to him. They were in the hospital parking lot. Sean hadn't yet started the vehicle.

Michelle said, "Just take deep breaths. And we need to get some ice for your face before it gets really swollen."

"This was my fault, you know that, right?" He kept staring straight out the windshield.

"No, I don't know that. I think it was the fault of the prick who shot her."

"She never would have been involved in this except for me, Michelle."

"Actually, I think I was the one who forced you into calling her. So if you want to place blame, lay it on me. But this kind of talk isn't getting us anywhere. If you really want to make it up to Dana, then I say we need to get to the bottom of what's going on."

Sean started the Land Cruiser. "Your logic is overwhelming, but logic is not going to cut it this time. We are going to attack this thing, though. Only not head-on."

"Why not?"

Sean pulled out of the parking lot. "Three guys at the mall. They weren't Feds. They looked to me like ex-military. They had the beef, the buzz cuts, the firepower, the veneer of authority."

"Ex-military. What would ex-military be involved in here?"

"Well, Sam Wingo wasn't in the reserves. He was regular Army. The DoD built a subterfuge and put him on a mission to deliver something. That mission got screwed and Wingo is off the grid. He contacted his son to tell him he was sorry. So, what was he delivering and who has it now?"

"Do you think Wingo took it?"

"I don't know. You vet a guy for a mission like that, you must feel he's pretty solid."

"So maybe the mission was a setup from the get-go and Wingo the fall guy. That might explain the email to Tyler."

Sean nodded in agreement. "The man Tyler described to us does not sound like a traitor. But if the mission *had* gone off as planned, what would the Army have told the Wingos? That Sam was KIA? MIA?"

"If that was part of the plan," said Michelle, "I'm betting a dad like Sam Wingo would have wanted someone there to be with Tyler. They don't have any other family, so …"

"So enter Jean Wingo as the stepmom."

"Which would explain the weird circumstances of the wedding. Tyler not even being invited. It being before a judge and all."

"Hell, they might not even be married," pointed out Sean.

"Right. I doubt Jean is even her real name."

He said, "So much deception, whatever that asset was it must've been really important."

"But now we have possible former military in the mix. What could they want?"

"You think they might have the asset?"

Michelle shrugged. "Maybe. But if so, do they also have Sam Wingo?"

"He got the email off to Tyler. What if he escaped and is now on the run?"

"Then he has the military and these other guys on his butt."

"Lucky him." Sean looked out the window. "We almost bit the bullet today too."

"I know. It was close."

"So these guys are good."

Michelle said, "More than good, I'd say."

"But we can take them. We did take them, in fact."

She glanced at him. "In the future it depends on how many of them there are. I left my superpowers back on my home planet."

"Well, they have three fewer bodies to throw at us after today." Sean rubbed his swollen jaw.

"When General Brown hears all the facts, Sean, he'll be sorry he punched you."

"I seriously doubt that. The next time the guy might just shoot me."

"So how are we going after this if we can't hit it straight-on?"

"Tyler is vulnerable, Michelle. If they went after us, they'll go after him in a heartbeat."

"So we stay away from him?"

"No, I think we need to be his protection detail."

"We can't cover him twenty-four seven," countered Michelle.

"No, but we can do our best."

"And solving the case?"

"I have an idea," he said.

"Care to share?"

"If Sam Wingo communicated with his son?"

Michelle caught on instantly. "Then Tyler can communicate with his dad by hitting reply."

"That's right. Only we'll be asking the questions."

"Sean, what do you think is going on?"

He drew a long breath. "Like Dana told us, I think the Army had some top-secret mission and it all went to hell in a handbasket. And whatever Wingo was brought in to deliver is out there in the wrong hands."

"But what could it be? A nuke? A biological agent?"

"I don't know, Michelle. I really don't know. But if it is a nuke or some turbocharged version of the Black

Plague, we might find out about it a lot sooner than we'd like."

"Why do we humans make things so complicated?"

"Because we're afraid that keeping things simple makes us unsophisticated. And uninteresting."

"You could be a philosopher. But how do we engage Tyler without making him a target?"

He said, "There's no way to do that. So we have to keep him safe at the same time he's helping us."

"But he lives with his stepmother."

"Did I say it was going to be easy?"

Sean gazed gloomily out the window. This was as bad as he had felt since, well, since watching Michelle fighting for her life in a hospital bed. He blamed himself for that one, too. If he had figured things out faster, she never would have been harmed.

"Why don't you text Tyler and see if he can meet us later? We'll have to keep it under the radar."

Michelle keyed in the text and fired it off.

Five minutes passed and then she got a response.

Michelle read it twice to make sure she was actually seeing what she was seeing.

"Sean?"

"Yeah."

"I think we might have a lot more access to Tyler than we thought."

"Why?"

"Because apparently his fake stepmom has disappeared too."

26

They didn't meet at the Panera, or at the pool.

It was a spot off a rural road about ten miles west of where Tyler lived. When he pulled up in his dad's pickup truck, Sean was already there.

Tyler climbed out of the truck and looked at him. "Where's Michelle?" he asked.

Sean pointed over his shoulder. "Right behind you."

Michelle pulled up in her Land Cruiser and got out. Sean eyed her. "Any problems?"

"No one followed him," she reported.

Tyler glanced sharply at her. "I didn't see you following me."

"That's sort of the point," she said, coming forward and standing next to them.

The air was chilly and damp and the sky overcast. They all shivered at the same time.

She said, "Let's do this in one of the vehicles."

"Not yours," said Sean quickly. "I hold the line against having meetings in Dumpsters. Let's use my sedan."

Giving him a brief scowl, Michelle followed them

over to the Lexus and they climbed in. Michelle sat in the back keeping watch out the windows while Tyler and Sean sat in the front.

"Tell us about Jean," Sean said. "Why do you think she's disappeared?"

"She's always at home when I get back from swim practice. She makes dinner. She nags me about homework. Always."

"But she wasn't there tonight?" said Michelle. "No dinner, no nagging."

"Not only that. Her car is gone. And her clothes too."

"Any note?" asked Sean. "Text, phone message?"

Tyler shook his head. "But I asked one of the neighbors. Mrs. Dobbers, the old lady across the street, said she saw Jean leaving around noon. She said she saw her put a suitcase in the trunk."

"Any reason why she would head out somewhere?" asked Michelle. "Sick relative somewhere close? Anything happen between the two of you?"

"I don't know about any sick relative. She never mentioned anyone. She and I had some words the other night. But it was nothing more than usual. She wasn't mad or crying or anything."

"What did she say exactly?" Sean asked.

"That she was sorry my dad was gone too. That we were all we had left. That got me mad. I told her I'd rather be an orphan." He looked embarrassed. "I shouldn't have said that. It was stupid."

"But she didn't break down crying or anything?" said Michelle.

"No. I just walked. Oh, I did tell her I was going to get to the truth. And that I was hiring you guys back to look into stuff."

"Bingo," said Michelle.

Sean nodded and looked at Tyler. "I think that's why she left."

"I don't understand. What does she have to worry about? I just want to find my dad."

"This is just speculation," began Sean.

"And we could be wrong," added Michelle.

"What!" Tyler snapped.

"Your dad married her really fast. They didn't seem to have a lot in common. You weren't even invited to the ceremony at the courthouse. That doesn't sound like your dad, does it?"

"No. That's what I've been saying." He stopped abruptly and his eyes widened in realization. "Are you saying it was all made up?"

"It *could* be," corrected Sean. "But right now it's just a theory. We have no proof. Not yet anyway."

"Why would my dad do that?"

"We learned some things about your dad today, Tyler."

"Tell me," he said quickly.

"He wasn't really in the reserves. He was still in the regular Army."

"What?"Tyler exclaimed, looking stunned. "My dad never told me that."

"He probably was barred from doing so," said Sean. "We believe he was on a special mission for the military in Afghanistan."

"But I don't understand. Why would he need to pretend to marry someone for that?"

Sean said, "There could be any number of reasons. He was going to be gone, Tyler. He had to have someone here to look after you. You couldn't really live on your own, not at your age. It might have been his only option. And they might not have even been married. You didn't attend the civil ceremony, right? You said they just showed up and said they were married."

Tyler looked away, his lips trembling. "So it was all a lie. He just lied to me."

Sean, seeing the hurt look on Tyler's face, added, "Which shows how much your dad cared about you. He didn't want you to be alone."

"That's bullshit," yelled Tyler. "If he really cared about me he wouldn't have pulled crap like this. He would have told me the truth. He told me he got married. He made me live with Jean for a freaking year. And it was all a bunch of lies?"

Michelle said, "We don't know that for sure, Tyler. Like Sean said, it's just one theory."

"I bet it's true," exclaimed Tyler. "I could tell my dad didn't really love her. They never held hands. I never saw them kissing. I never even saw them hug the whole time. It was all crap."

Sean looked at Michelle and drew a long breath. "The mission must have been really important, Tyler, and a long time in the making if he purportedly left the military a year ago and then 'married' Jean in preparation for it. You know when soldiers go into combat they can't tell anyone where they are, not even their families."

"I know that, okay? But this is different."

"It's a little different but not entirely. Apparently your father's mission was really dangerous and really covert. They chose him for it, which shows how much the Army thought of him. He sacrificed a lot. But most of all, leaving you."

"And not being able to tell you anything, Tyler," added Michelle. "I bet that was just eating away at him."

He glared at her. "You're just saying that stuff to make me feel better. Well, I don't feel better, okay? My dad lied to me. It's that simple." He was silent for a bit and then blurted out, "What sort of mission? And is it finished?"

Michelle said, "We're not exactly sure what the mission was. Apparently, to deliver something in Afghanistan."

"Will he be coming back home then? Is he really alive?"

Sean replied, "Unfortunately, I can't answer any of

those questions, Tyler, because I don't have the answers. I can tell you that apparently something went wrong with the mission. I can tell you that the Army believes your father is alive. They just don't know where he is."

"Was he captured?"

"Don't think so. If he'd been captured, I doubt he would have been able to email you."

"They could have captured him after he emailed me," Tyler pointed out.

"Yes they could," Michelle agreed.

Sean said, "There's something else you need to know."

Tyler looked at him apprehensively. "What?"

"A friend of mine who gave me the information about your dad was shot today at a local mall. Michelle and I were actually there. There were three gunmen. We managed to subdue all three."

"We managed to *kill* all three," Michelle corrected. "Before they could kill us."

"You killed people?" Tyler said, looking astonished. "At the mall?"

"I'm afraid so. And a police officer was also killed."

"And you think this had something to do with my dad?" Tyler said slowly.

Michelle said, "We don't have any other active cases. And the shooters did look like, well, like former military although they carried no ID."

Tyler looked at Sean. "That bruising on your face? Was that from what happened?"

"It's nothing for you to worry about," said Sean quickly.

"Will they be able to find out who the men are?"

"If they're in some database somewhere, the answer is yes. If they're not, there's no guarantee."

"So they came to the mall to get you and Michelle?"

"They wanted us to come with them. We just politely declined," said Michelle.

Tyler looked back at her, his face pale as cream. "I'm sorry. I never wanted anything like this to happen."

Michelle gripped his shoulder. "It's okay, Tyler. It's not your fault. It comes with the territory."

Tyler glanced anxiously at Sean. "I hope your friend gets better."

"Thanks," said Sean. "Me too."

They all sat in silence for about a minute.

Finally, Tyler said, "I'm not sure what to do now."

Sean said, "Well, the most pressing issue is, with Jean gone, what happens to you? You're sixteen. I don't think you can live on your own."

"But nobody knows that Jean is gone, not really," said Tyler.

Michelle said, "An excellent point." She looked at Sean. "He can stay with one of us."

"I have to go to school," said Tyler.

"That we can manage," said Sean. He looked at Michelle. "I think we need to double-team this. My place with both of us there. When Tyler's in school, we can do our job."

Michelle nodded. "Sounds workable."

Tyler said nervously, "Move in with you guys? Hey, maybe I could stay with Kathy's family?" he added hopefully.

"And maybe put them in danger?" pointed out Sean.

Tyler's face fell. "I didn't think of that."

"There is just one other thing, Tyler," said Sean.

"What?"

"Did you try to contact your dad? After you got the email?"

Tyler shook his head. "I thought about it. I wanted to, but…" His voice trailed off.

Michelle said, "But you were afraid he might not answer?"

Tyler nodded his head. "And if I try to email him now, other people might find out. They're probably monitoring my emails. You said he was on this important mission and everything."

"Probably," said Sean. "But you can write him from another email account. And you can use your code so he'll know it's you."

"How do you know about our code?" Tyler asked, looking suspicious.

"Didn't we tell you?" said Michelle. "We rock at code breaking."

Sean added, "Well, at least we know someone who rocks at code breaking."

"But then they could break the code too," persisted Tyler.

"Anything's possible. But we think it's worth the risk to contact your dad and see what he says."

"We can't be sure it's my dad, not just from an email."

"No, but I don't think a face-to-face is a possibility right this instant. For now, we need to get your things and take you where you'll be safe."

Tyler glanced up at him. "Where I'll be *safe*?"

Sean looked directly at him. "Yes. Because after what happened at the mall today we need to take every precaution we can. Right now, none of us is really safe, Tyler."

27

The man had a problem, a large one, but not unsolvable.

Forty-eight hundred pounds was a big part of it, but not all. At least it had gone where he had planned for it to go. But Sam Wingo was still out there. And then there was the son, Tyler Wingo. And on top of that he had lost three men at a mall.

He had assets but they weren't infinite, and it wasn't like he could hire the replacements he needed quickly and quietly. It all took time. That was the thing he didn't have much of: time. He had a lot left to do and the minutes were ticking fast. The window of opportunity was just that, a window. It closed at some point and would not come back. All elements of his plan had to come together at the exact right time.

At this moment he had the two faces imprinted on his brain: Sean King and Michelle Maxwell. Former Secret Service, now private investigators. They had royally screwed up his plans and cost him valuable assets on the ground.

Problems all around. He didn't like problems. He liked solutions.

He would figure out the solution to each of these problems, including King and Maxwell, and get this mission back on track. He had every incentive to do so. He had been planning this for a long time, assembling the pieces he needed. But soon, if things went as they should, he could finally let it go.

He took a cab to the airport and shortly was on a jet climbing into the sky. He arrived at his final destination and took a moment to slip on the lanyard with his ID badge and his creds settled against his chest. They marked him as a government contractor full of security clearances. He had once served his country in uniform. Now he was really serving only himself.

He picked up his car at the airport garage and drove to the "big house," as he always had referred to it. He passed through security. His creds would get him into many places here. All the ones he needed to get into, anyway. He walked down one long corridor, turned left, and kept going, passing military personnel all along the way.

Since he was no longer in uniform he never had to stop and salute. But there were so many enlisted personnel and officers here that there were designated "No Salute Zones." Otherwise, personnel would be spending all their time doing that.

He nodded to a few he knew but said nothing.

Everyone was bustling to get somewhere else. It was just that sort of place. No time for much chitchat.

He knocked before entering the office that was situated on the last corridor he had turned onto.

"Enter," said the voice.

He opened the door and looked around.

This was the outer office of the Army's assistant secretary for acquisition, logistics, and technology. The assistant secretary was a civilian now, a retired two-star who ran a program that decided how billions in defense money would be spent in the Middle East. There had been scandals and fraud and waste in this sector during the wars in Iraq and Afghanistan. Investigations and commissions had ensued and folks had lost their jobs and their careers; some had gone to prison. The current assistant secretary, Dan Marshall, was in his sixties and had a sterling reputation as a scrupulously honest administrator. He had come in and cleaned house, and things were running a lot more smoothly by most accounts.

The woman behind the desk looked up at the man, smiled, and greeted him. He asked for Marshall. She picked up her phone and buzzed the interior office.

A few moments later Marshall came out of his office. He smiled and came forward, not with an extended hand to shake but with both arms out for a hug.

"Alan, my favorite son-in-law, welcome back. How was your trip?" he said.

Alan Grant smiled, hugged his father-in-law back, and said, "Interesting, Dan. Interesting but productive."

"Come in and tell me all about it," said Marshall.

Grant followed him into his office and shut the door.

He would tell his father-in-law some, but of course not all.

He looked over at the shelf that housed an array of photos. His gaze locked on one—it always did.

Marshall followed his look and smiled sadly.

"I still miss your father greatly even though it's been so many years now. I was friends with your father long before you and my little girl were even born. He was the sharpest cadet in our West Point class."

Grant walked over to the photo and picked it up. His father was in his dress greens, his fresh oak clusters on his broad shoulders. He looked happy. That didn't last. Not after he became a civilian and had gone to work in D.C.

Grant put the photo back and turned to Marshall.

"Yeah, I still miss him too. Maybe more than ever."

"At some point, Alan, you have to let it go. Leslie's been telling me you've been on edge lately. Everything okay?"

"Your daughter is a great wife, Dan. But she worries too much about me. I'm a big boy. I can take care of myself."

"Well, you came back from Iraq alive. No one is questioning your toughness."

"Lots of very tough soldiers died over there. I was just one of the lucky ones."

"I thank the almighty you were. Don't know what I'd do without you. And Leslie would be lost."

"She's a strong woman. She'd be okay."

"Let's get off this morbid talk, Alan. But you really do need to move on from what happened to your parents. It's been over twenty years."

"Twenty-five," said Grant quickly. In a calmer tone he added, "And I am getting over it, Dan. In fact, before long I think I'll be completely over it."

"That's good to hear."

Yes it is, thought Grant.

28

The cargo plane bumped and bounced along crappy air at twenty thousand feet as it made its way over the Atlantic.

Sam Wingo sat tethered to a canvas sling seat. It had proved impossible to obtain a ride on a commercial aircraft coming out of India. Once he had made his way to New Delhi, he had spent a day changing his appearance as much as possible and then had identification documents created with the new image on them in a back alley store full of computers and high-res printers. Still, making his way through airport security had been problematic. He had heard rumors on the street that there was an official search on for an American solider; it was believed that he might have sought refuge in Pakistan or India.

Well, he hadn't been seeking refuge. He was trying to get the hell out.

After a day of trying every way he could think of to leave the country, an opportunity had presented itself. It had cost him some bribe money, but in Indian rupees the price was not bad. Thus, he was now sitting in his canvas sling seat trying to stop himself from being thrown into the sides of the fuselage and keep the little food in his belly from coming back up.

Nothing made sense right now. He didn't know who had taken his cargo or why. He didn't know what the U.S. government knew about it. He did know that they blamed him and that he would be arrested on the spot if they could only find him.

He didn't know that he had just received an email on his phone, because he had turned it off when the cargo plane lifted into the air. The email would have no response from him. At least for the duration of the long flight.

All the hours in the air would give Wingo some time to think about what he would do once he got back to the States. His options were limited. He had no doubt his son was being watched. They might have intercepted his email to Tyler. Hell, they might have his kid detained somewhere. That thought ate at Wingo so badly, he thought he might go berserk at twenty thousand feet. This mission had been a cock-up from the get-go. He had been in the crosshairs from the very first and he wondered how he had never seen it coming.

His guilt would have been established by his decision not to come in as ordered by his superior. In their minds he was already court-martialed. They probably thought he had taken the cargo for himself. Well, part of him wished he had. He could use it right about now.

But he didn't have it. Tim Simons from Nebraska did, whoever the hell that bastard really was. He was fairly certain his name wasn't Tim, and he seriously doubted he was actually a Cornhusker.

Wingo knew he had to get into contact with his son at some point and explain what had happened. Then he had to get a line on the hijacked cargo. If he could recover it, then maybe he could save his reputation and avoid spending the rest of his life in a prison cell at the United States Disciplinary Barracks in Kansas.

As the plane received a hard jolt from the turbulent air outside and dropped about a hundred feet, Wingo also received a jolt of sanity to his mind.

Everything he had just envisioned doing was impossible. He would not be able to get anywhere near his son. He had no way to get a line on the cargo. It was probably worlds away by now, and he had no means to get to where it might be. For all he knew the police would be waiting for him when he landed in Atlanta.

And he would spend the rest of his life in prison.

He put a hand to his head, closed his eyes, and prayed. For a miracle.

"Nothing," said Tyler.

He had been staring at the computer ever since he had sent an email to his dad. He had used a Gmail account set up by Sean. While his dad wouldn't recognize the account's sender, Tyler had used their code to write the message. He hadn't said much, though, in case others were somehow watching and had cracked the message.

He looked up at Michelle. They were at Sean's house in northern Virginia. Sean and Michelle had decided it was too risky to let Tyler go back to his home to get his things, so they had driven directly here. Sean had left to go to Tyler's house and pack him a bag.

Michelle had been constantly checking her watch for the last thirty minutes.

Tyler said, "You can call or email him."

"No, then he'd think I was checking up on him."

"But you would be."

"Exactly. He can get prickly about that."

It was dark outside now, and Tyler's belly was rumbling.

Michelle must have heard it because she said, "I can whip up some dinner. Although I'm not much of a cook."

"I can help," replied Tyler.

"Wait a minute. Kathy told me that you can cook. That you taught her mom a few dishes, in fact."

"I used to help my mom. She was a great cook."

"I'm sure she was, Tyler," said Michelle somberly. She brightened and said, "And for what it's worth, when you get out into the real world the ladies will really appreciate that talent."

"You think so?"

"Oh, trust me, I know so. There's nothing more attractive than a man with a spatula and a plan."

Then something occurred to her as she looked out the window. "You missed swim practice."

"It's okay. We don't have any meets coming up. I can slide for a bit."

"But will your coach call your stepmom or anything like that?"

"I already emailed him. Told him I was sick. He knows about my dad. He'll cut me some slack."

They decided on breakfast for dinner. While Michelle tried not to burn the bacon, Tyler whipped up a complicated omelet with numerous ingredients, buttered grits, and rolls he made basically from scratch in under an hour.

"Sean cooks too, right?" he asked her.

"Yeah, he's really good, which makes up for the fact that I can barely crack an egg properly. But how did you know?"

"His pantry and fridge are full of some really cool ingredients. And the layout of the kitchen and the types of appliances and cutting knives he has shows it." He held up a knife. "This is not for amateurs. And neither is that food processor over there."

"You'd make a good detective. Kathy said you were smart. Straight-A student."

"She did?" Tyler said, trying to hide a smile.

"Yes, she did."

They sat at the kitchen table and ate. Michelle had

coffee while Tyler drank orange juice. They finished, rinsed off their plates, glass, and cup, and loaded the dishwasher. Tyler cleaned the rest of the kitchen while Michelle checked her phone for messages.

"Sean will be here shortly."

"Where has he been?" asked Tyler.

"At the hospital to check on Dana, I suspect. And he was going to scope out a few things while I stayed here with you."

"I can skip school tomorrow."

"No. It's better that you keep to your routine."

"And what about Jean? When people realize she's gone?"

"We'll cross that bridge when we come to it, Tyler."

"It might be soon."

"It might be," she replied.

Twenty minutes later headlights hit the front window.

Michelle peeked out and saw that it was Sean getting out of his car.

A few seconds later he came in looking disheveled and depressed. He was carrying a large duffel bag and handed it to Tyler.

"I think I got everything you needed."

"Did anyone see you?" Michelle asked.

"Don't think so. Parked a block over and approached the house from the rear. Left the same way. I checked the front street for surveillance but didn't see any."

"Did you go back to the hospital?"

He shook his head. "I'm not family, not anymore. From what the surgeon said in the waiting room the next forty-eight hours will probably be critical."

"Well, there's nothing more you can do about that," said Michelle briskly.

"I've certainly done enough with Dana, including almost killing her."

That statement hung in the air like a ball of concrete until Michelle said, "Did you eat?"

"No, I'm not hungry."

"Tyler made a great dinner. We have some leftovers."

"I'm not hungry, Michelle," he said firmly.

She sat and stared up at him while Tyler hovered nervously in the background.

"Okay. Tyler has heard nothing back from his email. So what now? Did you exercise your little brain cells while you were gone?"

"I did. But I'm afraid not much came out of them." He glanced over at Tyler. "I'm really hoping that your dad gets back to us, Tyler. Without that we don't have much to go on."

"Anything on the three guys at the mall?" asked Michelle.

"I'm sure there's a lot, we're just not privy to any of it."

"McKinney sure as hell won't be keeping us in the loop," said Michelle dryly.

"All he wants to do is arrest us."

"Or shoot us," added Michelle.

"I've got a few contacts at the local police," said Sean. "They might know something about it."

"Even a name would be helpful," she said.

"More than we have to go on right now," added Sean.

Tyler said, "But if my dad contacts me, we might have a lot more to work with."

Sean exchanged a glance with Michelle.

Tyler saw this and said, "My dad didn't do anything wrong. And he's going to come back here and clear his name."

"I'm sure he would want to do that," said Michelle quietly.

Tyler scowled. "But you don't think he'll make it back. You think he's dead, don't you?"

Sean said, "The answer is we don't know, Tyler. We hope he's not dead."

Tyler looked away.

"I did get one bit of information," said Sean.

Michelle and Tyler perked up at this. "What?" they both said together.

"The name of someone at DTI who your dad worked with."

"How did you score that?" asked Michelle.

"Yeah," added Tyler. "He never talked about his work to me."

"Friend of a friend."

Michelle eyed Tyler and said, smiling, "Sean has lots of friends of a friend. He's very popular at parties."

Sean continued, "Your dad's co-worker was a woman named Mary Hesse. You ever hear him mention her?"

Tyler shook his head. "Like I said, he didn't really talk about work."

Sean slowly nodded. "Right. Well, I'm going to see her tonight. She might be able to tell us something."

"I can go too," said Michelle.

"No, you have to stay here with Tyler."

"Why don't we all go?" suggested Tyler.

"No," Sean said firmly. "I have no idea if Hesse will even give me five minutes. She sounded very reluctant over the phone. If we all show up, it might freak her out."

Michelle said, "Okay, that makes sense. I'll play bodyguard. You play detective."

Tyler said nothing, but he didn't look too happy.

A bit later Michelle walked Sean out to his car.

"I'm really sorry about Dana, Sean, but it wasn't your fault."

"Of course it was, but I don't want to get into that again." He fumbled with his keys. Michelle put a calming hand over his shaky one.

"You have to just let it go for now, Sean. If you keep up this way you'll be no good to yourself or anyone else."

"I know," he said resignedly. "It's just hard to shut it off."

"Secret Service. Tunnel vision. Block everything else

out. Like you said, these are dangerous waters. Bring your A-game all around. Right?"

He nodded curtly. "A-game, right. Thanks, Michelle, for a gentle kick in the pants."

"Any time. I can also do the hard kick in the pants if necessary."

"And don't I know it." He got into the car. "I'll call you when I'm on my way back."

"Okay."

He gazed at his house. "A-game all around," he said. "Including you. You've got the precious cargo."

29

After Sean drove off Michelle did a perimeter patrol then walked back to the house. She locked all the doors and made sure her pistol had a round in the chamber. She looked down at the kitchen table where Tyler sat with his schoolbooks piled everywhere.

"Lots of homework?" she asked.

"Always lots of homework," he said dully. However, he made no move to open a book or pick up a pencil.

"Shouldn't you be getting to it?"

"I suppose." He paused, gritting his teeth. "Where do you think my dad is right now?"

"Maybe on a plane back here from the Middle East."

Tyler listlessly thumbed through some pages in his math textbook.

Michelle doubted he was focusing on the formulas she could see on the pages. She eyed him more closely. "Before your dad deployed the last time, did he talk to you about anything?"

He stared at her blankly. "Anything like what? We talked about lots of stuff."

"Anything out of the ordinary? It could have been something seemingly innocuous."

Tyler thought about this and then slowly shook his head. "He told me to work hard in school and swimming. To mind Jean. And to keep out of trouble. Stuff like that."

Michelle nodded. "Well, keep mulling it over. Something else might strike you."

Michelle heard the noise before Tyler did. She pushed him down under the table and with one long leap reached the wall light switch and plunged the room into darkness.

Her Sig was in her right hand. She blinked rapidly to adjust her eyes to the absence of light.

Tyler whispered, "Michelle, what is it?"

"Someone outside," she whispered back. "You stay there. Get your phone out. Tap in nine-one-one. If I'm not back in five minutes call them."

"But—"

"Just stay down and stay quiet, Tyler. It'll be okay."

Michelle crab-walked out of the room, her gaze swiveling and taking in as much as her lines of sight would allow. She did not like noises in the night that she knew represented stealthy footsteps. Sean had neighbors on both sides of him, but there were buffers of trees on both those sides, too. A nice little screen for felons to do their work.

Michelle's immediate thought was that the three

stiffs at the mall had friends who had returned to finish the job.

She took a quick peek out the front window.

A sedan was there that hadn't been before. She couldn't tell if anyone was inside or not. Her Land Cruiser was parked in the driveway but she couldn't risk trying to reach it with Tyler in tow. She continued to watch out the window, all the while keeping her ears peeled for sounds of intrusion.

She stiffened when she saw the man come around the corner of the house.

"Shit!" she hissed.

She opened the front door and called out to him. "Is there something you wanted, Agent McKinney?"

He turned and saw her. Her manner had been jocular. When she saw his face, her jocularity vanished.

"What is it?" she asked.

He came toward her. "Can we talk?"

"What are you doing here? How did you even know to come here?"

"We're DHS," he growled. "We *do* have resources."

"Sean's not here. But you can talk to me."

He nodded and passed by her into the house. She glanced over his shoulder and checked the perimeter one more time before securing the door behind her.

Michelle called out to Tyler in the kitchen that things were okay. She flicked on the lights, and he came into the living room on wobbly legs. He flinched when he saw McKinney.

"Who's that?" he asked.

"Agent McKinney with Homeland Security."

"Homeland Security?" said Tyler. "Why are you guys involved?"

McKinney said, "We keep the homeland secure. Like the name implies." He stared hard at Tyler and then shot Michelle a glance. "Why is he here? Damn, can't you guys heed a warning?"

Michelle said, "It's a long story but Tyler is safer with us. So why are you sneaking around Sean's house?"

McKinney sat down and slipped out a pack of Marlboros. "You mind if I smoke?"

"Yeah, I do. And I know that Sean sure as hell would."

He put the smokes away and sat back. "Do you guys have any idea what you're involved in?"

"We're working on it," said Michelle. "Any help you'd like to give us would be appreciated."

"An international incident," said McKinney, who didn't seem to have heard her.

Michelle sat down across from him while Tyler remained standing and looked stunned.

"What kind of international incident?" asked Michelle calmly.

McKinney studied her. "I'm not sure I can answer that."

"Then why the hell are you even here?" she said hotly. "To tell us you can't cooperate with us? Trust me, we got that message loud and clear before."

McKinney cracked his knuckles. "The dead guys were former military."

"All of them?"

He nodded. "But they'd been out of uniform a long time and had gotten into stuff that men who wore the uniform of this country never should."

"Like what?" asked Michelle.

"Drugs and gunrunning, for starters. And some militia activity with maybe some domestic terrorism thrown in. The list only gets longer after that."

"Do you think that's what this is about?"

"I don't think so. But I can't be sure."

Michelle looked up at Tyler, who blurted out, "My dad wouldn't be involved in anything like that."

McKinney turned to him. "He seems to be right in the middle of it, whatever 'it' is."

"What was the mission, McKinney? What was Sam Wingo doing? We know he was delivering something but it never got there."

"Who the hell told you that?"

"Does it matter?" Michelle said.

"It might," snapped McKinney.

"Look, we're both trying to get to the truth."

He looked at Tyler again. "Your old man contacted you, didn't he? Slipped you a coded message?"

Tyler immediately looked at Michelle. She hesitated but then nodded.

Tyler said, "Yeah, he did. After he was supposed to be dead."

"And what did the message say?"

Michelle answered. "That he was sorry and wanted Tyler to forgive him."

"You're sure that was all?"

"Yes," said Tyler defiantly. "I wish it had been more but that's all there was."

"Sounds like a confession to me," said McKinney.

"Don't think so," said Michelle before Tyler could say anything.

"Why?"

"Just my gut."

McKinney snorted with derision.

She ignored this and said, "What was he delivering? And was it just him?"

"It was apparently just him. Which makes no sense at all considering the cargo. But then maybe the military does things differently."

"So what was the damn cargo?" asked Michelle.

McKinney cracked more knuckles. "Every alphabet agency and all the uniforms are mixed up in this shit. It's big, really big."

"I'm sure it is. Big enough for you to get a call from the Pentagon and read us the riot act. But that doesn't explain why you're here. Like you said, you're DHS. You have lots of resources. You don't need to come to us for anything."

"What you say is perfectly true," he said.

"And still, here you are."

McKinney let out a long breath. "I checked you

two out some more. You and King. That's why I'm here. People I respect say you're both the real deal. That you can be trusted. That you're sharp."

"Okay," said Michelle warily. "But why do I think one reason you're here is that you're having trouble getting straight answers from your side? And maybe there's a lack of trust going on."

McKinney hiked his eyebrows at this but said nothing.

Michelle said again. "So what was the cargo?" She added, "Come on, the suspense is killing me, Agent McKinney."

McKinney glanced at Tyler and then back at Michelle. He seemed to have finally made up his mind. "Forty-eight hundred pounds."

Michelle's brow furrowed. "That was the weight? Well over two tons?"

McKinney nodded.

"So what was it?"

"What do you know that weighs forty-eight hundred pounds?"

"What are we playing here, *Jeopardy!*?" Michelle snapped.

"A nuke or a dirty bomb?" said Tyler anxiously.

McKinney shook his head. "No."

She said, "Too light for a tank or a plane. Bio-weapons? Some off-the-rack centrifuges? A few hundred al-Qaeda terrorists?" she added sarcastically.

McKinney shook his head.

"Okay, we give, what is it?" said Michelle.

McKinney cleared his throat. "One billion euros."

30

Sean was seated across from Mary Hesse at a restaurant in Chantilly, Virginia. She was in her mid-forties, attractive with dark hair and a slim figure. She seemed to have a problem making eye contact with Sean. She wore glasses but kept taking them off and wiping the lenses with her napkin.

Nerves all around, observed Sean.

"So you worked with Sam Wingo?" he prompted for the second time. This was shaping up to be like pulling teeth, he thought. But in situations like this patience was a virtue even though it felt like an ulcer.

She nodded. "Sam was a really nice guy. It was just—" She broke off, looking slightly dazed.

"It was just what?"

He put a hand across and tapped her wrist. "Ms. Hesse, I know this is hard. But as I told you on the phone I'm working with Sam's son, Tyler."

"Sam spoke of him all the time. He was really proud," she said.

"I'm sure he was. Tyler is a great kid. But he's terribly worried about his dad."

"They said he had been killed in Afghanistan."

"We don't believe that to be true. And I think you were about to say that you thought something was off about Sam, weren't you?"

She looked surprised at his observation. "How did you—"

"I'm former Secret Service. We get really good at reading body language."

"Well, he just appeared one day at DTI. No one had seen him previously. No one that I knew had even interviewed him for the job. And while we're not that big a company we do have certain protocols."

"And these weren't followed with Wingo?"

"They didn't appear to have been followed," she corrected.

"What else?"

"He spoke Dari and Pashto, but not, well, not at the level of the other people at the firm."

"But I understood he was a salesman. He drummed up business for the company."

"We don't need drumming, Mr. King. We're swamped, even with the winding down of the wars in the Middle East. There's still a large military footprint. And commercial companies are starting to go there. They all need translators."

"So business is booming and you don't need salesmen. So what was Wingo doing for you?"

At this simple question Hesse seemed perplexed. "I'm not really sure."

227

"You're not really sure? You told me you worked with him."

Her face paled, and for an instant Sean thought she might be sick.

"Take a sip of water and catch your breath," he advised.

She gulped some water and wiped her mouth with her napkin.

"You okay?"

She nodded. "You see, he wasn't really working for us."

"So what was he doing?"

"I was teaching him Pashto and Dari. At least building on what he already knew."

"You were teaching him to speak the languages primarily used in Afghanistan?"

"And other countries in the Middle East as well, including Pakistan. And in Iran, Dari is known as Farsi. It's a very useful language to know over there, along with Arabic of course."

"So if he wasn't a salesman and he wasn't qualified to be a translator, were you teaching him to be one?"

"No. We have immersion schools for that. What I did was work with him one-on-one three hours a day, every weekday. I did that for nearly a year."

"Did you ever do that with anyone else?"

She shook her head.

"He was a reservist headed to Afghanistan. Maybe he wanted to speak the languages?"

"But he wasn't paying us to do it. We were paying him a salary to learn the languages."

Sean sat back, obviously flummoxed by this statement. "How do you know that?"

"Our company bookkeeper, Sue, is a friend. She told me. But the thing is we were getting fully reimbursed for his salary."

"Who by?"

"Some unit at the DoD. I'm not sure which, there are so many. But we were definitely getting paid back. It wasn't costing us a dime. Our company's owner is not known for his generosity. He wouldn't pay for an employee who had no duties."

"Did you ever talk to Wingo about this…this unusual arrangement?"

"I was told not to. I considered him a friend because we spent so much time together. He told me about his son. I told him about my family. I was stunned when he didn't show up one day. I knew he was leaving for Afghanistan at some point, but I didn't know he had been deployed. And I didn't know he was in the reserves."

"He was regular Army. I think you were helping prepare him for a mission that required those language skills."

"What was the mission?" she asked in a whisper.

"Good question. I wish I knew."

"You said you didn't think Sam was dead? But it was in the paper."

"No, I don't think he's dead." Sean leaned forward. "But that doesn't mean he's not in danger or trouble or both. Did he mention anything to you that might help me? Anything at all?"

"He told me he hoped to retire soon. He wanted to spend more time with Tyler."

"Anything else?"

"Well, there was something strange right before he left DTI."

"What?" said Sean sharply.

"He said he was going back to Afghanistan soon. I told him to be careful. That I didn't want him to die from an IED or a sniper. That I prayed he got back soon."

"And what did he say to that?"

"He said that IEDs and snipers were the least of his worries."

Sean rubbed his chin. "Meaning what? That something else even worse might happen to him over there?"

"I guess, yes." Her features shifted to alarm at what this actually meant. "What other things could be worse than being blown up or shot?" she asked.

"There might be something," replied Sean.

He confirmed some other information with Hesse and then left her there staring into her coffee cup.

He was halfway to his car when his phone buzzed. It was Michelle. She filled him in on her meeting with McKinney.

"A billion euros?" he said, his voice heavy with skepticism. "That's about a billion three U.S. dollars at current exchange rates."

"I'll take your word for it. And it apparently weighs forty-eight hundred pounds, crate not included."

"And why would McKinney come to us and offer up this information?"

Sean slid into the front seat and clipped his seat belt on before starting the engine, the phone wedged between his shoulder and ear.

"I think he feels hemmed in. Not trusting anyone, meaning on his side too," she said.

"Still, it was a stretch for a DHS guy to come to us and convey that sort of information. He could get his ass canned for that."

"No argument there. I was as surprised as you are."

"How did you leave it with him?"

"I didn't really. He just left and I got on the horn with you."

"I'll be there in about forty minutes. Hang tight."

Sean put the car in gear.

He didn't look in the rearview mirror.

If he had, he might have noticed the red dot flitting across his forehead.

31

Alan Grant lowered his pistol with the laser sight on the Picatinny rail as Sean drove off.

It would not be as simple as a trigger pull, although the time would come when it would be something that basic. He slipped his gun back into its shoulder holster and sat there with the engine running while he thought through some things.

Mary Hesse, a DTI grunt. Worked with Sam Wingo teaching him how to speak languages of the Middle East. She was a dead end. But there were other trails out there that could lead King and Maxwell somewhere.

He put his Mercedes sedan in gear and drove out of Chantilly, heading west toward the foothills of the Blue Ridge Mountains. The roads turned from interstates to highway to state routes and finally to rural road switchbacks.

He finally turned onto a gravel road, drove up a hill, turned left, and skidded to a stop in front of a small, ramshackle cabin. He climbed out of the car and checked his watch; it was nearing midnight. Time was

meaningless to him. He had long ago ceased to operate on a nine-to-five schedule.

He popped the trunk and looked down at the
woman lying there.

Her hands and feet were bound with flexi-cuffs,
mouth taped, eyes blindfolded. All these steps were
probably unnecessary since she was drugged. But he
was a cautious man. Cautious people, he had found,
lived to fight another day.

He lifted her up and carried her to the porch. He
set her down, unlocked the front door—triple locks
and a security system run off a propane-fired generator
that also provided lighting—picked her back up, and
carried her over the threshold.

There was nothing matrimonial about the gesture.

He walked into the back room where the window
had been blacked out.

There was a metal table in the middle of this room.
He laid her down on the table, removed her blindfold,
and stepped back. He took off his coat and laid his
pistol aside. It would just get in his way. He turned on
the overhead light.

As he watched, she started waking up. He looked
at his watch. Right on time.

Jean Wingo's eyes fluttered once, twice, and then
remained open. Her look was confused at first; then
she looked to the side and saw him.

She stiffened, her eyes instantly filling with apprehension.

Grant gently removed the tape covering her mouth.

She said breathlessly, "What are you doing?" She looked around. "Why did you bring me here?"

"To talk."

"You drugged me, tied me up, and now I'm lying on a metal table. You could have just called, for God's sake."

Grant could tell the woman's courage was returning.

She tried to sit up. He put on a pair of leather gloves and forced her back down on the table. With her legs and arms bound it was not a difficult thing to do.

"Please let me up."

"Not until we've talked. I need a debrief."

"Where are we?"

"In a safe place."

He pulled up a chair and sat next to her.

"Can I sit up, please?"

He put an arm under her back and helped her to a sitting position.

She eyed him warily. "What do you want to know that I haven't already told you?"

"For starters, why did you leave?"

"Tyler hired these detectives. I got nervous."

"You left without permission. You signed on for the mission. You can't change the rules midway through."

"I understand that, Alan, I'm sorry. But conditions on the ground change. And I had to change with them. These detectives—"

"I have that under control. Your leaving has complicated things. Tyler is now with King and Maxwell. I lost three men to them. This all could have been prevented if you had spoken up and controlled Tyler. If he hadn't gotten suspicious he wouldn't have hired anyone. He would have believed what the Army told him and that would be that."

"Wingo sent him an email."

"Which we know about. But it could have been sent by anyone. Not necessarily his father. Again, if you had stuck to the script, which had this contingency built in, it would have been taken care of."

"Look, I'm sorry, okay? Every plan does not go smoothly."

"Mine did. Until now."

"What, did you bring me here to torture me? Or kill me? How is that going to help things?"

Again, Grant could tell she was nervous but trying to cover that with bravado.

"No and no. And it wouldn't help things. I just want to see if you have any useful information to convey. Then I will redeploy you. But you need to understand that you screwed up. There have to be consequences, Jean."

"I think I more than carried my weight. I got designated as Wingo's 'bride.' I carried this whole thing pretty flawlessly the last year. The kid never warmed up to me. And Wingo was Wingo. It hasn't exactly been a walk in the park."

"I understand that. Just tell me anything you might have learned and we can head back to town."

"I left the house when things started to get hairy. I called you and told you what I was doing."

"And I told you to stay the course."

"Easy for you to say."

"What else?"

"That's pretty much it."

"Any more communications from Wingo on his son's email?"

"There was nothing. Wingo hasn't tried to contact him again." She looked curious. "What exactly happened over there? You never said."

"Wingo lost the cargo, but my people lost him. He's out there. Probably trying to figure out what happened and attempting to get back here. He has made contact with his immediate superior. Said superior did not believe his explanation. He is a marked man. DoD is putting major resources toward finding him. We're of course looking for him too."

"So he won't stay out there long."

"But we don't need the DoD to find him, because they might just believe that he didn't take the cargo. Then they start to look elsewhere. I want their focus on him."

"So you need to find him first."

"As you remarked before, easier said than done."

"Then we better get to it."

"Agreed."

He pulled his knife, cut her hands and feet free.

He flipped her his Glock 9mm.

She checked the mag, chambered a round, pointed it at him. "Sorry, Alan." She fired the weapon. Or at least attempted to. But there was no bang and no bullet was propelled down the barrel.

"Helps to have a firing pin," said Grant, who seemed unsurprised by her attempt to kill him.

He struck, the knife passing across her neck, severing all her major arteries. He backed away from the blood spray. Her gaze was on him and he continued to watch her. Waiting.

Jean fell to the floor and a few seconds later finished bleeding out.

He stared down at her for a few moments. "Consequences, Jean."

He wrapped her in plastic and tied her up tight like a present.

The dug grave was waiting in the woods a quarter mile away. As he put the last shovelful of dirt over the hole, he said a silent prayer and considered the fact that Sam Wingo was a widower for the second time.

He doubted the man would care about that right now. He had other things to worry about. He walked back to the cabin, cleaned up, and got back into his car.

He didn't like losing Jean, but some things were sacrosanct. You followed orders. You didn't make the rules up as you went along. There was a chain of command for a reason. A very sound, historically verified reason.

And Grant was, above all, a disciplined soldier. It didn't matter that he no longer wore the uniform. It wasn't about something you wore. It was all about what was inside the clothes. Discipline. Honor. Respect. Reliability. Professionalism.

Jean had violated all of these.

He didn't have the option of court-martialing her.

There was really only one option left. He had employed that option but only after she had failed his loyalty test. He was a fair man. If she hadn't tried to kill him, she would still be alive. She had and she wasn't.

He drove on.

He had a list. He had checked it twice. It was time to move the ball forward.

He had one billion euros. He didn't personally need all of it. He just needed a tenth of it.

But he believed it would be money very well spent.

32

The next morning Michelle dropped Tyler off at school.

She said, "If anything seems weird or if strange people show up looking for you, lock yourself in the principal's office and call me."

Tyler promised that he would, and Michelle watched him all the way into the school. She had never been a mother and had never really even imagined herself in that role. But she felt like an overprotective momma right now. In fact, the weight of responsibility she felt was even greater to her than when she'd protected VIPs at the Secret Service. Go figure.

She drove off and phoned Sean on her Bluetooth.

"Baby bird is dropped off," she said. "Where do we go from here?"

"You think McKinney will meet with us again?"

"I don't know. He left his card. I can call him."

"Do that."

"Why McKinney?"

"We need official access, Michelle. He provides it.

Otherwise we are cut out of the loop and have no leads to follow up."

"He's not going to just invite us to the investigation."

"You might be surprised."

"What do you know that I don't?"

"Just call him. Noon at our office."

"What are you doing in the meantime?"

"Checking on Dana."

"But you said you weren't family."

"There are always ways."

"What do you want me to do besides call McKinney?"

"Play detective and try to get a line on Jean Wingo."

"Okay. I'd say be careful but I know you will be."

He clicked off.

Michelle drove to Tyler's neighborhood. It looked just like thousands of neighborhoods that dotted the country. Working-class homes filled with working-class folks. Only this neighborhood was different. Certain people who lived here were definitely not who they appeared to be.

Michelle knocked on the door of Alice Dobbers, the neighbor who had seen Jean leave the previous day. Dobbers came to the door. She was well into her eighties, short, and about sixty pounds overweight. Her legs and arms were swollen and she looked to be in pain. She wore glasses; a hearing aid poked out of her right ear. Michelle explained who she was and what she wanted.

She added, "We're trying to help Tyler."

Dobbers nodded. "I know. Tyler told me about you and your partner. I can tell you what I told him. Saw her leave around noon, my soap was just about to come on. Aren't many of them left, soaps I mean, so I'm sure of the time. Just happened to look out the window, commercial was on. Coffee. Don't drink coffee anymore. Makes me hyper and pee at night. I don't like hyper, don't like peeing at night. Too much effort getting outta bed. Tried Depends. Didn't like 'em. Felt like I was being born again. Not in a good way, diaper, you see." She slid her glasses halfway down her nose and stared knowingly at Michelle.

"I'm sure," said Michelle quickly. "So she had her suitcase?"

"No, first she put out the recycling. Guess she forgot."

"Forgot what?"

"Yesterday was trash pickup day, not recycling. Why they can't do it all on the same day I'll never know. But I don't have enough time left breathing to worry about crap like that."

"Then what?"

"Then she came back out with a suitcase, popped the trunk of her car. Put it in there. No overnight bag. Big sucker. Probably everything she owned. Don't see her coming back. No loss there."

"What makes you say that?"

Dobbers gave her another knowing look. "I been married for fifty-seven years. Not to the same man, now. It was three of them, actually, but they totaled up to fifty-seven years of mostly good times until they weren't. So I know about love. Know about commitment. Know it when I see it. Know it when I don't see it."

Michelle glanced across the street. "And you didn't see it over there?"

"I knew Sam Wingo's first wife. Now, there was a woman in love and a man who loved her. Not the second time around. Don't know why he married Jean. But it wasn't for love."

"Did you talk to either one of them?"

"Talked to Sam a lot. Furnace is always kicking out on me when I need it the most. He'd come over and get it going. When I still used to drive, he and Tyler would change the oil, check the tires, give my car a good wash. Nice people. Now, Jean, not so much."

"You talked to her?"

"Tried to. Hard for me to get around. Got DVT, arthritis, Type Two diabetes, bad kidneys, and my liver's nothing to write home about. You name it I probably got it. Doctors going to pickle me after I'm gone so they can study all the things I got wrong." She stopped and looked questioningly at Michelle. "Brain fart, honey. Where was I?"

"You were trying to talk to Jean Wingo?" Michelle said helpfully.

"Hell yes, excuse my French. Now, going across that street for me is like running a marathon, but I did it, more than once. Even baked her a pie to welcome her to the neighborhood and I don't, as a rule, bake anymore because I'm just an Alzheimer's moment away from burning down the place. Now what did she do? Took the pie, thanked me, and shut the door in my face. Another time saw her out in the yard watering the flower beds. I started over to chat with her. She looked at me like I had dog poop on my face and went inside before I got halfway across the street."

"Not the friendliest of neighbors," said Michelle in a commiserating tone.

"Not a neighbor at all, least to my way of thinking."

"Any idea where she might have gone?"

"No. But good riddance, in my mind. I'm just worried about Tyler. Now, that boy loves his daddy. Now his daddy's gone and the woman his father was presumably hitched to is gone. Lots of turnover. Don't know what's coming down the pike next."

"Me either," said Michelle. "Well, thanks."

"Anytime." Dobbers squinted up at her. "Saw that feller of yours. Tyler said you were partners. Ex-super-spies or some such."

"Former Secret Service," corrected Michelle.

"Damn fine-looking man. If I were younger I might be shooting for hubby number four. Now, piece of advice." She looked the tall Michelle up and down. "You got all the goods right where they should be. So if I were you I'd bag and tag his cute buns, honey, before some hussy gets there first. And they will. Enough of 'em out there. So long, gotta pee."

She turned and waddled back inside.

Michelle just stood there, her notebook open and not a single word written on the page.

She walked across the street and stared at the spot where Jean's car had been parked. Michelle had a description of the car and its tag number from seeing it earlier. She just didn't have a way to run a BOLO on it. Only the cops could do that. But she agreed with Dobbers. She didn't think Jean Wingo was coming back. If Wingo's marriage had been a sham to provide cover for his mission, what was keeping her here?

She pulled out her phone and called McKinney. It went to voice mail. She left a message about meeting them that day at their office.

She walked around to the back of the Wingos' house. Tyler had given her a key and permission to enter. At least that would be her story if the cops showed up.

She started on the main floor and worked her way up. She didn't bother to check for prints; she had no database to run them against. That was another downside to being a private investigator. She would love to know what Jean's background was. If she'd been recruited to play a role, she might be in the military or a contractor thereto. That might give them a lead on her current whereabouts. Maybe McKinney could provide that service if he agreed to team up.

She took a few minutes to walk around Tyler's room. She imagined how much he was suffering, wondering whether his dad was alive or not. She hoped they could bring him some sort of resolution.

She entered the Wingos' bedroom. If they were simply playing a role, she assumed the two adults were not sleeping together, not an easy subterfuge in a house this small. She methodically searched through the bedroom and closet and didn't find anything very helpful. Jean Wingo had taken all of her clothes and apparently most of her personal possessions, since there weren't many feminine items left.

No computers. No hard-line phone. No cell phones.

She sat on a chair in the bedroom and stared around the space wondering if she had missed something. She looked out a window that gave her a view onto the backyard.

Green trash can by the back door. She might as well go through that while she was here. She heard a loud engine and the sound of hydraulics. She peered out another window in the bedroom that looked out onto the street. The trash truck was coming down the street. She looked at the blue container at the curb. Or maybe it was a recycling truck making its rounds.

The next instant Michelle was running flat-out down the stairs, out the front door, and leaping off the porch, landing on the front lawn. She reached the recycling bin seconds before the truck pulled up to collect it.

When one of the men jumped off the truck's rear and eyed her she said breathlessly, "Lost my wedding ring in here. You can skip me this week."

She rolled the bin up the driveway and into the backyard.

She closed the gate behind her and opened the top of the bin. It was half full.

Michelle had realized just in time that no sane person who was about to disappear would take the time to put out the recycling. So maybe there was something in there that she needed to get rid of and didn't want possibly found on her. Maybe that was what Jean Wingo had been thinking when she'd mixed up the trash and recycling days.

It took her twenty minutes of searching but finally her hand closed around the letter, or rather the envelope. It was addressed to Jean Shepherd, but not at this house. She folded the envelope and put it in her pocket.

A minute later she was racing down the street in her Land Cruiser.

33

Not that long ago Sean King had been cemented in a chair next to a hospital bed in which Michelle had been lying near death. Ever since that time he had loathed the inside of a hospital. If he could have avoided ever entering another one, he would have. But he couldn't. He had to be here.

Dana was still in the critical care unit and thus her visitors were limited to immediate family; one had to phone the unit to gain admission. He had lied and told the nurse who answered the phone that he was Dana's brother in from out of town.

He was directed to her room but stood by the door before going in. Dana was in the bed with IV and monitoring lines running all over her. The machine keeping track of her vitals hummed and beeped next to the bed. The blinds on the window were closed. The room was fairly dark. Dana wore a breathing mask, which was helping to inflate her damaged lung.

He took a few hesitant steps forward, hoping he wouldn't run into General Brown here. The last thing he wanted was an altercation. His face hadn't recovered from the last beating. And though Dana wasn't conscious, he didn't think something ugly like that would help her recovery.

He drew up a chair and sat next to her bed. Her chest rose and fell slowly, if unevenly. He slid a hand through the bed rails and gently gripped her wrist. She felt cold and for one terrifying moment he thought she was dead. But she was breathing, and the monitor showed her vitals, while weak, to still be recordable.

He bent lower, his head resting lightly on the cool surface of the bed rail. He had assumed this position for over two weeks while waiting for Michelle to open her eyes. He had never figured to be repeating this ritual so soon and certainly not with his ex-wife.

"I'm so sorry, Dana," he said softly. He let go of her wrist and let his hand dangle.

He closed his eyes and a few tears leaked out. He was startled when something touched him. When he opened his eyes he saw that her fingers had closed around his. He looked at her face. Her eyes were still shut, her breathing still weak. He stared down at her fingers once more, thinking he must have imagined it. But there they were, intertwined around his.

He didn't make a move until about twenty minutes later when her fingers slipped off his and she seemed to fall into a deeper slumber. He sat with her for another half hour and then made his way out, wiping fresh tears from his eyes.

He turned the corner and ran into the one person he had dreaded seeing.

General Brown was not in uniform today. He wore slacks and a blue blazer and assumed an angry expression as soon as he saw Sean.

"What the hell are you doing here?" he snapped. He looked over Sean's shoulder at the double doors leading into the critical care unit. "Have you been in there to see Dana? You bastard!"

He cocked his arm back to throw another punch. This time Sean didn't simply stand there and receive it. He hooked Brown's forearm, spun him around, and drove the arm up his back to such an angle that Brown cried out in pain. It was fortunate the corridor was empty at that moment.

Sean said into his ear, "Yes, I did see Dana. She moved her hand, in case you wanted to know. Now I'll remove *my* hand and let you go, but if you want to take another swing at me I suggest you wait until we get outside."

Sean stepped away and Brown, rubbing his arm and grimacing, faced him. "If you come back here again I'll have you arrested."

Sean eyed him. "The men came into the mall from the direction that Dana did. We arrived first. No one followed us, that I guarantee. So that means these men followed *Dana* there, not us. They asked me to call her and get her back after I sent her to get the police from the mall substation. They knew she was important."

"You sent her away to get the police?" said Brown, looking confused.

"Only she came back and helped us. In fact she ended up saving our lives. She's a very brave woman who I know loves you very much."

"And yet she betrayed me by telling you information that I gave to her."

"She did it because I asked her to. In hindsight it was both selfish and stupid of me to involve her. But I did it because I was trying to help a young man find his father."

Brown studied him. "Wingo?"

Sean nodded. "But how did those men know of Dana's involvement? I had dinner with her out of the blue. She had no idea why. And yet men start following her after she speaks with you. Men who used to be in the military."

Brown thought about this. "Are you suggesting that I might have a leak in my office? That's impossible," he added dismissively.

"Do you have another explanation?"

"I don't have to explain anything to you," Brown barked.

"No, you don't. But your wife is lying in there because a man who was following her shot her. And the only reason I believe he was following her was because she knew things about Sam Wingo that you told her. Now, we killed those three men. But that doesn't mean there aren't others out there."

"This is a classified military matter."

"Tell that to a sixteen-year-old kid who's been told his dad is dead even though he really isn't."

Brown's anger slowly faded. "I wasn't aware of that. But I still don't think I can help you."

Sean watched him, trying to detect any wavering in his features. "Your wife is lying in a hospital bed because a man shot her. If I were you, I would want to make sure that all the people responsible were appropriately punished."

Brown leaned against the wall and studied the patterned linoleum floor.

Sean moved closer. "The DoD is burying all of this. No surprise. But in doing so I hope they're also not covering up the truth. Because if they are this stops being a national security issue and starts becoming a criminal act."

Brown glanced up sharply. "I'm not hiding anything."

"By allowing others to hide it I lump you with them. Guilt by inertia."

"That's your opinion and I could give a crap what you think."

"It's not really an opinion, just a basic concept. Telling the truth is the best policy."

"That's a very naïve approach," Brown said in a sneering tone.

"I thought when you put on the uniform honor was a big part of it."

"It is a big part of it," Brown snapped.

"And if mistakes are made shouldn't they be corrected? Even if a secret comes out? Especially if we're talking about an innocent person's life?"

"I'm just one person, King."

"So you just put your head in the sand and look the other way? Is that what honor means to you?"

"What the hell do you want from me?"

"I want your help to set this right."

"My help? Do you have any idea what you're asking me to do?"

"I do, actually. And if you say no and walk away and sit with Dana, I'll completely understand. I'll work the case from another angle. But I will work it. I bear tremendous responsibility for Dana almost dying. I have to make it right."

"Then you might run right up against the Pentagon."

"I'm a licensed private investigator. And I know of no law that says I can't investigate a matter on behalf of a client."

"But national security."

"Yeah, I keep hearing that phrase. People use it like a get-out-of-jail-free card. But the more you use something the less effect it has, at least for me. And this is America. So when push comes to shove, liberty trumps all else."

"Until you lose that liberty."

"Been there, done that, General. And I'm still here."

"You're still taking a risk. A big one."

"I don't care. Comes with the territory. And I owe it to someone."

"Who? The kid?"

"No. Dana."

Brown glanced away, looking thoughtful. Sean could almost see the mental machinery humming through the man's scalp.

"No promises. But I'll see what I can do."

"I appreciate that." Sean handed him his card.

Brown took it and started to walk off but then stopped and turned back.

"When I put on the uniform, I *did* put on a sense of honor. And duty. Not just to the Army. But to my country."

"I felt the same way in the Service."

Brown twirled Sean's card between his fingers. "I'll be in touch."

He walked off to Dana's room.

As Sean left the hospital his phone buzzed..

It was Michelle. She spoke in terse, energetic sentences.

Sean listened and then ran flat-out to his car.

34

Michelle Maxwell was not good at waiting. In the Secret Service that had been one of the things that had most irritated her—the tedium.

She drummed her fingers on her steering wheel while she eyed the horseshoe-shaped motor court in south Alexandria, Virginia, right off Route 1, or Jeff Davis Highway, as it was known here. The area had once been nice but no longer was. And it was no longer that safe, either. The homes, strip malls, and other businesses around here had all seen better times. They were tired, used up, and, in some cases, abandoned and falling down.

Michelle was focused on the motor court. Specifically, room 14 at the Green Hills Motor Court. The name had made her smile when she'd first seen it since there were no hills, green or otherwise, around here. There was trash in the parking lot, mostly consisting of beer cans, used needles, empty condom packs, and smashed bottles of Jack and Black and gin. The paint on the doors and walls was peeling. The neon sign had long since lost its neon.

And yet Jean Wingo, or Shepherd, or whoever she really was, had letters addressed to her here. So presumably she had stayed here. Michelle kept drumming her fingers but the itch in her brain was telling her to act, to move, to knock down a door, to take somebody prisoner, or to kick someone's ass.

When the other car pulled into the parking lot she got out at the same time Sean did. They met in the middle of the nearly empty lot. She showed him the envelope with the address of the motor court and explained in more detail how she had discovered it.

"Really, really good work, Michelle," he said earnestly.

"And I really, really thank you," she said back jokingly until she noticed his still-serious expression.

"Is it Dana?"

"I saw her. She gripped my hand."

"Sean, that's great. Right?"

"Yes, it is. Really great."

"And yet you look so down."

"I ran into the general again."

"Did he take another swing at you? I hope this time you kicked his ass and—"

He put a hand to her mouth to stop her.

"Nobody kicked anybody's ass. No punches were thrown."

"So what happened?"

"He's agreed to help us."

Michelle looked dumbstruck. "Well, that's great too. So, why don't you look happy?"

"Because it might cost him his career."

"But it's his choice."

"I actually might have shamed him into doing it. And there's something else."

"What?"

"The Pentagon. They can come down on us like a ton of bricks."

"Wouldn't be the first time we've ticked off the high and mighty, Sean."

"This time might be different."

"What do you want to do then? Cut and run?"

He started to walk toward the building. "Not a chance. Just wanted full disclosure in case you wanted to call it a day."

She fell into step beside him. "You really think I'd just walk and leave you solo on this?"

"No. I didn't."

"Then why the little lecture?"

"Maybe it was for my benefit. To show that when it all goes to hell I had thought it through."

The rooms here were accessed directly from the outside. They walked up a set of rusty steps to a balcony that ran around the front and sides of the second floor. They turned to the left, and then turned right as it wrapped around the outside of the motor court's upper floor.

"Number fourteen is right down here," said Michelle.

They reached a wooden door that was badly in need of fresh paint.

Sean knocked.

"I didn't see Jean's car here," Michelle said.

"Just being sure," replied Sean.

He waited a few more moments then said, "Got your pick tools?"

Sean stood behind Michelle to cover her breaking and entering. Thirty seconds later she swung the door open with one hand. In her other was her pistol.

She entered, followed by Sean. He closed the door behind them. Michelle checked the small attached bathroom while Sean opened the tiny closet and then looked under the bed. There were no other places someone could be concealed.

Michelle was holstering her gun as she came back out of the bathroom. "All clear."

"She didn't leave much," he said as he opened a few drawers, revealing various articles of clothing. "There're a few hanging things in the closet."

Michelle flipped up the mattress and then checked the box spring for anything hidden there. Wiping the dust off her hands, she rose. "I doubt she left anything of significance."

"Yet her having this place is significant in itself," he replied.

She said, "How hard do you want us to look? We

can tear up carpet, peel off wallpaper, and dig the backing off the cheap prints on the wall. Check the toilet, the pipes, and the bath drain. The list goes on and on."

"Why have a second address at a place like this?"

Michelle perched on the edge of the bed. "As opposed to what?"

"Let's assume she was a DoD plant. Presumably Wingo would have known that."

Michelle saw where he was going. "So why a crash pad? If she was brought in from out of the area, the military had to have a better place for her to stay than this dump. I mean, the Pentagon has a lot of facilities up here. You can't turn around without bumping into space with their prints all over it."

Sean leaned against the wall. "Based on that, what's the logical conclusion?"

Michelle flicked her gaze around the room as she thought about this. When the answer dawned on her she said, "If you're right, this sucker just got really complicated."

"Because maybe Jean Wingo was playing a two-sided game. Working for DoD and pretending to be Wingo's wife."

Michelle picked up this thread. "And also working for the other side. The side that got the billion euros Wingo was supposed to deliver. So she's a spy?"

"I don't know what she is. A spy. A criminal. Both."

"But who would she be spying for?"

"Even our allies spy on us."

"Granted. But we have to make some progress on that question if we want to get any traction on this case."

"I'm hoping General Brown will come through for us there. And we might get really lucky and Sam Wingo will email his son back."

"Do you think Wingo went over to the dark side?"

"For Tyler's sake I hope not," replied Sean.

Michelle glanced toward the door. "Did you hear something?"

Sean ran to the window where he could see outside through a gap in the drapes. Whatever he saw made him leap across the room and push Michelle into the bathroom. He grabbed the mattress and threw himself through the doorway into the same bathroom, where Michelle was now lying on the floor.

"What the hell is going on?" she hissed.

In response he pulled her into the bathtub with him and threw the mattress over them both.

She didn't have time to ask her question again because the bedroom they had just been in disappeared in a vortex of shock waves, choking fire, and flying debris.

35

Sam Wingo was walking fast.

He was back on American soil. He crossed the street, dodging traffic, reached the other side, and picked up his pace. He turned up his collar and kept his gaze, concealed behind glasses, swiveling in a 180-degree arc. Every few seconds he would check behind him. If he was taken now, he was convinced no one would ever see him again.

And he would never see Tyler again.

He ducked into a coffee shop as the rain started coming down. He ordered a cup of coffee and carried it to the rear of the space. He sat with his back to the wall and his sight line to the door unobstructed.

He slid out a disposable phone loaded with minutes and data bytes that had been waiting for him in India courtesy of Adeel and gazed down at it. He had loaded his personal email account on the phone.

The message had come in as soon as he turned his phone back on after the cargo plane landed. Once they touched down he'd expected to feel a hand on his shoulder, a gun in his ribs, a voice in his ear saying, "You need to come with us, Mr. Wingo."

But none of that had happened and Wingo began to think that others truly believed him dead.

Well, let them.

He gazed down at the email message again. It had come in from an unfamiliar Gmail account. But he knew it was from Tyler. It was written in their usual code. He easily deciphered it.

His son wanted to meet with him, as soon as possible.

Wingo wanted the very same thing. Only he knew it wouldn't be that easy. His email account was known. There were others who had undoubtedly seen this message. Whatever he wrote back they would be able to see as well. There was no GPS chip in the phone he had so he wasn't unduly worried about them tracking him down that way.

But he would have to keep moving. He had drastically changed his appearance and was wearing clothing designed for maximum concealment. Yet he well knew the resources aligned against him. And it wasn't just his own government after him. There were others out there, and he wasn't even sure who they were.

He took a few minutes to drink his coffee and compose his response to his son's email in his head. Then he thumbed it in and hit the send key. He finished his coffee, rose, and headed out the other exit. He grabbed a cab and had it drop him off at a hotel near D.C.'s Chinatown where he had previously checked in.

He had cash and a set of credit cards under an alias. There would be markers in the system so he could no longer be Sam Wingo. He hoped one day to return to his normal life. But he was a long way from there yet.

Wingo went to his room, sat on the bed, and stared out the window. Across the river was the Pentagon, the world's largest office building, surprising since it was only a few stories tall. After the United States had been attacked at Pearl Harbor and needed a central-ized command and control facility, it had been built in a little over a year using wheelbarrows, shovels, and American sweat. It was an achievement of which to be tremendously proud.

Wingo was proud of his own service. He had always entered the doors of the Pentagon with an extra spring in his step. Now the thought of the place brought nothing but misery. He had a gut feeling that he had been set up somehow by folks in that very building. Why he didn't know. But certainly the motivation was there.

The journey of the forty-eight hundred pounds—representing a billion in unmarked five-hundred-euro notes that could be freely circulated—had been a complicated multistep mission. The delivery of the money had been the very first step. Wingo was one of the few privy to the entire scheme.

In a way that was a good thing because the number

of people who could have betrayed him had to be small. And he meant to find out who they were. He had tried to do his job. Someone had screwed him. He wasn't turning the other cheek. He was a soldier. Soldiers were not wired for compassion or forgiveness. They were trained to strike back when struck.

He left his room, walked four blocks to the west, and rented a car using his fake ID and a credit card that also had been provided to him in India. He drove out of the garage in his new wheels. The mobility felt good. He believed he could accomplish something now.

But he had to take care of something first. He drove to a police impoundment lot and scanned the area. He saw no dogs, and the lone surveillance camera mounted on a pole wasn't even connected to a power source. Budget cuts must be a bitch.

He scaled the fence and dropped down inside. Keeping an eye out for any uniforms, he searched until he found what he needed. A car in the back that looked like it had been here awhile, its front right fender and driver's door crumpled. He checked the plates—still valid. A minute later the plates were in his hand and he was back over the fence.

He replaced the plates on the rental with the ones taken from the car in the impoundment lot. Now if someone keyed on his plate number and tried to run it down, Wingo's alias would not be compromised.

He drove back to his hotel, went to his room, punched in a number, and listened while it rang.

The voice said, "South."

"It's me," Wingo said.

There were a few seconds of silence as Wingo heard the other man start breathing hard, working himself up into a fury, no doubt.

"Do you know what a shitstorm you're in?" barked South.

"Then you are too. It was your mission. The Army doesn't pick fall guys, Colonel. They just shoot everybody."

"And you think I don't know that, you son of a bitch? You have screwed me beyond belief."

"Did you find Tim Simons from Nebraska?"

"The CIA never heard of him. And they knew nothing of our mission in Afghanistan. Dead end."

"So he was a fake."

"If he ever even existed outside your own mind. Now where the hell is the money, Wingo?"

"I told you it was taken. Hell, you know it was."

"All I know is the team that was supposed to meet up with you was slaughtered. The truck with the money is gone. You're AWOL. Are you really surprised by what we're thinking about you?"

"If I had taken it, why would I keep calling you?"

"CYA."

"If I had a billion euros why would I have to cover my ass with anything?"

"If you're truly innocent, come in. I told you that

last time you called. We can sit down and evaluate what happened."

"You mean you'll bury me in some remote location somewhere so the truth never comes out."

"We're Americans. We don't make other Americans disappear."

"If the facts of this mission come out, you know as well as I do what will happen. It'll be felt not just at the Pentagon, but also across the river on Pennsylvania Avenue. I know where those euros were going and what they were going to be used for and so do you. And the last place they'll want to see it is on the front pages of the *Post* or the *Times*."

"Are you actually threatening me and by extension your government? What do you want, more money? Wasn't the billion enough? Or do you blackmail for the fun of it?"

"I'm just explaining to you why me coming in doesn't work. Even if I did nothing wrong, and I didn't, it won't matter. I'll never see the light of day again."

"Then why did you volunteer for the mission in the first place?"

"To serve my country. I didn't focus that much on the details of it not going according to plan. But now I've had the time to do just that."

"If you didn't steal the money, who did?"

"I'm going to find out. Count on it."

He clicked off and was about to put the phone back into his pocket when it vibrated. He read through the email that had just been deposited there.

Tyler had written him back.

36

Sean pushed the mattress off and gave a shuddering cough as the smoke engulfed them. "Are you okay?" he asked Michelle.

"Thanks to you," she said. "But we need to get out of here before we're not okay." She coughed, too.

They climbed out of the tub and staggered over to where the door was, or used to be. There were gaping holes in the wall between the bathroom and the front room. As Sean stepped to the doorway he immediately drew back. Michelle crowded behind him and then drew back, too.

The front bedroom was essentially gone. The edge of the bathroom was now the front of the room. An inch in front of them was a long drop to what remained of the unit on the first floor. They were cut off from the rest of the balcony so they couldn't escape that way. And flames were creeping up the walls of the bathroom, and the smoke was growing thicker.

Michelle peered over the edge.

"We have to get down there," she said.

"I know. But how?"

They could hear fire engine sirens. And a police car, its rack lights blazing, was powering down the road.

"If we stay here we're going to be burned alive."

The fire was starting to surround them.

Michelle saw a fire truck in the distance, but she figured they would be dead long before it got to them.

She grabbed up all the towels she could find in the bathroom. "Help me," she said.

They tied the towels together as tightly as they could, and then Michelle fastened one end around an exposed support beam in the wall.

"I'll go first," said Sean. "If it'll support my weight, it'll be no problem for you."

"And if it breaks, you're going to crack open your skull. Let me go."

But Sean had already clambered over the edge and grabbed ahold of the towel rope. "I hope they've maintained their towels better than the rest of this place," he said as he dropped over the edge.

He quickly climbed down and then Michelle even more quickly followed, letting go and dropping the last few feet.

The motor court must have been quite empty because there were only a few people in the parking lot, one of them barefoot in just his pants.

"Do you smell that?" asked Sean.

"Gas," said Michelle.

He yelled at the people, "Get back. Gas leak. Run."

They all sprinted away from the building. Sean and

Michelle found refuge outside the blast radius. Ten seconds later the gas ignited in the middle of the structure, blowing a yawning hole from the first to the second floor. Debris was thrown out thirty feet and rained down on the cars parked nearby.

The police car wheeled into the parking lot and two officers jumped out. The fire trucks came along a few minutes later, and the battle with the blaze began.

Sean and Michelle looked at each other.

He said, "I think it would be a lot better if we left now."

She nodded and they crossed over to their vehicles, which were fortunately undamaged. While the police and firefighters were engaged with the blaze they slowly pulled out of the parking lot.

They hit the road and accelerated, passing three more fire trucks and two police cars heading to the motor court. They stopped about five miles later at a 7-Eleven. Sean got out of his car and climbed into Michelle's Land Cruiser. He dusted off his clothes as best he could while she coughed violently.

"We both need showers and some oxygen," she said miserably. "What did you see out the window?"

"A pack of plastic explosives stuck to the door with a detonator attached."

"Who would put it there?"

"Friends of the three mall guys, I would suspect."

"But that means we were followed here. I didn't see anybody."

"Neither did I. Which means they're really, really good, Michelle."

He slumped back in his seat and rubbed his blackened face.

She said gamely, "Then we just have to be better."

"Easier said than done apparently. We almost bought it back there."

"What if they already knew about this place and were waiting for us to arrive?"

Sean said, "You mean they knew about Jean Wingo's involvement?"

"Maybe she was working with them, like we were saying before."

"And they wanted to get rid of any trace of that place, along with us. Two birds with one pack of Semtex."

She nodded. "Sounds pretty logical. And the motivation?"

"They have one billion reasons, Michelle."

"But if they already have the money, what do they care about any of this? They're long gone. Why come after us—or Dana, for that matter? Why not just disappear with the cash and go buy an island somewhere?"

"If they want to eliminate us, then they're afraid we're going to find out something with our investigation. Remember that Jean disappeared after Tyler told her we were back on the case."

"Maybe they found out we know about the money?" suggested Michelle.

"The money disappeared in Afghanistan, Michelle. They can't believe we're going there to check things out. So they can't be afraid we'd get a line on the cash."

"Then it must be about more than the money."

He rubbed his temples and gave another racking cough. "Why steal the money?"

"Obvious reason. To get rich."

"There's another reason."

Michelle thought about this for a few seconds. "You need to buy something with it."

"That's right. And not an island or a fleet of Bentleys."

"The cash went missing in the middle of Taliban land." She glanced at him. "You think we're talking terrorists?"

"Lots of cash has gone missing over there during the last ten years or so. They'd drive out with truckloads of it and who the hell knows where it ended up. Maybe our taxpayer money has been funding the bad guys for years."

"Okay, but what about *this* money?"

He said, "The mission was to get it from point A to point B. Wingo knew what those points were. He knew what the money presumably was for."

"Which makes him both valuable and a target."

"If he's innocent, he might want to clear his name. He wouldn't have been attached to this thing unless he came highly recommended. Tyler said his dad could run circles around guys half his age. The special language training? The fake marriage with Jean a year ago? Him leaving the Army a year short of his full twenty? A lot of planning and time went into this."

"Sean, if the mission went awry the government will obviously want to cover this up. Maybe years ago it wouldn't have mattered so much, but the last thing they need with all the budget cuts is to lose over a billion dollars of taxpayer money. They'd get murdered on Capitol Hill. And if they were going to use the money for a reason that the public would find whacko, that's even worse."

"The military may see us as a problem, Michelle. The three guys at the mall were all formerly in uniform. Maybe they were called back into 'duty' to take care of a problem, meaning us. Black, black ops."

"So our *own guys* are trying to put us in body bags?" she said incredulously.

"To them we're not on the same team. We are a threat to them. Threats have to be eliminated."

Michelle sat back with a look of despair. "So us against the Pentagon?"

"It may not be the entire Pentagon. In fact, I'm sure it's not. But it could be a small part of it looking to clean up this mess before it spreads."

"You said General Brown was going to try to help us."

Sean nodded slowly. "I wish I hadn't done that."

"Why?"

"Because if he helps us, he might just become a target too. And we can't count on these guys to keep missing."

37

Alan Grant kissed his wife Leslie goodbye that morning. In her arms was the youngest of their three children, a son. They were going to have more kids. He wanted a large family. To make up for the parents he had lost.

She said, "Alan, you're looking tired. Are you sure everything's okay?"

He smiled. "Your dad asked me pretty much the same thing."

"He cares about you. We all do."

Grant reached over and gently held his child's little fist. He looked at Leslie. "Things are fine, honey. I'm a little stressed, but then who isn't these days? I've just got some things to work through and then how about a vacation? Everybody. Your dad too. Someplace warm."

"Warm sounds wonderful."

He kissed her again and smiled. "Then it's a done deal." He let go of his son's hand. "See you, little guy."

He drove straight to the cemetery in Arlington from his home in western Fairfax. He parked his car and walked the rest of the way to the grave sites. He stood in front of them and read the names on the plaques.

Franklin James Grant, his father.

Eleanor Grant, his mother.

They had died on the same day, at the same hour, at the same minute, and in the same place.

A suicide pact. A car with a towel stuffed in the tailpipe, the windows rolled up tight, and the engine on while inside a rented storage space. A note was left trying to explain why they had done it, but the note was unnecessary. Everyone knew why they had decided to take their lives.

Grant had been thirteen years old when his parents had left him. Back then he didn't really grasp why they had done it. It was only when he reached adulthood that he came to understand the truth.

It was years later before he had settled on a plan to avenge his parents' sacrifice. He had long since forgiven them for leaving him an orphan to be raised by relatives who had not been pleased to have the added burden of another mouth to feed. But his rage over the reasons behind their deaths had increased with each passing year.

He set the flowers on the graves and stepped back. His father had been a soldier's soldier. A chest full of medals from Vietnam and stints stateside serving his country in various capacities, including time as a staff member on the National Security Council back in the 1980s. And then his life had gone to hell. And he had chosen to end it. And his wife had chosen to join him in death.

Grant could have blamed her for abandoning him. The shame had belonged to his father. It was misplaced shame, Grant felt, but still, his mother was untainted. She had chosen death with her husband rather than life without him. There was nothing wrong with this, Grant felt. A wife's place is with her husband. He had no doubt his mother loved him a great deal. She simply loved her husband more.

Grant had opted to stay in the military for only one tour. He had fought in a war. He had been wounded, not badly, but wounded just the same. He had displayed suitable heroics, saved the lives of his comrades in arms, and they, in turn, had saved his on occasion. All was as it should have been.

He had left with his own share of medals and an honorable discharge and a wide-open door into the Pentagon that had served him well as he built up his private contracting business in the military sector. He had beefed up his cyber skills over the years. And, as part of his plan, he had assembled a team whose collective hacking talents were far better than his.

At age thirty-eight he was not incredibly rich, yet he was affluent and lived very comfortably with his wife and children. He hoped to make more money in the coming years, but the truth was money did not interest him. Power did not interest him. This made him an unusual creature inside the Washington Beltway where others thirsted, plotted, and stabbed one another in the back to gain both money and influence.

He walked away from the graves thinking positive thoughts about his visit, the energy it had inspired in him to keep going. He got back into his car and drove to Reagan National Airport. He parked, walked into the terminal, passed swiftly through security, arrived at his gate, and boarded his flight right on time.

Later he landed in Florida. A car was waiting for him that took him well away from the city in which he had landed. The car pulled up in front of a home that was palatial by any standards. Grant wasn't enamored of the architecture or landscaping. It was all far too grand for his tastes, with too many pinks, salmons, and turquoises along with statuary lavish enough for a museum.

He climbed out of the car and walked up the wide marble steps to the front door. He knocked once and the door was almost immediately opened. He was escorted inside by a man dressed in black livery—a butler in the twenty-first century. Grant trusted he was well paid to re-create this archaic occupation.

He didn't dwell on the lovely paintings professionally hung on the enormous walls with two-foot-thick moldings. The ocean views did not capture his interest, either. Nor did the costly furnishings at eye level or the impossibly expensive Oriental rugs underneath his feet.

He was escorted into a wood-paneled room that

ought to have been a library, only there was not a single book on the shelves. In their place were collections of what looked to be paperweights, coins, timepieces, and model trains. The door was closed behind him as the butler receded to wherever butlers spent their time between duties. Perhaps polishing the silver, Grant idly thought, and then he thought no more of it.

He sat in the chair pointed to by the occupant of the large room that, too, looked out upon the Atlantic.

The man's name was Avery Melton. He had inherited a small fortune over thirty years ago and through hard work, occasional ruthlessness, and the more-frequent bribe, he had multiplied that inheritance a thousandfold. He was sixty-four years old but looked older. He spent too much time on the golf course where the sun beat as relentlessly down on him as it did on the laborers who maintained his lovely grounds. Nature played no favorites on that score.

He was five-eight, with a paunch and rounded shoulders, but his eyes were clear and his mind clearer still. He was a businessman with many interests and few scruples. He had products and services to sell and he needed buyers to complete the transaction. Grant was a buyer, Melton a seller. He did not make it any more complicated than that.

He said, "Good flight?"

"Always a good flight when the plane lands on its wheels," said Grant.

"Money?"

Grant opened his briefcase and slid out a piece of paper. They would not be using anything so coarse as money in rubber-banded bundles. He handed the paper to Melton, who studied it.

It was a wire transfer notification showing that twenty million dollars had been placed into an account controlled by Melton. He nodded. No grin, just a nod. This was business. He dealt in such numbers all the time. Some smaller, some bigger.

"I've already been told of the deposit confirmation, but it's good to see the paper too. I'm old school. Don't use computers."

Grant nodded and waited. The money had been delivered, but that was only one half of the transaction. Now he needed the other half.

Melton unlocked a drawer in his desk and pulled out a small hardback black book. He opened it, glanced down the first page, and then handed it to Grant, who performed a similar inspection.

Melton said, "The codes and other necessary details are all there. All your guys have to do is dial it up, input the codes, and you have an entire satellite all to yourself, the MelA3." He held up a cautionary finger. "For the stated time only. Then it's mine once more. The codes expire and the access is no longer valid."

"I understand."

"That's a lot of firepower," said Melton. "The A3 weighs two tons, cost over a billion dollars to build, launch, and maintain, and has fifteen more years of useful life in orbit. I'm glad to take your money but there's rental space on a lot of birds up there far cheaper than this one. And you don't have to lease the whole platform. On some of our birds we have up to five thousand lessees per platform. It's quite profitable but the upfront costs are enormous. You have to be patient to make your money—and I am."

"I appreciate your advice, but we like to have the whole pie. And there aren't that many up there that could do what the A3 can do," replied Grant.

"Such as?"

"I was hoping twenty million dollars would provide some degree of privacy," said Grant.

"But it's still my bird."

"The parameters of the rental have been hammered out. We will stay within those parameters at all times or find ourselves in litigation. And I can assure you, I have no plans to be in court."

Melton nodded. "Did you know the U.S. government is so broke they're renting space on my platforms too? 'Hosted payloads,' we call it in the industry. Military can't afford to send their own platforms up anymore. I'm bumping them off this one because of our deal, in fact. They were on the A3 but on a short-term lease that came up for renewal, only they wouldn't match your offer."

"Interesting," said Grant. "I didn't know that."

Except he did know it. In fact, it was the main reason he had rented the A3.

He rose and shook the hand that Melton had extended. The older man said, "The rental agreement has your company as Phoenix Enterprises."

"Yes it does."

"Phoenix, like in the city?"

"Phoenix like in the mythological bird that resurrects itself from its own ashes."

"Okay, whatever. My people tell me you're in some sort of contracting work. Defense intelligence sector."

"That's right."

"Then I can understand why you need work space up there."

"I was surprised you wanted to do this personally. I'm sure you have a team of executives who could have met with me and closed the deal."

"Piece of advice, young man. In business, when you do a deal of this size, and I've done bigger and I've done smaller, I like to look the man in the eye and shake his hand. Good for me, good for him. And we could be doing business together again."

"Yes, we could," replied Grant. But he was thinking, *No, we never will.*

He took the next flight north. He arrived back in D.C., drove straight to his office, and sat at his desk. He opened the small black book Melton had given him and looked at the series of codes and authentication keys that were critical for him to gain access to the A3. It was quite a unique bird, he knew, for a variety of reasons. And while the military and other federal agencies had been kicked off the platform, they weren't really. Not really. They always left a little fragment of themselves behind.

And a fragment was all Grant needed.

38

"Hey, Wingo!"

Tyler looked over as he was leaving school. The group of senior boys was watching him. Some had big duffels they carried over their shoulders. One held a football helmet and shoulder pads.

One of them shouted, "Heard your old man's not dead. Heard he went AWOL. And he's a crook."

Tyler's face flamed red and he shouted, "That's a load a' shit."

The seniors came over to him, each towering over him. Tyler recognized them all as being on the varsity football team.

The largest senior said, "My old man told me. He's in the Army. He should know."

One of the other seniors shoved Tyler. "So you calling his dad a liar?"

"If he says my dad is a crook, I am."

"AWOL, that's like being a coward, right? Your old man a chickenshit, Wingo?" said a large, big-bellied eighteen-year-old named Jack. He shoved Tyler so hard he fell back on the dirt, which made all of them laugh.

The other boys crowded around. One jerked Tyler up and held his arms, while Jack cocked his fist back and was about to punch Tyler in the gut.

"Don't think so."

A hand grabbed Jack's fist and ripped it backward.

The boys all turned to see Michelle standing there. She let go of Jack's hand and said, "You guys like ganging up on people?"

"What's it to you?" snarled Jack.

"Tyler's a friend of mine."

Jack guffawed as he looked Michelle up and down. "You mean you're his bodyguard? You need a chick to guard you, Wingo?"

The other boys all laughed.

"I can take care of myself," snapped Tyler as he quickly got to his feet and glared at Michelle.

"I know you can. But six on one isn't fair for anyone. So let's see." She looked at the other boys one by one, her gaze finally coming to rest on Jack. "You play football, right?"

"Starting left tackle," bragged Jack.

"Which means you're big and strong." Jack's smile grew larger. "And slow and fat and you have no stamina because you can't run more than three yards without collapsing."

Jack's smile disappeared.

Michelle looked at Tyler. "Now, Tyler isn't nearly your size, but he's wiry and quick and he swims, which means he has great endurance. You fight him, and you don't take him out fast, he'll dance around, popping away until you get so tired you won't be able to stand up, much less hit anything with force. And Tyler's dad, the so-called coward, is Special Forces, and those guys are in another world when it comes to close-quarter combat. You think MMA guys are tough? They wouldn't last a round with a SEAL or a Ranger. And Special Forces guys don't just beat you up. They kill you. And I bet Tyler's dad taught him a few things."

She glanced at Tyler, who was staring furiously at Jack.

"And Tyler looks like he wants to take your head off," said Michelle, turning back to Jack. "So why don't we just let you two go at it. But just the two of you. Any of your buddies try to help you, Slick, I'll step in, and even though I *am* a girl, I don't fight like one."

Jack eyed Tyler and Tyler stared back at Jack. Jack finally dropped his gaze and said, "Screw this. I'm not getting kicked off the football team for kicking this punk's ass on school grounds."

He turned and walked off with his buddies.

Michelle and Tyler stared after them and then Tyler turned to her. "Thanks for doing that," he mumbled.

"You didn't really need me. In fact if it were just one-on-one you could have taken him."

"You really think so?"

"You have fire in the belly, Tyler. That jerk just has a big belly."

"What are you doing here?" he asked.

"I dropped you off. Now I'm here to pick you up."

"But I've got other plans."

"Like what?"

"Just other plans."

"We've had this discussion, Tyler. We stick together for now."

"I don't want to stick together."

She eyed him intently. "What changed from then to now?" She eyed the phone gripped in his hand, and the truth dawned on her. "When did your dad email you back?"

"Just leave me alone."

"No can do."

"I'm outta here."

He started to walk off but she grabbed his arm. "Let me clue you in to something really fast, Tyler. This morning Sean and I went to check a lead. It was a lead I picked up at your house and it led to a motel that your fake stepmom was using as a drop point."

"A what?"

"Doesn't matter. While we were there someone stuck a pack of probably Semtex on the front wall of the unit and detonated it. If not for Sean's quick think-ing I wouldn't be here and those guys would have kicked your ass. As it was, most of the motor court burned down. Luckily, no one was hurt."

"A bomb?"

"Yeah, a bomb. So when did your dad contact you?"

"I saw the message right before lunch."

"And what did it say?"

"Nothing much." Tyler looked down at the ground as he said this.

"You really suck at lying."

"I'm not lying!"

"Okay, if it was nothing much why can't you tell me?"

"Why would Jean have another place to live?"

"We told you we think she and your dad might not even be married."

"Right. You said he might have brought her home so I'd have an adult to live with while he was gone. Did you change your mind about that?"

"No. But we've modified our opinion somewhat. We think she was a plant."

"A plant?"

"We think she might be working for the people who set up your dad. That's why she's disappeared now. She got scared and took off with us back on the case. She had this address at the motor court where mail was sent. We checked the place out but didn't find anything except nearly a fiery death."

"But who was she working with then? Not the Army?"

"Don't think so, but the Army is definitely mixed up in all this. We think there's another factor. Maybe the factor that made your dad's mission go wrong."

His face brightened. "So you believe my dad is a good guy?"

"I think we're both coming around to that, yeah."

"Well, he *is* a good guy."

"Even though he lied to you? You were pretty mad at him for that."

"I guess he had to do that. He was serving his country."

"Come on, let's go see Sean. He'll want to hear this too."

Tyler's face screwed up. "I don't want to go with you. How many times do I have to say it?"

"So what will you do? Hook up with your dad?"

"Maybe. I don't know."

"And if it wasn't your dad who sent you that email, you'll be walking right into a trap."

"It was in our code."

"Which, like we told you, we broke in a few seconds. You don't think other people can too? This is the big league, Tyler. They have resources you won't even see in a Hollywood film because the movie guys can't come close to imagining what some folks already have for real."

"I can take care of myself."

"You mean like you did with those idiots back there? The dudes you'll be facing by yourself will put a hole in your head and not think twice about it."

"You're just trying to scare me."

"No, I'm just trying to be straight with you."

Tyler hesitated.

Michelle seized on this. "I tell you what. We go see

Sean. Let him talk to you. If you still want to go, you go. We can't keep you against your will. That would be a crime."

"Are you being straight with me now or is this a trick?"

"Ever since we got hooked up with you we've almost been killed twice. I don't think we'll survive another attack. So, yeah, I'm being straight with you. And you're the client. You want to go it alone, there's nothing we can do about it. Except attend your funeral later. Which would have been more than Sean and I would have had after this morning."

"What do you mean?"

She put a hand on his shoulder and guided him toward her Land Cruiser. "Semtex doesn't usually leave enough of you behind to bury."

39

They drove to Sean's house and filled him in. Michelle was surprised by what he wanted to focus on.

"Why did those punks at school say your dad was AWOL and a crook?" he asked.

Tyler stared at him angrily. "My dad is not—"

Sean cut him off. "I didn't say he was. That's not my point. What I'm asking is *where* did they get that idea?"

Tyler now looked puzzled. "One of them said his dad told him. And his dad is in the Army. That I know for a fact. He's a lieutenant colonel."

Michelle said, "Or they might have made it all up just to harass you, Tyler."

"No," said Tyler. "Those jerks don't have that much imagination." He paused and added, "If he heard it from his dad and his dad's in the Army, I guess it might have come from there."

Sean shook his head. "I don't think so. The Army has put the kibosh on this whole thing. They're coming down like an Abrams tank on us and we're not even in uniform. I don't see them letting the rank and file flap their mouths. Actually, I don't see the rank and file even being in the loop on this."

Sean pulled out his laptop and started clicking keys. He looked at the results, clicked some more keys, and then nodded.

"I Googled your dad's name. And this came up. There's a leak," he said. He spun the computer around so they could see.

He continued, "Not the mainstream media yet, but there are three articles dealing with this. They're actually the same article just repeated in strings. Meaning other online media outlets are picking it up now."

Tyler and Michelle read the pages on the screen.

Tyler said, "Shit, they know that Jean is missing too. How did they find that out?"

Sean replied, "Maybe because the source behind this story was the one who made her disappear."

After they were finished Michelle sat back and summarized the articles. "So, missing money. Unauthorized money. And a missing soldier named Sam Wingo smack in the middle of it. The White House refuses to comment as does the Pentagon, which means everyone will assume they're covering it up. So that's obviously what the punk's dad was referring to. He'd read this article."

"Right. But who the hell was the source?" asked Sean.

Michelle eyed the byline of the first article. "If this was the original that the other outlets just copied, it was George Carlton. He has a blog devoted to military and political matters." Michelle looked at Sean. "You know of him?"

"No. I'm not much into the blogging world, but I wonder if Mr. Carlton has received a visit from DoD?"

"He's local. Bio says he lives and works in Reston, so maybe he has. But they surely wouldn't have wanted him to write this."

"Not saying they would. I meant after the fact, to find out his source." He read over the article again. "The White House refuses comment. I wonder why they were even asked?"

"The White House?" said Tyler. "What does that place have to do with my dad?"

"That's for someone else to know and for us to find out," observed Michelle. She glanced at Sean. "You think we should check out this blogger?"

"After this story he might be lying low."

"How low? Like in a grave low?" asked Michelle.

"Shit," exclaimed Tyler. They both looked at him. "Are you guys being serious?" he asked.

"Serious about what? How dangerous this is?" said Sean sternly. "Then yeah, we are serious as shit."

"What about Tyler's dad contacting him?" asked Michelle.

"Next point on my to-discuss list," said Sean. "Does he want to set up a meeting?"

Tyler shrugged. "I don't know. He didn't say."

"Sure he did, Tyler," said Sean.

"What do you mean?"

"I set up the Gmail account for you. And I added a back door."

Tyler stared at him. "So you already read the email?"

"And decoded it," added Sean.

Michelle looked at him in amazement. "Sean, I'm seeing your Steve Jobs side and liking it. Very sexy. But I am pissed you didn't tell me before now."

"I just saw it five minutes before you got back." He looked at Tyler. "So he wants to meet with you. He set a time and place. He's just waiting for your response."

Tyler looked uncomfortable. "I'm not sure my dad would be cool with you guys coming too."

"So you were just going to meet with him alone?" said Michelle. "And who would be covering your back?"

"I…I mean, I guess I hadn't thought about that yet."

She said, "Well, if your dad is the kind of guy I believe he is, he'll think about it. And he won't do anything to put you in danger. So why don't you write him back and tell him we've got your back and we're part of the team and he needs to meet with all of us. Face-to-face."

"But what if my dad won't do it?" said Tyler.

Michelle shook her head. "I'm not sure he has much choice. We can't let you go and meet with him alone. It's too dangerous."

Tyler said quickly, "I guess you're right. My dad wouldn't want me to get hurt."

"Glad you see our point," said Sean. "So send him another email. Tell him you can meet him tomorrow night at the place he gave you. You can tell him we're investigators you hired to help him. Then we'll go and see what he has to say."

"Okay," agreed Tyler.

"Sean, look at this."

Michelle was pointing at the computer screen where she had pulled up the latest on the bombing at the motor court in south Alexandria.

"The police are looking for two people seen leaving the blast site. A man and a woman."

Sean said, "Maybe we should have stayed and told the cops our story."

"Hindsight is twenty-twenty," she replied. "Too late now."

"Uh, guys," said Tyler. He was peering out the front window of the house. "There are like some dudes in your yard."

Sean and Michelle exchanged another look, then strode over to the window and looked out.

Michelle sucked in a breath while Sean let one out.

"Shit!" they said at the same instant.

"Is that kind of like a SWAT team?" asked Tyler, backing away.

Sean shook his head. "No, that's *exactly* like a SWAT team." He turned to Michelle. "Take your gun out, remove the clip, and put it down on the table over there. Quick." She did this and Sean followed suit with his weapon.

Sean said, "Tyler, go into the kitchen and sit at the table. Keep your hands in plain sight. And whatever they ask you to do, you do, understood?"

Tyler's face was so pale Sean was worried he might pass out. He put a hand on his shoulder and smiled reassuringly. "Been through stuff like this lots of times, Tyler. It's going to be okay."

"You swear?"

"Absolutely. Now go into the kitchen."

As soon as he was gone Michelle said, "When have you confronted a SWAT team before?"

"Never in my life."

"Great."

"I'm not waiting for the warning," he said. He moved to the front door.

"Sean, wait."

But he had opened the door and stepped outside with his hands up.

Sean was confronted by a dozen armed and armored men who had their assault weapons pointed at him.

"Is there a problem?" asked Sean.

One of the men came forward. He had on body armor and a face shield. He drew up the shield so Sean could see who it was.

Agent McKinney of DHS said, "Oh, yeah. A big one. And you're it."

40

Sam Wingo sat on the bed in his hotel waiting for his son to email him back. Tyler, he noted, had used a new email account. That was smart thinking on his son's part. But Tyler had not written him back about the meeting he wanted. And as every minute passed Wingo's concern grew. He wanted to go to his home and see that Tyler was okay. But the place, he knew, was surely being watched. He would be arrested before he even got to the front porch.

It was maddening to come all this way just to sit and wait. Wingo could be patient when it was necessary, but that didn't mean it was easy.

A burn phone that he had been given in India vibrated, and he snatched it up. This could only be from one person, the man who had arranged for the phone.

Adeel, his Muslim contact in the Middle East, the man who had gotten him through Pakistan and into India. But Wingo had almost been killed on the Khyber Pass. He still didn't know if he'd been betrayed by Adeel. Maybe this email would answer that question.

He read the message: *Bodies discovered at target site. Identified as all Muslims. Interestingly enough, a group of Western males arrived in Afghanistan on charter flight from States on the day before and took transportation in vicinity of target site. Heron Air Service, based in Dulles, Virginia, was the charter service they flew in on. Preliminary investigation indicates that some of the Westerners had U.S. credentials. Exact agencies unknown. They were given passage by various tribal chieftains. Usual financial arrangements meaning cash so no trace possible. No other information obtainable on my end. If you are back in States, you may follow up. Good luck. And I hope you see your son. A.*

Wingo deleted the message from both his inbox and trash. He lay back on the bed and stared at the ceiling. A group of Westerners, some with U.S. creds, had flown into Afghanistan on the day before he was to deliver one billion euros to a group of Muslims. The Muslims had been slaughtered and these men had hijacked the shipment from Wingo, again while flashing U.S. creds. The money was gone and so were the men. Wingo was the fall guy and running for his life.

He had another thought, sat up, and clicked on his phone pad. He was Googling his own name. The same three articles that Sean had found—now expanded to ten—came up.

He read through them all quickly. They seemed to be a string, each merely regurgitating the facts of the others. Collectively, they were devastating.

Missing money, missing soldier.

Me.

How the hell had that leaked? Colonel South hadn't mentioned anything about the story getting to the media. He wondered whether to call the colonel but ultimately decided the man would not be helpful. He was convinced of Wingo's guilt. Maybe everyone was.

But then that meant Tyler probably knew about it too. What must his son think? That he was a thief or a traitor?

The news story went on to add that the missing money and soldier might have something to do with some classified operation that led all the way to the White House. However, neither President John Cole nor anyone at the Pentagon would comment, which of course was just creating a vacuum that was being filled by increasingly strident and hyperbolic voices.

Then he wondered about something else.

Where was Jean? Had she been pulled by the DoD after the mission overseas had gone to hell? If so, who was with Tyler?

That had been the hardest thing about this whole task for Wingo. Pretending to remarry and bringing what amounted to a complete stranger home to be his son's new stepmom. But it had been unavoidable. Tyler needed a grown-up with him. Wingo had refused to leave without that condition met. Unfortunately, the simplest way to achieve it was to fake a marriage. And so he had. But he had regretted it from the very first instant Tyler had laid eyes on Jean and been told that this woman, in essence, was taking his real mother's place.

Wingo turned on the TV in his room to see if there was any more news about the missing money. Every local station was chasing the same story, but it wasn't *this* story.

There had been an explosion at a motor court in south Alexandria. The cause of the explosion was unknown as yet. But he sat up when the news anchor mentioned something else, namely that the room had been rented long-term to a Jean Shepherd, whose whereabouts were currently unknown.

Jean Shepherd? That was Jean's real name.

He thumbed in another message to Tyler, urgently asking his son to contact him. He waited. And then waited some more. His phone never vibrated.

He debated whether to drive over to the house and see what he could find out. But that would be suicide, he knew. Yet he seriously thought about chancing it to make sure his son was okay.

He contemplated Adeel's email. Westerners coming into Afghanistan on a charter flight. Heron Air Service based out of Dulles, Virginia, which was not that far away. Could he maybe get a line on Tim Simons from Nebraska? It was the only lead he had right now. He rose, slipped his gun into its belt holster, and headed out.

★

Later, from inside his car, Wingo watched a jet lift into the air away from a storm approaching from the west. It made a graceful ascent, then performed a long bank to the south before leveling out and continuing its climb out from Dulles Airport.

Wingo took the fork to the right and made his way to the general aviation section of the sprawling 12,000-acre airport. It had been opened in 1972, and for many years had been largely unused by the flying public, which had preferred closer-in Washington National Airport. Now Dulles was one of the busiest terminals in the country, with short-haul flights to New York and nonstop routes to Tokyo. Its terminal roof, roughly in the shape of a wing, had been ultra-modern when it was first built, though now it looked dated. The original control tower with the enormous pearl-white ball on top was no longer used. It had been replaced by a new tower about five years ago, and there were currently six air traffic controllers stationed there to keep the busy area skies safe.

Wingo had flown out of Dulles many times over the years. He had landed in a cargo plane here not that long ago. His name had been on the flight crew manifest, something that had cost him quite a bit of money. With private flights, the CBP, or Custom and Border Patrol agents, would meet the deplaning passengers at the front door of the fixed-base operator, or FBO, operating the flight. With cargo flights they came directly to the plane. They would check the people on board, but their chief concern was the cargo. It had been an ignominious homecoming but at least he had arrived back in the country safely. Before the CBP agents had even arrived he had walked directly out of the FBO, into a parking lot across the street, and from there to the rental center where he'd picked up his car.

Now Wingo parked his car, partially slid down his window, and took up observation with a pair of binoculars. He kept looking around for anyone watching him. He knew there were surveillance cameras everywhere, and he tried to keep out of the direct sight lines of the ones he could see. He knew there was a ramp tower that housed individuals whose job it was to keep things safe on the ground, looking for anything out of the ordinary that would require airport security to be called in. Wingo kept low in the seat for this reason.

People came and went from Cargo Buildings One through Four. These narrow warehouses, barely sixty feet deep, were home to mom-and-pop cargo consolidator companies. They packaged freight and loaded it into the bellies of planes.

Heron Air Service was located next to one of these cargo facilities. In the restricted lot behind the building Wingo could see jets of varying sizes either sitting with wheels chocked or else being prepped for departure; there was one jet heading in after taxiing off the runway. This was how the rich and well connected flew. No security lines, no parking problems, no dealing with the little people.

Wingo didn't know if Heron was simply a charter company or did any freight business, but he had situated himself to be able to see both sectors of business conducted there as best he could. Still, Dulles Airport had over half a million square feet of cargo warehouse space and nearly a million square feet of cargo ramp. Hundreds, maybe thousands, of employees worked here, Wingo thought. Not to mention all the millions of people who came through as passengers. And while there might not be as many charter flights and passengers as on the commercial side of the airport, he was still looking for a needle in a haystack.

And then a miracle happened right in front of him.

He stiffened when he saw the man exit the offices of Heron Air Service. He wore a pilot's uniform. He headed across the parking lot to his car.

Wingo snapped a picture of him with his cell phone.

The man climbed into a late-model Audi.

Wing noted the license plate and took a picture of it and the car. When the man drove off, Wingo fell in behind him.

The man was not Tim Simons from Nebraska.

But he was one of the men in that stone building in Afghanistan. And thus he represented the best and only lead Wingo had right now to uncover what the hell was going on.

41

"Do you even realize how much trouble you're in?"

The person asking this was not Agent McKinney. It was FBI Special Agent Dwayne Littlefield—or so said his ID badge. He had not bothered to formally introduce himself.

He was in his early forties, black, about six feet tall, with wide shoulders, big arms that strained against the dress shirt holding them in, and a thick, heavily veined neck. He looked strong enough to punch a hole in the metal door of the room they were in, and pissed off enough to do it.

Sean and Michelle sat stonily in their chairs at the FBI's Washington Field Office in downtown D.C. Tyler was not with them. He had been led to another room, they assumed for a debrief or possibly interrogation.

Littlefield leaned into Sean's face. "I asked a question."

"I assumed it was a rhetorical one," replied Sean. "But in case you were really wondering, I would say that we are duly aware of our surroundings and circumstances, yes."

"Why in the hell did you think it was necessary to send an army of agents to come get us," bristled Michelle. "Don't you have a cell phone?"

Littlefield wheeled around on her. "Are you telling me how to do my damn job?"

"Actually, yeah, I am."

"You have got some balls, lady."

"Not the first time I've heard that."

Sean said, "Let's try and keep this on a professional level. First things first—why are we here?"

Littlefield stared back at Sean. "You are really asking me that, to my face, really?"

"Yeah, I really am. We were sitting in my house with a client not doing anything illegal as far as I'm aware when we looked out the window and saw Patton's Third Army surrounding the place."

"Well, let me refresh your memory then," said Littlefield. He picked up a remote and pointed it at a screen hanging from one wall of the room.

On the screen an image popped up.

It was Sean and then Michelle climbing down out of the wreckage of the destroyed motel room and then running off. Littlefield hit a button on the image, freezing it, and then tossed the remote down on the table and said, "Nothing happens anymore where there's not someone or something around to record it."

He plopped down into a chair, put his hands behind his head, and said, "So unless you're claiming that's not you on the video, you have damn sure got some explaining to do."

Sean and Michelle stared at the screen and saw themselves staring back.

Sean said, "Someone tried to blow us up. I don't suppose your 'camera' got a shot of him?"

"Why would someone want to kill you?"

"Have you spoken to McKinney?"

"I know about the mall incident. I know a two-star kicked your ass in the waiting room of a hospital because you got his wife nearly killed. And I know you've got a kid for a client whose dad is MIA and maybe for all the wrong reasons." He leaned forward and placed his palms on the table. "What I don't know is why to any of it. And McKinney doesn't seem to know why either."

Michelle said, "There's a lot of that going around. We seem to have the WTF virus too."

Littlefield glanced at her. "Former Secret Service, both of you. Only drummed out for messing up big-time."

"Ancient history," said Sean. "If you check our more recent past, you'll see we're legit and good at what we do. Lots of people will tell you that."

"They actually have. Because I'm good at my job too, and I asked around before your butts ever got to my playground."

Michelle said, "So why are you hassling us?"

"Because you left the scene of a bombing without

talking to the police. You both know better than that. What the hell were you thinking?" Before Sean could answer he went on, "And now the kid's stepmom is missing. So that means he's an adolescent on his own. You knew that too and didn't tell anyone."

"Sorry, I didn't realize it was our job to do your job," retorted Michelle.

Littlefield stood and leaned against a wall, his arms folded over his chest. "So the bottom line is, I don't know what to do with you two."

"You could release us and let us get on with our work," suggested Sean.

Littlefield smiled and shook his head. "Don't think so. Two loose cannons out there is not something I need."

"So you've been assigned to find Sam Wingo?" asked Michelle. "And by the way, we're not loose cannons."

"I'm not going to tell you what I have or haven't been assigned to do."

Sean shook his head wearily. "Let's cut to the chase. You've been tasked to find Sam Wingo. This is becoming an international incident. It's too hot for DHS to handle so the Bureau's been called in. An explosion occurred. Until it's determined to be solely from domestic sources, it's the Bureau's jurisdiction. Whatever Wingo did or didn't do over in Afghanistan has everybody over here white-knuckling their chairs and considering the impact on their careers."

"We know what he lost," added Michelle. "Over two tons of euros. A billion three in U.S. dollars."

"Who the hell told you that?" barked Littlefield.

"Sorry, lips are sealed," said Michelle. "Secret Service drills that into you."

"And how about if I see whether a grand jury subpoena drills it out of you?"

Sean said, "We can do the macho dance or we can work together on this."

Littlefield said incredulously, "Work together? You out of your fricking mind? Does it sound like I want to partner with *you*?"

Michelle stood and fixed her gaze on him. "We've been lied to, almost shot, nearly blown to hell, and pushed around by dickheads from the Army, DHS, and now the FBI. So I can tell you flat-out that whether you want to 'partner' with us or not, we're working this case. So stick that up your ass and see how it fits"—she glanced at his ID on a lanyard around his neck—"*Dwayne*."

Sean muttered, "Holy Mother of God," and put his hand over his eyes.

Littlefield looked ready to pull his gun and open fire. Then he did something that made Sean glance up in amazement. The FBI agent started laughing.

"You are something. I heard you were hell on wheels, but seeing it for myself, you are really something."

He sat down and grew serious as he studied them

both. "This shit goes so far up the food chain that it's like surfing the Net and reaching the end of it. There is no higher-up to go to."

"We heard on the TV that the White House has refused to comment," said Sean. "Is that how high?"

Littlefield gave a barely perceptible nod.

Michelle was still standing. Littlefield looked up at her and said, "You gonna join the party or what?"

Michelle sat down. "Why send one soldier out with all that money? Who couldn't see only bad things happening with that?"

"Apparently everybody except the stars and bars over at the Pentagon," replied Littlefield. He opened a file in front of him. "You two figured out what Wingo is or was?"

"He's not an Army reservist," said Sean. "Nobody exits the uniform one year before a full pension to take a sales job at a translator firm with DoD secretly footing the bill."

"You have done your homework," said Littlefield, looking impressed. He glanced down at the file in front of him. "You two familiar with DIA?"

"Defense Intelligence," replied Michelle. "Like CIA but in uniform."

"DIA has a bigger budget than CIA and they actually do more in certain parts of the world. But post-nine-eleven the two agencies have learned to play nice." He paused. "You two don't have security clearances anymore."

"So just leave out the juicy parts," said Sean. "And be clever enough to work them in some other way."

Littlefield chuckled. "It's not a secret. It was in the papers not that long ago. DIA has bulked up its clandestine field units big-time. They're working closely with Langley overseas in certain hot spots. We can all guess where those might be."

Sean said, "But I didn't think DIA was authorized to conduct covert operations that went much beyond your basic intelligence gathering, drone strikes, or getting guns into the hands of our enemy's enemy."

"That's true. But that's also where CIA comes in, because they *are* authorized to do that and a lot more. However, they've also had their budget slashed and committed some very public missteps lately. And even with defense cuts and sequestration the DoD has the funds to do more stuff."

Michelle said, "Are you saying that CIA provides the cover of their station platforms overseas—"

Littlefield broke in, "And training at the Farm in Virginia."

Michelle continued, "And DIA provides the field operatives?"

"DIA has even copied Langley on their Persia House initiative, creating a body to merge resources on problem countries around the planet. The difficulty has been how to leave soldiers behind after their units have been called back home. One way was to take the uniform off but not for real—train the solider up and deploy him directly into the field of concern with an appropriate backstory that CIA would support."

"So Wingo is recruited for a mission for DIA and CIA. He sets off with a billion in euros and disappears," said Sean.

Michelle added, "Any idea where he is now?"

Littlefield shook his head. "Still in the Middle East? India? Back in the States? Your guess is as good as mine."

"Who was he supposed to meet?" asked Sean. "And deliver the money to?"

"Been trying to get that info. So far, no answers. But we did get something in, not in the CIA/DIA loop."

"How?" asked Michelle.

Littlefield looked disappointed by the question. "Hey, CIA and military aren't the only ones playing overseas; the Bureau has resources there too." He lifted out a piece of paper from the files. "Wherever Wingo was heading to, there were bodies found. All of them had been shot."

"Who were they?" asked Sean.

"Muslims."

"From where?" asked Sean.

Littlefield put the paper back in the file. "Don't know. But let me clarify. They weren't from any official government over there. They were insurgents."

Sean and Michelle took this in and Sean said, "Insurgents? So are you saying…?"

Littlefield nodded, a grim look in his eyes. "The euros from us might, and I emphasize might, be going to a group that wants to topple an Islamic government."

"Which one?" asked Sean.

"Don't know. We're funding Syrian rebels publicly now, with both weapons and other supplies, so I don't think it's them."

"That narrows the choices," said Sean. "To some really bad ones."

"And if that became public? And the identity of the country?" said Michelle.

"Not good," answered Sean.

Littlefield said, "We've been known to send aid to the enemies of our enemies before. But we do try to keep it on the QT. In this situation that's not a can of worms anyone wants to open. Unfortunately, this can has been partially opened. Somehow the story about the money and Sam Wingo made it to the press. That's another reason we need to keep a tight lid on the kid. The press will be all over him otherwise. We have an agent with eyes on the Wingo house. There are media trucks all over the place. It's all starting, and once the press is on the hunt they don't quit until a bigger story comes along. And I don't see that happening."

"Good thing we got Tyler out of there when we did," noted Sean.

"But the money never made it to where it was supposed to go?" said Michelle.

"Apparently not. Either Sam Wingo stole it or somebody took it from him."

"And why are you really looping us in on all this?" said Sean. "I doubt it was my partner's eloquence about sticking something up your, well, you get the point."

"It wasn't her eloquence, although it was good, I have to admit. It was the kid."

"What about him?" said Sean.

"The only people he'll talk to are you two. And we need him. Or at least the Bureau believes we do, to get to the bottom of all this, because he's the only connection we have to his old man. And the Bureau doesn't want to be seen as manhandling a kid who might have lost his soldier dad in combat."

"All of which means you need us," said Michelle.

"For now," replied Littlefield, who then smiled stiffly at her. "Until we stop needing you."

He rose. "Now let's go."

"Where?" asked Sean.

"To see the man."

"FBI director?" said Michelle.

"Aim higher," said Littlefield cryptically. "A lot higher."

42

"Congratulations, it's all yours," said the man.

Alan Grant shook the man's hand and looked up at the building he had just purchased. It was an old AM radio station in rural western Fairfax County complete with a two-hundred-foot-high transmission tower. It had once broadcast crop and farm animal prices along with local news and weather on weak AM frequencies, but it had been unused for years.

The man looked at Grant. "This thing is sort of a historical landmark around these parts."

"I'm sure," said Grant.

"Hope you're not going to tear it down."

"Wouldn't think of it," said Grant.

"Going to run your own station? You'll need to jump through lots of hoops with the FCC."

"Got it all covered, thanks."

The man walked to his car and drove off, leaving Grant alone with his unusual purchase. He walked the perimeter and then stopped at the tower, gazing up at its two-hundred-foot height. Parts of it were rusty and some cross members needed repair. He had been inside the building, which was brick with few windows and a partially rotted front door. There was lead paint and asbestos ceiling panels, but that was okay, too. He didn't need to make structural changes to the place, but there would be changes, lots of them. And they needed to be done quickly.

He checked his watch and then sent a text.

Five minutes later the two tractor-trailers came rolling up the winding road to the building. Three men sat in the front seat of each rig. The trucks stopped and the men got out. They opened the rear doors of the trailers, and five more men jumped down from each one. With sixteen men in total working, it wouldn't take them long.

A ramp was dropped from each trailer, and the men started off-loading building materials.

Grant unlocked the door to the station and the men began carrying in all the materials, including twin gas-powered generators.

Grant consulted with his foreman and then walked around inside the station directing the placement of the materials. Some of the other men began collecting junk and other debris from inside the old radio station and carrying it out to the trucks. The men worked steadily and methodically, and hours later what had been in the station was now in the trucks and what had been in the trucks was now in the station.

Grant studied some plans that had been set up on a long piece of plywood laid on sawhorses in what had once been the lobby of the radio station. He consulted with the foreman, made notations on the construction plans, and gave some suggestions.

They were on a tight schedule, and Grant was pleased to already hear the whine of power tools as the men commenced preparing the building for the required rehab.

He again walked the interior with the foreman, pointing out where he wanted the vestibule walls to be.

"Five layers of SID," he said, referring to "security in depth." "From the controlled perimeter of the guts to layer five."

The other man nodded and pointed to various spots. "Intrusion detection points."

Grant nodded and pointed out spots for more. They would be taking a six-sided approach to this project, meaning all four walls, the ceiling, and the floor. Construction would be from true floor to true ceiling. There would be special insulation and slip-proof acoustic fill between the first and second layers of gypsum board, with fire-rated plywood over that.

Every penetration into the secure space, whether it was ductwork, utility lines, or any others, would be sealed off with acoustical foam. All ductwork would have metal bars to prevent access. All penetration lines would be configured to come in at only one juncture point and be properly sealed off to prevent unauthorized entry or electronic surveillance.

The windows would be covered and sealed and would not open. They would be alarmed and outfitted to pass TEMPEST certification, as would the entire facility. There would be one rear emergency exit with no external hardware on the door; it would carry deadlocked panic hardware and be alarmed 24/7 with local annunciation.

All doors would be nearly two inches thick, made of eighteen-gauge steel, have acoustic sweeps and seals, be self-closing and locking, have RF shielding, and be connected to alarms. The door hinges would be reinforced to seven-gauge steel, lock areas predrilled to ten-gauge steel, and the door closure to twelve-gauge.

Grant continued to walk the interior, seeing in his mind all that would be there very soon. Motion sensors, emergency backup power, access control. No one without a key card, a PIN, and the requisite biometrics on the security checklist would be admitted. Anyone else approaching the building would not have a pleasant time.

A perimeter gate would be set up two hundred yards down the road and a guard stationed there. For five hundred yards on all sides of the building there would be sensors implanted in the ground, laser lines, observation posts, and every other intrusion detection device that Grant could reasonably deploy here.

The exterior of the building would have enhanced noise generators and sound-masking devices that would defeat any attempts to capture sensitive information.

Grant ventured to the very center of the building and visualized where the vault would go. It would be a steel-lined modular room with a Class 6 entry door. This was the guts of the operation, an operation that would be taking place fairly soon.

He walked outside and studied the perimeter. The best place for these types of facilities was on a military base where you could have a dedicated response force. However, Grant did not have that option. He needed to work with what he did have, and an army he did not.

He ventured over to the transmission tower. Very soon it would have a number of satellite dishes tethered to it. They would all be beaming and receiving information through a concrete electronic pipeline of Grant's own fashioning. With that technology he could have made billions in the business world because no one, as yet, had been able to truly protect electronic data—particularly from mobile devices—as it went from point A to point B.

Wars in the future might still be fought on dirt and in the air and on the seas, but probably the most critical confrontations would take place in cyberspace as countries used armies of cyber soldiers to attack infrastructure, power grids, financial markets, transportation and energy hubs, and more, all through the click of computer keys instead of the pull of a trigger or the drop of a bomb.

What Grant was doing was akin to this type of futuristic warfare. But his target was fairly specific. In fact, it was about as focused as one could get.

He finished walking the perimeter, spent a few more minutes with his men, and then drove off. He noted with satisfaction that the security perimeter was already being installed. Along with the building Grant had also purchased a hundred acres. The closest home or business was miles away. He liked his privacy.

He reached the main road and sped up. He turned on the radio and found the all-news station he had been searching for a few seconds later. He waited until the top of the hour and then smiled as the lead story came on.

It was the old story of a missing billion euros along with a missing soldier. But now that story had new elements. The anchor paused for emphasis here and then announced with a flourish that:

"Information has just come to light that hints at the possibility of an illegal plot emanating from deep within the power corridors of the U.S. government, which might have serious international ramifications."

Grant was glad that the story had hit all of the salient and salacious points. That had been his hope when he had it planted.

He turned off the radio and sped up. He had some confidential information to purchase. But with enough money there was nothing on earth anymore that could be truly kept secret.

43

They were in downtown D.C. now, and the car Wingo was following swung into a parking garage. Wingo hesitated and then pulled in after it. It was a pay garage, and each driver had to get a ticket before the gate would lift. Wingo parked about six car spaces over from the other man.

Then things got dicey. There was a bank of elevators. People were waiting for the next one. The man walked up to the queue, and Wingo followed. He pulled his ball cap down tightly over his head and adjusted his sunglasses. He was not about to take them off. He'd changed his appearance since Afghanistan but he couldn't take a chance on being spotted.

The group stepped onto the elevator car. It carried everyone to the lobby, where they all clambered onto another elevator. In the back Wingo saw that the man he was following pushed the button for floor six. When the doors opened on that floor several other people got off as well. Wingo was the last off. He watched as the man walked down the hall and turned left. Wingo followed, stopping at the intersection of the two corridors.

He watched as the man entered a door. It closed behind him. Wingo continued on, passed the door, and looked at the name on the wall next to the door.

The Vista Trading Group, LLC.

Wingo continued on down the hall and then stopped, wondering what to do. He had a gun. He could perhaps burst in and make a citizen's arrest. That, of course, would be stupid. He had no evidence. He was a wanted man himself. He had no permit for his gun. The police would come and he would be the one arrested.

He rode the elevator back down and returned to his rental. He did an Internet search on the Vista Trading Group, LLC. He got the perfunctory website that told him nothing much of interest. They were engaged in defense contracting as consultants. He looked under personnel but did not find the picture of the man he had been following. He could simply have been going there for a meeting. He didn't have to work there, Wingo concluded.

This had been a dead end, but Wingo wasn't done with it yet. He would wait out on the street; when the man left, Wingo would take up the trail once more. It was then that Wingo noticed a shop across the street. He got out, ran across, and entered. Thirty minutes later he came back out and walked into the parking garage.

He went over to the man's car, looked around to ensure no one was watching, and then knelt down and attached the surveillance bug under the man's bumper.

Wingo quickly left the garage and got back to his car. He slid in and then powered up the device he had purchased. The shop had been one of those places that sold police scanners, handheld electronic wands that detected metal, handcuffs, police batons.

And tracking devices.

An hour later the man pulled out of the garage and passed Wingo on the street. Wingo had been watching in his side mirror and sank down in his seat before the car passed.

He put the car in gear and followed. He lost the car a couple of times in traffic and once when he hit a red light. But with the tracking device, he managed to regain sight of it each time.

It was rush hour now; traffic volume was heavy, and corresponding speeds were slow. Wingo kept his eyes on the car as it moved along with the other traffic. He was thinking maybe the man was going back out to Dulles Airport again because he seemed to be making his way to Interstate 66, which would tie him into the Dulles Toll Road in Virginia. If that was his destination, Wingo wasn't sure what he was going to do.

When he checked his rearview mirror, he suddenly realized he would have to do something. Something drastic. It seemed that while he'd been following the guy up there, somebody else had been tailing him.

SUV. Black. Tinted windows all around. The Feds had a million rides like that. Was that who was back there? His own guys? After screwing him half a world away?

He lost the car up ahead when he hung a left. He decided it was better to live than keep up the tail.

The SUV also turned left.

Okay, confirmation was nice, thought Wingo. He could almost hear the camera taking pics of his car, his plate, and the back of his head.

If they were Feds back there, they could pull him over and wave their badges; he would disappear forever. Never see Tyler again. Never prove his innocence.

He sped up, took a right and then a quick left. The SUV mimicked his maneuvers. He pushed the pedal down and risked being pulled over for speeding. He eyed up ahead, then looked to his left.

To the left looked promising for three reasons: traffic, a traffic light about to go from green to red, and, most important of all, a tractor-trailer about to make a wide turn.

He cut the wheel and made the left. He punched the gas, eyeing the rearview at the same time. The SUV was coming on strong. They were probably planning to end this little chase right now. But Wingo had a few seconds. He would need every single one of them. He gauged the traffic light timing, the cars aligned on all sides, and the big rig making a left.

The light turned yellow. One car zipped straight

through the intersection, beating it. Wingo didn't want to go straight. He wanted to go left. And he wasn't waiting for the rig. In fact, he was gong to jump to the front of the line.

He punched the gas as he saw the yellow light flickering.

Red here we come.

He laid the gas pedal flat to the floor and cut his wheel hard to the left.

He shot through the intersection in front of the rig, blocking it. The truck driver slammed on his brakes, cut his wheel to the right, and laid on his horn. The semi slid sideways.

The light turned red. Oncoming traffic started up but went nowhere. The big rig was blocking the entire intersection. Horns started up from all quarters. The truck driver was no doubt delivering a few choice words in Wingo's direction.

Yet Wingo was all smiles as he hung another right, then a left, and quickly made his way back to his hotel. And if they ran the plates, which he was sure they would, they would lead to a wreck at the D.C. impoundment lot.

This round to me.

44

The chopper swept over the bucolic Maryland coun-tryside.

Sean gazed out the window and then down below.

"Damn," he muttered.

Michelle was sitting next to him. "What's wrong? Don't like flying in whirlybirds?" she said sarcastically. She well knew that as a Secret Service agent Sean had flown in more copters than just about anyone outside the military.

"I don't like our particular destination."

"Which is?"

"Camp David."

Michelle shot him a glance, leaned over him, and looked out the window.

"Damn," she said.

"I thought I already said that," Sean shot back.

She flopped against the seat. "We're going to see POTUS? *He's* the man?"

"Apparently so."

"Remember the last president you met with?"

"I'm hoping this one is a little better."

The chopper landed and they were escorted to the main building of heavily fortified Camp David, named after Dwight Eisenhower's grandson and situated in Maryland's rustic Catoctin Mountains.

They sat in a large room with knotty-pine paneling.

"You ever pull protection detail at Camp David?" Sean asked Michelle.

"Once. I watched the king of Jordan do some putting on the one hole they have here. It would make you wish for milk curdling as a distraction."

"I'm sure it would," said the man.

Both Sean and Michelle instinctively sprang to their feet when the man entered the room. Old habits died hard.

President John Cole was a bit under six feet and obviously fighting the battle of the waistline at age fifty-five. Still, his shoulders were broad, his face ruggedly good looking, his smile infectious, and he radiated impressive health and confidence.

"Mr. President," Sean said while Michelle respectfully nodded.

"Please, sit," said Cole.

Sean and Michelle eyed the two Secret Service agents who were escorting Cole. They had obviously been told of Sean and Michelle's Secret Service past; Michelle even recognized one of them as a former colleague. But they also knew that both agents would regard them with suspicion and would have no problem firing bullets into each of their brains if the conditions warranted such extreme force.

The president was dressed informally in slacks, a polo shirt, and a blue blazer. His guards were similarly outfitted; you followed the president's fashion lead. Cole sat behind a desk while Sean and Michelle sat across from him.

Cole eyed them intently. "I know you had dealings with my predecessor."

Sean nodded and said, "Unfortunately, yes, we did."

"The truth is the truth," stated Cole. "And the public, at the end of the day, demands that. And well they should."

"Is that why we're here?" asked Michelle.

"I think you both know that it is." Cole eyed one of his bodyguards. "Billy, you know Ms. Maxwell, I take it?"

Billy eyed Michelle, gave a curt smile and a nod.

Michelle skipped the smile and just returned the curt nod.

Sean said, "How can we help?"

"Sam Wingo?"

"We know about his disappearance."

"With over a billion dollars of this country's treasure."

"We've been working with his son."

"I'm sure the young man is terribly worried about his father."

"And you're worried that his father is a traitor, a killer, a thief, all of the above?" said Sean.

Cole put his feet up on his desk and steepled his hands. "This is not how I envisioned my first year going. I have a lot I want to do. I have some political capital with which to do it. This sort of potential scandal takes all the wind out of one's sails. Media has already started speculating. My friends on the other side of the aisle smell blood and are circling. I'm not saying anything. Want to see how it shakes out. At some point I have to make a public statement. But before I do I'd like to have something to say, something positive, that is. Right now I have nothing."

"Where was the money supposed to go?" asked Sean. "We understand that a bunch of Muslim insurgents from an unknown country were found dead at the rendezvous spot."

"We prefer to call them freedom fighters," said Cole. "Although over there your ally at breakfast is your enemy before dinner, so I'm not sure how valid that description of them is. Nonetheless I made the bed, now I have to sleep in it."

Sean said, "So the money was meant for them. To help in the fight against an Islamic government? Which one?"

"I can't disclose to you the name of the country. I'm sorry. Neither of you would be privy to any of this but for your relationship with Tyler Wingo."

"And you need him?" said Michelle.

"I need his father. I need his father to tell me where the hell the money is and what the hell happened over there. If he's turned against us, we have to track him and the money down. If he's innocent we still need him to come in and explain what happened."

"Do you think he's innocent?" asked Sean.

"The betting here is running about nine to one against him," said Cole frankly. "Personally, I don't know. He was vetted for the mission. Outscored everyone else. Patriotism above reproach, all that. But the proof is in the pudding. The money is gone. The freedom fighters are dead. And the longer Wingo stays away, the more we're going to assume he's against us. Just human nature."

"He might be afraid to come in," said Michelle. "He might believe he was set up and doesn't know who to trust."

"Has he made contact with anyone at DoD?" asked Sean.

"His field superior, Colonel South."

"And what did he tell South?" asked Michelle.

"He told South that he was set up. That someone ostensibly from the CIA met him at the rendezvous spot, told him the mission had been changed, and demanded the money. At gunpoint."

"Was the person from the CIA?" asked Sean.

"Not that we've been able to discover. Wingo was attached to DIA. And while DIA has been working more closely with CIA, they were not in this instance. The loop was small and closed: DIA and me. And while it's true that Langley is always demanding more budget dollars, I can't believe they would resort to stealing from Peter to pay Paul in order to get it," Cole added dryly.

"Did Wingo give any indication to South where he might go or what he might do?" asked Michelle.

"Apparently, he wants to prove his innocence. Where that takes him I don't know."

"I guess that partly depends on who set him up," reasoned Sean.

"*If* someone set him up," amended Cole. "We only have his word for that. And I'm still missing a billion euros."

"And euros were used for an additional layer of cover," said Michelle.

"Ben Franklins might have been a little too obvious. And there was a very practical reason. A billion bucks in hundred-dollar bills, which is the largest denomination we use, would have weighed a lot more than forty-eight hundred pounds."

"Which brings us back to what you want us to do," said Sean.

"You have Tyler Wingo's loyalties by all accounts. We believe that his father will try to contact him again. They'll want to meet. We need to be there when they do."

"So you want us to deliver Sam Wingo to you, using his son to do it?" said Michelle.

"That's basically the plan, yes. I've been told the boy

will say nothing to my people. You're the only ones he trusts."

"And if we betray that trust?" said Michelle, her voice rising just enough for the two Secret Service agents to draw a step closer to them.

"Better than betraying your country," pointed out Cole.

"Was Jean Wingo part of this?" asked Sean.

Cole nodded but tacked nothing on in speech.

"She's disappeared."

"We know that."

"But she didn't come in to you?" asked Sean. Cole shook his head. "So she might have another partner in this deal."

"Like Sam Wingo?" shot back Cole.

"I didn't say that."

"No, I did. So, will you help me?"

Michelle looked at Sean and Sean looked at her.

He said, "We need to talk about this."

"I can give you a few minutes alone," said Cole.

"We're going to need longer than that," said Michelle while Sean looked at her nervously.

Cole raised both eyebrows and then gazed for a long moment at the ceiling. He rose with an extremely disappointed look on his face. "I expected better, I really did. I assumed that a direct appeal from your commander in chief would carry the day. I could have pushed you off to a lower-level flunky, but I flew you up here to go eyeball-to-eyeball. To tell you that your country needs you." He paused. "And you tell me you have to talk about it." He shook his head disgustedly. "Well, I guess they don't make them the way they used to."

"We're between a rock and a hard place, Mr. President," Sean said by way of explanation. "It's not as cut-and-dried as it may seem."

"Billy here will show you out. Thanks for humoring me. I'll await your...answer."

With this curt dismissal, Sean and Michelle turned to the door.

As Billy walked them down the hall Michelle said, "How is your family doing, Billy?"

"Fine."

"I remember your wife had a rough pregnancy."

"She's fine."

"Okay."

Michelle waited but the question never came.

Finally she said, "Just so you know, I'm fine too."

They got back on the chopper. As soon as the door closed it lifted off.

Sean and Michelle settled into their seats and strapped on their belts.

"Well, now I know what it's like being cold-cocked by the president," she said.

Sean shrugged. "What did you expect? A medal for meritorious service? His ass is in the fire. He's looking for any way to put the flames out. That's why he let us leapfrog the normal chain of command."

"And it's our fault all this shit happened?"

"We made the choice, so I'd say we're partly accountable."

"We were helping a kid find his dad, Sean. I never expected this to become an international incident."

He sighed. "I know. Neither did I. But now we've got the most powerful man in the world pissed off at us. That's cause for worry in my book. A big worry."

45

When they returned to FBI headquarters, Sean asked Agent Littlefield to take them to see Tyler. The expression on Littlefield's face was not encouraging.

Sean said angrily, "Look, you have no right to keep us from seeing him. He's probably scared out of his mind right now."

"I wouldn't know if he was or not," said Littlefield evasively.

Michelle said, "And why would that be? Can't you just ask him?"

Littlefield said nothing. He simply aimed his gaze at a spot on the ceiling and seemed to be pretending Sean and Michelle weren't even there.

Sean looked at her. "I think he's sending us a telepathic message."

"Okay, let's see if we can grab the signal." She put a finger to her forehead and closed her eyes. "Wait for it, wait for it, okay, it's coming." She leaned down and got right in Littlefield's face, her hands on her hips.

"How the hell did the FBI manage to lose a sixteen-year-old kid?"

Now Littlefield met her eye. "We had no reason to believe he was going to make a break for it."

"And you had no reason to believe he wasn't either," Sean pointed out. "But from the WFO? Really?"

"How?" demanded Michelle.

"Does it matter?" asked Littlefield.

"It might just help us find him."

Littlefield slumped in his chair.

"He said he was hungry. Wanted a hot dog and curly fries from the vendor outside. He also wanted some air. Sent one of the old codger uniforms with him. Our guy had two dogs and a pack of fries in his hands and was trying to pay for the food when the kid took off across the street like a rocket. Right in the middle of rush hour. In less than a minute he was gone. Our guy said the boy could flat-out run."

"Uh, yeah, he's sixteen freaking years old with long legs," said Michelle. "And he's on the swim team, which means he has tons of endurance. But I'm sure you knew all that. Which makes me wonder why you sent an old codger out with him in the first place!"

"He wasn't under arrest. He wasn't being detained."

"It was your job to keep him safe. Now he could be anywhere," said Michelle. "Including dead."

"Okay, I get all that," said Littlefield miserably. "I screwed up." He looked from one to the other. "So what now?"

"Now we find Tyler before some other folks do," said Sean. He added, "I'm assuming we're free to go?"

"For the time being. But I'll feel a lot better if I send some agents with you. For personal protection, of course."

"No offense," said Michelle. "But the Secret Service does personal protection a lot better than you, so we're good to go."

"So what did the president want with you two?" asked Littlefield.

Michelle said, "To congratulate us on our work to date."

"Cut the crap. What did he want?"

"He wants us to do something," said Sean. "And we're thinking about it."

"The president asks you to do something and you're *thinking* about it?" Littlefield said incredulously.

"You know," said Michelle. "That's exactly how he sounded too. Well, take care, we'll be going now."

She put her hand on the knob and eyed Sean. An invisible message seemed to have been telegraphed between them.

Sean said, "We'll keep you abreast of our investigation if you do the same."

"You know I can't promise that," said Littlefield.

"Good," said Sean. "Then we'll keep you in the dark on ours too."

They left.

As they walked down the hall Michelle said, "Where do you think Tyler went?"

"He got a message back from his dad. My guess is he got another one."

Sean was already pulling his phone out and checking the back door he had established on Tyler's Gmail account.

"And there it is. And unfortunately it's not in code."

"Why unfortunately?" asked Michelle. "If it's not coded we should be able to break it easily, even without Edgar."

"You'd think, wouldn't you?"

He handed her the phone.

She eyed the screen, reading the short email.

Tonight at ten. Usual place.

"Usual place," said Michelle, her brow furrowed.

"Seemingly straightforward information without context is better than code," noted Sean. "There's no logical way to crack it because we don't know where the usual place is."

"Sure there is," countered Michelle, tossing him back his phone.

He caught it and stared at her as she sped up on her way out of WFO.

They had to take a taxi back to Sean's house because the FBI had refused, or at least Littlefield had refused, them a ride back.

Michelle sat impatiently in the backseat, urging the cabdriver to run red lights, break the speed limit, and come as close as possible to sideswiping cars that refused to get out of the way.

"In other words," said Sean, "you want him to drive just like you."

"Basically, yeah."

"And why the rush?"

"Got an idea. We need to talk to someone."

"Who?"

"The only person I know who can give us some context and help us understand that email."

They returned to Sean's house and climbed immediately into Michelle's Land Cruiser. Sean had to kick junk and trash off the floorboard so his feet would have a place to rest. Some of the stuff fell outside on the driveway as he closed the door.

"Just so you know," he said, "I am not picking that up."

"Good boy, Sean. Glad to see you're being a little less of a neatnik. It shows personal growth and maturity."

"You know that was not my poi—"

He didn't finish because she had backed the truck out of his driveway at about eighty miles an hour before slamming it into drive and hurtling off. She started tapping the steering wheel with her fingers, moving her head from side to side and smiling.

"You really get high from this stuff, don't you?" he observed, watching her.

"What stuff?"

"Speed, danger, being stupid."

"You lost me on the last one."

"So the context? Fill me in."

"Kathy Burnett. They grew up together. They're tight. I'm betting if anyone can tell us where the 'usual place' is for Tyler and his dad, it will be her."

"That's actually quite insightful, Michelle," he said.

"I thought so." She glanced at him. "But if we do guess right and we catch up to Sam Wingo, what then?"

"I've been running those scenarios in my head. He's officially wanted by the authorities. Our duty should be clear."

"Our duty is *never* clear."

"This is very true," he agreed.

"So again, what do we do?"

"I don't have a clear answer. A lot depends on what Sam Wingo's story is."

"He's Special Forces, Sean. Selected for a pretty classified project. And survived what looked to be an ambush and a bunch of people dead. Guy clearly has incredible skills. If he's gone bad—"

"Then we'll have to tread carefully."

"Maybe more than that."

He looked at her. "What do you mean?"

"Sean, we might have to be prepared to kill him. Before he kills us."

"Kill him? Right in front of his son?"

"It's not my first choice, obviously."

Sean stared at the scenery passing by them at eighty miles an hour.

46

"Usual place?" repeated Kathy Burnett.

She was standing on her front porch while Sean and Michelle stood opposite her.

They had gotten here in record time. Once Sean thought a cop was going to take up the chase when they flew past his position, but he just stayed where he was. Sean thought it might be because he was doubtful he could catch them.

"Right. The usual place," said Michelle. "Someplace that Tyler and his dad might go to. To meet, talk, do something together?"

"Why don't you just ask Tyler?" she said, a bit suspiciously, Sean thought.

Before Michelle could answer he said, "This is for down the road, Kathy. It's just background work that all detectives do. We're simply building a file on everyone and that includes their likes and dislikes, preferences, typical meeting places. It might not matter now, but it could later on. It's as much for Tyler's protection as anything."

Michelle shot him a glance, but his gaze remained

fixed on Kathy. He was hoping she would not think too much about this avalanche of words, because if she did the girl would realize they made no sense at all.

Kathy nodded slowly. "Okay, I guess I can see that."

Sean let out an inaudible breath of relief. "But nothing is coming to you?"

Michelle said, "I saw fishing poles leaning against the wall in the laundry room when I was over there."

Kathy looked exasperated with herself. "Of course. They used to go to fish at a place on the river near here. Well, it's not much more than a creek really, but they've caught stuff there. And Tyler and his dad would just hang out and talk. I've been there twice with Tyler, but I'm not into fishing. I'd just watch and we'd talk."

Sean whipped out his notepad and a pen. "Can you tell us exactly where it is?"

She gave them directions. They thanked her and headed back to the Land Cruiser.

"Give me the keys," Sean said.

"What?"

"The keys," he said again, snapping his fingers.

"Why?"

"Because our timetable does not allow for us to be stopped by the police for speeding or otherwise reckless driving."

"We weren't stopped on the way over here, were we?"

"By the grace of God. I can't count on that happening again. Keys please."

She tossed them to him so hard one of them cut his finger.

"Thanks," he said tersely.

They climbed in and drove off.

Michelle checked her watch. "Seven thirty already. It's going to be tight. Sure you don't want me to drive?"

"Very sure, thanks."

He sped off and followed the turns Michelle fed him from his notes.

"What's our plan?" asked Michelle as Sean hung a hard left and pressed the gas pedal back down.

"We have to assume Sam Wingo will come in armed and paranoid. He'll trust his son, of course. But he won't trust anyone else."

"We can't play judge, jury, and executioner, Sean, not on the spot."

"Hell, you were the one saying we might have to kill him."

"I also said it was not my first choice."

"We have to control the situation. Then we have to get him to trust us."

"I don't see either one of those objectives being easily accomplished."

"They won't be."

"But if he came back for his son, isn't that pretty strong proof he's innocent?"

Sean looked at her. "Maybe. But it's not conclusive proof, Michelle. And don't forget, if he was set up then whoever did set him up will not want him to be able to come back and talk to anyone."

"And if we're in the middle of that?"

"Hell, we're already in the middle of that."

Michelle pulled her gun from its holster, checked to make sure a round was chambered, then put it away. She let out a long breath. "What if Wingo doesn't come alone?"

"Who else?"

"Assuming he's not innocent."

Sean nodded, looking thoughtful. "The problem is he knows this fishing hole place better than we do."

"Yeah, but I bet he hasn't been trained to scope a place in about six seconds, like we have."

"We're going to have to split up on this. I'll be the contact person. You cover me."

"Why not the other way around?"

He smiled. "I'm not too proud to admit that you're a better shot than I am."

She looked in the back of her truck. "I've got my sniper rifle back there."

"Good. We might just need it."

"You think Tyler has doubts about his dad?"

Sean shook his head. "No. He obviously idolizes the guy. I just hope the sergeant doesn't disappoint in the hero department." He looked up ahead. "We're going to find out soon enough. That's the turnoff for the road to the fishing hole. We're going to park up the road a ways. The last thing I want is for Tyler to spot your truck. We'll backtrack, do a recon, set up an observation point, and wait."

"Sam Wingo might already be here waiting."

"He might. And there's nothing we can do about that." He looked at her. "Can you do it?"

"Do what?"

"Pull the trigger on Wingo if it comes to it. With Tyler there?"

Michelle didn't hesitate. "I'm not going to let anything happen to you, Sean. You can take that to the bank and cash it."

47

The man said, "This is more valuable than gold, you know that? Than platinum. Than, hell, I don't know what."

Alan Grant sat in the car and stared over at him.

"I understand that," said Grant. "More than platinum. And yet you're only charging for platinum. Thanks for the deal."

The other man was Milo Pratt. He was short, chubby, and had a lot of years in places that had allowed to him to get the platinum Grant needed.

He smiled at Grant. "Do you know what the price of platinum is?"

"High. Higher than gold, probably."

"Gold isn't even in the ballpark. What's your name again?"

"Not important."

"Why do you want it?

"I'm curious, always have been," said Grant. "It's just my thing."

Pratt smiled more broadly. "But why this thing? Why this info? Guy has to ask. You understand, right?"

"Perfectly. I would have been disappointed if you hadn't asked."

"Good, good. So why? Really?"

"Isn't it obvious?"

"You a traitor? I mean, I got no problem with that, but I would like to know."

"Not a traitor, quite the opposite in fact."

"You a Fed? Got some squirrelly covert op going on?"

Grant pointed at him and smiled. "You have a quick eye."

"It's subject to change, of course. Nothing I can do about that."

"I completely understand that. I'll simply have to build that into the op."

Pratt held up a flash drive. "It's all here."

"I'm sure it is." Grant held out his hand and took it.

"I know the money is in my account, or you wouldn't be holding that," said Pratt.

"If I were you, I'd do it exactly the same way. But with just one small difference."

"What's that?"

Grant slammed Pratt's neck against the steering wheel, crushing his windpipe. He watched as Pratt suffocated and then died, collapsing sideways in the seat.

Grant said to the dead man, "I would never do the exchange face-to-face in a lonely spot because I might end up dead. Like you."

He got out of the car and walked away. A minute later he climbed into his car and drove below the speed limit to his next stop. The retrofit on the old radio station was progressing nicely. He knew his men were working hard, but they would have to work still harder. After the rehab was done he would bring in his tech team. They were a multinational bunch. Not a single one was committed to anything other than himself. No flag-wrappers in the lot of them. He liked that. When money was the motivation, you knew exactly where you stood. They were the best he could find, and Grant knew where to look.

The Pentagon was as busy now as it was during the day. It truly was a building that never slept and where people visited, ate, and worked at all hours. He cleared security and went directly to his father-in-law's office once more. He was admitted immediately because he was expected. He and Dan Marshall were having dinner tonight, and Grant expected to get some scuttlebutt about things he needed to know about.

Marshall greeted him as enthusiastically as before, first gripping his hand and then giving him a bear hug.

"Leslie says you're keeping really busy lately, Alan. You remember you have to keep some time open for those grandkids of mine."

"I will, Dan. I promise. Just got quite a few things in the hopper right now. Want to build a good life for us. And Leslie and I want to give you more grandchildren too. We're not stopping at three. We're still relatively young."

Dan beamed. "Never hear me complaining about more rug rats to pal around with."

The two men walked to a restaurant in the Pentagon and sat at a table well away from others.

"You look worried about something," said Grant, observing Marshall closely.

Marshall chuckled, rubbed his face, and took a sip of the Coors draft he'd ordered. Grant drank only water. When Marshall put the glass down he had stopped chuckling and looked far more serious.

"You've been reading the news?" he asked.

Grant nodded. "Bizarre to say the least. How over a billion bucks of Treasury money ended up going missing in Afghanistan along with a reservist?"

Marshall looked around to make sure no one was close enough to overhear. "It was actually in euros."

"Euros? Why?"

"Can't really say."

"What the hell was the money for?" Grant then quickly added, "Sorry, I'm sure that's classified."

"There're rumors all over the press now. Really bad ones. Conspiracy. Breaking the law. Misuse of funds. And it all goes up very high."

"Rumors with some truth to them?" asked Grant quietly.

"Let me put it this way, Alan. I can't say unequivocally that they're not true."

You haven't seen anything yet, thought Grant.

He reached over and put a hand on his father-in-law's arm. "Dan, you're in procurement. You buy stuff for the Army. You control a lot of money. But you're not getting caught up in all this, are you?"

Grant liked Dan Marshall, he really did. But he didn't like him well enough to *not* sacrifice him in order to achieve his goal. There was no one in the world he liked that much.

Marshall passed another hand over his face, as though he were trying to rub a layer of skin off. "Well, Alan, I'd say this sucker is big enough to catch a lot of folks."

Grant withdrew his hand. "I'm sorry, Dan." And in a way he was sorry. But that was all. He had put his father-in-law in this situation. He knew it would come to this. He hoped for his wife's sake that her father would be mostly spared.

But my father and mother hadn't been spared. They were ruined, crushed, and then they killed themselves. The only casualties. The only ones when there should have been far more.

He said, "What about this reservist, Sam Wingo? What's his story?"

"Who knows? The son of a bitch hasn't been seen since he drove off with Uncle Sam's money."

"I saw on the web that some of the money was going to Muslim insurgents. But it didn't say which country."

Marshall looked at him miserably. "I saw that too."

"That will not sit well with some over there."

"From the little I've been told, the diplomatic channels are being used so much they're molten hot. I still have no idea how the media caught on to it. It was highly, highly classified."

"It's a mystery to me too," lied Grant. "But I'm sure if you catch Wingo you'll be able to put all this to rest quickly. Any leads there?"

"There might be, actually. I've been kept in the loop on this for a number of reasons, mostly because my ass is tied up in the outcome. Wingo has a son, Tyler. His mom died but Wingo remarried." He lowered his voice. "Now, the marriage was not a real one."

"The hell you say," exclaimed Grant, who knew this perfectly well.

"No, it was just a sham. Part of the mission Wingo was going on. Convoluted but he also just couldn't leave his kid on his own. Now the wife has disappeared. No one knows where she is."

In a proper grave in the middle of nowhere with her throat slit because she disobeyed and then tried to kill me, Grant said to himself while he kept looking straight at Marshall with polite interest on his face.

Marshall continued, "And there are two investigators that somehow got involved. A Sean King and Michelle Maxwell. Former Secret Service who've been poking around even though they've been warned off."

"But no news on Sam Wingo's whereabouts?"

"It's believed that he made it back to the States, probably on private wings or maybe a cargo plane. He might have had fake IDs no one knew about. From all the reports I've read on him the guy is good, real good. That's why he was picked for this mission."

"He could have stolen the money," Grant pointed out.

"Yes he could. And if he did he might have come back to get his son and then disappear. And actually that's what he might have done." His voice sank to a whisper. "I just got an email that said Tyler Wingo had disappeared from FBI custody."

This statement did startle Grant. "What?"

"Yeah, I know. They had taken him and King and Maxwell into custody or protection or some such because a motel they were at blew up. I don't know all the details but you probably saw that on the news. Over in south Alexandria?"

"Right, I did see something about that. I thought it was a gas leak."

"Don't think so."

"And where are King and Maxwell?"

"If I had to guess they're trying to find Tyler. They're probably thinking if they find Tyler, they'll find the dad."

And that's exactly what I think too, thought Grant. *Which is why I'm having them followed right now.*

48

Michelle never would have planned an operation this way. It was way too fast and loose, little prep and no real evaluation of the pros and cons. And no true Plan B when something unexpected happened. Her cover spot had several weak spots, any one of which a guy like Sam Wingo would be able to exploit in his sleep.

She was twelve feet up in the crook of a tree with her sniper rifle making wide arcs over the landscape below. Sean was taking up his position near where they believed the father and son might actually meet. But they could be way off about that. And they could be really way off if the fishing hole didn't turn out to be the right spot at all.

He was communicating with her via an earwig and power pack. She carried the same equipment. It felt like they were back in the Service. And in a way this was very much like protection detail. She wasn't going to let anything happen to Sean or Tyler. Sam Wingo was still not a sure thing for her. He could go either way. And depending on which way he did go, she might have to put a round in him. Right in front of his son.

Michelle looked down at her trigger finger and wondered if she could do it. But she already knew the answer. She could. And would. Right now Sean was her protectee and she would take a bullet for him if it came to it.

Over her earwig she heard Sean say, "Got an eyeball on something. But I can't make it out. Just a glimpse."

"Where?"

He gave her the coordinates and she swung her scoped rifle in the direction. She saw something. It flitted in and out among the trees, almost like vapor.

Then she locked in on it.

"It's Tyler," she said. At least they had come to the right place.

"And his father?"

Michelle scanned the area. "No eyes on him yet."

"He's probably reconning right now."

"That's exactly what I'm doing," said a voice.

Sean began to turn toward it when the voice said, "Don't."

Sean froze.

In his ear Michelle whispered, "Ten yards to your right, behind the oak. Can't confirm it's Wingo."

Sean gave a bare nod.

"Where's your partner?" asked the voice. "I want her down here right now."

Sean said, "Why's that, Sam? Want to gun us both down?" He said this in an overly loud voice.

"Who are you?" asked Wingo, who had revealed just a sliver of himself behind the oak.

"Someone trying to help your son." He added in a very loud voice, "Isn't that right, Tyler?"

"Shut up," barked Wingo. "Or I'll put a round in your leg."

"Didn't you come to meet Tyler? He's right over there. Tyler, join the party."

"I said shut up!" yelled Wingo. He edged out past the oak, his gun pointed at Sean.

Michelle said into Sean's earwig, "I have a clean shot, Sean."

He gave a curt shake of his head, and Michelle's hand moved away from the trigger guard.

"We could have taken you out right now, Wingo. But that's not what we're here for."

"Bullshit!"

"Then here's proof," said Sean.

Michelle fired a round that struck a branch two feet above where Wingo was standing. It fell to the ground a foot away from him. Wingo jumped back behind the tree.

"Now do you believe us?" asked Sean.

"Dad, Dad!"

Tyler came rushing into the clearing and then pulled up short when he saw Sean.

"What are you doing here?"

"Trying to talk your dad out of shooting me."

Tyler looked around, "Dad? Dad, are you here?"

Sean knew why Wingo was hesitating. "If you come out I'll have my partner come out too, Wingo. We *are* here to help."

Tyler added, "They are, Dad. They've really been helping."

A few moments later Michelle appeared at the edge of the clearing, her sniper rifle pointed down.

Sam Wingo saw this and slowly stepped clear of the oak. They all stared at each other.

Sean said, "Uh, you might want to hug your son, Sam, just to prove to him you're not a ghost."

Father and son eyed each other for what seemed an impossibly long moment. Then Wingo holstered his gun and spread his arms wide. Tyler rushed to him. The two hugged for a long time. Tears ran down both the Wingos' faces.

Michelle drew closer to Sean and said quietly, "This whole thing just got very complicated."

He nodded. "That's the face of a guy who got set up and doesn't know what the hell is going on."

"Which means he may not know any more than we do."

"Maybe, maybe not. But now we can at least ask him."

Wingo finally stopped hugging his son, but kept one arm protectively around his shoulders. He wiped his face of the tears while an embarrassed Tyler did the same. Wingo walked toward Sean and Michelle.

"How did you two get involved in all this?"

"Just saw your kid running down the street one dark and stormy night after the Army told him you were dead," said Michelle. "Total coincidence."

Wingo slowly nodded. "I appreciate your not shooting me when I came out from cover."

"And I appreciate your not shooting me," said Sean.

"Dad, you look…different," noted Tyler.

Wingo rubbed his shaved head and new beard and said, "Have to when people are looking for you."

"What people?" asked Sean.

"Good question," shot back Wingo.

"Your people?" asked Michelle. "The military? You've apparently created a huge buzz at the Pentagon and the White House."

"Wasn't supposed to go down like that."

"How then?"

"Classified."

Sean looked disappointed. "After all you've been through you're going to pull the classified crap?"

"Look, I could be court-martialed for discussing any of this with you."

"You been listening to the news?" asked Michelle.

Wingo nodded.

"Then you know a lot of it has become unclassified."

"DHS told us about the nearly five thousand pounds of euros."

"Over a billion dollars' worth that you somehow managed to lose," added Michelle.

Tyler looked at his dad. "Is that true, Dad?"

Wingo looked uneasily from Michelle to his son but said nothing.

"If we work together," said Sean. "We might make some progress."

"But you said DHS had looped you in. So you're working with them."

"No. And we've been to see the FBI. And the president," said Michelle. "And we decided not to work with any of them. At least not yet."

Wingo looked shaky. "You met with the president? Over this?"

"Apparently on his big-item to-do list, you are at the numero uno spot," said Michelle. "Congratulations."

"Shit!" said Wingo, putting a hand over his eyes. "I can't believe this is all actually happening."

"Well, it is happening," snapped Sean. "And we have to address it."

"How?" asked Wingo. "What can you do?"

"Dad, they're investigators. They used to be with the Secret Service. They're really good. They can help."

"I'm not sure anyone can help me, son."

"So you're just giving up?" said Michelle. "After

dragging your butt back here from Afghanistan? You're going to let them get away with it?"

Tyler angrily looked at her. "My dad is not a quitter."

"I'm not saying he is or he isn't, Tyler. But the real answer is up to him."

Sean added, "We'll help you, if you'll let us."

"Why?" asked Wingo. "Why open up a can of worms that isn't your problem?"

"I think we've already made it our problem," he answered. "And we can't put our heads in the sand and hope it goes away. So the only way it gets resolved is to pool our resources and figure it out."

Tyler took his father's arm. "Come on, Dad. Do it."

An instant later Michelle said in an urgent tone, "Someone's coming."

49

Wingo and Tyler went left.

Sean and Michelle darted right.

The block of men with guns came at them from east and west, converging on the four fleeing people. Yet Michelle's keen hearing had given them a bit of a head start. Hopefully, it would be enough. Right now it looked too close to call.

Michelle pushed Sean ahead of her. "Take the next left down that path. It'll take you to the truck. Get in, start it, and wait two minutes for me."

"I'm not leaving you here to go against these guys alone, Michelle."

"I've got the sniper rifle. Just be prepared to drive a lot faster out of here than you did getting here. Now go!"

"But—"

She gave him another hard shove. "Go!"

Sean sped down the path and turned left.

Michelle wheeled around, did a quick calculation of the terrain, and raced off to the right, taking up position behind a fallen tree. Using that as her cover and the trunk as the support for her weapon, she readied her rifle and set her crosshairs on the spot from where she believed they would be coming. She calmed her breathing, relaxed her muscles, and waited.

The first man veered into her line of fire and paid the price for that with a shot to the knee. He went down screaming and clutching at his ruptured joint.

Michelle immediately sprang up, ran to her right, and took up a new position at the confluence of two trees that were leaning against each other.

She readied her rifle and swung it across the terrain in front of her. They would be proceeding with caution now, she knew. She acquired the next target and fired before it could disappear on her.

The slug ripped into the man's arm where he had left it exposed by a couple of inches. He dropped, gripping his limb, trying to stanch the blood flow.

Again Michelle moved as soon as she had fired. She was listening for the sound she needed to hear, so desperately wanted to hear. A few seconds later it came.

The sound of her Land Cruiser starting up.

That meant Sean at least had gotten to safety. Now she needed to get there, too. The next sound she heard was a bullet whistling past her head and blowing off a chunk of wood from the tree she was standing near. A piece of bark hit her in the head, and blood started flowing down her face. She staggered back, regrouped, took aim, and sprayed five shots across the field in front of her.

Another shot rang out and she watched in amazement as a man fell from a tree about fifty feet away from her. When he hit the ground his rifle flew from his hands, bounced along the dirt, and shattered against a tree.

She looked behind her from where the shot had come.

Sam Wingo was lowering his weapon. He locked gazes with her for a second.

She nodded in thanks and then Wingo was gone from her view. She had no idea where Tyler was. Maybe Wingo had gotten him to safety and then come back to help. Whatever the reason, Michelle was grateful.

Michelle wheeled around and sprinted flat-out toward the engine sounds of the Land Cruiser that she knew as well as she did her own name. When she broke into the clearing she saw a man lying facedown. For a moment she was paralyzed because she thought it was Sean. Then the Land Cruiser flew in reverse toward her and the passenger door was thrown open.

Sean yelled, "Get your butt in here!"

Michelle jumped in. Sean shifted to drive and mashed down the pedal. The truck flew forward, its back wheels slipping a bit in the dirt before gaining traction, and then they were racing down the road. When they hit asphalt again Sean looked at her and exclaimed, "You're bleeding."

"Thanks for noticing," she replied. She reached

down to the floorboard and picked out a tattered towel from the jungle of items and trash there. She rubbed the blood off.

"I doubt that's clean," he noted.

"I doubt I care," she replied.

"Are you okay?"

She looked in the vanity mirror, moving her hair out of the way to reveal a cut along her scalp. "Just a shallow bleeder. Blowback from tree bark, not a bullet," she added. She rummaged in the glove box, pulled out some antiseptic, sprayed it on the wound, and then covered it with a Band-Aid. She sat back against the seat and let out a long breath. "We just used up all of our nine lives back there."

He nodded. "And lost Wingo and Tyler in the process. I hope to God they didn't get killed or captured." He suddenly slowed. "Do you think we should go back?"

"No. I think they got out okay."

"How do you know?"

"He saved my life," Michelle said quietly.

Sean shot her a glance. "Who did?"

"Sam Wingo. One of the guys after us got a sight line on me from a tree with a sniper rifle. Wingo got the kill shot on him before he could take me out."

"Well, maybe he is on the right side after all."

She glanced at him. "What about the guy back by the truck? What happened?"

"I figured they followed one of us here. Either us

or Tyler. I didn't think they would have gotten a lead on Wingo that fast. I assumed they'd station someone at the vehicle in case we got back to it. I took him out before he could take me out."

"I didn't hear a shot."

"That's because I hit him in the head with a rock."

"You got close enough to do that?"

"No, I hit him from about thirty feet away."

"With a rock?" she said in amazement.

"I never told you I was a pitcher in college?"

"No, you never did, Sean."

"Well, it was good to see I still had some stuff."

"What do we do now?"

"Our problem is I think they followed us to get to Wingo."

"You think he thinks we did it on purpose?" she asked.

"No. Not with the other guy drawing down on you. And I heard other shots."

"I got two of them. Non-kills, but they'll be out of action for a while."

"Then Wingo must know we were ambushed too," Sean replied.

"Which still doesn't answer my question. What now?"

"We need to hook back up with Wingo and Tyler. He's the only path forward that I can see. Otherwise we'll keep going around in circles until one bullet or bomb doesn't miss."

"So how do we 'hook back up' with them?"

"You ask a lot of questions. Want to give some answers a try on your own?" he said grumpily.

"Well, we know what Wingo currently looks like. He changed his appearance quite a bit."

"So?"

"If we can get ahold of some footage at the airports we might get a line on how he got back in the country. He had to come by plane. Ocean freighter would've taken a lot longer."

"Good idea."

"Thanks," she said curtly. "I have one a year."

"So do we go to McKinney or Littlefield with the request?"

"Oh, why let one have fun over the other? Let's go to both and hit them together."

"Okay, sounds like a plan."

"Let's hope," said Michelle doubtfully.

50

Alan Grant had been listening to the news with great interest. Milo Pratt's body had been discovered in his car, his throat smashed, his life gone. The police had no clues and no suspects and were hoping the public would come forward with some leads to help them track down the murderer.

Grant knew there would be no public coming forward and no leads to help track down the suspect. He had not allowed himself to be seen. He did not leave evidence behind.

The body of Jean Shepherd had not been discovered. He doubted it ever would be. But even if it were, he was not unduly worried. He had effectively covered his trail. There would be no way for the police to connect him with her.

He continued driving out of the city until he reached his final destination. He passed the checkpoint, drove up the steep, narrow road, and got out of his car. Grant walked around the perimeter of his new purchase. The radio station looked remarkably different than it had a short time ago. The electricity had been turned on. His men were moving with precision and urgency. When they were done, the tech team would come in and work their magic.

The transmission tower was being outfitted with satellite dishes. He watched as one of his men rode high up in a cherry picker, a dish next to him in the lift bucket. Grant then turned his attention to the electronic tablet sitting on his car's hood. He needed a bit of quiet to compose this email, and the sounds of construction going on within the old radio station would not provide it.

He was using an untraceable email portal. It didn't seem like anything was really untraceable these days. But that wasn't the case if you knew what you were doing. And he did.

He wrote out the email, editing it over the next several minutes. As his fingers typed in the words *Afghanistan* and *poppies* he smiled broadly. Then, satisfied with the email's contents, he hit the send key. It was like launching a torpedo. He expected this one to slam into its target with even more devastating results than had the first one, about certain rebels being funded by the U.S. government.

He performed an NSA-level wipe on the tablet, obliterating any trace of the email on it, and then slipped the device into his pocket. His phone buzzed. He pulled it out and looked at the screen. His smile quickly became a frown.

King and Maxwell were true escape artists, it

seemed. Maxwell had shot two of his men while King had incapacitated a third. A fourth man had been killed by Sam Wingo, who had also managed to escape with his son, Tyler.

Grant put the phone back into his pocket, leaned against his car, looked at the dark sky, and shut his eyes. He hummed the melody from *Rhapsody in Blue*, a favorite method of his to relax. When he finished he opened his eyes, looked over at the radio station, and calmly thought about his next move.

The email he had just sent would detonate like a bombshell in D.C. Then the shock waves would emanate out from there. It was so easy to get a message to go viral these days what with all the outlets on social media, and with all the idle eyeballs looking for the next big thing to pass on through the digital spectrum.

So his plan was good there. Not so good on other counts.

The former Secret Service agents were seriously hampering his efforts. But for them, he would be much farther ahead. And Wingo now would go deep under. And take his son with him. It made no sense to go full-bore after him right now. Better to go after a target that wasn't as hardened or as elusive.

King and Maxwell were the low-hanging fruit. The pair obviously wasn't an easy target, but Grant played the percentages. And that way of looking at things told him they were the ones to focus on. And there were ways to do that without necessarily going after either of them directly. He didn't want any more casualties on his end.

He pulled out his tablet and entered some search terms. The response was fast and illuminating. He looked at the Facebook page of the person—young, sweet, innocent. She could have no idea what was about to hit her like a tsunami.

King and Maxwell would be his go-to target. Once he got to them he could leverage them to get to Wingo. With him off the board Grant could feel far more confident about his plan succeeding.

He made a call and conveyed his instructions. They would be carried out quickly and efficiently, he was certain of that.

Then he looked at his radio station. This was the key. This was the whole ball game right here. If he could make this work, nothing else really mattered.

51

Tyler sat on the thin mattress and stared over at him.

Sam Wingo was at the window of the hotel room peering out, a gun in one hand, his other hand curled around the window drape.

"Dad?" said Tyler in a shaky voice.

Wingo held up a hand to quiet his son. He lingered at the window for a few more minutes, his gaze running up and down the streets, to the tops of the buildings and the windows facing him, to the cars parked down below, to the people moving along the sidewalks.

Finally, he closed the drapes, slipped the gun into his holster, and turned to his son. Wingo started to say something but then stopped as he saw the terror in his son's eyes. He drew up a chair next to the bed and sat down in it, his knees nearly touching Tyler's.

"I'm sorry, Tyler. I'm sorry for all of this. Everything I've put you through."

"I'm…I'm just glad you're alive, Dad."

Wingo wrapped his arms around Tyler, and they sat

there swaying a bit. When Wingo drew back, he took a deep breath and began speaking.

"First, I know all the stuff you've heard on the news. I didn't steal the money. And I'm not a traitor to my country. I was set up."

"I know that, Dad. I never thought you did any of that stuff."

"I'm going to find out who did set me up, though."

"I know you will."

They grew silent, each staring at the other intently. Wingo finally rose and paced the small room.

Tyler looked around the space. "Are we going to stay here? I mean, I've got school and a swim meet coming up."

Wingo stopped pacing and looked over at him.

"We can't stay here, no. And as for school and swimming…." He started pacing again.

"What about Jean?" asked Tyler.

His father sat down in the chair. "What about her?"

"Who was she?"

Wingo looked markedly uncomfortable by this question.

Tyler hurried on, "See, I heard she was a plant. That you thought she was working with you. But maybe she was really working for someone else. Like a spy."

"Who told you that?"

"Sean and Michelle."

"King and Maxwell, the PIs?"

"Yeah. Is it true? Was she a plant?"

"It's complicated, Tyler."

Now Tyler frowned and sat up straighter on the bed. "No, it's not, Dad. Either she was or she wasn't."

Wingo pressed his palms against his thighs. "Jean was assigned to stay with you while I was away."

"Assigned to stay with me? Were you two even married?"

Wingo shook his head. "No. It wasn't like that. It was just her mission. Her job was to be with you while I was gone."

Tyler looked dully at him. "So Mom was replaced with somebody who was doing a *job*?"

Wingo flushed. "It wasn't like that at all, son."

"And you kept all of this from me? Your son? For almost a whole year? I couldn't know about any of it?"

"It was classified, Tyler. I couldn't tell anyone not in the loop."

"Great, I was out of the loop. Glad to know you had a good reason."

He stood and went over to the window, looking out.

"Tyler, keep away from there!" exclaimed Wingo.

"Don't worry about me, Dad. I'm not in the loop. I'm not part of the mission."

"Tyler, please. I couldn't tell you."

"Couldn't or wouldn't?" Tyler turned to face him. "I didn't even know you were still in the Army. I thought you had a job at some company."

"That was also part of the cover," Wingo said miserably.

"Right, cover. From everybody, including me."

"I took an oath, son. To serve my country to the best of my ability."

"Yep, and country trumps family every time, right. Maybe I'll join the Army when I get out of high school. Then I can keep shit from you and you won't be able to complain. Because I'm *serving* my country."

"I'm not proud of how I handled this, son. I feel awful how this turned out."

"Not as bad as me."

Wingo started to say something and then closed his mouth.

Tyler looked back out the window. "What do we do now?"

Wingo glanced at him. "I need to find out who set me up."

"How?"

"I've got a few leads."

"And what about me?"

"You can't go back to school. Not now. You have to stay with me. I'll be able to keep you safe."

Tyler turned to face him. "You killed a man. I saw it."

Wingo rose and stood next to him. "I'm sorry you had to see that. But I had to do it. He was going to shoot her."

"Michelle Maxwell. I like her. I like them both."

"Do you trust them?"

"Yes. And you should too. They can help you. They're smart."

Wingo pulled his son away from the window and sat him back on the bed.

"I'm not sure we can trust anyone, Tyler."

"They can help you, Dad!"

"They led those men right to us."

"That wasn't their fault."

"There's no room for mistakes, Tyler."

"Will you let them help?"

"I don't think I can," said Wingo.

"Then I'll go to them."

"I said you had to stay with me."

"That's what you said. That doesn't mean I have to."

"You're my son! I didn't travel seven thousand miles to get back to you only to lose you again."

"But I'm out of the loop. You can't tell me anything. So how can I help you?"

"You need stay with me so I can keep you safe."

"They can keep me safe."

"Tyler, this is not open for discussion."

"How can you keep me safe and find out who set you up? You'll be putting me in danger if I come with you."

Wingo pressed his hand against his temple.

"Face it, Dad. You need help. You *need* Sean and Michelle."

Wingo slowly sat down in the chair. "Do you really think they can help?"

"Yeah, I do."

Wingo looked up at his son. "Do you trust me?"

Tyler stared at his father. "I believe you when you said you did nothing wrong. But I'm not sure I trust you. At least not yet."

Wingo nodded and looked down. "After all this I guess I can't blame you."

"But you're still my dad. And we have to get through this. Okay?"

"Okay."

52

Sean and Michelle were on one side of the table while Agents McKinney and Littlefield were on the other. It was the next morning and they were in a conference room at a DHS satellite office in Virginia. Both agents looked dour.

Sean said, "So still no Tyler Wingo?"

Littlefield said, "We'll get him."

Michelle interjected, "You better hope you do before somebody gets to him first."

"What's that supposed to mean?" said McKinney.

She replied, "Pretty simple, actually. People are after his dad. Means they might use his son to get to the father."

"Yeah, we've considered that," said Littlefield. "So why the face-to-face now?"

Sean said, "You know we met with POTUS. He made a request. We're going to accept that request."

Littlefield and McKinney sat up straighter.

"Okay," said Littlefield.

"But we have a little problem," added Michelle.

"What's that?" said Littlefield.

"The president wanted us to use our relationship with Tyler to get to his father."

Sean added, "But you lost Tyler. Now, I'm sure the president knows about that, right?"

McKinney glanced at Littlefield, who directed his gaze at the floor.

"Agent Littlefield?" began McKinney.

Littlefield said, "The president is a busy man. We can't interrupt him with every little thing."

"Little thing!" said Sean. "Tyler Wingo is the most important teenager in the country right now."

"Shit," muttered McKinney, but a tiny smile escaped his lips, probably at the thought of the FBI's plight in this case.

Michelle focused her attention on him. "And I don't think the president, when he finds out, will take the time to specifically assess blame, Agent McKinney. FBI? DHS? To him, it will all be the same. Alphabets that royally screwed up."

The smile faded from McKinney's lips.

Littlefield said, "Okay, you've shown your hand and it's a strong one. What do you want?"

"Some cooperation and information sharing," said Sean.

"Such as?" asked Littlefield warily.

Michelle answered, "Such as all surveillance camera footage from Dulles, Reagan National, and BWI for the last five days."

"Why?" asked McKinney.

"If Sam Wingo is back in the country we figure he came by plane—commercial, private, or cargo."

"We've already run that with facial recognition software," said Littlefield.

Sean looked at Michelle. "I'm not feeling the love here. What say we go back to the president and see if he'll authorize it if these guys won't?"

"Sounds good to me," said Michelle. She started to get up.

"Wait, wait," said Littlefield, holding up his hands. "I guess two more pairs of eyes on it won't hurt. But it's a lot of footage."

"Not if you know what you're looking for," said Michelle.

"And you do?" asked McKinney suspiciously.

"Secret Service. We've got the best eyes in the business," answered Michelle.

"Right!" snorted McKinney.

Sean pointed to McKinney's ear. "You got some shaving cream in your right ear. Guess you missed it this morning. Surprised your DHS buds didn't point it out." He looked at Littlefield. "Or your good friend at the FBI."

McKinney stabbed his finger in his ear and looked at the shaving cream on it.

Michelle smiled. "That one was free of charge."

An hour later Sean and Michelle were sitting in front of a bank of computer screens.

"Which airport first?" said Michelle.

"Let's dial up Dulles. It's closest. And Reagan doesn't handle international flights from the places Wingo would be coming from."

Six hours and three cups of coffee each later they sat back looking defeated.

Michelle said, "Without facial recognition software this is going to take forever. There are just too many faces to do manually."

Sean nodded in agreement, thinking hard.

"Let's focus on cargo. Even with his new look I don't think Wingo would chance flying commercial."

They dialed up that segment of the footage.

They started watching when Sean realized something. "This footage is probably too recent. Wingo was probably already back in the country by then."

Michelle grabbed his arm. "Wait. Check out the car."

Sean sat back and focused on a car that was parked outside one of the cargo terminals. "That's Wingo," exclaimed Sean.

"And it looks like he's watching someone. Can you adjust the angle?"

Sean hit some keys and the screen changed to show Wingo's sight lines. A man was coming out of a building. He got into a car and drove off. Sean hit some more keys and they watched as Wingo pulled onto the road and started following the other man's car.

"He's tailing the guy," observed Sean.

Michelle was typing in something in her phone. "License plate of both cars," she explained.

Sean nodded while he again changed the footage angle. "Heron Air Service," he said, reading the sign on the side of the building from where the man had come.

Michelle saw this and hit some more keys on her phone. "You think that's the folks he rode back in on? I just Googled them. Among other things they run an international cargo service."

"But if he'd gotten a ride with them, why tail them?"

"That's true."

"Maybe he was running down a lead on the money," said Sean. "Maybe Heron had something to do with transporting the billion euros."

"We need to run down the same lead then. How do you want to go about it?"

"Deceit and lies, the usual template," replied Sean. "I could go on bended knee to Edgar and see if he can run these plates for us."

"Good idea. And I'll find out all I can on Heron Air Service."

"And the Feds?" asked Michelle.

"We tell them we found nothing on the footage and we eat our humble pie."

"Not in a trusting mood?"

"I haven't been in a trusting mood for twenty-five years." He leaned back in his chair. "But we have to keep in mind that those guys followed us to Wingo, Michelle. They're still gunning for us. Which means we have to take evasive action."

"Tough to do while we're investigating this," she noted.

"But we have to. Unless and until Sam Wingo wises up, we have to follow up everything solo."

"And wall the Feds off at the same time. And the president. Tall order, Sean."

"Where's your usual can-do spirit that I know and love?" he said with a smile.

"I think I left it back at either the blown-up motel room or the woods where we nearly got shot."

He shrugged. "You were the one who got us involved in this sucker. So, in for a dime, in for a dollar."

She drew a long breath. "Yeah, I know. I'm just wondering when we're going to run out of change."

53

Michelle sat in the passenger seat of the car staring down at her phone.

Sean was in the driver's seat. It was a vehicle they had borrowed from a friend. They had stayed the night at a motel, paying in cash.

"And?" he asked expectantly, looking at her.

"Edgar came through. The plates on Wingo's car belong to a vehicle that was impounded by the D.C. cops about a month ago."

"He stole the plates off it to replace the ones on his. Probably a rental. He's using a fake ID and didn't want anyone to be able to trace it back and blow his cover."

"That's right," said Michelle absently. "He's probably only got one ID and a credit card pack based on that. That gets blown, he's out of resources."

"What about the other vehicle?"

"Registered to a Vista Trading Group, LLC, based in D.C. Their office is over off L Street, Northwest."

"And what do we know about Vista Trading Group?"

"Consultants in the defense contracting arena. They operate in lots of countries but they seem to have a specialty in the Middle East."

"Special enough to steal a billion euros?" asked Sean.

"Maybe."

"Connection to Heron Air Service?"

"Nothing mentioned on the site."

"Did you dig deeper on Heron?"

"They're a private charter service. They've got ten aircraft. All have the capability to fly across the pond and then beyond with a jet fuel fill-up."

"And the guy driving?"

"No clue. His photo wasn't on any screen page. The president of Vista is someone named Alan Grant. His bio's on here. Late thirties. Family man. Former military. MBA from Wharton." She held up her phone. "Here's his picture. Nice-looking guy."

Sean glanced at it. "But no picture of the guy in the car we saw?"

She shook her head. "Nothing on Vista's website. And Heron didn't have a site, which seems odd."

"Well, if he is involved in this, his mug shot will soon be posted in lots of places."

"How do we hit Vista?"

"Tricky because some of them might have already seen us. So my usual plan of hitting them head-on is probably out."

"We can establish an op post and see what falls out."

"Or we can do some digging on this Grant guy.

Background, business associates. What he's done in the past. You said he was former military?"

She nodded. "Doesn't say where or what on the bio, though."

"The Pentagon keeps meticulous records. I can check on that discreetly."

"So, they took the money why?"

"Well, a billion in cash has its own built-in motive, doesn't it?"

"But what about the blogger that dropped the bombshell on the money being funneled to Muslim rebels?"

"That does make it more complicated, I grant you."

"The White House is taking it on the chin. I don't think this is just about stealing money, Sean."

"Maybe we should follow up with the blogger. What was his name again?"

"George Carlton. Address in Reston. But you said he might be lying low."

"Well, then we'll just have to dig deep. But if he's getting his info from a source, we need to find that source. And the most direct way to do that is to get to Carlton."

"Do you want me to get Edgar to dig into Grant and Vista?"

"Do you think he will? He got in trouble last time."

Michelle looked at him. "I think he will if we both ask him."

"Both of us. Why?"

"He looks up to you, Sean."

"He's six foot nine. He doesn't look up to anyone except NBA centers."

"You know what I mean."

"I'm surprised Bunting will let us near him after what happened."

"Well, we saved Edgar's life. And Edgar is a very special and good person. He will never forget that."

Sean glanced out the window. "Okay. Call him and see if he has time to meet. Maybe we can very discreetly involve him in this. But he needs to understand he can leave no trail. I don't want Bunting jumping down my throat again."

"Well, we have the president behind us now. That trumps DoD and Peter Bunting, doesn't it?"

He smiled. "Good point."

"Let's just make sure we're not followed."

He put the car in drive while Michelle made the call to Edgar.

Two hours later they were staring across at Edgar Roy, who sat opposite them at an outdoor café many miles from where he labored on behalf of the U.S. government.

"We're sorry about what happened before, Edgar," began Michelle.

"Mr. Bunting was very upset," said Edgar as he stared off. "I don't like it when people scream like that."

"Me either," chimed in Sean. "And we appreciate

your running down those plates for us. I hope Mr. Bunting doesn't find out about that."

"Mr. Bunting is very smart. But he's not that smart," replied Edgar.

"Meaning you covered your tracks well?" said Michelle.

"I like helping you both," said Edgar. "I know you're trying to help other people. Just like you helped me."

Sean glanced at Michelle. "That's right, Edgar. And we wouldn't come to you unless we really needed the kind of help you can provide. It's important. We're actually working for the president of the United States on this."

"Then I'm sure Mr. Bunting will have no problem at all with me helping you. What do you need?"

They explained about Vista Trading Group and Alan Grant.

Michelle added, "Really, all you can find out about the company and the man."

"He's mixed up in all this?" asked Edgar.

"We *suspect* he might be," corrected Michelle.

"I can get to work on this today."

"What about the Wall?" asked Sean.

"Maintenance issues, so I have some spare time."

"A break from saving the world?" said Michelle, smiling.

"What?" said Edgar, looking at her strangely.

"It was just a little joke," said Michelle, looking embarrassed.

"Oh, okay," said Edgar, and he attempted a smile. "But it will probably take some time."

Sean said, "That's okay. We have some leads to follow up at the Pentagon. Whatever you find you can just email to us."

"Do you have good encryption on your end?" asked Edgar.

"Uh, password-protected," he replied.

"Your password is oh-five-oh-eight. That's not very strong."

A stunned Sean said, "How did you know my password?"

"It's your date of birth backward. I got it on the third try when I hacked you a while back. I would have gotten it on the second attempt, but I didn't think you would be so obvious."

"Why did you hack me?"

"I didn't know you as well back then. I didn't know if you were my friend or not. I never hack my friends."

"So did you hack Michelle too?" he asked.

Edgar glanced at Michelle. "No."

"Why not?" demanded Sean.

"I knew right away that Ms. Maxwell was my friend."

"Thanks, Edgar," said Michelle, giving Sean a poke in the ribs with her elbow.

"I'll change my password to something stronger," groused Sean.

"All right. But don't simply add your year of birth. That's not good enough."

Sean's expression made clear that was precisely what he was planning to do.

"What exactly would you suggest then?" he asked in an exasperated tone.

"Random numbers and letters, uppercase/lowercase-sensitive, that do not correlate to any of your personal data in any way. Thirty-character minimum. And don't write it down anywhere."

Sean looked dumbstruck. "Great, but how exactly am I supposed to remember thirty random characters without writing it down, which sort of defeats the whole super-duper secret code thing?"

Edgar looked perplexed. "You can't remember thirty random characters?"

"No, I can't," snapped Sean.

Michelle chimed in, "He's older, Edgar. Losing brain cells at a daily rate you can't even imagine."

"I'm very sorry to hear that," said Edgar somberly. "Then, if you really must, you can cut it to twenty-five characters but no less than that," he suggested.

"Thanks," said Sean curtly. "I'll get right on it."

54

He was at the cemetery again staring at the same two graves.

The inscription on the grave on the left said that Franklin Grant had been a wonderful husband, loving father, and true patriot.

"I miss you, Dad," said Grant. "I miss you more every day. You should be here. You should be a grandfather to my kids."

He turned to the other grave. Loving Wife and Mother, read the inscription.

He had tried to keep the image such inscriptions inspired in his head. But he had been unable to for a very good reason.

As a thirteen-year-old he had inadvertently seen a picture of his parents dead in their car, their asphyxiated features deadly pale, and their bulging eyes wide open as they sat slumped against each other, their suicide pact complete.

"Miss you too, Mom," Grant mumbled. And he did.

But his gaze and his thoughts turned back quickly to his father.

He had been a true patriot who had bled for his country. He had risen far. He had worked in the White House. As a boy Grant had gone there with his father, shaken the hand of the president of the United States at the time, seen the center of power of the strongest nation on earth. It had left an indelible impression on him. It had been a compelling reason he had joined the military. But the truth behind his father's tragic end had left a far deeper mark, like a third-degree burn. He doubted it would ever fully heal.

The one thing that kept Grant going was that he had his plan. It was being executed and it was succeeding, albeit with some bumps along the way. He'd expected that. Plans this complex could not unfold free of problems. He had been ready for such an eventuality. And it was a good thing.

He placed the flowers on his parents' graves, said a last goodbye, then turned and walked back to his car.

An hour later he was walking into his house and greeting his children. His seven-year-old son was in school, but his five-year-old daughter and two-year-old toddler came hurrying over to him. He scooped up his son in his arms, took his daughter by the hand, and walked into the kitchen, where his wife was making lunch.

Leslie Grant was in her middle thirties and as lovely as the day he had proposed to her. They kissed, then Grant snatched a cucumber from the salad she was preparing and walked into the adjacent living room carrying his son.

Dan Marshall was sitting in front of the large-screen TV dressed in khaki pants and a flannel shirt with tasseled loafers on his feet.

Grant put down his son, who quickly raced off to join his sister in the playroom. Grant turned to Marshall, who was cradling a beer and watching ESPN on the TV.

"How're the Wizards doing?" asked Grant.

"Better. Nets drilled us last time. Hopefully, we can return the favor tonight."

Marshall handed Grant a beer. Grant popped it and took a swig before sitting down in the recliner and studying his father-in-law.

"How are you doing?" he asked.

"Been better," said Marshall.

"Work?"

Marshall sat back and turned his attention from the ball game to Grant.

"I've never stopped missing Maggie," he said, speaking about his late wife. "But this is the first time I'm also glad she's not around to see this."

Grant put the beer down. "When we last spoke I didn't take away from your comments that it was that bad."

"Well, we were at the Pentagon. One has to watch what is said there."

"So it's worse?"

Marshall sighed, drained his beer, and put the empty bottle down. "It's bad, Alan. I signed off on this mission. I had my doubts, but the orders from the top were crystal clear. It was going to happen, with my rubber stamp or without."

"So why would the blame fall to you then?"

"You obviously don't understand how government, and the DoD in particular, works."

"I was in the military."

"But never in the military *bureaucracy*. It has its own rules, and many of them don't make sense. But one you can count on is that when the civilian leadership screws up a matter connected to the military, folks in uniform are going to be left holding a big part of the blame."

"But you're not technically in uniform."

"Doesn't matter. I've got the office and the title and the ball weighs about one ton and is heading right for me. Worst case I'm squashed. Best case I'm severely wounded."

"So what outcome do you really see?"

"I'll spend my remaining days testifying in front of Congress. If I'm lucky I'm not indicted. If I'm not lucky we might be talking prison."

"Jesus, Dan, I had no idea."

Grant of course had every idea, but, still, he felt badly for the man. "Is there anything I can do for you?"

Marshall patted his arm. "Look, we all have troubles.

Now, you've got a great family and you've made my little girl very happy. You just keep doing what you're doing. Things will shake out one way or another."

I plan to keep on doing what I'm doing, thought Grant.

They had lunch and neither of the men made any mention of Marshall's dilemma in front of Leslie and the kids.

After the meal was over Marshall said his goodbyes. Grant gave him a handshake and a hug.

"I'm sorry, Dan," he said. And he actually meant it. But when it came to avenging his father's death, there was no one Grant was not willing to sacrifice. And that included himself.

He walked out into the backyard, sat in a lawn chair, and stared at the sky. He watched a plane begin its final descent into Dulles Airport.

He, too, felt as though he were in his final descent. The radio station was coming along. His itinerary seemed to be rock-solid and very promising. The satellite he had leased was perfectly situated to do what needed doing. And the fragments left on there would be very helpful in getting him to the necessary outcome.

And that necessary outcome was that someone had to pay for a wrongful act committed twenty-five years ago. That injustice had cost his father his life. His father was the only one who had really paid a price. Now it was time for others to do so. It had become the most compelling force of Grant's life. It was not a goal of his. It was an obsession. And obsessions tended to blind one to all other things. Grant was aware of this, but he also found he could do nothing about it. That's what an obsession was, after all.

Thus, he had chosen to risk his father-in-law's career and perhaps his life to attain this goal. He would even sacrifice his family's happiness if it came down to it. Because Grant could not be happy unless the wrong was righted. And he knew of only one way to do it. Nothing could get in the way of that. And if something did it would have to be removed, with force if necessary.

Just like he had done with Jean Shepherd and Milo Pratt. Just like he would have to do with Sam Wingo, and perhaps his son. And Sean King and Michelle Maxwell. He was pretty certain they would have to die before this was all over.

He drew his gaze from the plane overhead as it disappeared down past the trees. In a few seconds its wheels would hit the tarmac and the reverse thrusters and brakes would be applied. Another safe landing, just as happened millions of times a year.

His own landing would probably not be so smooth. But Grant had a chance, a real chance to make it all work, achieve his goal of justice, and then slip back into a normal life. That would be the ideal. With the burden gone he could live again.

Others were not to be so fortunate. More people were going to die before this was all over. And Grant knew exactly who most of them were. It would be a historical event in the eyes of the world.

But for him, it would just be avenging the memory of the man he held most dear.

55

"Yes, sir, thank you, sir."

Sean clicked off the phone and looked up at Michelle.

Keeping on the move, they were in another motel room they had paid for in cash.

Sean had just gotten off the phone with President John Cole.

She said, "Are we good to go with POTUS?"

"I think so. At least with him behind us we can go pretty much anywhere and ask pretty much anything."

"I noticed you handled the question of Tyler Wingo very smoothly."

"I'm not looking to derail McKinney's or Littlefield's careers. They might prove useful. The president is expecting us to deliver Tyler at some point. We just have to executive-lag that."

"So where do we go first?"

"Pentagon. We're meeting with the head of procurement who was involved in the cash-in-Afghanistan program, and Colonel Leon South, who was Sam Wingo's immediate superior in the field."

"Let's roll then."

An hour later they were being escorted down a long corridor at the Pentagon. In fact, every corridor at the Pentagon was long. It was a labyrinth beyond all labyrinths. Indeed, it was rumored that employees from the 1960s were somewhere in the bowels of the place still looking for an exit.

They reached an outer office and then were escorted into an adjacent conference room. Two men were waiting for them. One was in uniform, the other was not.

Dan Marshall rose and held out his hand. "Mr. King, Ms. Maxwell, welcome to the Pentagon. I'm Dan Marshall, assistant secretary of acquisitions, logistics, and technology. I'm the one who spends a lot of the taxpayers' dollars around here."

They shook hands.

Colonel South did not rise to greet them. He merely nodded and said, "Colonel Leon South. I understand you're here with the president's blessing."

Sean, Michelle, and Marshall sat at the table.

Sean said, "That's right."

South said, "I'm not sure how private investigators figure into a classified mission, I'm really not. Can you explain that to me?"

Marshall said, "Leon, surely with the president's authorization we don't need to get into that."

Sean said, "I can understand the query. We stumbled into the case mostly by accident. By a series of fortuitous events we ended up becoming close with one of the main players in this little saga. The president deemed that valuable, and that's why we're in the loop."

South nodded slowly but his features remained inscrutable. "So what do you want from us?"

Sean said, "Some background on the mission? Some insight into Sam Wingo?"

"Wingo is a traitor," began South.

Marshall held up his hand. "We don't know that, Leon. We don't know a lot of things, actually."

"A billion euros gone missing, along with Wingo? I think we know all we need to know."

"But he contacted you," said Marshall. "And protested his innocence in the strongest possible terms."

"Of course he did, to throw us off," retorted South.

"When did he contact you?" asked Sean.

"Shortly after the mission cratered."

"What did he say happened?" asked Michelle.

"That there were strange men at the rendezvous spot. They said they were CIA and had the creds to prove it."

"Have you spoken with Langley about this?" asked Sean.

South looked at him contemptuously. "No, I just took him at his word."

Sean said, "Okay, what did Langley say when you contacted them?"

"That they had no idea what the hell he was talking about. They had no agents anywhere near this mission."

"How many times did Wingo contact you?" asked Sean, changing gears.

"Twice. Both times to moan about being innocent. And about finding out who set him up."

"And you obviously didn't believe him," said Michelle.

"No, I didn't."

"Did you know Wingo before this mission?"

"By reputation. Which was a solid one. Otherwise, he would not have been selected."

"And yet you just assume he's guilty?" said Sean inquiringly.

"Missing money and missing man, yeah, I do," South replied in a curt tone.

"Let's assume for the moment that he is telling the truth," began Sean. "Who would benefit from setting him up?"

Marshall said, "Anyone who wanted a billion euros. I said all along that we should have at minimum sent in a three-man team, but I was overruled. It was too much for one person, even someone as skilled as Sam Wingo."

Sean looked at him. "Did you know Wingo beforehand?"

"Just by reputation, like Leon."

"And you don't think he's guilty?" asked Michelle.

"I haven't formed a conclusion one way or another. I know he went through a tremendous vetting process and had to endure a year's worth of setting up an arrangement with another field agent that impacted his private life."

"That would be Jean Shepherd," said Michelle. "His supposed second wife."

"Yes."

"And she's disappeared too," said Sean.

"Right," interjected South. "Maybe they're on the Riviera right now enjoying the fruits of their theft."

"So you think they were in on it together?"

"Why not? They had a year to plan it. A billion euros sets them up for life."

"I might agree with you but for one thing," said Sean.

"What's that?" asked South.

"Tyler Wingo."

Michelle added, "We don't think he would ever abandon his son. By all accounts they were incredibly close."

South shrugged. "Maybe he plans to come back for the kid."

"So that also makes his son an accessory after the fact. A fleeing felon at age sixteen," said Michelle.

"That much money will make people do strange things," replied South.

"We understand that the money was intended for

certain Muslim freedom fighters to use to purchase weapons. Is that true?" asked Sean.

South and Marshall exchanged nervous glances.

"Is that a yes?" asked Michelle.

Marshall cleared his throat. "It's not untrue."

"Good, because that's what the president told us," added Michelle.

"So why ask us?" South groused.

"Just making sure everyone's on the same page," said Michelle.

"So a mess for the White House?" said Sean.

"Not just the White House," said Marshall. "Technically, such funds are not to be conveyed in that manner. So we're all in the same boat. I doubt whether Congress will take a scalpel to this."

"More like a meat cleaver," said South.

"So you mean *technically* it might be illegal?" said Michelle.

"That argument could be made," said Marshall. "The freedom fighters may be fighting against a regime that is not our ally. But it's not as though most of those rebels are knights in shining armor."

"Many of them want to bring sharia law to prominence in the secularized Arab countries," added South. "And in the countries that already have sharia law they could still be as bad as or worse than the regimes in power now. So it's a shitty situation all the way around."

"Like us supporting Osama bin Laden and the mujahideen in Afghanistan against the Soviets in the

1970s," noted Sean. "They later used the weapons we bought them against our troops."

"Geopolitics is not and never will be an exact science," noted South.

"Some might say common sense might be enough," said Michelle.

"Well, they'd be wrong, wouldn't they?" snapped South.

"So your career will take a hit over this, right?" said Sean, staring at him.

South's face turned red. "I'm more concerned about making this right than whether my next promotion will come through."

"So if the mission had gone according to plan, what was Wingo's role?"

South said, "To accompany the money to its end source. The freedom fighters. There was a group of them who were supposed to meet him at the drop spot. He was to follow them with the money out of the country. We had the route planned out and the proper authorizations needed with the tribal chiefs along the way."

"Why Afghanistan? Why not just bring the money directly to the freedom fighters?" asked Michelle.

"We couldn't be that transparent," said South. "In fact, the money technically wasn't going directly to the freedom fighters. There was an intermediate step where the funds were going to go to purchase weapons and ammo."

"From whom?"

South and Marshall exchanged another glance but said nothing.

Sean said, "Unless my memory fails me, there's one big country directly next to Afghanistan that isn't exactly our friend."

"And that would be Iran," said Michelle.

Sean looked squarely at South. "Please tell me we weren't dealing with freedom fighters to overthrow the government in Tehran?"

"Neither confirm nor deny. And I doubt the president gave you a direct answer on that," added South.

Sean looked at Marshall. "We really need to know."

Marshall nodded and rose.

South put a restraining hand on his arm. "Dan, think about what you're doing."

"Leon, they have the president's blessing. And how can they figure this out without knowing the whole story?"

He went to a wall where there was a paper map of the world. He pointed to several spots. "The actual plan was to loop north. The euros would be laundered in Turkmenistan and Kazakhstan."

"And the Russians were okay with that?" Sean asked quickly.

Marshall looked at South. The colonel said, "They were on board. It's complicated geopolitics for a neophyte like yourself, but rest assured that they're as tired of Iran's chest-thumping as we are."

Sean shook his head. "I don't think so."

"What?" snapped South.

"The Russians like saber-rattling particularly when it gives us grief. Prime example, Syria. In addition, Russia's economy is based largely on oil and gas, of which they have a ton. If the hardliners in Tehran get ousted and their oil comes back on the world market, the price goes down. That would hurt Moscow big-time. Their economic stabilization plan is actually destabilization in the region. The more fragile things are the more money they make on their natural resources."

Marshall smiled and Michelle looked impressed. She said, "How do you know all that?"

Sean shrugged. "Hey, I enjoy the *Economist* as much as the next neophyte."

Marshall continued, "The weapons were to be purchased through intermediary arms dealers in Turkey and then brought over the border there and into Syria and then onward to the freedom fighters."

"In Iran?" said Sean. "The freedom fighters were from Iran?"

Marshall nodded.

"Okay, and Wingo was to ride shotgun over all of it?" asked Sean.

"That's right," replied Marshall as he sat back down.

"An Army solider involved in something that smacks of the intelligence world?" observed Michelle.

"Talk to us about the DIA," said Sean.

"I'm with DIA," said South. "So was Wingo. Most people don't realize that DIA dwarfs CIA in manpower and resources. We've been recruiting and training thousands of new field agents for missions worldwide. We drop them into regular Army units that are dispersed worldwide and then keep them there after the units pull out. It's terrific cover, actually. Our enemies have long since caught on to the fact that State Department cover is for intelligence operatives. We work with the CIA on many joint ops. But this one we were heading up." He paused. "And we blew it big-time, which means it might be our last mission lead."

Sean looked at him curiously. "Which means Langley would be the boss in any future operations?"

"Probably."

"So they have a motive to blow this up?"

Marshall shook his head. "I highly doubt that. Before this is over everybody will have egg on their faces. And if they did and the truth came out, the CIA would be emasculated for decades to come. Far too risky."

"What steps have you taken to track Wingo?" asked Michelle.

"Every step we could think of," said South.

"And you think Wingo is a lone wolf on this?"

"Yes."

"Then we know he's innocent," said Sean.

"How?"

"There're quite a few people involved in this, actually. Several of them have tried to kill my partner and me. And not one of them was Sam Wingo."

"Well, with the money he has now he can hire whoever he wants to do his dirty work," replied South.

"My gut is telling me otherwise," Sean said.

"Oh, well, that makes all the difference to me," said South sarcastically.

Marshall said, "Do you think you can find Sam Wingo?"

"We're going to do our best. And we have great incentive."

"You mean because the president is counting on you?" said Marshall.

"No," said Sean. "Because it means we'll probably get to keep living."

56

Sean sat in his car and gazed over at the building. A voice crackled in his earwig.

"Vista Trading Group is on the sixth floor," said Michelle, who was sitting at an outdoor café near the next intersection.

"Got it."

"Edgar was very helpful in getting us so much information so fast."

"Yeah, but it *wasn't* all that helpful," said Sean. "Vista is a legit business. Alan Grant comes from a good family. His dad was in the military, then in civilian government. And Grant doesn't have a blemish on his record. Former soldier too. Now a successful business-man. Not even any parking tickets."

"Yeah, he's clean. Too clean in my opinion."

"Can't convict a guy for being *too* law abiding."

"But one of the men who works there has Sam Wingo's interest for some reason."

"We don't know what that interest is. It would be nice to ask Wingo directly."

"Have you emailed Tyler?" she asked.

"Twice. No response yet."

"Someone might be monitoring the new Gmail account."

"I used his code. Just asked if he was okay. That we wanted to be in touch."

"Wingo might not be letting him respond. He might not trust us."

"If I were him, I wouldn't trust anyone," replied Sean.

"So what do we do about Vista?"

"We wait."

Four hours later, when Michelle had ordered but not touched her fourth cup of coffee, their patience was rewarded.

Sean's voice crackled in her ear. "Alan Grant and our bogie on your three."

Michelle imperceptibly turned to look in that direction. She had on a ball cap pulled low with her long hair bundled up inside it. Wide sunglasses covered the top half of her face.

"Eyeballs on," she replied.

Grant and his colleague looked like young, successful businessmen having a quick meeting on the street. Michelle couldn't hear what they were saying, and she didn't want to risk getting up and crossing the street to get closer. If they spotted her, it might blow their only chance to advance the investigation.

"Plan?" she whispered.

"If they split up, I'll take Grant, you take the bogie. If they both go inside the office building, follow them in, see and hear what you can. Same if the bogie goes in alone."

"What if they ID me?"

"You're pretty well disguised, and there are a lot of people around. I think we just have to risk it."

"And you?"

"If one or both leave in a car, I'll follow Grant while you're on the bogie. You got your wheels nearby?"

"Around the corner. But I miss my Land Cruiser."

"Look, just throw some trash around the car's interior and you'll feel right at home."

"God, you are so funny you could go into stand-up," she snapped.

"Everyone needs to have a backup career."

"You really think this is going to lead somewhere?"

"If Wingo is interested in these folks, then we are too."

"They're heading into the building."

"Good luck."

"Roger that."

Michelle rose and took up the tail. She wedged herself in with a group of people who were entering the building after Grant and his colleague.

She just managed to jump onto the elevator with Grant, the other man, and ten more people. She pushed to the back, keeping Grant and his companion in front of her. She caught snatches of their conversation but doubted they would be discussing anything sensitive in public.

They got off, as she knew they would, on the sixth floor. Four other people exited the elevator car there, so she decided to chance it. She followed them down the hall and passed by them as they entered the offices of Vista Trading Group. It was a double-door entry and looked impressive. Grant must be pretty successful because this was a Class A building and rents were not cheap in this area of D.C.

She slipped around the corner and then doubled back.

And got the shock of her life.

She darted back around the corner before the man could see her.

"I just saw a guy going into Vista," she said to Sean through her comm pack.

"Okay, who was it?"

"You are not going to believe this."

"With this case I'm starting to believe anything is possible. Who did you see?"

"The guy we met with earlier at the Pentagon."

"Colonel Leon South?"

"No, the other one. Dan Marshall, assistant secretary for acquisition, logistics, and technology. The same guy who lost a billion euros of taxpayer money."

"Holy shit."

"That's what I thought."

"What's the connection with Vista?"

"Coincidence?" said Michelle.

"If it is, it's the size of Texas. We need to dig a lot deeper."

"Edgar?"

"He already dug into Grant's background. I'm surprised he didn't find the Dan Marshall connection."

"Even geniuses miss things."

"Or maybe he's losing a few brain cells too."

"Don't worry, he has tons to spare."

57

Michelle contacted Edgar and conveyed the particulars on what they needed. He promised to get right on it and call her back with his results. In the meantime Sean and Michelle headed over in Sean's car to Reston, Virginia, to meet with the blogger, George Carlton.

Sean phoned ahead and Carlton met them outside his town house—which was also his office, he told them, as he escorted them inside.

"I'm surprised there aren't news trucks parked out here," said Sean. "After your big scoop."

Carlton was short and portly and around fifty. His beard was trimmed close to his chin and his mustache drooped partially over his upper lip. He looked at them strangely and then apologized.

"My right contact has a scratch. Trying to get in to see the eye doctor."

He showed them into his office, a small room off the foyer. It was piled high with books, newspaper articles, magazines, and DVD cases. A large computer sat on the top of his desk while a server hummed below in the kneehole.

They all sat. Carlton rubbed his mustache and looked at them thoughtfully. "Media trucks here would validate the world of the blogger, so that will never happen."

"The two worlds don't get along?" said Michelle as she perched in a chair, sharing space with a stack of magazines.

"The two worlds don't recognize each other. I'm about the truth. They're about entertainment, ratings, and the almighty dollar."

"I'm all for the truth," said Sean.

"In your call you said you might have some information for me?" said Carlton.

"Quid pro quo," said Sean.

Carlton frowned. "I'm in the business of gathering and reporting information en masse, not in dispensing it individually. And I'm certainly not going to pay for it."

"Well, we're in the business of digging down to the truth," said Michelle. "And we need your help to do it."

"Who are you?"

Sean showed Carlton his ID card.

"Private investigators?" sniffed Carlton. "And who is your client?"

"Confidential," said Sean. "But depending on what you tell us, we might have some things to tell you."

"Like what?"

"Like some more background on the story you're

already reporting on with the missing billion euros."

Carlton smiled. "You obviously have not read my most recent blog. It went up just thirty minutes ago. I expect it to go viral anytime. The eyeball rate is already through the roof."

"No, we haven't seen it," said Sean. "But I'm not a regular blog reader."

"And he thinks viral is an infection," added Michelle.

Carlton chuckled. "Well, I *am* surprised that the media trucks have not swooped in after this one. Or at least the Feds."

Carlton hit some keys on his keyboard and swung the screen around so they could see it. Sean and Michelle swiftly read through the contents of the most recent blog. Carlton was watching them closely. "You don't seem too surprised."

Sean glanced at him. "That the billion euros was going to fund weapons for people seeking to topple the Iranian government and that an intermediate step to funnel the money involved poppies from Afghanistan that you use to make heroin? Yeah, it's a big surprise to us." He added, quite truthfully, "Especially the poppies and heroin part."

Carlton looked at him slyly. "I thought you were into the truth. Because what you just said was bullshit."

"Who was your source?" asked Michelle.

Carlton did an eye roll. "Please, don't even go there."

Sean swiftly counted on his hands and then looked

at Michelle. "Is it six people killed and five severely wounded so far in this whole thing or do I have the numbers backward?"

Michelle did a quick mental count. "I think it's five killed, six critically wounded. And don't forget the woman who's missing and probably dead. That's all in this country. But that doesn't take into account all the men killed in Afghanistan. That was a real slaughter."

"That's right. I had it backward. Well, in my defense, the body count keeps changing day-to-day. I can't keep up."

A startled Carlton looked between them. "What the hell are you talking about?"

"And you know the bombing at the motel in Alexandria?" asked Sean.

"That's connected to this?" said Carlton in a shaky voice.

Sean said, "Well, since we were there and were almost killed, yeah, it is. So what you have to take into consideration, George, is that whoever is behind this is feeding you information for some purpose that is not exactly clear yet. But what is clear is that they have a habit of cleaning up leave-behinds." Sean stared pointedly at him. "Do you get what I'm saying?"

"That I'm a leave-behind? But I'm just a blogger. I don't know anything that could hurt anyone."

"Well, if the source is emailing you, that leaves a trail. And that trail starts with you and ends with the source."

"But I'm sure my source is taking pains to cover that trail."

"Doesn't matter. Can't take the chance. I would expect that once your usefulness is over he'll come kill you, take your computer and your phone and your e-tablet and the server I see under your desk, and burn down your house and your bloody remains just to be extra sure." He looked at Michelle. "What's your take? You'd do that, right, if you were the source? No trace?"

She replied, "Absolutely. But I'd dismember him first, then burn him. Then use acid. Makes identifying the murder victim much harder."

Carlton looked ready to throw up but said weakly, "You're just trying to scare me."

Sean slowly shook his head. "I don't have to try. You *should* be scared. I am. And I was with the Secret Service. Not a lot can scare me, but this sure as hell does."

Michelle said, "You need to think about this very seriously, George. Very seriously. All those connected to this are dropping like flies. We've almost been killed three times and we can take care of ourselves." She looked at his small, chubby frame. "I don't think you're in the same situation."

"But what can I do?" wailed Carlton.

Sean said, "Download your emails to a flash drive and give it to me right now. Then pack a bag and buy a plane ticket that will take you far, far away from here for about a month. Check the papers or, better yet, the blogs for what's going on back here. If we're all still alive at the end of thirty days, then come back. It should be safe."

"You're shitting me!"

Sean looked at Michelle and then back at Carlton.

"Or you can stay here and die," she said to the blogger.

Carlton said nothing.

Finally, Sean rose. "Let's go, Michelle. Waste of time here."

Michelle stood. "Lead a horse to water. Sorry, George. Don't know what to tell you. Pay up the life insurance. Notify next of kin of the cash coming their way. And make sure your homeowner's insurance is paid up. For when they come and burn this place down with you in it."

They started to leave.

"Where would I go?" yelled Carlton.

Sean turned back. "Where would you like to go?"

Carlton thought for a few moments. "Always wanted to see the Sydney Opera House."

"Good choice," said Sean.

"Great choice," added Michelle.

"Flash drive?" said Sean, walking back over to the desk.

Carlton fumbled for one in his desk drawer and slipped it into the slot on his computer.

"Can you guys drive me to the airport? I can book a ticket online and it'll take me no time to pack and snag my passport."

"Why not?" said Sean.

"Are you armed?" asked Carlton.

Sean pointed to Michelle. "I have her, so the answer is yes, *I'm* armed."

He watched as Carlton downloaded the emails onto the flash drive and then popped it out and handed it to Sean.

They drove Carlton to the airport and dropped him off there.

"Good luck," said Sean.

"I think you'll need it more than me, pal," said Carlton before he hurriedly disappeared into the crowds at Dulles.

As they drove off Michelle said, "Think Edgar can trace the email back to the source?"

"If anyone can, he can. The IP address and all the other junk that I don't understand will be on the email trail. Whoever sent it will have done all they can to shut off the route, but Edgar may find something."

"Find *someone*, you mean."

Sean glanced at her. "That trip to New Zealand is looking better and better."

"Yes it is," said Michelle as they drove on.

Sean's phone buzzed. He answered it, listened, said thank you, and then turned the car in the other direction.

"What's up?" asked Michelle as he punched the gas.

"Dana's awake and wants to see me."

"I'm surprised the hospital would notify you. You're not family."

"That wasn't the hospital. It was her husband, General Curtis Brown. And he also wants to talk to us."

58

Curtis Brown, Dana's two-star husband, stood in the corner of the room with Michelle while Sean sat next to the bed and spoke to Dana. She was groggy, in pain but alive. She even managed to smile a few times, though she winced each time she did.

"Should have listened to you, Sean," she said slowly. "Should have just left the mall."

"Why didn't you?"

"Old habits die hard, I guess. Didn't want you to get hurt. But you look okay. And Michelle?"

"Standing right over there with the general, fit as a fiddle."

"I'm glad. I'm so glad," she said breathlessly.

"You should rest."

She gripped his hand more tightly. "Those men?"

"Taken care of."

"Have you figured out what is happening yet?"

"Getting closer every minute," he lied. He glanced at Brown. "I know your hubby has been here every second. I think you got the marriage thing right this time. You guys were definitely meant to be together."

She smiled while Brown looked down, embarrassed. Michelle patted him on the shoulder and gave him a reassuring look.

Dana said, "I feel okay, just so tired."

"That's the morphine drip. Enjoy it while you can."

Her eyes closed and her hand slipped away as she fell back asleep.

Sean rose and went over to Brown and Michelle.

Brown said, "The doctors said it'll take time but she should make a nearly complete recovery."

"That's great news," said Sean.

Brown glanced at him and then looked away. He said, "About what we talked about before."

Sean said, "You found out something?"

"The coffee shop, if you've got a minute."

"We've got all the time you need. Let's go."

They got their coffees and took a table far away from all others.

Brown swirled a pack of sugar into his cup and stirred it slowly.

"The Pentagon has shut up like a clam on this," he said.

"That's what we heard."

"But there's been a fresh leak," Brown said.

"That says we're trying to overthrow Iran by laundering funds for weapons with poppy shipments?" said Michelle.

He glanced at her sharply. "So you saw it?"

"We saw it on a blogger's site."

"Well, that blogger is in big trouble."

"I think he knows that."

"Free speech is one thing. But you can't print stolen national security secrets and get away with it."

"So it's true? About Iran?"

Brown took a sip of his coffee. "People look at the slaughter in Syria and think it's bad. But they don't see what's happening in Iran. Or in North Korea. Those countries have shut down all communication with the outside world. Bodies are piling up like you wouldn't believe."

"So we're going after Iran first. And North Korea second? I didn't think North Korea had any opposition forces in country."

"You'd be surprised. Many of them are displaced into South Korea, but want to go back home and change it. Iran was a test to see if something like this could work. If so, it would be deployed in North Korea."

"Long shot," said Michelle. "Even a billion euros might not buy you an overthrow of an entire government."

"Didn't have to. Just shake it up. If Iran or North Korea thought they were vulnerable from the inside they might tone down the rhetoric, come to the bargaining table, start to act like adults. Like you said, it's a long shot but economic sanctions and threats from the outside didn't work. We like to call it war on the cheap." He shook his head. "I can't believe I'm telling you this. I only found out recently. This is classified as classified can be. If it's discovered I told you I'll be court-martialed."

"No one will find out from us, Curtis, I can guarantee you that," said Sean.

"I appreciate that."

"So Sam Wingo?"

"Pentagon thinks he's dirty."

"He's not," said Sean.

"How do you know that?"

Sean looked at Michelle and said, "We've met him. He saved Michelle's life when some guys attacked us."

"What? Where? What guys?"

"Probably from the same group that shot Dana. But Wingo was set up."

"So you're working with him?"

"We're trying to, but, as you can imagine, he's not in a real trusting mood."

"And his son?"

"With the father. But please keep that to yourself."

"I have to even if I didn't want to. If I admit to knowing that, I'll have to tell them I met with you and then it's all over for me." He took another sip of coffee. "And the money?"

"Gone."

"Does he know who set him up?"

"He has some theories. And he's been doing some legwork to run down those theories."

"Does he think it's an inside job? You thought there was a leak at my office. But I checked, Sean, there wasn't. There couldn't have been."

"I'm starting to think the leak is coming from another place. What do you know about Heron Air Service or the Vista Trading Group in D.C.?"

"Nothing. Are they involved somehow? I can check into it for you."

"We have somebody doing that. How about Dan Marshall at the Pentagon? You know him?"

"A little. We've sat in on some meetings together. He heads up acquisitions. By all accounts, including my own, a straight-up guy. Please don't tell me he's mixed up in what's going on?"

"That's still an open question," said Michelle. "His career will take a hit with the missing money. And even more so with where that money went. At least that's what he told us."

"I'm surprised he opened up to you."

Michelle said, "We forgot to tell you, we have a brand-new BFF."

"Who?" asked Brown.

"President John Cole."

Brown gaped at her.

Sean asked, "How about Colonel Leon South? You know him?"

"No. Is he Army?"

"DIA."

"I don't have much to do with the military spooks."

Brown sat back, obviously out of ideas. "What else can I do?"

"Keep your eyes and ears open. I'm always available by phone. But I think Dana will be keeping you pretty busy now."

Brown smiled. "I hope so."

"And keep an eye on her, Curtis. Whoever's involved in this may come back to her at some point."

"They'll have to go through me to get to her."

"Oh, I have no doubt of that."

Outside the hospital there were two SUVs parked next to their vehicle. Two men and a woman in suits and shades stood in front of them.

Sean looked at Michelle. "Look familiar?"

"Yeah, they look just like we used to look."

"You know where we're going?" Sean asked.

"I know where we're going," answered Michelle.

59

Alan Grant and Dan Marshall left together from the offices of Vista Trading Group.

"Thanks for making the trip downtown," said Grant.

"No, thank you for getting me away from the Pentagon," replied Marshall.

"Rough times continuing?" asked Grant.

"Getting rougher every hour, it seems. Have you seen the recent news?"

"Feeding off that same blogger. Iran? Afghan poppies? Really?"

"That's what the media says. I can't comment on it, not even to you."

"Anything I can do to help?"

"Just take care of my daughter and the grandkids."

"Maybe this will blow over, Dan."

"Yeah, and maybe the sun won't come up tomorrow either."

They had a meal at a nearby restaurant and talked of things other than the disaster confronting Marshall. They said their goodbyes on the street.

"There's going to be some diplomatic blowback from Iran on this," observed Grant.

"No doubt. This will give Tehran an excellent opportunity to stick out its chest and start screaming at us. It'll also give fodder to the whack jobs wanting to do us harm. Well, back into the fire pit I go."

"Take care, Dan. Let's talk soon."

They shook hands, and Marshall walked off.

Grant watched him go for a bit and then headed to his car in the underground garage and drove off. The drive took longer because of construction shutting down lanes on Interstate 66. He finally got off at his exit and drove for a while longer. He had exchanged the hustle and bustle of the capital city for the bucolic peace and quiet of the rural countryside in less than 150 minutes.

He cleared the guard checkpoint and continued driving up the hill. He pulled his car to a stop in front of the old radio station and got out. He looked up admiringly at the transmission tower. It was now bedecked with satellite dishes hanging off it at precise angles. There was a hum of power emanating from there.

He walked the perimeter of the station and noted that the exterior construction was all done. He went inside and gazed around at all the activity. Portable generators droned away. Power tools popped and clacked. Walls were going up. The interior vault was nearing completion. Men were moving rapidly in a choreographed construction dance with the thoughts of their bonuses for early completion firmly in their minds.

Grant looked over the plans with his construction foreman and then walked the interior with the foreman, making sure that everything in the plans was actually being carried out in the execution phase. He made some modifications as they surveyed the construction and then walked back outside.

He stared at the foothills of the Blue Ridge Mountains in the distance. Directly east was Washington. He could see none of it from here, of course. Although he did watch as a commercial jetliner made its way toward Dulles Airport. He drew in a long breath and then exhaled.

Shortly they would be online and in the game. His hackers would be in their seats clicking away on their keyboards. They would be forcing themselves into where they needed to go like explorers used to do with their machetes when working through dense jungles or forests.

He had handpicked these people. He had their undivided loyalty because of money he had paid them for their services. They didn't care about geopolitics and had no horse in any international game of chicken. Grant did have horses in that game, but he was not a traitor to his country. After this was all over, America would pick itself back up and keep moving forward, of that he was certain.

I'm simply righting a wrong.

He put his hand in his coat pocket and pulled out his precious document, the one he had received from Milo Pratt. This document had cost Pratt his life. But without it Grant's plan would not have a chance. There were many things that could go wrong, but at least this one piece probably would not.

He could not say the same for other elements. Sam Wingo was still out there somewhere. As were Sean King and Michelle Maxwell.

Yet Grant had some ideas on how to take care of that.

He glanced down at the paper. But he couldn't take his eye off the endgame, the real prize. He just had to nail it and then he would wrap up this operation, leaving no trail behind. And he would continue on with his life. At least that was the plan.

He looked to the sky and angled his face in the right direction. His rented satellite was up there in its nice, safe orbit. The fragments his people had found on there were enough to get him where he needed to go.

He looked at a different spot in the sky. Another platform was circling the earth at that spot. So much crap up there. Debris and working platforms. The Space Station. Soon, even the paying public—well, at least the rich paying public—would get their own ride into space.

But for him it was just the two platforms, circling

the earth in precise patterns. They had nothing to do with each other. At least not yet. But soon, they would be inextricably intertwined, at least in his own mind. As for the rest of the world, they would never know of the "twining" of the two hunks of metal. All signs would be eradicated because of a particularly ingenious execution method he had conjured that would literally bounce any evidence all over the digital space and then explode it into a trillion pieces.

Humpty Dumpty sat on a wall...

He dropped his gaze back to the ground.

If only the problems down here could be so easily dealt with.

He checked his watch as he turned to look back at all the construction activity. He glanced at his phone as the message came in. The task was complete. What Grant had ordered done had been done.

That meant he had somewhere to go.

He had someone to see. If the person refused his request, that meant he had someone to kill.

Someone *else* to kill.

60

"Haven't been here in a while," said Sean as the SUV they were riding in pulled through the gates that were capable of stopping a runaway tank.

"Yeah, and the last time wasn't very pleasant," noted Michelle.

"Yeah, that I remember."

They were escorted into the West Wing of the White House.

"You never pulled presidential protection duty, did you?" said Sean.

"My career ended before I got there," she said. "One of my few regrets."

"It's not all it's cracked up to be."

"Liar," she said, flicking her elbow lightly into his side.

They were shown into the Roosevelt Room and told to wait.

As Sean wandered the room gazing at several famous paintings on the wall, Michelle said, "Recognize any of the protection detail?"

"Been gone too long. All my contemporaries are off double-dipping at other agencies. You?"

"The woman outside the hospital looked familiar, but I never knew her name."

"Jealous?"

"Yeah, why wouldn't I be?"

"You get to work with me full-time."

"Doesn't change my answer."

"Thanks a lot."

The door opened and the lead agent walked in, followed by President Cole and the rest of his detail. Sean and Michelle instantly rose to their feet and waited until Cole sat across from them before resuming their seats.

Cole stared across at them.

"Blogger?"

"Yes, sir," said Sean.

"What do you know about it?"

Sean didn't answer right away. He was trying to size up the question and the intent behind it. "George Carlton. Independent. Not tied to any news agency."

"You went to see him?"

"So your people have been following us?" asked Michelle.

"No. They had Carlton's place staked out. You showed up. One reason that prompted this meeting."

Sean studied Cole. The man seemed to have aged ten years since they had last seen him at Camp David.

He's thinking this is his Watergate, thought Sean.

"I'm surprised that the Feds hadn't already visited him."

"Free speech. Fourth Estate," responded Cole. "Tricky thing. I'm not looking to censure the media. I get accused of enough crap without fueling that fire. But you're not the government. You maybe can do things we can't do."

"And then share them with you?" asked Michelle.

Sean glanced nervously at her.

Cole said, "I thought we agreed that that's exactly what you would do? Work this thing together. Starting with finding Sam Wingo by using your connection with the son."

Sean glanced again at Michelle but said nothing.

Cole added, "And if you're covering for your buddies at Hoover, I already know the FBI lost the boy."

"We apparently don't have buddies at Hoover, sir," said Michelle.

Cole shrugged. "This ends right, it's no harm no foul, as far as I'm concerned."

"That's very generous of you, sir," said Sean, although the look on his face did not match his words.

Cole did not seem to notice, or if he did, he did not seem to care.

Sean said, "So Iran? That's what we were doing?"

"Not as simple as that, no."

"Money for weapons to fuel insurgents in Iran. With North Korea next on the drawing board?"

"Who told you that?"

"Private investigators, sir. We have to maintain confidences."

"Just as we are with you," added Michelle.

"So if it's not that simple, can you enlighten us?" asked Sean.

"Why?"

"We have to know the big picture if we're going to make a dent in this, Mr. President."

Cole stared at him for a few seconds before leaning back against the couch. "As was mentioned in that stupid blog, the euros were going to purchase poppies for heroin production. Not really, of course, the poppies would never be used for drug making. At least not by us."

"But you needed a way to launder the euros," speculated Sean. "Before they got to their final destination."

Cole nodded. "The purchased poppies would end up in a third party's hands."

"Let me guess," said Sean. "An international arms dealer?"

"And then the weapons obtained in return for the poppies would make their way to Iran."

"And what would the arms dealer do with the poppies?"

"I said the poppies would not be used by us for making heroin. I can't speak for anyone else."

"Permission to speak candidly, Mr. President?" said Sean.

"Considering you're no longer in the Secret Service, you can speak candidly whenever you want."

"Whoever came up with this plan needs to be fired, sir."

"It's idiotic," added Michelle. "With so many ways it could go wrong. And did."

Cole's face flushed but then his anger quickly subsided. "I accepted the person's resignation two days ago. Not that that matters. The buck stops with me. I authorized it. I own it."

The room was quiet for a few seconds.

Cole said, "The blogger?"

"Out of the game," said Sean. "He knew nothing about his source."

"You believe him?"

"I can read fear in a man's eyes," said Sean. "He was clueless. Just looking for the next big scoop."

"Do you have leads to the source?"

"Working on that right now."

"If it came by email my people could work back to the source, but—"

"That tricky balance thing," said Michelle. "Free speech, the Fourth Estate."

"Right. A scandal is one thing. Perhaps survivable. Covering up the scandal is unforgivable."

"Then let us do our thing, Mr. President," said Sean.

"Can you find Sam Wingo?"

"I believe so."

"Do you think he's involved in this?"

"We think he was set up."

"By whom?"

"Not clear yet. But we have some leads and we're running them down."

The president rose. "Then I should let you get on with it. I have an appointment outside the office."

Sean and Michelle stood.

"Thank you, sir," said Sean.

"Anything I can do, let me know. I can't drop everything I'm doing, but this is a priority for me."

"Understood."

Sean and Michelle followed at a distance as Cole and his protection detail, surrounding him in a hard diamond pattern, walked down the passageway.

They went outside where the motorcade was waiting.

The presidential limo, known as the Beast, sat there with its engine running. D.C. cops had already cleared all roads the motorcade would travel on. The Beast did not stop for red lights or anything else.

Before the door was closed Cole looked up at them. "I'm counting on you both."

Then the motorcade was off.

Michelle looked wistful as the long line of vehicles sped away.

"It *is* impressive," said Sean.

"Yeah," said Michelle.

"But it gets old fast."

She snorted. "Right."

"This way," said a Secret Service agent.

They were driven back to their vehicle outside the hospital.

As they climbed into the Land Cruiser, Sean, noting his partner's subdued look, said, "That was your past, Michelle. You can't live in the past."

"Sure you can, Sean. If you're not too thrilled with your future."

61

"His father-in-law?" said Sean.

He and Michelle were sitting across from Edgar Roy at his farmhouse west of D.C. The place looked asymmetrical in that the interior and furnishings were rustic, but there was gleaming computer equipment everywhere.

Edgar had texted them on their way back from the hospital that he had news to share. They had immediately headed to his farmhouse.

Edgar sat at his desk, which was actually a large rectangular section of sanded and painted three-inch-thick plywood painted black that rested on four sawhorses. Sitting on it were three giant computer screens set next to one another.

Edgar nodded but looked oddly chagrined. "Yes, Dan Marshall is Alan Grant's father-in-law."

"His father-in-law?" exclaimed Sean again.

"Yes. Alan Grant married Leslie Marshall nine years ago. They have three children. Dan Marshall is a widower. His wife, Maggie, died of cancer two years ago."

He paused. "I'm sorry that I didn't find this connection earlier. I can't believe I missed it."

"It's okay," said Michelle in a soothing tone. "It just shows you're human like the rest of us."

"Yeah," agreed Sean. "Only you have four times the brain power of the rest of us."

This seemed to perk up Edgar's spirits and he continued in a firmer voice. "Alan Grant served in the Army and was honorably discharged. He heads up Vista Trading Group. I could find no connection between Vista and Heron Air Service."

Sean said, "And Grant's parents? You said you'd found something there?"

"A suicide pact. They killed themselves back in 1988 when Grant was thirteen."

Michelle said, "Suicide pact? What was the reason?"

"Franklin Grant served as an assistant to the NSC back in the 1980s. He became embroiled in the Iran-Contra affair and I guess he couldn't live with it and neither could his wife. All very, very sad."

Michelle looked at Sean. "Okay, is that significant?"

"Maybe."

Sean looked at Edgar. "What else can you tell us about Franklin Grant's duties at the National Security Council?"

"Most of it, Sean, is still classified. But from what I could gather Franklin Grant might have been in the loop on the scheme but wasn't in favor of it. I dug a bit deeper than just the papers and other media reports at the time. It seems that Grant tried to speak out against his superiors but they used him as a scapegoat." Edgar looked down for a moment and said, "I know what that feels like."

"We know you do, Edgar," said Michelle. "So a scapegoat and leaving behind a young and suddenly orphaned Alan Grant."

Sean looked thoughtful. "I remember reading about Iran-Contra in the papers, of course, although I came to Washington after it was over. I don't remember the name Franklin Grant."

Edgar glanced at his screen. "There wasn't much to find. There were juicier parts out there. Reagan and all his high-ranking administration officials. Oliver North. North's secretary. Manuel Noriega. Franklin Grant seems to have simply gotten lost in the history shuffle."

"But he was the only one who paid the ultimate price, right?" Michelle asked.

Sean added, "From what I remember, even though a ton of documents ended up somehow being lost or withheld during the course of the investigation, quite a few administration officials were indicted and/or convicted, including the then-secretary of defense. But a bunch of the convictions were either overturned on appeal or vacated. And those that weren't were pardoned by the next administration. I think North got jail time but he was pardoned too, or something like that."

Edgar said, "He actually received a suspended sentence and probation and did some community service. But his conviction was later vacated and all charges were later dropped."

"So Franklin Grant was really the only one who bit the bullet," said Sean.

"Maybe despite trying to be a whistleblower he had a guilty conscience," reasoned Michelle.

"Or more integrity than some of the others involved," replied Sean. "But the bottom line is, this gives Alan Grant a great motive to have planned what is happening now."

"I'll confess I was too young to really follow Iran-Contra. What exactly happened?" asked Michelle.

Sean looked at Edgar. "I wasn't too young. But you've just done the research. You can probably explain it better than I can, Edgar. The details are a little fuzzy for me."

Edgar looked at him sadly. "Your massive brain cell loss."

Michelle coughed to cover her laugh.

Sean looked indignant. "Okay, listen up, I have a *normal* brain cell loss for someone…for someone of my age."

"There are medications that can help," offered Edgar sincerely. "And I know some specialists in the field."

Michelle had to stifle another laugh.

"Iran-Contra, okay? Can we get to it?" said Sean expectantly. "Because we're wasting time focusing on my brain shrinkage."

Edgar sat back. "It sounds complicated, but it's actually very simple. It started out as a way to free American hostages held by a radical group with ties to Iran. The original scheme was for Israel to ship weapons to Iran and then the U.S. would resupply Israel and receive payment from them. Then it devolved into a straight arms-for-hostages scheme in which weapons would be sold to Iran, something that was banned under U.S. law, and the hostages would be released in return for those sales. Then the plan was later modified so that an intermediary in Iran was used to sell the weapons and a portion of the resulting proceeds was used to funnel money to the Contras in Nicaragua. This was done so that Manuel Noriega and his Panamanian Defense Forces could help overthrow the Sandinista leadership, which was no friend of ours. But additional support to the Contras by American intelligence agencies had been prohibited by an act of Congress. Thus, the reason for the clandestine plan to get around that prohibition while at the same time trying to gain release of the hostages from the Iranian forces through the parallel arms sales."

"And you call that *simple*?" exclaimed Michelle.

"Well, yes," said Edgar matter-of-factly.

"As simple as politicians seem to be able to make anything," noted Sean. "And Noriega later turned out not to be such a good friend."

Edgar nodded. "Not unusual. After all, we liked Saddam Hussein until we didn't like Saddam Hussein."

"Remind me never to run for public office," said Michelle.

"Or become a dictator," amended Sean.

Sean leaned back in his chair and looked at Michelle. "Iran-Contra back in the 1980s. And now George Carlton's blogger source has alleged that the U.S. has attempted to funnel money through sales of Afghan poppies to anti-Iranian forces to buy weapons in an effort to overthrow the government there. It's not an exact parallel."

"But maybe the best he could do under the circumstances," said Michelle. "He didn't initiate the scheme, Sean. Maybe he just found out about it and that was the catalyst for him to do what he's doing."

"Are we talking about Alan Grant?" asked Edgar.

Sean nodded. "He's in cahoots with someone with connections to Heron Air Service. Sam Wingo was following that guy. He might have led him to Grant for all we know."

Edgar said, "But I could find no connection between Vista and Heron."

"There might be no discoverable connection. Or they might have covered their tracks really well. They might even have been the air service that was used to get the cash out of Afghanistan. Wingo said men flashing CIA creds took the shipment from him."

Michelle said, "But then the cash probably didn't end up in Iran."

"No. I think it might have ended up back here."

Michelle said, "Look, maybe this is just a very complicated robbery. Grant is Marshall's son-in-law. Marshall knew about the euros. Maybe he let it slip to Grant and Grant plans the heist and nabs the cash."

Sean shook his head. "I would've thought that but for the history of the parents. Pretty strong revenge motive there. I don't think it's as simple as a billion euros. If it was a simple robbery, why give George Carlton all that ammo for his blog? No, he's discrediting Cole and his administration. And Grant doesn't need the money, does he, Edgar?"

"His business appears to be very successful with several significant clients in the government sector. His home is worth nearly a million dollars, and the mortgage was paid off three years ago. His credit history is excellent and he has no outstanding judgments or pending lawsuits against him. I even hacked into his tax returns; his income places him in the top tier of earners."

"You hacked into his tax records?" said Michelle. "Isn't that illegal?"

"Not really. I have pretty much carte blanche to go where I need to go. National security is a very large hall pass. And I just sort of extended that privilege to the work I was doing for you," he added, a bit lamely.

Sean slipped the flash drive from his pocket. "And now we have this."

"What's on it?" asked Edgar eagerly as he took it from Sean and popped it into his computer's USB slot.

"The blogger's source's emails. There's the usual IP trail on there. We're hoping you can tell us where it came from. I doubt the sender made it easy, but if at all possible we need for you to track it back."

Edgar pounded his keys at speed as his eyes darted over the screen. "Usual protocols didn't work."

"How do you know that?" asked Michelle.

"Because I just employed them."

Sean and Michelle stared at each other. In a low voice Sean said, "I think he's actually growing more brain cells every day, not losing them. Maybe he's taking some of mine by like osmosis or something."

"Do you even know what osmosis is?" she hissed back.

"I did back in high school." In a louder voice he said, "If you figure it out, let us know ASAP."

Sean and Michelle got up and left.

"Why do I feel so stupid every time I'm around him?" said Sean.

"Because by comparison, we are."

She stopped walking and Sean bumped into her.

"What the hell? he exclaimed. "Michelle, are you ..."

He stopped talking when he saw what she was looking at.

Sam Wingo stared back at them.

62

"You're a hard man to find," said Sean.

"Well, here I am," said Wingo. He took a step forward.

"Yes, here you are," said Sean. "And how did you come to be here?"

"I followed you. But no one else did in case you were worried about that."

"Then you're really good because we didn't see you," said Sean. "Where did you pick us up?"

"At the hospital. Tyler told me about your friend. I gave a stakeout a shot and you two popped into it. Was that the Secret Service dropping you off?"

"The very same," said Sean.

"Where were you?"

"Classified."

Michelle looked over Wingo's shoulder. "Where's Tyler?"

"In a safe place. I needed to make sure of things before I brought him out."

Sean said, "You mean you needed to make sure of us. Are you?"

"I need help. And I don't say that lightly. And Tyler thinks you're okay. So I think you're okay."

"What if I said the jury is still out for us on whether we can trust you?" noted Sean.

"I guess I could understand that."

"We saw you following the guy on the airport surveillance feed," said Michelle. "Heron Air Service. Which led you to the Vista Trading Group?"

Sean glanced nervously around. "I'm feeling a little exposed here. Can we move to other surroundings, preferably with four walls and a door that locks?"

Michelle pulled out her keys and smiled at Wingo. "Hope you can keep up."

They drove back to the motel where Sean and Michelle were staying and went inside Sean's room. Sean sat in a chair, Michelle perched on the bed, and Wingo stood next to the door.

Sean said, "We're listening."

"You know a lot of it already."

"But not the most interesting parts certainly," replied Michelle.

"I saw the news. The Iran thing."

"Did you know that was part of the mission?" asked Sean.

Wingo nodded.

"And how did you feel about that?" asked Michelle.

"It wasn't my job to feel anything about it. I'm a

soldier. I volunteered for a mission. My only concern was to carry it out successfully."

"Which you didn't," Sean pointed out.

"Trust me, that one I get," snapped Wingo.

"Vista?" began Sean.

"Don't know much about it. Tyler Googled it but there wasn't anything there."

"But some connection to Heron Air Service presumably," said Michelle.

Wingo nodded. "Like you said, I followed a guy from Heron to Vista. That was the connection."

"And the guy from Heron was of interest why?"

"He was with the people who jumped me in Afghanistan. I figured having a private air charter was a good way to move money around, particularly over two tons' worth of it. I also had a tip from a friend overseas that Heron was involved. That's what put me on to them in the first place."

Sean said, "Alan Grant heads up Vista Trading Group. You know him?"

"No. What's his interest in all this?"

Michelle answered, "It might be quite personal, actually, going back several decades."

Wingo looked confused.

"Long story," said Sean. "But Grant might have some personal vendetta, and he might be using the billion euros to carry it out."

"Okay," said Wingo slowly. "But do you have any proof?"

"Not a shred," said Michelle.

"Do you know what his overall goal might be?" asked Wingo.

"Not a clue," said Sean. "But if it required stealing a billion euros and publicly exposing the United States in a way that might lead to a war with Iran or fresh terror attacks that could kill a lot of people, then I don't think it's something to be taken too lightly."

"So how do we stop it?" asked Wingo. "Whatever it is?"

"If Grant or a colleague of his was the source for the blogs about the missing money and the overthrow of the Iranian government, then that's something we can take to the authorities. Then they can bring the hammer down on Grant."

"How did he even know about the euros?"

"We just found out his father-in-law is Dan Marshall."

"Assistant Secretary Marshall?" exclaimed Wingo.

"One and the same."

"He was in the loop. That I know for a fact. You think he's working with Grant?"

"I don't know," replied Sean.

Wingo said, "So what do we do in the meantime? Just sit around and wait for something to happen?"

Michelle answered. "Personally, I don't like to wait."

"She's more of a kick-ass-and-take-responsibility-later sort of gal," elaborated Sean, drawing a scathing look from his partner.

Wingo eyed Michelle with admiration. "I kind of like that in a person."

She smiled. "And thanks for saving my butt back at our first meeting. Never saw the guy in the tree."

"You had your hands full," said Wingo. "And the way I see it you saved my ass too."

"We can pat each other on the back later," said Sean. "I'm thinking of a plan to flush Grant out and see if he's up to what I think he is."

Wingo's phone buzzed.

"It's from Tyler."

He looked down at the message. "Oh, shit."

"What is it?" asked Sean.

Wingo didn't answer. He sent a text back and then punched in a number. "Come on, come on, answer the damn phone."

It went to voice mail. Wingo said, "You stick tight and we'll be on our way. Do not do anything or go anywhere, okay? Do you hear me? Do not go anywhere."

He put his phone away and looked up.

"What is it?" asked Sean.

"Kathy Burnett called him. She said she needed to see him right away at Tysons mall."

"Why?" asked Michelle.

"She said the CIA has been to see her. And they want me to come in and talk to them."

"How did they key on Kathy?" asked Michelle.

"I don't know."

"And it's probably not the CIA," said Sean.

"No, it's probably not."

"But you said she called him and presumably talked to him. Did she sound coerced? Scared?"

"He didn't say in the text."

"You think he's already headed out to meet her?" asked Sean.

Wingo calmed and stared over at Sean. "Yeah, I'm really afraid he has." He looked down at the text. "Damn, it didn't go through. It's still sending. Useless piece of crap."

Michelle said, "We've found the area around here bad for electronic signals too."

"But you left a voice message," said Sean.

"Tyler never turns his ringer on. He may not know I've even called."

He slammed his fist against the wall. "Why the hell don't kids call their parents anymore? Why don't they answer their phones? Why all this crazy texting shit?"

"Did he say where at Tysons mall?" Michelle asked in a calming voice.

"Starbucks near the Barnes and Noble bookstore."

"Let's go."

The three of them raced out of the room.

63

Earlier that day Kathy Burnett had stepped out of her house and headed down the street. She had a tennis racket under her arm and a can of balls in her hand. She was planning to hit the balls against the wall in the park three blocks down.

And she wanted to think about Tyler. He had not been at school, and she wondered why. She had gone by his house but there had been no one there, although the Wingos' truck had been in the driveway.

All the Wingos, it seemed, had disappeared.

She turned the corner and reached a stretch of trees that carried over to the next block. She was so focused she never heard the van pull up next to her, and didn't hear the door slide open.

The next instant she was off her feet, a hand holding a moistened cloth around her face. She took a deep breath and then fainted. The van door closed and the vehicle drove off. Kathy's racket and can of balls were all that was left on the sidewalk.

The van drove for well over an hour, winding through back roads and keeping well away from populated areas. Its destination was the little cabin in the woods where nearby Jean Shepherd was buried. The cabin was dark, but there was a car parked outside it.

The van slowed to a stop and a man climbed out, opened the sliding door, lifted out the still-unconscious Kathy, and carried her into the cabin.

She was tied to a chair and blindfolded. Her mouth was not taped shut. They wanted her to talk. And there was no one nearby who would care about her screaming.

The van driver stepped back and put his shoulder against the door into the cabin. Alan Grant drew up a chair and placed it about a foot away from where Kathy sat slumped in her seat. He studied her features, prepared his line of questioning. He was not desperate in his search to find Sam Wingo, at least not yet. But he was running out of time and he hoped Kathy Burnett could provide him a shortcut.

He waited patiently until she came around. Her head flopped from side to side as she regained her senses, and then she held her head up and looked around. Obviously, all she could see was the inside of the cloth covering her face.

Grant touched her on the arm, which made her jump and scream.

He had done that deliberately. He needed her to have a measure of calm, but he also wanted her to feel scared, intimidated, and desperate.

"Who are you?" Kathy said in a quavering voice.

"Someone who just wants to talk, Kathy."

"Please…please don't hurt me."

"No one is going to hurt you, Kathy. I just want to talk. And I need you to do something for me."

"What?"

"Tyler Wingo. He's your friend, isn't he?"

She nodded, her body shaking so badly the legs of the chair were shifting slightly.

"Well, I want to help him."

"No, you don't. Why would you kidnap me and tie me up if you want to help him?"

Grant smiled. She was showing some spirit now. But the fear would return. It always did. "It's complicated, Kathy. Very complicated. These things are. You know what Sam Wingo is accused of doing?"

"I don't believe it," she said heatedly. "He's a good man. He would never steal that money. He was a sol-dier."

"I actually believe you, Kathy. I don't think he did it either. But others do. And those others can harm him and Tyler. I'm here to prevent that."

"No you're not!" she snapped. "You want to hurt them."

"I'm going to take your blindfold off and show you something, okay?"

Grant nodded to the other man, who turned and left the room. Grant moved behind Kathy.

"Do not turn your head around, Kathy. Stare straight

ahead. What you'll see hopefully will convince you of my good intentions."

He held something out in front of her and with his other hand removed the blindfold. Kathy blinked her eyes rapidly and then focused on what was in front of her.

"You're with the CIA?" she exclaimed breathlessly as she stared at the cred pack held in front of her.

"Yes. Undercover, which is why I can't let you see my face. What Sam Wingo is involved in is very serious. We believe he was set up, but we have no proof. Wingo is not going to trust anyone, including us. But we have to communicate with him somehow. Make him come in and work with us."

"But why do you need me to do that?"

"We tried to reach out to him, but like I said, he's not trusting anyone. I think he'll trust you, Kathy."

"What do you want me to do?"

"Can you contact Tyler and let him know that you want to meet with him? You pick the place. Make it very public so you'll both feel safe."

"But what do you want me to tell him?"

"That his father needs to contact us. That he needs to come into Langley. You know about Langley, right?"

"It's your headquarters."

"That's right, Kathy. There are people there who care about what happens to Sam Wingo. They want to make this right. But the longer he's out there, the worse it's going to get. You can see that, right?"

She slowly nodded, still staring at the CIA badge he kept holding in front of her. This was a very deliberate action by Grant. He needed her to believe he really was with the CIA and a "good guy."

"So you'll do it? You'll call him?"

"I guess I can. But I can't guarantee that he'll meet with me."

"I know that. But I think he will. I think he likes you and trusts you. I know he wants the best for his father, and so do we. And his father will trust Tyler. I'm sure of it."

Grant held up her phone, which had been taken from her previously.

"I'm going to hit Tyler's number."

"I could just text him."

"I think he needs to hear your voice. If you text him he can't be sure it's from you."

"Oh, right. I forgot about that. But where should we meet?"

"How about Tysons mall? There's a Starbucks there, right? I know it's not that close to where you both live, but it's a central place with lots of people."

"Yeah, we've actually gone there sometimes."

"We'll take you to the mall and drop you there. You meet with him. Deliver the message. And then you go home. And we'll take it from there. How's that sound?"

"That sounds really good," she said, relief in her voice.

Grant smiled. "I thought it would. And your country really appreciates your help."

He hit the key for Tyler's speed dial.

He had to call the number twice before Tyler picked up.

"Kathy?"

She delivered the message as calmly as possible.

"I'll meet you there," said Tyler. He clicked off.

Kathy looked at Grant.

"You did the right thing," he said. *For me.*

64

Tyler hurried into the mall and looked around. Hearing from Kathy had floored him. The CIA wanted to talk to his dad! He could hardly believe it. Kathy had said they thought he'd been set up. If he could get to the CIA, maybe he had a good shot at getting all this sorted out.

The Starbucks was up ahead. He looked cautiously around again. He trusted Kathy completely, but with all the crazy things happening he knew he needed to be careful. The mall was pretty full, though, and thus he felt safe.

He felt the hand on his arm and whirled around. He was staring up at a police officer.

"Tyler Wingo?" the man said.

Tyler stammered, "Yu–yes?"

"You need to come with me, son."

"Why?"

Another man in a suit appeared behind him. He held out his ID card.

"FBI. Special Agent Martin. You need to come with

us, Mr. Wingo. Down to the WFO in D.C. for questioning."

"What about?"

The man looked at him incredulously. "About your father, Mr. Wingo. What else would it be? You running a drug ring or something?"

"No. But I'm meeting with someone at Starbucks."

"We know all about Ms. Burnett. We have already collected her. She's in big trouble, Mr. Wingo. Do you know what accessory after the fact means?"

Tyler looked like he might throw up. "N-no. Is it bad?"

"It could be very bad, depending on how this turns out. Now let's go."

They escorted Tyler out of the mall and the three climbed into a black SUV with tinted windows. It immediately drove off.

Tyler's phone vibrated in his pocket. His father's text had finally come through. He did not have a chance to answer it. The text sat there unanswered, as did the message his father had left on Tyler's voice mail.

Thirty minutes later Sean, Michelle, and Wingo rushed into the mall.

Michelle held up a warning hand. "Wait. Let's do this right. They could have used Tyler to flush you, Sam, which means they could be waiting to ambush us."

"In a crowded mall?" said Wingo.

Sean said, "They've already done it once to us. These guys don't seem to care where they hit you or who gets hurt in the process."

They spread out and advanced on the Starbucks that Tyler had mentioned in his text. When they arrived it only took a few seconds to see that neither teenager was there.

Wingo said, "They've already got them."

"We don't know that for sure," said Michelle.

"The hell we don't. They've got my kid. Shit!" He slumped against a wall and put a hand over his face.

Sean put a hand on Wingo's shoulder. "We'll get him back, Sam. We just need to keep calm and think of a way."

"I can't think straight. Not with Tyler..."

"Which is exactly what they want to happen," observed Michelle.

"Let's continue this discussion outside," advised Sean.

They returned to Michelle's truck and climbed inside.

Sean was in the passenger seat and Wingo in the rear. He turned to look at Wingo.

"Assuming they have Tyler, they'll contact you to make a deal."

"Right, me for Tyler."

"That's what they'll offer."

"And that's what we'll give them. Tyler goes free. There's no debating that. And Kathy too if they have her."

"They may not want that. They might want you both."

"Tyler knows nothing about any of this."

"They can't be sure of that. They might be afraid you told him something."

"Look, I'm just the scapegoat. They're planning to dump this whole thing in my lap."

Sean said, "But they can't count on that working perfectly. Tyler is insurance."

Michelle said, "What did you see over there in Afghanistan?"

"A bunch of guys. They flashed CIA creds. The leader's name was Tim Simons. At least that was on his ID. They said the plan had changed. That I was to turn over the cargo to them."

"How did you get away?"

"The truck was wired with explosives, and I had the detonator set with the button depressed. If they shot me, my finger would release."

"And boom," said Sean. "Idiot switch."

Wingo nodded.

"So you could recognize him? This Simons guy?" asked Michelle.

"Yeah. But I also already told that to my superior."

"Colonel Leon South?" said Sean.

"Right."

"What else?"

"I had a contact over there who helped get me out of the Middle East and back here. He told me that there might be a connection with the missing cash and Heron Air Service."

"Which was why you were staking out the place at Dulles," noted Michelle.

"That's right. That's when I saw one of the guys who jumped me in Afghanistan come out of the Heron Air Service building." Wingo slapped his thigh. "I forgot."

"Forgot what?" asked Michelle.

"When I was tailing the guy from Heron, he drove into D.C. and went into the offices of the Vista Trading Group, like I said. When he left there I followed him. But then I picked up a tail and had to shake it. Only did so by the skin of my teeth."

"So they know you're on to them. That you know of the connection to Vista and Heron. That alone was enough to get you on their hit list, Sam," concluded Sean.

"I guess so," said Wingo glumly.

Sean looked at Michelle. "Do we call in the Feds on this? If the kids have been kidnapped?"

"No! If you do that they'll just kill them, Sean," said Wingo. "This is not a simple kidnapping. The stakes are a lot higher. These guys are not concerned with ransom money. They want me. Like you said, collateral damage means nothing to them."

"Then the question becomes what do we do when they make their demand," said Sean.

"We have to make sure that when I give myself up, Tyler and Kathy get out of there safely," said Wingo.

"Easier said than done," observed Michelle.

"But there are ways," said Sean. "And the ideal plan would be to walk away with all three of you safe."

"When do you think they'll call?" asked Wingo.

"Not right away. They'll want to make you sweat. Think about the consequences of noncompliance."

"But that will give us some time to prepare," noted Michelle.

"Yes it will," said Sean. "And we need to put that time to good use."

"Are you guys expert with kidnapping situations?" asked Wingo.

Sean and Michelle exchanged a glance. "Suffice it to say, this won't be our first time," said Sean.

Michelle put her truck in gear and they drove off.

65

"Whoever you are, you're not with the FBI!" yelled Tyler.

Tyler and Kathy sat bound and blindfolded in chairs.

Alan Grant sat across from them. "It's more complicated than that."

"You're bad guys," said Tyler angrily. "You set up my dad."

"But he's back now. He was with you. That's good news, right?"

"You're trying to kill him."

"You're wrong."

"That's bullcrap."

Grant glanced up at one of his men who had hovered in the background but now stepped forward and gripped Tyler's shoulder so hard he gasped in pain.

"Enough," said Grant simply and the man let go.

Grant looked back at Tyler.

"Why do you think we want to harm your father?"

"Because you've already tried to kill him."

"How do you know that was us?"

"I just know. Who else could it be?"

"Maybe his own government. And you're right, we're not with the government."

"Then who are you?"

This question came from Kathy, who had not spoken before.

Grant focused on her. "Ah, now that's a good question. Who are we? Who do you think we are if we're not with your government?"

"Spies, terrorists," exclaimed Tyler. "Which makes you bad guys."

"Sometimes spies are on the right side," said Grant. "Even spies who have to kidnap children because there is no other way to proceed."

"Bullcrap," Tyler said again.

"You're as stubborn as your father."

"You don't know my dad."

"On the contrary, I know him very well. And the woman who was pretending to be your stepmother."

"Pretending?" said Kathy.

"She's missing," said Tyler.

"I know she is. Do you have any idea where she went?"

"No. Do you?"

"You're very brave, Tyler, even though I know you're very scared." Grant reached over and gently gripped Tyler's arm. The teenager flinched.

"I have no idea how this will turn out, Tyler, but I do know that you will see your father at some point. I can guarantee you that."

"Why?"

"Like I said, I need to speak to him. And once that is over, you and he can be reunited."

"Just like that?" scoffed Tyler.

"A call will be made. He will ask to talk to you."

"Then I'll tell him to keep very far away."

"Are you sure of that?"

"I'm not afraid of you."

Grant let go of Tyler, placed his hand on Kathy's head, and squeezed slightly. "But your friend is, Tyler. Remember, you need to think of your friend here."

All of Tyler's courage seemed to drain away at this remark.

Grant let go of Kathy, turned, and left the room. The other man followed, locking the door behind him.

When he heard the door close behind the footsteps, Tyler said, "I'm really sorry, Kathy. I never meant for you to get involved in all this."

Kathy fought back tears but managed to say, "It's okay, Tyler. You had nothing to do with this." A sob escaped her lips and Tyler tried to reach out to her, but his bindings held him back.

"We have to get out of here because I know they're never going to let us go."

"How?" asked Kathy.

"We have to think of a way. Both our parents are in the military. They taught us stuff. At least I know my dad did me. How about your mom?"

"She made me take Tae Kwon Do. And I know how

to survive in the woods with no food and water. But that doesn't help us right now."

They listened as a car started up and drove off.

Tyler said, "I can sense you're right next to me. If I lean my head toward you, do you think you can use your teeth to get my blindfold off?"

"I can try."

It took five minutes but Kathy finally clamped her teeth onto the knot behind Tyler's head and worked away at it.

"I can feel it coming loose," she said at last.

Another minute passed and then the cloth slipped off Tyler's face and fell into his lap.

He blinked and looked at her. "Great job," he said quietly. He looked around the room. It was small, and the only pieces of furniture were the two chairs in which they sat. There was a window, but it was blacked out.

"Okay, I'm going to get your blindfold off. Lean your head toward me. It'll be easier now that I can see."

In less than a minute Kathy's cloth dropped away.

They sat there staring at each other, visibly heartened by this small victory.

"Now we have to get these bindings off," said Tyler.

"How about if we sit back-to-back? I can work on yours. I have really strong fingers."

"All right, but we have to take it slow. They might hear the chairs scraping the floor."

They managed to turn their chairs around as quietly as possible until they were back-to-back. Tyler could feel her fingers clenching and unclenching around the rope holding him.

"They're tight," she said, "but I feel them giving a bit."

It took about thirty minutes, and Tyler could hear Kathy breathing hard with the effort. But then his hands were free. He undid the rope around his feet and then quickly freed her.

"Now what?" she said in a whisper.

Tyler pointed at the window. "If we can get out there, we can make a run for it."

"What if they have someone posted outside?"

Tyler slid up his baggy pant leg. Strapped to his calf was a cylinder.

"Pepper spray. My dad. He's kind of paranoid."

They eased across to the window, taking their time because the floorboards were old and had a tendency to squeak.

Tyler slipped aside the black cloth covering the window and peered out.

"It's dark outside," he whispered. "That's good for us."

He examined the window lock. It was a simple one. He had the window up in another minute, taking care to slide it slowly in case it made any noise.

He passed through the open window first and then helped Kathy.

They stopped to look around. A black SUV was parked in the front. It was the same one Tyler had climbed into at the mall. They had driven away and then a cloth had been placed over his face and he had quickly fallen unconscious.

"Looks like we're in the woods," he said quietly to Kathy. She nodded, shivered, and said, "Which way?"

"Hey!"

They turned and saw a man standing on the porch.

"Run, Kathy," yelled Tyler.

She turned and raced away. The man hoofed it after her. Tyler stepped in front of the man and blasted him in the eyes with the pepper spray. The man screamed, staggered, collided with Tyler, and they both went down in a tangle of arms and legs. Tyler punched and kicked at the blinded man until he saw something. Kathy was not running anymore.

A man shrouded in the darkness had placed a gun against her head.

Tyler instantly stopped struggling.

"Big mistake, Tyler, an unforgivable mistake," said Alan Grant.

"Please, don't hurt her," Tyler yelled, tears flooding his eyes.

The gun fired.

66

"It's been twenty-four hours!" exclaimed Sam Wingo.

"Yes it has," replied Sean calmly.

They were at the motel where they had stayed the night, waiting for the phone to ring or a text to come from Tyler.

Michelle was leaning against the wall of the motel room. "And we told you they would do this to string you out, to make your nerves get the best of you."

"And we know Kathy is with them," added Sean. "The news story confirmed that she's missing."

Wingo looked miserable. "I know her parents. Her mom's in the Air Force. All that was left…was a tennis racket and a can of balls on the sidewalk."

"No one saw or heard anything," said Michelle. "Which tells us these guys are pros."

"But the good news is that although they're aware we met, they don't know that we've officially hooked up," said Sean. "We're going to provide backup that they might not anticipate."

"We'll have little time to prep," added Michelle.

"They'll call and expect us to be there shortly thereafter."

"How do we get back on the offensive?" asked Wingo. "I don't like reacting to others, particularly when they have my son."

"We've still got prep work to do," said Sean.

"Prep work based on what?" asked Wingo.

"On being Secret Service agents," replied Michelle.

"I'm Special Forces. If it comes to it, we're used to close-quarter combat a lot more than you guys."

Michelle looked at him. "But you liked all the guys you fought with?"

"Of course. You go in willing to die for the guy next to you."

"Did you ever have to eat a bullet for someone you didn't like?" asked Sean.

"No," said Wingo.

"It kind of sucks," added Michelle. "But it's in the job description for the Secret Service."

"And it gives you perspective," amended Sean.

"Such as?" asked Wingo.

"Such as never let the other guys see what you're looking at. It's why we all wore reflective shades. Now let's get to work."

Grant was at the radio station.

The construction work was done. Those workers were now gone and had been replaced with another set. These were not muscular young men. They didn't carry guns. They did not act macho. Their weapon was their brain. Their bullet was their keyboard. They were cyber warriors.

He made his way around the interior of the old building with the new guts that had transformed it into a state-of-the-art tech center with only one goal.

Focused mayhem.

That meant one act that would bring cataclysmic events across the globe. Grant didn't really care about that part of the equation. Others could reap the benefits from that. He was just righting a wrong. It was that simple. He was not going to let his focus waver from that.

A reader outside the vault scanned his retina and he entered the space, the only one with access here. He sat in front of a bank of computers and studied each of them. Progress was being made. His bird in the sky was searching for what it needed. It was like a private detective looking for a thread that would provide him a solid lead, which would coalesce into a suspect that could end in an arrest and a conviction.

Only the elements were bunches of ones and zeros instead of flesh and blood, and his sleuthing was confined to wireless data zipping across the ether. The system they were trying to crack had more than thirty million lines of code. There were many ways inside, but once inside the malware to be planted had to remain hidden. And that limited the possible ports of entry.

Grant continued to watch the unique confrontation

taking place on the computer screen. It was a delicate ballet of choreographed movements, feints, probes, counterattacks, and more sparring. It was actually far more intriguing than any clash on the ground involving guns and bombs. They were brutally efficient killing devices. But they lacked the intellectual purity, the high level of sophistication needed to carry off something like this.

With any other target Grant would have been successful by now. But his target wasn't just any target. It was heavily protected. It was known to have threats against it. It was one of the most famous targets in the world, in fact. And it had never been seriously threatened. But that didn't make it invulnerable. That just made it challenging, and Grant loved a challenge. Even the best security sometimes grew lax as year after year passed and no successful attack was ever launched against it. That was why he had a chance to do what no one else had ever done before.

And he noted, with a degree of confidence, that the barriers to entry depicted on the screen were falling one by one. In fact, given this burn rate, he would be through in a shorter period of time than he thought.

He drew out the itinerary for which he had killed Milo Pratt. He ran his eye down the column and finally settled on one that appeared to be in the window of possibilities. He sat back in his chair and dreamed what had for so long seemed the impossible dream.

Revenge. And justice. Two of the most potent desires in the world. They were not mutually exclusive. In fact, thought Grant, they went hand in hand extremely well. His father had killed himself over a scandal |not of his making. Now the current president was attempting a similar and equally misguided maneuver on the world's geopolitical stage. Well, this time the administration would pay the price. Grant's learning of the plan had been the prime reason behind the timing of his operation. It had come none too soon. The grief over his parents' deaths was becoming unbearable.

Well, it was finally about to end.

67

"Where do we do the exchange?" said Wingo.

The call had come at last, the next night when the rain was howling outside and the temperature had plummeted as the storm system struck the region.

The filtered voice was mechanical, but the words it spoke were stunning. "There will be no exchange."

Sean and Michelle, who were listening in because Wingo was using the speakerphone feature on his cell, exchanged a sharp glance.

"What the hell are you talking about?" snapped Wingo. "I'm willing to come in if you let my son go."

"That may have been your thinking, but it isn't ours."

"What then?" barked Wingo.

"Keep calm, Wingo. All you have to do is stand down. You do nothing. If you do that, you will see your son alive. If not, he's dead."

Wingo covered his face with his hands and took a deep breath. Michelle put a supportive hand on his shoulder.

"How do I know I can trust you?" said Wingo.

"How do we know we can trust you?"

"Even if I stand down, how will you know I am?"

"We'll know, Wingo. We have assets in place. You talk to anyone, go anywhere, tell the FBI about your son, give anyone something that will help them on this, we'll know. And then your son is no more. That is a guarantee."

Sean pointed to the phone and then his ear. He mouthed the name, "Tyler."

Wingo said, "I want to talk to my son. Right now. Or no deal."

A few moments passed, and then Tyler's voice came on the line.

"D–dad?"

"Tyler, are you all right?"

"I'm really scared. These people—"

There were sounds of a scuffle and Tyler's voice broke off.

"Tyler? Tyler!" yelled Wingo into the phone.

The mechanical voice came back on. "Stand down, Wingo. Then you get him back."

"What about Kathy Burnett?"

"Just stand down. And you get your *son* back."

The line went dead.

Wingo slowly sat up.

Sean rubbed his jaw and said, "Okay, that was an unexpected development."

Michelle was eyeing Wingo. "We're going to get him back, Sam."

"You have no way of knowing that," said Wingo bitterly. "And it sounds like Kathy is dead."

Michelle looked at Sean but said nothing. It did sound like Kathy Burnett was dead.

Wingo looked up. "So there's nothing more to do. Except wait and hope to God they keep their word."

"That's you, not us, Sam," said Sean. "We have to keep working this thing."

"But it might put Tyler in danger."

"He's already in danger," said Michelle. "And let's be brutally honest here. I don't see them voluntarily letting him go whether you stand down or not, do you?"

Wingo stared at her, the lines in his forehead hardening for a moment and then going lax. "No, I don't."

"Our best chance to get Tyler and Kathy back is to find them."

"How?" barked Wingo. "You have nothing to go on."

Sean sat down next to him. "I know you're under incredible stress. I've never been a dad so I can't possibly know what you're really feeling. But I'm asking you to trust us, Sam. We know what we're doing. And we will do our best to get them both back. Alive."

Michelle knelt on Wingo's other side and said, "The only reason I got into this case was because of Tyler. I could feel something was off with him. I knew how much he missed you, Sam. How much he didn't want you to be gone. I will do anything, risk my life even, to get him back to you."

Wingo slowly nodded. "Okay. Okay, I do trust you. Please, just get them back safe."

They left Wingo in the motel room and climbed into Michelle's Land Cruiser.

"We promised the man a lot," said Sean. "And now we need to deliver on that promise."

"What about Kathy?"

"We said both of them. That means what it means."

"But if she's dead?"

"We can only try, Michelle. That's all we can ever do."

"Is Edgar our next stop? If he's been able to track the IP address of Carlton's source?"

"If he had he would've contacted us. It won't do us any good looking over his shoulder. Geniuses work best alone."

"What then?"

"We have a lead we haven't followed up yet."

"And what would that be?"

"Heron Air Service's connection to Vista Trading Group."

"Edgar couldn't find any dirt."

"He was just looking at the pixels. We have to get in the dirt to find dirt. The way investigators used to do it."

"How? We were worried that someone there would recognize us."

"We do it by stealth."

"Again, what's the plan?"

"Conditions on the ground will dictate the plan."

"Translation—you haven't thought of a plan yet and you're buying time until you do."

He scowled. "Feel free to jump in with one anytime you want."

She sighed and looked out the window. "We can't screw this up, Sean. There's too much at stake."

"There's always a lot at stake."

"I meant with the kids."

"We've been down that road before too. And we didn't let them die. We found them and brought them home safely."

"I know. I just hope we can do it this time."

A few seconds passed and then Sean said, "Actually, I think we can."

She glanced sharply at him. "You just thought of a plan, didn't you?"

"I just thought of a plan."

68

Sean drove while Michelle kept an eye out.

"Nice neighborhood," he said as they passed by some large homes with expensive landscaping. He looked at a few of the homes. "Very nice."

"Yeah, if you go in for that sort of thing," replied Michelle.

"What, no heaps of trash?"

"You're a riot."

They left that neighborhood and entered another.

"It's coming up on the left," noted Michelle. "Third one down."

Sean eased his car to a stop at the curb behind a pickup truck and killed the engine and the lights. Michelle took out a pair of night-vision binoculars and pointed them across the street.

"So Leon South's house?" she said. "And what do you hope to find here?"

"Hopefully, a clue that will take us where we need to go."

"I thought our leak was Dan Marshall, not South?"

"The more I think about that, the more I think it's

too obvious. And we met with them both. You read the body language of each guy. What did you think?"

"That Marshall was on the up-and-up. South was curled in. Gaze to the right and down. Arms folded. Too much posturing. Too much defensive blustering."

"That was my take too. The leak had to come from somewhere, and my money is on Colonel South."

"Motive?"

"Marshall made his pile of money. He can retire anytime he wants. South is still on the ladder heading up. But he's fifty-one so maybe he feels topped out rank-wise. Maybe he wants a better retirement plan than Uncle Sam is offering."

"And our watching his house?" asked Michelle.

"To see if something pops. He's divorced and his two kids are grown and gone. So we see if someone comes by on this dark and stormy night who might lead us where we need to go."

Two hours later no one had come or gone. The house lights were on and they had seen movement inside, but it was only one person, presumably South, whose government car was parked in the driveway.

Sean stretched. "You want to call it a night? Doesn't look like he's going anywhere."

Michelle was about to say something when head-lights broke the night.

Sean checked his watch. "Nearly midnight. Maybe it's a neighbor coming home."

They both ducked down in the car as the vehicle passed by slowly.

Michelle pressed her optics to her eyes and did a sweep.

"Shit!"

"What?"

"That's the guy from Heron Air Service."

"Are you sure?"

"Pretty damn sure."

"But he's not stopping at South's."

"Sean, it's him."

Sean started the car, eased out, and took up the tail. He said, "We're the only two rides out here. He's bound to spot us."

"Just keep it up a bit. There's a major intersection coming up. There should be some traffic there we can hide in. I don't want to lose this guy."

He did as she asked.

"He's making a left."

"Got it."

They reached the intersection. Luckily the light was green and they didn't have to stop behind him where he might have gotten an eyeball on them despite their headlights boring into his line of vision. Both cars turned right and Sean backed off, sliding in behind a green Chevy to give himself some distance but keeping the other car in sight.

Michelle put down the optics and opened her laptop. She started fiercely clicking keys.

"What are you doing?" asked Sean, glancing over at her.

"Hacking into the DMV."

"You can do that?" he said, looking surprised.

"Edgar showed me recently how to do it. I know, I know, it's not exactly legal."

"Actually, legally speaking, it's not legal at all."

"Look, I'm just trying to get some traction on this case. So don't read me the riot act."

"No. I think it's very cool. Can you show me how to do it?"

She shot him a look. "Show *you*, Mr. Computer Illiterate?"

He scowled. "I know my way around Internet… stuff."

"Sean, you just discovered emoticons last week."

She continued clicking, and then a page opened up. "Trevor Jenkins, age forty-one. He lives in Vienna."

"Can you do a Google-thingy and find out more about him?"

"A Google-thingy?"

"Just do it, Michelle. I'm following a suspect here. That's apparently all my shrinking brain can handle."

She clicked more keys. "Not finding much. Guy's not a celebrity with his own website and Twitter account. Hold on, he does have an account with LinkedIn, of which I'm a proud member."

She accessed that and read down the page.

"Well?" said Sean expectantly.

"Former military. West Point. Hundred and First Airborne. He's now president and CEO of Heron Air Service. Single. No kids. Has a commercial pilot's license. He belongs to a number of industry trade groups. Spent time in the Middle East, presumably during combat tours."

"Alan Grant is also former military. I wonder if he was in the Hundred and First?"

Michelle hit more keys and found that Grant also had a LinkedIn page. "Nope. Grant was infantry. But soldiers in the air and soldiers on the ground could still know each other. It's still the Army."

"True. Okay, he's turning."

Sean hooked the same left as Jenkins had.

Michelle looked around. "I think he's heading home, Sean. The address in his DMV file is right around here."

"I'll pull off the tail and come back around, then, so he won't get suspicious."

Sean backtracked to the address in the DMV file and got there in time to see Jenkins's car pull into the garage of a fairly new home with older houses on either side.

They passed by and kept going.

"What did we learn from that?" asked Michelle. "Besides Jenkins's identity, background, and where he lives?"

"He was in South's neighborhood."

"But he didn't go to see South. He drove right by it."

"That is a puzzler. Maybe he was just keeping eyes on it."

"Maybe," said Michelle doubtfully.

"Yeah, I don't believe that either," said Sean, noting her dubious look.

"But we know there's a connection between Jenkins and Vista and presumably Alan Grant. They're both former military."

"And Wingo identified Jenkins as one of the guys in Afghanistan who took the euros from him."

"And a Heron Air Service plane might have brought that cash back here."

"Not sure. I guess one of their bigger jets could carry over two tons' worth of cash. You think the whole company is in on it?"

"Jenkins is the top guy. He could have flown the sucker in himself. He has his pilot's license. And what better way to get something like that through customs? The guy probably knows a million ways to hide stuff coming in."

"But this is getting us no closer to finding Tyler and Kathy."

Sean said, "It's a mosaic. We have to find all the pieces and then we can see the whole picture."

"I'm not sure we have time to find all the mosaic tiles, Sean."

"Do we sit on Jenkins all night and see where he goes tomorrow? He might lead us to the kids."

"Or it might be a big waste of time."

He glanced at her. "You got another idea?"

She sighed and shook her head. "No. There's an all-night Dunkin' Donuts two blocks over. I can run and get us some coffee and food while you stay here and keep eyes on Jenkins."

"Okay," Sean said absently.

She undid her seat belt and looked at him. "What?"

"Don't know. Just something back there."

"Back where?"

"Back at South's. No, before South's neighborhood."

"What about it?"

"I just felt like I knew the area. Been there before."

"When? Why?"

Sean shook his head. "Can't think of it." He smiled resignedly. "Brain cell loss. Maybe it's for real."

"Well, stick your fingers in your ears and try not to let any more out. We're going to need all the thinking we can muster to get to the bottom of this sucker."

69

Sean felt the nudge against his shoulder. His brain misfired for a second as his mind toggled between sleep and consciousness. Another nudge and he was awake. He looked around and saw Michelle next to him, her camera with long-range lens in hand.

She said, "Hello, Sleeping Beauty. Ready to go to work?"

They had taken shifts, two hours on, two hours asleep.

"What time is it?" asked Sean as he blinked, yawned, and sat up straight.

"A few minutes after eight."

Sean gazed outside. The rain and gloom were still with them. It still felt dark.

"Any movement on Jenkins?"

"Not yet. Lights went on at seven sharp. Probably had his alarm set. I've been snapping pictures of anything relevant."

"Action on the street?"

"Early-morning commuters, sleepy kids straggling

to bus stops. Couple of joggers running in the rain to stay healthy before they drop dead from pneumonia."

Michelle reached into the console, took out a protein bar, ripped off the cover, dropped the plastic on the floorboard, and bit into the chocolate. She eyed Sean, who was staring at the trash on the floor. She held out the protein bar.

"Want a bite?"

"I'd rather eat mouse droppings. Actually, that's probably what's in there. Lots of protein in poop."

"What do we do when he comes out?"

"Tail him."

"He might spot us."

"He might. But we have to risk it. He's the only viable lead we have right now."

"Are we making a huge mistake by not calling in Littlefield and the FBI?"

Sean rubbed the kinks out of his neck, slapped himself a few times in the face to come fully awake, and then leaned back against the seat. "Half of me says we're idiots for not doing exactly that."

"And the other half?"

"I haven't figured the other half out yet."

"Here he comes."

They both slid down in their seats as Jenkins's garage door rolled up and his car backed out. He passed by them and headed out of the neighborhood.

"Hey, you have your pick gun?" Sean asked.

"I have a pocket, so I have my pick gun."

"Hit the house, see what you can find. I'll tail Jenkins and then we'll hook back up."

"Okay, but how do I get back?"

"Call a cab."

"Gee, thanks."

"And don't get caught. Breaking and entering is very bad. It's a felony, in fact."

Michelle climbed out of the Land Cruiser and watched for a moment as Sean sped off in pursuit of the other vehicle. She looked both ways and was pleased that the morning was gloomy and ill lit, with even tendrils of fog drifting through the trees that were spaced in between the houses. She walked up to the front stoop of Jenkins's house and knocked, just in case anyone was watching her.

She gazed through one of the side windows next to the door and saw the alarm pad on an interior wall. It was blinking red, which meant it was engaged.

It can never be easy, can it?

She slipped around the back, keeping to the shadows thrown by the house.

Because of the alarm system the front and rear doors were out. Her pick gun was useless.

That left one alternative.

She eyed a small window that was reachable by the rear deck.

Bathroom, she deduced.

She looked behind her. No homes here. There were

just stands of trees dense enough to provide good cover.

Her knife made short work of the window lock. She slid it open, praying that the windows weren't wired to the alarm system, and clambered inside, dropping quietly to the floor next to the toilet. She closed the window behind her and went to the doorway, peering out. She eyed the ceiling and the corners of the hallway, looking for motion detectors.

Seeing none, she moved carefully out into the hall. She froze when she heard scurrying feet.

The little dog scooted around the corner and came to a stop in front of her, yapping. Then it rolled over onto its belly and she knelt down to scratch its stomach.

"Okay, little guy, want to tell me where all the deep, dark secrets are hidden?"

She quickly searched the rooms on the main level and found nothing.

It was on her search of the top floor that she found Jenkins's home office.

It was small, with a desk and chair and a shelf filled with books, mostly on planes and FAA requirements.

An Apple computer sat on the desk. She sat and hit some keys but a password was required and she didn't have one. She tried half a dozen based on Jenkins's birth date and other personal data, which she had gotten from the DMV records. None of them worked, which didn't surprise her.

She tapped her fingers on the desktop. If she had her truck she could just sneak the whole computer out and let Edgar break into it. But she couldn't walk down the street with a twenty-four-inch Apple computer under her arm and hail a cab.

Edgar!

She called him.

She said, "I have a little problem. I'm house-sitting for a friend of mine and he said I could use his computer, but he forgot to give me the password. And he's not answering phone or email. Anyway, can you help me out?"

"What brand of computer is it?"

"An Apple."

"It'll take some time."

"Great," she said despairingly. "How much time?"

"At least a minute."

Michelle smiled. "I love you, Edgar."

There was a long moment of silence.

"I'm actually seeing someone, Ms. Maxwell."

"Uh…good for you, Edgar. My loss."

He took her through a series of assaults on the computer. In less than a minute the hard drive came to life.

"I'm in. Thanks."

"You're welcome. And Ms. Maxwell?"

"Yes?"

"You're not really house-sitting, are you?"

"Um…"

"I didn't think so. I just helped you break into someone's computer, didn't I?"

"It's all for a good cause, Edgar."

"Okay, if you say so."

"Goodbye, Edgar."

"Goodbye. And I'll let you know if things don't work out with the person I'm currently seeing."

"Uh, okay, thanks."

Michelle clicked keys and accessed as many files as she could. She also found a flash drive in the desk and downloaded to it as many files as she could find that seemed pertinent.

She jerked around when she heard a siren in the distance. She ejected the flash drive, used her jacket to wipe her prints off the keyboard, rose, and ran back out of the room. She hurtled down the stairs even as the siren grew closer.

Did I trip some silent alarm?

The little dog yapped at her heels as she raced to the bathroom, opened the window, and cantilevered over the sill, landing on her feet. She jumped off the deck and ran not toward the street, but into the woods behind the house. She came out on the other side and fast-walked to the same major intersection from last night.

She didn't see a cab but she did board a bus that carried her to the Metro. From there she grabbed a cab and rode that back to their office. Along the way she called Sean.

"Where are you?" she asked him.

"Just pulling into Heron Air Service at Dulles. Traffic sucked even heading out of town. What about you?"

She quickly explained to him what she had done and where she was. She fingered the flash drive.

"I'm going to take the rental car we left here and see Edgar. Maybe he can find some stuff on the flash that will make sense."

"Good idea. I'll join you as soon as I can."

Michelle clicked off.

Sean put his phone down just about the time the gun was placed against his head.

70

Peripheral vision. It was a necessity for many jobs.

NFL quarterbacks had to have it so they wouldn't be crushed by charging defenders.

Basketball referees needed it to cover all the goings-on around the court.

And Secret Service agents needed it to prevent harm from coming to their protectees and themselves.

Sean saw the gun and eyed the person holding it all without moving his head.

His elbow hit the horn, and the sound shattered the relative morning quiet around the airport. At the noise the gunman's hand flinched just a bit, but it was enough to give Sean the space he needed to do what he did next.

He grabbed the man's shirt and jerked him forward.

His head collided with the hard metal of the Land Cruiser's door frame. Blood spattered on Sean along with bits of a tooth from the man's mouth; then the gunman slumped down to the asphalt.

Sean already had the vehicle in gear and the wheels spinning. He punched the gas to the floor, and the truck shot out of the parking lot. He looked in the side mirror and saw the man slowly get to his feet and stagger sideways before falling down again.

It wasn't Jenkins. It was someone else.

"Shit," Sean muttered. He'd been spotted. That did not bode well for anyone he cared about, particularly Tyler and Kathy.

He got on the phone and called Michelle. He talked as he drove, filling her in.

"I never saw the guy until the last second. It was my screwup."

She said, "I distracted you with my call."

"I can chew gum and talk at the same time," he snapped. "At least I used to be able to," he added darkly.

"Should we tell Wingo?"

"No, he's already close to going off the deep end. This will send him there for certain."

"So what now?"

"I'll meet you at Edgar's. Hopefully, he can flesh out some of the computer files for us so we can get a direct line on these bastards before it's too late."

An hour later Sean pulled to a stop in front of Edgar's farmhouse. The skies had partially cleared and the sun was doing its best to poke through the clusters of gray clouds. He noted that Michelle's rental vehicle was already there. He would have expected no less with the way she drove. He touched the hood of her car as he passed. It wasn't even warm. She'd been here awhile, probably smoked her wheels the whole way. And never gotten a ticket. He shook his head and kept going.

He knocked and then walked into the house.

Michelle was hunched over Edgar's shoulder as he was gazing at his multiple screens on his plywood desk.

Edgar said, "She wasn't house-sitting. She was breaking and entering. That's a felony."

"Yeah, I told her the same thing. Is the coffee fresh?" asked Sean, eyeing the cup in Michelle's hand. "My brain is mud."

Edgar gave him a significant look. Sean started to say something but then obviously decided not to even bother.

Michelle said, "He has a Keurig. Take your pick."

Sean left the room, made his cup of coffee, rejoined them, and perched on the edge of Edgar's desk.

"So what do we have?"

"A lot of files to go through," replied Michelle.

"What about the other stuff?" asked Sean. "The IP trail on the email from the blogger's source?"

"I've broken through three of five barriers," answered Edgar.

"Hey, that's great."

Edgar said, "The remaining two are proving hard to crack. The person knows what he's doing."

Sean's excited look faded. "Well, if you can't crack it, I don't think anyone can, Edgar."

"I didn't say I couldn't. I just said they were proving difficult."

Michelle cradled her cup of coffee and pointed at the screen. "But there might be something here."

Sean squinted at the screen. "What am I looking at?"

"On the surface it's an invoice for jet fuel," said Edgar.

"But looks can be deceiving," added Michelle.

"What do you mean?"

In response Edgar hit a few keys. The page they were looking at turned into a jumble of symbols that made no sense at all.

"I've seen that before," said Sean. "When my computer goes haywire and turns my document to gibberish."

"It's simply a failure of the computer to read the document coding properly," explained Edgar. "And that can happen for any number of reasons, including damage to the file or a problem with your processor. And if you know what you're doing you can disable your computer's ability to read the code properly. That's what I just did. But it's also something else."

"What?"

"A code," said Michelle.

"You mean they hide the code in the gibberish?" said Sean.

"*Gold in the trash* is a phrase we use in the cyber security field," noted Edgar. "It's actually pretty cool because everyone's had that happen to them. It's just a software glitch. You don't think it's anything more than that."

"But you obviously saw there was more to it," said Michelle.

"Well, with the Wall, you pretty much see everything," said Edgar modestly.

"So what does this code say?" asked Sean.

"It's a communication to an unknown party, but one I strongly suspect is the same one on the IP trail from the blogger because the exact same barriers have been set up to block access to the source at the other end."

"But what does it say?" persisted Sean.

"It's a series of numbers," he replied.

"Numbers meaning what?"

"If I had to guess, it's satellite coordinates because I've seen them before," said Edgar. "I haven't fully deciphered the message, so I don't know the location of the satellite yet if that's what it is."

Sean looked upward. "A bird in the sky? What does that have to do with anything?"

"Eyes in the heavens," said Michelle. She looked thoughtful as she took a sip of coffee. "How much does a sky bird cost?"

"It could be a lot," said Edgar. "You have to build it first and that's not cheap. Then you have to get it up there, and that's not cheap either. Most people with such a need just rent space on an existing platform."

"You can do that?" said Michelle. "Rent space on a satellite just like you would an apartment?"

Edgar nodded as he kept clicking keys. "Done all the time. There are businesses devoted to it. Some of the satellites the government uses are rented from commercial companies."

"The government?" said Sean. "But how do you maintain security?"

"There are a number of ways. Sometimes you rent the whole satellite."

"Must really be big bucks involved," said Sean.

"Like a billion euros?" replied Michelle.

That comment drew a sharp glance from him. "Is that what you're thinking? Someone bought a satellite? Why?"

Michelle took another sip of coffee. "I don't know. But if sats are expensive, a billion euros would certainly come in handy."

"Yes they would," added Edgar.

Sean said, "Edgar, what would it cost to buy or rent a satellite?"

Edgar used his left hand to start clicking keys on another keyboard, with the results popping up on another screen. All the while his right hand clicked away on the first keyboard. His gaze darted between the two screens.

"A lot depends on the size and reach of the satellite," explained Edgar. "Building one can cost from half a billion up to two billion. They can be as small as half a ton all the way up to the size of a truck weighing a couple of tons. But there are other varieties. I call them burners."

"Why is that?" asked Michelle.

"You can build them on the cheap, say a million bucks or less, get them up to position on a rented rocket along with other payload. You lease the platform out to as many paying customers as you can get, sometimes for a few hundred bucks a week to get your investment back plus a decent profit, and a couple of years later the bird drifts back to earth and burns up in the atmosphere. Hence the term *burner*."

"But these cheaper satellites, they wouldn't have the reach of the more expensive ones."

"Of course not. Even in space you get what you pay for. Gravity not included." Edgar smiled and looked at Sean. "That was a joke."

"Yeah, I got it. So how many satellites are in the sky?"

Edgar clicked more keys. "Over a thousand. Most are owned and operated by the U.S., Russia, and China divided among civil, commercial, government, and military applications. But lots of countries own all or pieces of satellites. Most commercial satellites are in what is called geosynchronous orbit, as opposed to low-earth orbit where governments have the most platforms."

"And satellites are used principally for…?" asked Michelle.

"Communications," answered Edgar promptly. "Moving information around the world at speed. Phone service, navigation, computer networks, whatever. The Wall depends on them, which means so do I."

Sean looked off, thinking. "If Alan Grant bought or rented a satellite, what would be his reason?"

"Spying?" said Michelle.

Sean looked doubtful. "For whom? And why the billion-euro theft? Edgar said you could rent space on a satellite for a lot less than that. And Grant has to be the source for the blog. The administration is taking incredible heat over it. You saw how worried President Cole looked. And if this whole thing is payback for what happened to Grant's father during Iran-Contra, then the satellite must figure into the plan the man has."

Sean put down his coffee cup and pointed at the screen. "Edgar, can you find a list of commercial satellite operators?"

"Yes."

"Can you find out who might have rented space on one of them in say the last few weeks or so?"

"I can try."

"Okay," replied Sean, picking up his coffee cup again.

Michelle said, "What are you thinking?"

"Communication, that's what satellites are for. What I'm thinking is Grant is into communicating, running the show. He fed George Carlton all the secrets about the debacle in Afghanistan."

Michelle nodded, a glimmer of understanding coming into her features. "You think he's using the satellite for communicating something else?"

"Yeah, I do. I just don't know what. And it might not simply be information." He looked at Edgar. "Using a satellite, you can control things on the ground, right?"

"Yes. The government uses it to operate the power grid, the nuclear arsenal, command and control functions, lots of things we all depend on."

Michelle interjected. "You think he's trying to take over the U.S. nuclear arsenal?"

"No. Those would be on government birds and protected as well as anything can be. Plus you have manual safeguards for those suckers back on the ground."

"Well, what then, Sean?"

"I don't know," he said, visibly frustrated. "But whatever it is, I know it's going to be pretty damn significant."

"While Edgar is working on all this, what do we do?"

"We have to talk to Wingo. Tell him what's happened."

"Like you said, he might go off the deep end."

"It's all in how we phrase it, Michelle. It'll take some diplomacy."

"So you want me to talk to him?"

"Uh, no."

"Why not?" she wanted to know.

"Don't take this the wrong way, but you're about as diplomatic as the punk running North Korea."

"Maybe so, but I'm also a lot tougher."

71

Alan Grant was not pleased by the day's developments.

Sean King had been at Heron Air Service but had gotten away yet again.

The home of Trevor Jenkins had been broken into, and while nothing appeared to be missing, he couldn't be sure of that.

He picked up the burn phone and made the call using an electronic filter to disguise his voice.

Sam Wingo answered on the first ring.

"Yes?"

"We have a problem, Wingo."

"What is that?"

"Two problems, actually. King and Maxwell."

"I don't know what you're talking about."

"I asked you to stand down."

"I am standing down. I haven't moved since you called me last time."

"But your friends have."

"They are not my friends."

"Do you want me to send a body part from your son to get my point across?"

"Listen, please, just don't hurt him."

"I know that you're working with King and Maxwell so don't try to bullshit me. And if you think I'm going to stand by and do nothing while they seek to find me, then you've made an egregious miscalculation."

"What do you want me to do?"

"Put them out of commission."

"How?"

"I'll leave it to your imagination. You can kill them if you want. I don't really care. If I find them interfering one more time, Tyler gets delivered to you in a body bag. Are we clear?"

"Yes," Wingo replied in a hushed voice.

Sean and Michelle pulled into the parking lot and climbed out of the car.

Sean said, "I'm really not sure how to approach Sam on this."

"Don't ask me. I'm down there with the punk from Pyongyang on the diplomacy scale."

"Look, I didn't mean it exactly like that."

"You meant it exactly like that."

Sean knocked on Wingo's motel room door. "Sam, it's us."

"Come on in, the door's unlocked," Wingo called out. They opened the door and walked in. Michelle closed it behind them.

When she turned back around she saw that Sean had his hands in the air. She looked across the room.

Wingo was standing there, his gun pointed at them.

"Is there a problem?" asked Sean.

"I got a call. You two have been snooping around. They said if you keep it up, Tyler comes back in a body bag."

Sean eyed the gun. "Sam, we told you what we were going to do. We agreed that was the best plan to get them back safely."

"No, *you* agreed that was the best way. I didn't really have a say." He flicked the gun. "Now I do."

Michelle said, "You're playing right into their hands, Sam. If we all stand down, Tyler is never coming back."

"Let me tell you what I do know. If we don't stop he's dead. If we do stand down, he might have a chance."

"You don't really believe that," said Sean.

"Don't tell me what I believe or don't believe," barked Wingo. "I am not going to let you give my son a death sentence."

She said, "You already have, Sam, by doing what you're doing."

"We have leads," added Sean. "Good ones. We're getting closer."

"You can say whatever you want to say. I have to think of my son."

"And you don't think we are?" said Sean. "The only reason we took this case was because of your son."

Wingo glanced down for a moment. "Look, I'm not blaming you, okay? I know you're trying to help. It's just that I'm caught between a rock and a hard place."

Michelle said, "Well, you made that situation. Not us. And certainly not Tyler. It was your choice to take this mission."

Wingo's features hardened. "You think I don't know that? I've regretted that decision from the instant I made it."

Sean sat on the edge of the bed. "So the answer is to just sit here and wait and hope these people who have already killed will let your son free? Is that your strategy?"

Wingo sat down heavily in a chair against the wall, but kept his gun on them.

"What choice do I really have?"

"What say we turn the tables on them."

"How?"

"We're sure Alan Grant is connected to this."

"Okay, how does that help?"

"He has a family too."

"So?"

Sean stared at him. "You've been pushed against the wall. You have no other way out. You're a desperate man."

"I'm not following you."

"He's threatened to kill your son."

"Yeah he has," snapped Wingo. "But what do I do about it?"

Sean said, "I'm tired of always reacting to these assholes. Let's go on the offensive."

"How?" asked Michelle.

Sean said, "Sam can threaten to kill Grant's family."

Michelle froze. Wingo looked confused.

"He'll never believe that I would do that."

"Are you desperate?"

"Of course I am."

"Then desperate times call for desperate measures."

"Even if I were inclined, how would I communicate with him?"

Sean pointed to Wingo's phone. "With that."

Michelle said, "Sean, we're not harming Grant's kids."

"Of course not. I said threaten. That's all."

"But—" began Michelle.

"Let's send the threat," interrupted Sean. "And see what happens."

Michelle got an understanding look on her face. She glanced at Wingo, who sat there still looking confused. But finally he put his gun away and held up his phone.

"Tell me how to do this."

"First, we have to go somewhere," replied Sean.

72

Alan Grant was staring at a computer screen inside the vault at the radio station when the burn phone in his pocket vibrated.

He slid it out, glanced at it. Then his gaze became riveted to it.

Child for a child. You take mine, I take yours. And, unlike me, you have three to choose from.

Grant leapt up so quickly he banged his knee against the desk edge.

Limping slightly he left the radio station and hurried to his car.

He phoned home while he drove. There was no answer. He tried his wife's cell phone. There was still no answer.

He drove fast, but it still took more than two hours before he pulled into his driveway and jumped out of the car. He was heading to the house when he saw them.

His wife had the two youngest kids and their black Lab. The youngest child was in his stroller. His five-year-old daughter was helping to push it. They had obviously been for a walk.

When she saw her husband, Leslie Grant looked surprised. "Alan, what are you doing home?" She saw the concern on his face. "Is everything okay, honey?"

"Where's Danny?" he asked, referring to their oldest child.

She looked confused. "He's still in school. The bus will drop him off this afternoon." She drew closer as their daughter ran forward to her dad.

Grant rubbed his face and forced a smile as he picked her up.

Leslie drew next to him. Grant patted the Lab and tried to look unconcerned.

"Alan, is everything okay?" she said in a low voice.

"Daddy's okay," said their daughter, whose name was Margaret, but who went by Maggie, after her grandmother. She cupped her dad's face in her hands. "Daddy's okay," she said again.

"Daddy is very okay," said Grant, wrapping an arm around his wife as he held Maggie with the other.

"Look," he said. "How about I take you three out to lunch? Sound good?"

"You'll have to give me a few minutes to put myself together," said Leslie.

"Okay. I've got some stuff to get from the car. Say twenty minutes?"

"Fine."

She took the kids and the dog into the house but

shot a nervous glance back at her husband before shutting the door.

Grant was standing next to his car when he felt the burn phone vibrate.

He looked at the text that had just appeared there. *Nice-looking family, Alan. Let's keep it that way. Don't worry, I won't hurt the pooch.*

Grant spun around in all directions, attempting to get eyes on the text sender.

But he saw no one. He put the phone away.

This complicated things. They had a stalemate on the kids, but that had no impact on his overall plan. All elements were in place. And even if Wingo had managed somehow to trace things back to him, he had no proof of anything that could stick. Grant could pull the trigger and there would be no evidence that he had done anything illegal.

After it was all over he would figure out what to do about Wingo. And King and Maxwell.

Far down the block, behind a line of parked cars, Michelle lowered her binoculars and glanced over at Sean, who sat in the driver's seat. Wingo was in the backseat with optics on Grant as well.

"You were right, Sean," said Michelle. "That really flushed him out. Like a bird dog into the thicket and the quail spilling out."

"What I was hoping for," said Sean with a pleased look.

"You think he's standing down on this?" asked Michelle.

"He's got a family, just like me," said Wingo. "He doesn't want anything to happen to them."

"That I get," said Michelle.

"But I doubt he's standing down on his overall plan," noted Sean. "That's what you mean, right?"

Michelle nodded. "So that means the hostage situation will have no impact on what he wants to do."

"Satellite, missing money, government conspiracy, leaks," said Sean.

"And the motive being his mother's and father's suicide after Iran-Contra," added Michelle. "Seems like a lot."

"But there's zip there we can take to the FBI," said Sean. "Littlefield will look at us like we're nuts. Or worse, he'll make some inquiries and maybe blow everything up."

"This satellite," said Wingo. "You trying to get a fix on it?"

"Trying. We're also trying to find the blogger's source, but something tells me we're staring right at his house. So that part is solved."

Michelle said, "But if Edgar can establish a link between Grant and George Carlton, that is evidence."

Sean said, "Evidence of a leak, not evidence of a major crime. And unless it can be proven that Grant stole classified information, his free speech rights might bar any prosecution."

"So what do we do?" asked Wingo.

"We have to find out what the satellite is for. If we can do that, we might just be able to jump a few spaces and take his king."

"You're mixing checkers and chess," observed Michelle.

"Yes I am, because I'm not yet sure what game Grant is playing."

"What can we do?" asked Wingo.

Sean thought for a moment. "Satellite."

Michelle looked at him quizzically. "Yeah. We already covered that point."

"No, I'm not talking about *that* satellite. I'm talking about another one."

She touched his forehead. "Do you have a fever?"

"I wonder where Grant just came in from? It wasn't his office downtown. It took him well over two hours after we sent the text for him to get here. This time of day the trip out of D.C. would take him thirty minutes tops."

"That's true," said Michelle, looking thoughtful. "Well, he's driving a pretty new Mercedes. GPS comes standard on those models."

"And GPS is controlled by satellite," remarked Sean.

"So how can we possibly get a satellite to follow his—?" Michelle stopped herself when Sean gave her a knowing look.

"Edgar," she said.

"What is this Edgar you keep mentioning?" asked Wingo. "Is it an acronym for a computer system or something?"

"Or something," replied Sean.

73

They dropped Wingo off at the motel and then drove out to Edgar's farmhouse to meet with him. After coming to understand what they wanted, Edgar agreed to help.

"You really should be on our payroll, Edgar," Michelle joked. "I think we're using you more than the U.S. government. What a team we'd make."

Edgar looked at her strangely. "How much do you pay?"

Sean interjected, "I doubt we could match what you're making. We don't have Uncle Sam's pocket-book."

"Or his debt, thankfully," added Michelle dryly.

"What benefits do you offer?" asked Edgar. "I get four weeks' paid vacation and a 401(k) plan. And catered breakfast and lunch. And a rental apartment in the city with nice views."

"Uh, I think Michelle was just making a joke, Edgar," added Sean, who looked perplexed.

However, Edgar didn't appear to be listening to him.

"I'll think about it," said Edgar while Sean gave Michelle an anxious look.

"What just happened?" he mumbled to her.

"I'm not sure," she whispered back.

He said in a normal voice, "So you think you can do it, Edgar? This tracking thing?"

"You gave me the license plate number of Grant's vehicle. From that I can easily get the VIN. And from there lots of things open up."

His fingers were flying over the multiple keyboards.

"Just curious, you ever get repetitive motion injuries?" asked Michelle as she watched him work away.

"No," said Edgar.

"How long will it take to track him via the GPS?" asked Sean.

"Not long," replied Edgar. "I'll contact you when I'm done."

They walked back to their car and drove off.

Michelle said, "I think that he thinks we offered him a job."

"You mean he thinks *you* offered him a job."

"I wasn't being serious. And we can't afford him."

"I know that," said Sean. "But we can't just keep asking the guy to do all this stuff for us for free." He paused and added with a tinge of hope, "Can we?"

"No, we can't," she said firmly.

Sean turned the radio on, and they caught the top-of-the-hour news feed. It was dominated by the growing scandal surrounding the Cole administration.

The political opposition in the Congress was strenuously calling for investigative hearings; subpoenas were already being drawn up. One congressman had even mentioned impeachment as a possibility. The government of Iran was also rattling the sabers and denouncing the U.S. actions. And America's allies were distancing themselves from the situation. Cole's spokesperson was offering the standard spin, and all of it seemed weak and evasive.

"Pretty bleak," commented Michelle.

"Well, what they did was pretty stupid," said Sean. "You can't buy a democracy, even with a billion euros."

"Very eloquent of you," she said.

"I have my moments."

"So what now? Just twiddle our thumbs waiting for Edgar to do his thing?"

"No. We're going to split up."

"Where are you going?"

"I'm going to babysit Wingo so he doesn't do something stupid."

"And me?"

"Can you go by the hospital and check on Dana for me?"

Michelle looked slightly panicked. "Me? Sean, they won't let me see her."

"They will if she wants them to."

"But why not you?"

"I'm...Can you just do it for me, Michelle?"

She started to protest again but when she saw the

look on his face she said, "Sure, I'll go. Just drop me at my truck. But if something goes down you call me, okay?"

"You got it. And, Michelle, thanks."

"You're welcome."

An hour later Michelle walked into the hospital and made her way to the ICU. She was dreading running into Curtis Brown. She discovered, however, that the general was not at the hospital. A nurse informed Michelle that he had left earlier but planned to be back soon.

The nurses' station buzzed Dana's room, and she agreed to see Michelle.

The nurse admonished, "You can't stay long. She needs her rest."

"Absolutely," said Michelle.

She entered Dana's room and took a moment to look around at the array of tubes and machines hooked up to her, helping her to get better. It had not been that long ago that Michelle had been in a hospital bed with nearly the identical medical equipment hooked up to her as she fought for her life.

She drew up a chair and sat down next to the bed.

Dana looked over at her. Her coloring was better today, Michelle thought, even if she still looked very weak.

"Sean's not with you?" she said.

"Not right now. I know he'll be coming by to see you later."

Dana slowly nodded but looked disappointed all the same.

"I understand that the general was here earlier?"

Dana tried to sit up a bit, but Michelle put a restraining hand on her shoulder. "I'll raise the bed instead, okay?"

Michelle hit the lift control and Dana's torso rose a few inches.

"Curtis has been great through this," said Dana.

"I'm sure he has. But so have you." Michelle gave her a reassuring squeeze on her arm.

"Have you found out anything about all this?"

"Still trying. But we're getting there."

"Sean will get there, I'm sure of it."

"You seem to have a good relationship with your ex," said Michelle, with just the tiniest of bites to her words.

"Actually, we had no relationship at all. Not until he contacted me. I hadn't heard from him since the divorce."

Michelle started to say something else and then caught herself. She glanced at the monitors and the drip lines and decided not to push it. The woman was still in precarious shape.

"You can ask what you want to ask, Michelle."

She glanced over to see Dana's gaze on her.

"He's a good man and I screwed up big-time in letting him get away."

"So, regrets?"

"I'd prefer not to use that word. I have Curtis. I have to look forward, not back." There was a minute of silence until Dana said, "Are you two more than just business partners?"

"Does it matter to you?"

"Could you hand me that cup of water please?"

Michelle held the cup for her while Dana sipped on the straw. She sat back and took a few deep breaths. One of the monitors started alarming and Michelle quickly stood. "Should I get a nurse?"

"No. That thing's been chiming the last two days. They have the parameters set too low, or so they told me. No one's been in to adjust it yet."

Michelle sat back down.

Dana stared at her wrist, where an IV line was inserted. "I guess it does matter to me, Michelle, but probably not for the reason you think." She eased her head to the right and looked at her. "I'm very happy with Curtis. I would like Sean to be happy too."

"He is happy."

"Being happy alone and being happy with someone are two different things. So are you more than business partners?"

"I don't know what we are, Dana."

"Is that your version of the facts or Sean's?"

Michelle scowled. "Look, I know you've been shot and everything, but this isn't really your business, is it?"

"Did Sean tell you why we split up?"

"No, not really."

"Entirely my fault."

"Being married to a Secret Service agent isn't easy."

"I cheated on him. Multiple times. I'll never, ever forget the look on his face when he found out. I know he felt so betrayed."

Michelle eased back in her chair. "We don't really have to go into this."

"If you love him, Michelle, make it easy on yourself and just tell him. I saw how he is around you. I know him. I know what he's feeling for you."

"You just saw us together the one time and it wasn't for long."

"I didn't need long."

Michelle looked down and rubbed a hand through her long hair. "Thanks for the advice."

"But you won't take it?"

"I can't make promises, sorry. But you delivered the message really well."

Michelle's phone buzzed. She slipped it out, hoping it was Sean.

It wasn't.

The name on the caller ID would have gotten anyone's attention.

It was the White House.

74

Sean was sitting across from Sam Wingo. They were in Sean's car staking out Jenkins's house.

"What good will this do?" asked Wingo.

"Three-quarters of what PIs do comes to zip. But you have to go through that to get to the other twenty-five percent that actually will result in something. Same sort of deal at the Secret Service. Ninety percent tedium, ten percent bedlam."

"Well, I don't see this resulting in anything more than a waste of time."

"Are you telling me that when you were soldiering, you didn't have to show patience?"

Wingo sighed and shook his head. "Actually, it was ninety-nine percent tedium and one percent chaos." He looked at Sean. "Sorry, guess my nerves are just running away with me."

Sean patted him on the shoulder. "Your son is safe for now. We bought some time. If we can just—"

Sean broke off when his phone buzzed. He looked at the screen.

"It's Edgar. Maybe he worked his magic with the satellite or found a way to track Grant's car."

Edgar, however, had not accomplished either of those things. Yet he did have something else.

"I was looking through Jenkins's file and found something that might help you."

"What?" asked Sean.

"Real estate tax bill for a piece of property other than Jenkins's home."

"Where is it?"

"Ten acres in Rappahannock County, Virginia. I looked it up from an old real estate listing online. It's a cabin. Very remote."

"Does it have an address?"

"I'll email you the directions right now. Good luck."

Sean clicked off and filled in Wingo on what Edgar had just told him.

"You think it could be where they're holding Tyler and Kathy?"

"Rural and isolated. Maybe that's where Grant was when our email flushed him out. It's well over an hour away."

"What do we do? Go charging in?"

"No. We have to do this the right way."

He glanced at his phone and then called Michelle. It went straight to voice mail. She might still be at the hospital with Dana, he thought.

He punched in another number. A voice came on the line.

521

"Special Agent Dwayne Littlefield," said the voice.

"Agent Littlefield, it's Sean King."

"Did you just drop off the planet or what? My ass is sitting out with the president of the—"

Sean broke in. "I think I might have a lead on Tyler and Kathy."

"Where?"

"There's going to be firepower if the kids are being held there."

"We have people who specialize in this, King. How solid is your info?"

"Won't know until we get there."

"We? No, you let the Bureau handle this."

Sean had the phone on speaker mode, and when Wingo heard this last part he snatched the phone before Sean could stop him.

"It's my kid and I'm going to be there. I don't give a shit what you say."

"Who the hell is this?" Littlefield paused. "Sam Wingo? Is that you? Do you know how much trouble you're in? And Sean King? Harboring a fugitive? Obstruction of justice. And I'm not even warmed up yet. Your ass is mine, King."

Sean jerked the phone back from Wingo and gave him a withering look.

"Look, Dwayne, let's just focus on getting the kids back safe and sound. You do that, I think the president will once more look favorably on the FBI. And then we can work out these other little details."

"Little details?"

"Focus, Dwayne. The kids?"

"I can send in HRT. They got firepower like nobody else."

"No, we're not going to do it that way. You fight fire with fire, everybody ends up getting burned."

"Are you trying to tell me how to do my job?" snapped Littlefield.

"The former president's niece was kidnapped. Remember that?"

"Yeah."

"Well, my partner and I were the ones who got her back safe and sound, so we're not exactly thumb suckers on this. We can help."

"This is way out of protocol."

"This whole damn thing is way out of protocol."

"So how do you want to do this then?" asked Littlefield.

"Me and Wingo. You and McKinney. We go in fast and with no warning and we get the kids."

"What about your partner, Maxwell? I hear she can kick ass like nobody's business."

"I tried to get hold of her. But we need to move fast."

"I'd rather go in at night."

"And that's right when they would be expecting something. We go in while it's still light, we catch them off guard."

"I don't like this."

Sean looked at Wingo. "We got a guy here who's Special Forces. We got you, me, and McKinney. Not one of us is an amateur. These guys have to be running out of manpower by now, so I think the guns on their side might be a little light. We can do this, Dwayne. I'm getting floor plans of the cabin sent to me right now. We'll walk through it, do our recon, and then hit it."

"If you're wrong—"

"Then my ass is yours. But for now, we do it my way."

"Okay. Tell me where and when."

Sean did and then put his phone away.

Wingo looked over at him. "You as confident as you sound?"

"Not even close." Sean put the car in gear and tore off.

75

Two hours later the skies opened up and Sean looked to the heavens and thanked the man upstairs. It was a quick thunderstorm but it was making a lot of racket. It would be over and done in about thirty minutes; the skies would clear to a spectacular, cleansed blue, and the winds would calm. But right now bucketing rain, heavy, howling winds, and booms of thunder were covering every sound of their approach to the cabin.

He and Wingo had hooked up with Agents Littlefield and McKinney. The man from DHS had been even more skeptical than his FBI counterpart but came around when Sean pointed out the likely scenarios for him. They rescue the kids, they're heroes. If the kids weren't there, then they had Wingo, and Sean as an aider and abettor.

But as Sean made his way slowly up the hillside to where the cabin stood in its tiny footprint, his gut was screaming at him that the kids were inside its walls.

Wingo was on his right flank. They had their guns inside their rain jackets to keep them dry. McKinney and Littlefield were approaching from the other side.

Edgar had emailed him the interior floor plans of the cabin that he had dug up somewhere online. It was amazing what the gentle giant could do with his keyboard and a mind filled with more stuff than just about anyone else's.

Sean wished they *could* afford him.

There were two rooms in the place of equal size. Sean was pretty sure the kids would be held in the back room because the front had the only exit door to the place. You didn't put prisoners in a room with a way out. And when Sean drew near enough to the cabin to see the rear window, his deduction was confirmed. There was plywood nailed over it.

He looked at Wingo. "You see that?"

Wingo nodded. "Problem is, we try and get the boards off, the guards will gun them down."

"Not if we take care of the guards first."

"There might be one in the room with the kids."

Sean eyed the vehicle parked in front of the cabin. It wasn't Grant's Mercedes, unfortunately.

"Four-seater," said Sean. "Chances are we have two guards. They have to move the kids, that makes four seats."

Sean had a comm pack that was wired to units McKinney and Littlefield had. He spoke into his headset.

"We're in position."

"Roger that for us too," replied McKinney.

"Looks like we got two guards and the hostages in the back room."

"We have eyes on it. How do you want to do this?"

Sean edged closer to the cabin. What he was trying to get was a direct sight line through one of the front windows. But the storm, while covering their approach, was making a visual pretty hard to come by.

He looked back at Wingo and waved him forward. The soldier scampered toward him seeking cover along the way, just as he no doubt had done in the Middle East.

He stopped next to Sean. "What's the plan?"

"Treat it like combat. What would you do?"

Wingo eyed the surroundings. "Normally, you'd want to draw fire, revealing their position, and then follow up with focused fire or call in an airstrike."

"Fresh out of F-16s, my friend. Too bad one of our Federal friends didn't bring a thermal imager. We could see where the body heat was arrayed in there."

A jagged strip of lightning struck a tree in the distance, severing it in half and setting it on fire. A deafening boom of thunder followed. The split tree toppled to the ground, where the flames were quickly doused by the heavy rains.

Sean watched the smoldering tree for a few moments and then looked at Wingo.

"Here's what we're going to do. Thank you, Mother Nature."

★

Michelle was being escorted to the White House in a black SUV with four Secret Service agents, two of whom she knew.

"What's the deal?" she asked one of them as they drove along.

The man shrugged. "Not my place."

The other added, "You'll know soon enough. The Man will tell you himself."

The Man was President John Cole. And from the grim expressions of the four agents, Michelle did not think the Man was in a particularly good mood.

They had made her turn off her phone. No communications. No pictures. No recordings of any kind. She hoped Sean didn't call while she was out of the loop.

They pulled into 1600 Pennsylvania Avenue and Michelle was taken to the Oval Office. She was told to wait; the president would join her shortly.

"Tell him to take his time," Michelle said to herself as the door closed, leaving her alone. She looked down at her phone. She was itching to turn it back on but she knew there were eyes on her in here. This was a White House under assault, with leaks coming from somewhere, and it was making them all paranoid. If she tried to get her communications lines back up, they might just make her disappear. Well, maybe not that drastic, but she didn't want to add fuel to what looked like a bonfire in the making. She sighed, sat back, and waited for the most powerful man in the world to walk in and further ruin her day.

Edgar Roy's fingers were hammering the keyboards with—even for him—unusual ferociousness. But things were not going well. Edgar had almost never been beaten when hunting down something electronically. People tried to hide things from him but they never could. He could stare at a wall of screens with information coming in digital packages from the four corners of the earth, and make sense of it while just sitting there. His mind was uniquely designed to function at a high level in complete chaos. He could bring order, reason, and results to situations that seemed impervious to any of those things.

He had been able to track Grant's Mercedes—that was relatively easy. It was right now parked in a very rural spot more than sixty miles farther west from the address of the cabin that he had given Sean earlier. He had emailed Sean with the information and then turned to his next task. The satellite.

And yet he couldn't find the eye in the sky that Alan Grant had presumably leased. He might have used an alias of course, or more likely a shell company. Edgar had looked at purely commercial satellites and then government platforms and now he decided to look at the category in between—commercial satellites leased to the government. Sean had told him that

Grant was mad at the government. So maybe he was trying to get back at it.

As he was clicking away something caught his eye. He hit other keys, his gaze flitting across two screens. To the casual observer this would be quite a feat, but for Edgar it was actually a break. He was used to staring at fifty screens at the same time. He thought about the request that Sean had made—to track Alan Grant's Mercedes using GPS. He had done that. Police did that all the time. The GPS chip in a car's computer brain made such a task relatively simple. The onboard computer systems in cars these days were extraordinarily complex. Yet since they were tied to other systems, they were vulnerable to hacking, just like Edgar had done.

But as the data kept flying over the screen, Edgar Roy got a very concerned look on his face.

This couldn't be possible, could it?

76

"Do you smell smoke?" the man said.

The pair sat in the front room of the cabin. Each sported shoulder holsters. One had been reading a magazine. The other had been playing a video game on his phone.

The other man looked up and inhaled. "Yeah, I do."

They each glanced to the window. "Lightning struck that tree a little bit ago. Could be that."

The other man shook his head. "Too far away. And with all the rain coming down the fire went right out. Not much smoke."

They both rose and looked around.

"There!" the first man exclaimed. Smoke was coming through a crack in the wallboard. They both rushed over and examined the area.

"I'd try to put it out but I think it's in the walls. Piece-of-crap place. Maybe the storm caused an electrical short." He looked anxiously at his companion.

"We better move to the backup place. I'll get them."

He raced into the other room and came out a few moments later with a gagged, blindfolded, and bound

Tyler and Kathy. Kathy had a bandage wrapped around her arm where Alan Grant had shot her. He had done so in a way that the wound was only a crease in her arm. The slug hadn't gone in. But it had burned her skin, bled a lot, and hurt badly.

"Let's go," said the man as he pulled them along. "Move it!"

His partner was already at the front door. He said, "I'll check in on the way, let him know what we're doing."

They stepped outside onto the porch and prepared to get very wet running to the car. They would not have to worry about that, because they were never going to make it to the car.

A fist crushed the first man's jaw. He toppled as if he'd been clubbed by a grizzly. The second man yelled, let go of the kids, and reached for his gun. When he saw three guns pointed at his head from inches away, he wisely decided to put his hands up instead.

Sam Wingo stood over the man he had just knocked out, rubbing his fist.

He looked at Sean. "That felt really good."

"Dad!" Tyler had managed to spit out his gag when he heard the voice.

Wingo ran to his son and untied him.

Sean did the same for Kathy. She was teary and holding her arm.

While Wingo hugged his son, Sean held Kathy. "It's okay, Kathy. Everything's going to be okay now."

She whimpered and said, "He shot me."

Sean looked down at her bandaged arm and then held her tighter. "And he's going to pay for that. He's going to pay for a lot."

They loaded the kids into the car.

Sean doused the small fire he had built using rags, papers, and a bit of gasoline that he'd found in a can behind an old lean-to on the cabin property. Wingo came up to him.

"Brilliant tactic," he said.

Sean stamped the last of the fire out and poured some water on it to make sure. Although the rain had left everything wet, he didn't want to take any chances with the cabin really catching on fire.

"Any tactic is brilliant so long as it works."

Wingo gripped his shoulder. "Thank you, Sean. I…"

Sean put a hand on Wingo's shoulder. "I know, Sam. I know."

McKinney and Littlefield had the two men cuffed and in their SUV. Sean poked his head in.

In a low voice he said, "I just checked my email. Got a lead on our guy using the GPS in his car. It was parked at an old AM radio station in the middle of nowhere."

Littlefield nodded and pulled out his phone. "Give me the address and I'll have an HRT team check there ASAP."

Sean did so and then added, looking at the two prisoners, "Spilled their guts yet?"

"They want to lawyer up," Littlefield replied. "And I don't blame them. Kidnapping. Attempted murder. Conspiracy to commit a terrorist act." He said all this in a loud voice so the two prisoners would be sure to hear. He turned to McKinney. "Hey, if we classify them as terrorists or even enemy combatants do they even have the right to a lawyer?"

Sean said, "Well, I used to practice law. You guys might have a shot at taking them straight to Gitmo."

"I'm an American citizen," yelled one of the men.

"Doesn't matter," said McKinney. "If you were planning to attack this country, there's precedent." He smiled at Sean. "This might get really fun."

"Maybe," said Sean. "But he's still out there."

"But we got the kids back," pointed out Littlefield.

"I know. And that's the most important thing."

"But?" said McKinney.

"But kidnapping wasn't the real plan, was it?"

Alan Grant stared at the computer screen for what would surely be one of the last times. He was inside the vault at the old radio station. The frenetic activity in the other part of the station had ceased. It was empty. He was the only one left. His team had done what they came to do.

He looked at the itinerary one last time and confirmed the schedule. He checked his watch. Soon it would all be over. His decades-long nightmare finally laid to rest. He had not escaped unscathed. And he wasn't sure he would be able to avoid a jail cell. But in the end, it would be worth it. His kids would still have their mother. She had plenty of money. They would be okay. Scandalized by what he'd done, but only he could understand truly the justice in all of it. But he felt fortunate in a way. Fortunate that the current president had made the same blunder as his predecessor all those years ago. But for that, this moment might never have come.

He called the cabin to check in. There was no answer. He called again. No answer. Slightly panicked now, he downloaded what he needed to his laptop, grabbed his keys, and ran to his car. A semi and accompanying crew would arrive in twenty minutes to undo everything that had been done here, leaving the place scrubbed.

He drove to a prearranged spot in D.C. near the Virginia side. He would do what he needed to do from this spot using a remote feature he had built into his plan. From here he had a nice view of the capital city. Soon it would be a capital city in chaos.

He readied his optics and checked his watch. Nearly there.

Edgar had just finished clicking keys and now he sat back stunned at what he was seeing. It was an electronic back door the likes of which he had never encountered before. He had to marvel at the ingenuity of the people who had done this. They had taken what amounted to electronic DNA fragments from a satellite once leased by the government and used that to disguise themselves, almost like a virus or cancer cell, in order to infiltrate another satellite, a very special satellite, that was relegated to one user, and one user only. And for a very good reason. Otherwise something catastrophic could happen.

It might already have.

77

"I'm sorry to keep you waiting, Ms. Maxwell."

President Cole looked harried and distracted as he entered the Oval Office.

"No problem, sir," Michelle said, quickly rising to her feet.

"And Mr. King?"

"Not here. We split up. You just get me today."

Cole nodded, but said nothing. He looked deeply preoccupied.

"Bad day, sir?" she said, trying to bring his thoughts back around to this meeting.

He started, turned to her, and attempted a smile. "You could say that. But in this job, it's all relative. A really bad day is sending off brave young men and women to die for their country."

"So I guess a garden-variety scandal isn't so bad."

"No, but it is distracting. And it gives my political enemies powder for their guns. Not that they seem to need any to fire away at me."

"What can I do for you, sir? I know every minute of your day is planned out."

"Well, I'm afraid that we're going to have to make this meeting a mobile one."

It was then that Michelle fully focused on the fact that Cole was wearing a tuxedo.

"Sir?"

"Formal event in Virginia tonight at Mount Vernon. I'm the keynote speaker. You up for a ride in the Beast?" He smiled. "My people will give you a lift back."

"Yes, sir."

As she walked out to the waiting motorcade she slipped her phone out, powered it up, and quickly thumbed in a group text to Sean and Edgar. She hit send, smiled, and put the phone back in her pocket.

A Secret Service agent she knew held open the limo door for her. The president always got in last. When his butt hit the seat the motorcade would leave. Michelle couldn't hide her smile as she climbed inside and took the seat opposite the president, facing backward.

As soon as he climbed in the door thunked closed and all outside noise vanished. It would not reappear until the doors opened once more, because the phone-book-thick windows did not roll down. The motorcade started off.

The Beast looked like the Caddy DTS it was on the outside, but it was unique in all other respects. Three hundred thousand bucks allowed some interesting optional features. It weighed more than eight tons and was completely sealed in case someone tried to hit it with biochemical weapons. The fuel tank was foam-sealed. Even if it got struck, it wouldn't explode. It had an oxygen supply and fire extinguishers in the trunk along with a supply of the president's blood type. Built into the front bumper were night-vision cameras and tear gas cannons. The vehicle's shell was a combination of ceramic, titanium, and the old reliable steel. The tires had a Kevlar skin and were run-flat. The doors were as heavy as a large jet's cabin portal because of their eight-inch armor plating. The windows' first few layers were bulletproof to absorb a round while the inner layers were a special type of plastic that would catch any bullet like a fly in a web.

Two drawbacks were speed and fuel consumption. The Beast topped out at sixty miles an hour and got only eight miles to the gallon because of all the weight.

Michelle noted the driver and other agent in the front seat. She then gazed out the window, taking in the thirty-vehicle motorcade. Then she looked over the plush interior of the rear compartment.

Cole looked at her in slight amusement. "First time in the Beast?" he asked.

She nodded. "I left the Service before I could rotate to protection detail at the White House."

"I remember my first time. I thought I was in a dream."

"Must feel pretty old hat by now."

"Not a chance. It's an honor and a privilege and it's

539

pretty damn cool." He settled back in his seat and gazed out the window. "I can never go anywhere on the sly. I'm not even allowed to drive on a public street."

Michelle sat back, too. "Probably a good idea. You don't want to have to talk your way out of a speeding ticket."

He smiled and then gazed at the agent in the front. "Window up, Frank," said Cole.

The partition glass separating the two sections of the Beast slid up.

Cole waited for it to finish its glide and then focused on Michelle. "I'm going to speak frankly, Ms. Maxwell."

"Yes, sir."

"My administration is in a world of trouble."

"I sort of got that impression."

"The thing is we were trying to do something positive, something that would help another country become free."

"The best of intentions, the worst of outcomes."

"My opponents are always screaming at me to send in troops, use America's massive military. But when we actually do something, the effect of which would be the same at far less cost to us, they threaten impeach-ment."

"I think it's called politics, sir."

"Only this time I think I went too far out on a limb. And it's about to snap." He eyed her with desperation. "Have you and your partner been able to find out anything?"

"We have, sir." She took him through all that they had learned, including the kidnapping of Tyler Wingo and his friend Kathy.

"My God, I knew nothing about that. And you think Sam Wingo was set up and that this Alan Grant is behind it all? For a political scandal that led to his parents' deaths over two decades ago?"

"That's what we believe."

"And he's the source of the leaks to that blogger?"

"We believe that too."

"And your proof?"

"We're collecting it. In fact, if you let me make a call to my partner he may have an update."

"Please."

Michelle dialed Sean. He answered on the second ring.

"I got your text," he said. "The Beast, huh? With the president?"

"Yes I am," she said happily.

"Well, we have great news too. We got Tyler and Kathy. They're both okay. They're at Fairfax Hospital. Kathy was wounded in the arm, but she'll be okay. They've got heavy FBI security. Her parents were notified and are at the hospital with her."

"Sean, that is fantastic news."

"And we got two of Grant's thugs. Littlefield and

McKinney are going to put the screws to them. If they talk, we may have a direct line back to Grant."

"Better and better." She turned to Cole. "Sir, they got the kids back. They're safe. And they got the kidnappers. The FBI has them in custody. It may lead us directly to Grant."

"Thank God," said Cole. "That's a miracle."

Michelle glanced out the window. They were just heading over Memorial Bridge into Virginia. There were no cars on the road other than the motorcade, because the Beast did not share the road with mere mortal cars and drivers. It was a beautiful evening now that the rains had passed and the descending sun shimmered off the frosty surface of the Potomac.

"So why are you meeting with the president?" asked Sean.

On Michelle's screen a text from Edgar popped up. Her eyes widened and her gut clenched.

"Michelle?" said Sean.

"Oh, shit!" exclaimed Michelle.

"What is it?" said Cole.

"Michelle, are you okay?" said Sean.

Michelle turned to the president. "We have to get—"

She never got a chance to finish.

78

The steering wheel of the Beast was ripped out of the driver's hands and cut a sharp turn to the left. At the same time the gas pedal hit the floor and the sixteen-thousand-pound vehicle accelerated and hit the bridge's stone balustrade at close to its maximum speed. The stone railings were strong, but they were never designed to stop a car that heavy going that fast. The front end of the Beast burst through the stone and its front wheels cleared the pavement. The rear wheels kept spinning, retained their traction, and with another burst of power the Beast cleared the bridge entirely and was suspended in midair for a moment. Then its nose pointed downward, and that was the direction it headed. It hit the water a few seconds later. The rear end came down and the car settled on the surface of the Potomac.

The Beast could do many impressive things. Floating was not among them. It quickly sank.

"Michelle!" Sean yelled into the phone. There was no response.

He turned to Wingo. "Something is very wrong. She's with the president and—" His phone buzzed. It was another call coming in. It was Edgar.

"Edgar, what is going on?"

"I just texted Michelle," he said. "She's with the president."

"I know that. She called me. But then something happened. I can't get through to her." Edgar said nothing. "Edgar, are you there?"

When Edgar next spoke, his voice was strained. "Sean, I just got a news break on my screen."

"What is it?" Sean said, his heart pounding.

"The presidential limo just ran off the Memorial Bridge and plunged into the Potomac."

"What? How?"

"That's what I just texted her about."

"What are you talking about?"

"The satellite, Sean. They hacked the satellite that the presidential limo uses for navigation and communication. It's too complicated to explain how they did it."

"Okay, they hacked it, so what?"

"The limo has over thirty million lines of code, Sean. The computers run everything on that vehicle. You hack the brain—"

Sean finished for him. "You control the car," he said dully.

"Yes. Speed. Steering. Brakes. Everything."

"Grant," said Sean looking at Wingo. "That son of

a bitch just got his revenge on a president who had absolutely nothing to do with his parents' deaths." He added in a shaky voice, "And Michelle is with him."

Edgar said, "What are you going to do?"

Sean dropped the phone, punched the gas, and the car flew forward.

Wingo had turned the radio on and they listened to the just-breaking news story. It sounded grim. Rescue operations were quickly being assembled, but they would need heavy equipment to get the car off the bottom of the river. The good news was that the limo had its own oxygen supply and was completely sealed so no water could get in.

Wingo said, "The Feds will be doing everything they can. And you heard the radio. The vehicle is sealed, and they have oxygen down there."

Sean stared straight ahead. "First, crashing through the barrier might have 'unsealed' the Beast. It's a tank, but even tanks can be damaged."

"And second?"

"The computer controls everything in the Beast, Sam. You own the computer, you own the Beast. And Alan Grant is way too smart to have missed something like that."

As the limo hit the bottom of the river Michelle undid her shoulder harness and checked the president. He was unconscious. She checked his pulse. It was strong, though his face was pale. She cupped her hands around his neck, feeling for fractures or bulges, but found none. She next did something she could hardly believe she could even think about.

She slapped him in the face, not once but twice.

He came around on the second strike. He looked dully at her.

"What the hell just happened?" he gasped.

"Are you hurt, Mr. President? Does anything feel broken, bruised, sore?"

He gingerly moved his arms and legs. "Sore but everything feels intact," he replied. "What happened?"

Michelle drew a short breath. "We went off the bridge. We're in the Potomac." She glanced out the windows and saw nothing but black. "The bottom of the Potomac, actually," she amended.

"In the Potomac?" he said incredulously.

Michelle found the control in the console for the window partition. Miraculously it still worked. The Beast still had power, but down here that probably wouldn't last. The motor had cut off, though, and she doubted it would restart underwater. Besides, where would they drive?

The glass slid down and she crawled through to check on the agents in the front. The air bags had deployed, she immediately noticed, which gave her hope.

The hope faded when she saw the blood and open eyes.

She checked their pulses but already knew the answer. The bags had deployed when they'd struck the railings. They had probably survived that. What they hadn't survived was the impact with the water. There were no more air bags left to save them from that. She looked at the side windows and the steel frame around them. They were bloody. Impact had probably been there. Death had probably been immediate.

She and the president were alone at the bottom of the river.

She slid feet-first back out and returned to the rear compartment.

"How are they?" Cole asked anxiously.

Michelle shook her head. "They didn't make it, sir."

"Oh my God."

Michelle looked around at the comfy leather with the thick cushions and padding. This little cocoon had saved their lives while the agents up front had taken the full brunt of the collision.

Michelle looked down at her phone. No bars, obviously.

Sometimes her service was spotty on land, much less underwater. But—

She opened the center console. There was a phone there.

She pulled it out. "This will test the manufacturer's warranty," she said.

The president undid his bowtie and unbuttoned his top button. "Getting a little close in here," he said.

"I'm sure they're assembling a rescue team as we speak, sir. Divers will be on the scene soon."

Michelle had rowed all over the Potomac. She knew the river well. She knew it was very shallow for the most part. The mean depth of the nearby Chesapeake Bay was only twenty-one feet. The spot they were in right now wasn't much deeper than that. But sitting in what was basically a tank with twenty-plus feet of water over them, a rescue attempt would be complicated.

She glanced at the doors. Eight inches of armor plating. They were not easy to open, even with hydraulic assistance. With tons of water pushing on them, they would be impossible to open without heavy machinery. And that would take time. And water would come in. She could see a scenario where water would fill the compartment as the door was slowly being forced open. They might drown with their rescuers barely inches away.

They might get equipment like you would see at a car junkyard with a magnetized end in an attempt to lift the car out. But would it work underwater? And would it be strong enough to lift an already superheavy car out of twenty-plus feet of water?

The best bet might be to tie a cable to the front of the Beast and pull it to shore with equipment that remained on land.

But again, all of that would take time.

Although this was her first time riding in it, she knew that the Beast had a portable oxygen supply that would be deployed automatically in the event the air supply in the cabin was compromised. So they should have some time. Now she was grateful for the vehicle's seal. She looked around. No water was coming in that she could see.

She looked at the phone again. She would try to contact—She drew a breath. She was startled to see it catch in her throat.

She looked at Cole. He seemed to have turned a shade paler. Now she focused on what he had said before.

Getting a little close in here.

"Sir, can you move to the rear-facing seat?"

She helped him undo his shoulder harness and aided him to the other side of the cabin. She popped the backseat down and crawled into the armored trunk. She saw the fire extinguishers and the blood supply canister. She crawled through and unhooked the trunk's floor covering. There were the oxygen tanks. She examined them closely. They seemed to be full, but they didn't seem to be deployed. She rapped on one of the tanks with her knuckles and then bent her ear to the pipes running into the cabin. She could hear no air flowing through them.

Most people would be panicking by now. But like pilots trying to save a plunging plane, Michelle had been especially trained for crisis situations. She was too busy trying to save the president and herself to start screaming.

There was no manual wheel on top of the oxygen cans that would allow her to open them herself. She cursed this obvious flaw in the plan. She took a shallow breath and felt herself becoming a little light-headed. It was maddening to think that ample oxygen was right here but they couldn't get to it.

She kicked it with her foot in the hope that it might start flowing, but when she put her ear to the lines she heard nothing. How could the fail-safe have failed? It was like all engines on a plane stopping at the same time. It just didn't happen.

Then she remembered Edgar's text. *Get out of the limo. There's a problem with it.*

Somehow, against all odds, the mighty Beast had been sabotaged.

She climbed back into the rear compartment.

The president looked at her. "The oxygen isn't working, is it?" he asked.

She shook her head. "No."

"Did the driver have a medical emergency?"

"I don't think so, sir."

"Then how did this happen? Were we hit by something?"

"I think the Beast was…somehow taken over by a third party."

"Taken over? How?"

"I'm not sure." Michelle looked back at the phone, then snatched it up and dialed the number, praying that the Beast's world-class communications system would live up to its billing.

"Hello?" The voice sounded panicked, desperate.

"Sean, it's me."

"Michelle, talk to me. Give me the status."

She did so. Two agents dead. President okay. Oxygen not working.

"Grant took control of the Beast," Sean said. "And he ran it off the bridge."

"Edgar sent me a text while I was talking to you that there was a problem with the limo. What's going on up there?"

"I just got on the scene. It's barricaded off, as you can imagine. I managed to get hold of Littlefield, and he got me through to the bridge. I'm looking down at you right now. Dive boats are on their way, but they have to come up from the Anacostia. It'll take a little bit of time but they're trying to get them faster. They've got a police boat on the surface getting a radar fix on your location. They have choppers coming in with grappling hooks too."

"The Beast weighs eight tons."

"I know. They'll need military transport choppers and even then I doubt they could do it. You've got tons of water over you."

"Then it's the divers we have to wait on," she said, the hope in her voice fading. "But if they can attach a cable to the bumper and then winch us out from the riverbank—"

"Michelle, listen to me very carefully. You don't have time for them to get you out. You have to get yourself and the president out."

"Great, Sean, just tell me how," she snapped.

"It's a long shot, but it's the only chance you've got. How much air do you think you have left?"

She glanced over at the pale Cole. "If we breathe shallow, a few minutes, max."

"Okay, here's what you have to do."

79

Alan Grant had watched in uneasy fascination as the presidential limo crashed through Memorial Bridge's side and plunged into the murky waters of the Potomac. He had clicked some more keys on his laptop disabling the car's oxygen supply. He didn't bother with the communications capability of the vehicle. He wanted them to talk to each other. He wanted them to hear the desperation. It wouldn't do any good. It was too late. It would take thirty minutes to get a rescue operation together. By then the president and anyone else in that limo would be long dead, poisoned by the carbon monoxide released from their own mouths, with no fresh air to replenish it.

He closed his laptop and watched for another few seconds as utter chaos continued on the bridge and riverbanks. The media trucks were already converging. The public had clustered near the scene as closely as they could. Police and news choppers were in the air, for all the good that would do them.

The mighty Beast, killed by its own weight, along with the president inside it.

The FBI, DHS, Secret Service, Metro Police, military, and probably half a dozen other agencies were scrambling around trying to do something. All they were doing was absolutely nothing.

If it weren't so pathetic, it might even be funny, he thought.

Grant put his car in gear and slowly drove off. He had tried to call his men again at the cabin and still had gotten no answer. That was very troublesome. His phone rang. He answered it. It was Trevor Jenkins. He had posted him at the radio station.

"Have they gotten everything out yet?"

Jenkins's voice was strained. "No. And I don't think they will."

"Why?" snapped Grant.

"Because a convoy of SUVs is flying up the road. I think it's HRT."

"Get yourself out of there, now, Trevor," yelled Grant.

He put the phone down, his panic rising.

His discreet exit from the scene was now gone. They had cracked his nut.

But he had gotten his man. He had obtained his goal.

The president was dead. His father was avenged. It had only taken twenty-five years and a son's nearly lifelong obsession to get it done. But now it was done.

Finally.

★

Michelle had gotten the president into the front seat with her after sliding the bodies of the two dead agents onto the floorboard. She had made him take off his lightweight body armor. In the water, that would be a death sentence.

She held a Remington shotgun that she had taken from a compartment next to the driver's seat. Sean had told her about it. He had also told her something else. A plan, one she was just about to execute.

She had flipped down the forward-facing rear seats, exposing the trunk area. She had explained to the president what she was going to do. He had accepted the strategy as the only chance they had. But she knew what he had been thinking by the look in his eyes.

She was young, fit, and strong.

He, on the other hand, was a middle-aged man with a slight paunch. And while he probably engaged in light exercise, what he was going to have to do in order to live was something more than that.

Michelle had taken all of this into account after Sean had talked to her and built her own plan around his. She went over in her mind what was about to happen. They had light now because of the Beast's sealed power unit. But once she did what she was about to do, they would be plunged into darkness. So she had to graft onto her brain both the way out with the president and then the way up, to the surface.

Twenty-four feet, that was how far it was to the surface at this point in the river. It didn't sound like a long way, but when you were holding your breath and struggling upward, it might as well have been a mile, especially with someone holding on to you.

She looked over at Cole. She had found some rope, Velcro straps, and an emergency flashlight behind a seat panel that Sean had also told her about. She tied one end of the rope around the president's waist and then attached the other end to her waist. She purposefully kept the rope length short. They could not afford to get it snagged on something in the dark as they were fleeing the car. The result would be both their deaths. She unlatched the trunk, but the water pressure was keeping it firmly shut. At least it wasn't locked.

"Sir, when I fire the lights will probably go out and the water will flood in. Take three deep breaths and hold the last one. Then I'm going to move forward and out and then up. You can kick your feet and move your arms once we're out of the car. Then we go immediately up. I'll be right with you the whole way. I will not leave you. I will not let you die. Okay?"

He nodded as beads of sweat collected on his brow. "Okay."

She had Velcroed the flashlight around her head. She prayed it worked underwater.

"On the count of three," said Michelle as she aimed the Remington. "One…two…three."

She fired at the oxygen tanks. There was an explosion and a flash of light. The gas tank had been sealed against an explosion and its tank was full so very little vapor was present. And while the Beast was designed to withstand an RPG round coming from the outside, an oxygen-fueled explosion coming from the inside had not been contemplated by the architects of the car.

The unlatched trunk blew off and the water poured in.

Michelle dropped the shotgun and shot forward, pulling the president behind her. She met the cold water head-on. The light continued to work, although weakly. But it was enough illumination.

The Potomac had underwater currents as well as surface ones that were surprisingly strong. Many an unwary swimmer had died because of them. But Michelle was not unwary and she was a strong swimmer. She pushed hard through the car's interior, using the seats and frame to propel forward.

She stood inside the trunk for only a moment, something she could now do because it no longer had a lid. Then she planted her feet firmly and pushed off strongly, aiming herself and the president upward. The trunk height was about two feet off the river's floor. That meant twenty-two more feet to go.

She kicked powerfully with her legs and arms. She could feel the president doing the same right behind her, if somewhat more feebly.

Twenty-two feet became fifteen. Michelle could feel her arms and legs begin to ache with the cold and the effort it was taking to pull a full-grown man along with her.

Fifteen feet became ten. She could see a bit of light above her.

She gave another mighty kick and tried not to think about her lungs bursting.

Ten feet became less than six. But her head was throbbing so badly she thought a vein would burst. She also felt the president faltering. He was no longer kicking with his feet.

She could feel herself being pulled downward.

She gathered all of her strength and pushed upward, kick after kick, stroke after stroke. If she was going to die she was going to leave it all on the table, just like she had in the Olympics. Her crew team had lost in the final and gotten the silver, but it had still felt incredible. Well, tonight second place was not good enough. She was going for the gold.

Six feet became three, then two. She gave a tremendous kick and broke the surface of the water. She grabbed the end of the rope and pulled with all her might. The effort caused her to go under but the president's limp form shot past her and his head rose above the surface. He coughed and vomited.

Suddenly, strong hands were grabbing them both. Michelle was pulled nearly out of the water by a grip that felt like steel. She looked around and saw the police diver next to her. Other hands latched on to her and she was pulled cleanly out of the water and into the rescue boat.

A moment later President Cole slipped into the boat next to her. She coughed up some water, took great gulps of air into her lungs, and sat up on one shoulder.

"Mr. President? Are you okay?"

He tried to sit up but two medics kneeling next to him gently pushed him back down. As they worked on him he looked at Michelle and smiled weakly.

"You can be on my protection detail anytime you want, Ms. Maxwell," he croaked.

As blankets were wrapped around her Michelle lay back and closed her eyes. And then she smiled.

At least I finally got to ride in the Beast, she thought.

80

In a private White House ceremony Sean and Michelle received the country's thanks for saving its leader from certain death. And fortunately for President John Cole, this latest attack on the country's highest officeholder and his dramatic and heroic escape from death had rallied all around him. Even his most ardent political opponents had dropped their cries for investigation and impeachment, at least for the time being.

After the ceremony was concluded, Cole shook hands with Sean, thanking him for his quick thinking and sound advice to Michelle. And then Cole broke protocol and gave Michelle a heartfelt hug, while Mrs. Cole did the same to both Michelle and Sean.

"Thank you," both the president and First Lady said together.

Littlefield and McKinney had attended the ceremony. Both agents had been given commendations for their work in busting up the conspiracy to first embarrass the nation and possibly draw it into a war, and then to kill its leader.

On the downside, the kidnappers had not yet broken their silence. And the team of movers at the AM station did not know anything about what they were moving. Or at least that's what they claimed. The billion euros, or what was left of it, was still missing. And, most significantly, Alan Grant had not yet been found.

As they walked to her Land Cruiser after the White House ceremony Michelle said, "You look nice in a suit. You should wear one more often."

Sean smiled and shook his head. "Had enough of that in the Service. My battle armor was a Brooks Brothers off-the-rack, tie, and wing tips. And sunglasses. The rest of my life will be spent in casual mode."

She held up the medal the president had bestowed on them. "Except when you get one of these, you mean."

"Except then. How're the shots feeling?"

Michelle and Cole had undergone a series of antibiotic treatments, some of which had been by injection. They had both been in the Potomac and had swallowed some of the water. And while the river was cleaner than it had been decades ago, when it had been semi-radioactive, one still wouldn't want to drink it.

"My butt has felt better, let's leave it at that."

They climbed into her truck.

"Been meaning to ask you something."

"Okay," said Sean.

"How did you think of blowing the oxygen tanks to get us out of the Beast? I can't believe you guys practiced that scenario when you were on protection detail."

"We didn't," Sean admitted as he put on his seat belt. "Nothing close. Air Force One has water-landing scenarios, but not the Beast."

"So how, then?"

"Can we leave it at my brilliantly incisive mind that can size up any critical situation and move like a laser to the solution?"

Michelle belted up and then started the truck. "Don't make me get physical with you, Sean."

He sighed. "Okay, but this is only for your ears." He paused. "I remembered it from *Jaws*."

She leaned on the steering wheel and stared at him. "*Jaws*?"

"Yeah, the movie *Jaws*. Roy Scheider's character is the small-town sheriff stuck in the middle of the ocean and the shark is bearing down on him. But the shark has an oxygen tank wedged in its mouth from where it sank a dive boat. Scheider just happens to have a gun. He shoots, hits the tank. Boom. No more shark."

"So I'm sitting here talking to you instead of lying in the morgue because of a Spielberg flick?"

"What can I tell you? It made an impression on me when I first saw it."

She patted him on the shoulder. "Well, thank God it did."

Once they got out of the city she said, "So what will happen to Sam Wingo?"

"Nothing. They know he was set up. They know he's innocent. They know his son was kidnapped to keep him in line. Hell, the guy deserves a medal like us, and the military knows that. He'll be just fine. And Tyler got his dad back."

"Well, I think Cole is both happy to be alive and thrilled that the missing euro scandal has disappeared at least for now."

"All you need is a bigger story to cover. Remember Chandra Levy and the congressman some thought had killed her?"

"No, not really."

"That's because it was 'the' story until nine-eleven happened shortly thereafter."

"So the missing piece is—"

"Alan Grant, yeah. His wife has been questioned, of course. From what Littlefield could tell me she's as stunned as anyone else. But his guilt is pretty well established."

"And Dan Marshall, his presumed leak and partner in this?"

"He's been questioned and will no doubt be questioned some more."

"By the cops?"

"Yes. But also by us."

"What?"

"We were hired to do a job, Michelle. We have not finished that job, at least not to my mind."

"I didn't think you wanted any piece of this case to begin with."

"It's grown on me. And I take great exception to anyone who tries to kill the president." He turned to look at her. "Or you."

"So we go and see Marshall?"

"Yes, but I want to talk to Edgar first."

"He figured out how Grant hacked into the satellite used for the Beast."

"I know. The stuff they found at that old radio station was state-of-the-art equipment. I bet that's where some of the billion euros went. In addition to leasing a satellite. And the guy who leased it to him recognized a picture of Grant. He just had no idea what he was going to use it for."

"Then he needs to screen his customers better," she said.

"I'm betting Grant did not do this alone. He must have had serious computer hacking talent in place. The FBI is checking out movements of known bad guys with computer skills."

"They're probably long gone."

"Probably," conceded Sean. "But I really hope they find Grant. He was the one who shot Kathy. She identified his picture too. And that tells me he had no intention of letting either of them go."

"How about our old pal Trevor Jenkins?"

"Gone like a ghost by the time HRT got to the station."

"You think he and Grant are on the run together?"

"I wouldn't bet against it. But they're going to have a hell of a time getting out of the country. Everybody's looking for them."

She put the truck in gear and hit the gas. "God, it's good to be back on dry land."

81

"I'm very glad that you lived, Ms. Maxwell," said Edgar with as much emotion as he was apt to show.

"I am too, Edgar, thanks. And you know you can call me Michelle."

They were seated around the kitchen table at Edgar's farmhouse.

"You figured this out before anyone," said Sean. "And we told the president that. Don't be surprised if you get a call."

"I already did," said Edgar. "He wanted me to come to the White House, but I told him I had to feed the chickens."

Sean blanched. "Edgar, please tell me you did not tell the president of the United States that you couldn't come to the White House because you had chickens to feed."

"Actually, I didn't."

"Thank God for that."

"I told his chief of staff, who I presume told the president."

Sean wearily shook his head while Michelle bit her lip to keep from laughing.

"Chickens take a lot of time to care for properly, Sean," explained Edgar. "It was just a question of timing. I'll get by the White House at some point."

Sean asked, "How did you track down what Grant had done?"

"It was more by chance than anything intentional. But your asking me to find Grant's car by using the GPS chip in it made me think about things from that angle. Cars these days have a great deal of computer hardware and software to make them function the way people need them to. There're approximately one hundred megabytes of binary code in high-end models that runs over fifty computer units. But this also allows hackers numerous points of entry. Telematics, Blue-tooth, keyless entry, even tire sensors that utilize wireless connections. Or you can be hacked through your CD or DVD player. But most hackers will attack a vehicle through something called the On-Board Diagnostics port. It's an access port where repair shops hook up their diagnostic computer to a car's computer so they can talk to each other."

"Sounds like a patient and his doctor," said Sean. "Not a car."

"We've apparently come a long way since the 1966 Mustang," added Michelle. "I drove my brother's hand-me-down in college. It had something called an eight-track player."

Sean stared at her. "These are the moments where I realize how much older I am than you."

She smiled sweetly. "You're not in bad shape for a man of your advanced years."

Sean turned to Edgar. "The FBI's having their guys tear the Beast apart to see where the attack came from," said Sean.

"It started with a commercial satellite that had once been leased to the government," said Edgar. "They're supposed to be scrubbed of any sensitive material once they're no longer used by the government, but Grant apparently found some remnants. He used those remnants as a way to infiltrate the satellite that is devoted to the GPS navigation and control functions of the presidential limo. I'm betting that the FBI technicians will find malware placed on there that allowed Grant to remotely control all functions of the car."

"I bet they will too," said Michelle. "The car just started driving itself. The agent at the wheel could do nothing about it. It just happened. It changed course, accelerated, and into the water we went. And then the oxygen system didn't work."

"The malware I'm sure had a part in that," noted Edgar.

Michelle said, "If they could hack the Beast, no car is safe."

"Absolutely true," said Edgar matter-of-factly. "It really does show the good and bad of technology. We rely on it at our peril."

"We still haven't determined who the leak was," said Michelle. "Grant knew about Wingo's classified mission in the Middle East. He had to get that from somewhere."

"What about the president's itinerary?" asked Edgar. "Grant knew precisely when he was going over the bridge."

"It was public knowledge that the president was attending the event in Virginia that evening," said Sean. "But he couldn't have known when the motorcade was leaving the city. Although he could have had eyes on it."

Michelle said, "But unless he had inside information he probably wouldn't have known until that day about the event. It's not like the schedule is heavily publicized. Or the route the motorcade would take. And he might have wanted several options to nail Cole and picked the best one."

"Well, he might have gotten the president's schedule from someone. But that someone probably would be different from the person who knew about the mission in Afghanistan."

"My money is still on it being Dan Marshall," said Michelle. "He's Grant's father-in-law. I'm not saying he knowingly did it. Grant had some access and he might have exploited that access. And if he's good enough to hack the presidential satellite, then maybe he hacked Marshall's computer at the Pentagon."

"If he did they would know," opined Edgar. "The

Pentagon does get hacked, but they quickly realize if they have been."

Michelle looked doubtful but said, "Okay, if that's the case what do we do now? Who's our focus? Do we go to Trevor Jenkins's place and poke around?"

Sean said, "The FBI has been all over it. And I highly doubt he's going to come back there to pick up some clean clothes. He's probably in Venezuela by now on his way to disappearing permanently. His share of a billion euros buys that kind of vanishing act."

"Couldn't hurt," said Michelle. "Unless you have a better idea."

"I knew you were going to say that," he replied.

She rose and pulled out her keys. "So let's go fishing."

82

They drove toward Jenkins's house. It was dark now and the wind was picking up. The skies promised more rain and soon. Michelle shivered a bit and glanced over at Sean.

"I never thanked you properly," she said.

"For what?" he asked curiously.

She looked incredulous. "Oh, I don't know. Saving my life?"

"You saved your own life, Michelle. I just suggested how you might want to go about it."

"You're a hard man to compliment."

"At least you weren't stabbed this time. It was just the threat of drowning."

"Are you going to go all grim on me again?"

He sighed and tried but failed to force a smile.

"Sean, we've had this discussion before."

"And never had a resolution to it."

"There is no resolution to it if we keep doing what we're doing. And forget your suggestion that you keep being a PI while I go bake cookies."

"I didn't suggest that you bake cookies."

"Good, because I suck at baking. You're the cook, not me."

He was about to respond to this when he glanced out the window and it finally hit him.

"Damn," he muttered.

"What is it?" asked Michelle.

"You remember when we staked out South's place before and I said it felt funny when we were driving through some of the neighborhoods?"

"Yeah, like you'd been here before but couldn't remember when or why."

"Well, I think I just remembered both. Only I really hope I'm wrong."

"Is this about Grant?"

"No, this is about the leak."

He pulled out his phone and punched in a number. "Edgar, it's Sean. You think you have one more hack left in you tonight?" He added, "The Pentagon. Here's what I need."

It took two hours but Edgar came through and gave Sean the answers to his questions. He'd also managed to discover some additional information on the person in question. "People need to hide their tracks better online," said Edgar. "Two proxy servers, three ghost IP addresses, a manufactured digital confluence in Hong Kong, and a byte dispersal program randomly free-riding on excess data streams with reassembly on a platform in Dubai just doesn't cut it anymore."

Sean rubbed his temple. "Okay, Edgar, I have no idea what the hell you just said, but can they track it back to you?"

"I'm cool," said Edgar. "National security—"

"Trumps all," finished Sean.

He put away the phone and looked at Michelle.

She said, "From your scowl I deduce your wish did not happen. You were really right, not really wrong."

"I'll give you directions to where we're going."

"Sean?" she said quizzically.

Sean looked grim. "Not now, Michelle. Not now."

They walked up to the door of the substantial house set on a corner lot. Sean rang the bell. They heard footsteps approaching. A few moments later Curtis Brown, Dana's two-star husband, opened the door. He looked surprised to see them.

"Jesus, I thought you guys would be making the major news show circuit by now. National heroes. Pretty damn impressive."

"Can we come in, Curtis?" asked Sean somberly.

Brown took a step back. "Sure, what's up?"

"I know it's late, but I just wanted to ask you a few questions. About Dana."

"Okay. She's doing much better. Docs think she can be discharged in a week or so to rehab."

"That's great news."

He closed the door behind them and led them into the living room.

Sean looked around at the comfortable furnishings. Everything had been done in fine taste.

"Do I detect Dana's work here?" he asked.

"Yes. I can lead soldiers into battle. I cannot decorate a room or match colors to save my soul."

Curtis sat and motioned for them to do so. "Now, what can I do for you?"

"You didn't tell us you were retiring from the Army," began Sean.

Brown looked surprised. "How did you find out about that?"

"Is it true?"

"Yes. Two stars are enough for me. I'd have to keep making the circuit if I wanted to keep moving up and getting one or two more. And I'm tired of the game."

"And you're moving to Malaysia?"

Now Brown stood and glared at Sean. "You've been spying on me. Hacking my personal records."

"Not me, no, I wouldn't know how. But a friend of mine is really good at it. Only Malaysia isn't your final stop. You're only there for a few weeks. You bought property, through a shell company, on an island in Indonesia. A lot of property, all oceanfront. Way more than a two-star should be able to afford even though you do have a trust fund."

"And interestingly enough Indonesia has no extradition with the U.S.," added Michelle.

Brown sat back down and said nothing.

Sean rose and looked around the room. "When we

were staking out Leon South's home we passed through this neighborhood. I recognized it, though I didn't know from where. But I had driven by it once years ago."

"Why?"

"I'd heard Dana had remarried. Did some checking, got the address. Just wanted to see if she was okay."

Sean stopped and looked down, a hint of incredulity at his own words on his face. Michelle was watching him closely.

She said, "Are you all right?"

He straightened. "I'm fine. Anyway, drove by here. Nice neighborhood, beautiful house. You had a good, solid rep. Seemed like she had married very well."

"And so had I."

Sean turned to face him. "Then why the one-way plane tickets, Curtis? And why are you the only one booked to go? Where's Dana's ticket? You leave in two days. According to what you just said she won't even be out of the hospital by then, much less rehab."

Brown kept silent.

"We saw Jenkins pass by South's home that night, only he didn't stop there. That's because Jenkins was coming from your house, Curtis. He'd already met with you. You were Grant's leak at the Pentagon, not Dan Marshall. You told us you'd sat in on some meetings with Marshall. You neglected to tell us that you were also privy to the mission Sam Wingo was undertaking.

And I'm not just talking scuttlebutt that Dana weaseled out of you."

"And the price Grant paid for that is buying you a new life on your island in Indonesia. A life for one," Michelle added.

"Funded by fifty million bucks placed in an offshore account after Sam Wingo was ambushed. The transfer was done through a shell that we also traced back to you. That was part of the billion euros, right? Any idea where the rest of it might be?"

Brown just stared at them.

Sean drew closer to him. "When Dana started poking around for me, did you think you'd just had the worst luck in the world? Your wife's ex had come around asking questions about the very scheme in which you were neck-deep. That must have freaked you out. Did you arrange the hit at the mall? Take out all three of us at the same time? Later, did you sit by her bedside at the hospital praying she wouldn't make it?"

Brown said dully, "I love Dana. I'm going over-seas to get things set up. Then I'm coming back for her. I did not arrange for anyone to shoot her. When you told me that she'd been followed to the mall—" He broke off here, and the tears spilled down his face.

"Your partner double-crossing you?" asked Michelle.

Sean added, "When he found out you'd talked to

Dana about Wingo's situation, he must've been really upset."

"I didn't know she was doing it for you," said Brown. "I didn't even know you two had met until—"

"Until your partner told you. And he sent the kill squad to the mall."

Sean said, "Did Jenkins come to read you the riot act that night, General? Or did he just want to make sure you were pretending to work with us to throw off suspicion?"

"I…I don't…"

"Did you know what Grant was going to do with the information you gave him?" asked Michelle. "Kill the president? That's treason. That's the death penalty."

Brown started and seemed to realize what he had been saying. He said firmly, "I don't know what you're talking about. Now I'd like you two to leave."

He stood.

"You're not going to make the flight to Malaysia," warned Sean as he faced Brown.

"Why not? You have no proof of anything. So I bought some property, so what? The fifty mill in the offshore account? Don't have a clue what you're talking about. I just made good investments and got a really good deal on some land."

"You punched me for putting Dana in danger," said Sean.

"So what?"

Sean swung his fist and knocked Brown over a chair.

"I just returned the favor," he said, rubbing his hand.

Brown jumped up. Sean braced for his attack when a voice froze all three of them.

"Enough!"

They turned to see Alan Grant standing by the doorway.

In his hand was a small box with a button on it. His finger was pressed on the button. With his free hand he swept open the front of his coat. Three C-4 packs were strapped to his torso.

83

Sean and Michelle immediately moved away from Grant and his explosive belt, but Brown stood rooted to the spot. "What are you doing here?" he said slowly.

Grant pointed at Sean and Michelle. "Following them. Are you the one who stabbed me in the back, Curtis? Because without somebody's help I don't see how they could have done what they did."

"I don't know what you're talking about, Alan," replied Brown, eyeing the detonator in his hand.

Grant observed this. "Idiot switch. Fitting, actually, since I've learned this is what Wingo used in Afghanistan to escape. Otherwise, he would have been dead as planned and I wouldn't be standing here now as a flesh-and-blood IED." He eyed Brown. "Pity you didn't have the intelligence about Wingo's fail-safe, Curtis. But then again you've failed me in so many ways."

"It doesn't have to end like this, Grant," said Sean.

Grant looked at him. "Nice to finally meet you face-to-face, Mr. King. We seem to communicate too much these days with texts and emails." He paused, and his calm face finally showed a flash of anger.

"Twenty-five years. A quarter century I've lived with this hurt, this shame. This injustice."

Michelle said, "But how exactly is it justice to kill a man who had nothing to do with your parents' suicides?"

"Well, I couldn't kill the man in office at the time could I? Because he's already dead. So it's symbolism that matters, Ms. Maxwell. This all began with Iran and now it will end with Iran. Or at least that was the plan. President Cole's heroic escape with your help apparently will allow him to suffer no consequences for his actions. The guilty once more go free and brave, honest people die."

"I was the one under the Potomac," Michelle snapped.

He looked directly at her. "I should have thought of the oxygen tanks being used as an explosive device, but I didn't. I commend your ingenuity." He gave a mock bow in their direction.

"Is this how you want your family to see you go out, Grant?" asked Sean. "In a flame ball? Like a suicide bomber? You fought against those guys when you were in uniform. Now you're taking a page from their book. Is that how you want to be remembered?"

"My options are limited."

"I didn't betray you, Alan," said Brown.

"I don't believe you. I paid you well for your services. Was it too much to offer loyalty in return?"

"I didn't betray you," shouted Brown.

"He's telling the truth, Grant," interjected Sean. "We figured it out for ourselves. Wingo followed Jenkins to Vista Trading. That's the link to you. We knew about what happened to your mom and dad. That was public information. That gave us the motive. We tracked your lease of the satellite through a shell company. Jenkins had purchased the cabin, which we found out from his computer records. By the way, the police found a shallow grave up there with the remains of Jean Shepherd."

"Another one who lost her way," said Grant.

"We were on to her," said Michelle. "That's why she ran."

"Then why are you here?" said Grant. "If not to hook back up with your confederate?"

"We're here to tell him why the FBI is going to be showing up here any minute," said Sean. "To arrest him for being a co-conspirator with you to assassinate the president." He stared at Grant. "What, did you think I slugged him because he's my buddy?"

Brown paled. "The FBI?"

Sean looked at him. "Did you really think we just came over to blow a lot of hot air and then let you walk? The FBI used our intel to do their deep dig. They have the evidence to nail you to the wall."

"You're lying," barked Brown.

"Now you know how it feels, Curtis, to have your life ruined," said Grant.

Brown turned to him. "Did you order the hit on Dana? Are you the reason she nearly died?"

"She was working with these two. And what did you do? Blab to the bitch about Wingo. *That* was the betrayal."

"So you were just going to kill her? For that?"

"I've killed for a lot less than that. Just like right now."

Sean said, "Grant, you don't want to do this."

Grant hadn't noticed that Michelle had edged close enough to strike.

She hit him chest-high, her long, strong fingers clamping over the detonator, keeping the button pressed down. But Grant was also strong and agile. He spun around and threw her off. He had not anticipated the next attack, though.

Curtis Brown screamed and hit Grant so hard the two men flew backward and crashed right through a window, toppling into the front yard.

Sean grabbed Michelle from the floor, and they hurtled into the kitchen. He pushed her down and she landed on the floor and kept sliding. Sean threw himself forward and covered her body with his.

When the C-4 detonated it blew out the entire front of the house. The walls collapsed and the roof toppled downward. Glass shards and other debris thick as fists hurtled in all directions.

"Move, move, move!" shouted Sean. He grabbed Michelle's hand and they burst out the back door, jumped off the deck, and ran across the back lawn. Sean gave her a leg up over the fence and then scrambled over it, too. He landed face-first in the grass on the other side at just the moment when the severed gas lines in Brown's house erupted.

In a blazing flash the entire house was leveled. The explosion was so huge that it blew out windows in the houses next to Brown's even though each was over a hundred feet away and there were stands of trees in between. The remains of the destroyed house quickly caught fire.

The fence Sean and Michelle were behind was impaled with glass and metal shards. Part of the top was sheared off.

Michelle helped Sean up. "You okay?"

He nodded, holding his hand at an odd angle. "But I think I fractured my hand," he said.

She dialed 911 and reported the explosion.

"Is the FBI really on the way?" she asked him.

He shook his head.

She drew a long breath and leaned against a tree for support.

"Is this sucker over yet?" she said, in a husky, drained voice.

Sean shook his head.

"One more to go."

84

It felt like the longest walk Sean King would ever have to take.

The hospital corridor was mostly empty. Michelle was not with him. She was waiting outside in her Land Cruiser. She had offered to come with him, but this was something Sean had to do by himself. He *had* fractured his hand when he'd jumped over the fence. It was in a soft cast. He would take that over getting his head blown off.

He turned down the last hall and proceeded to her room.

Dana Brown had been stepped down to a regular hospital room. She was finally out of danger. She would make it. At least physically she would. Sean wasn't sure about mentally.

He knocked, heard her say "Come in," then opened the door and stepped into the room.

One look at her face told him all he needed to know. She had been told about her husband's death and his involvement with Alan Grant. As he approached the bed Dana slowly sat up. They hugged for a long time. He let her cry and he felt the tears trickle out of his own eyes.

When they drew apart he pulled up a chair and sat down next to her. He held her hand and watched her closely. She had aged much in the last few weeks. Anyone would have. But even though she'd been shot and had nearly died and now had lost her husband, he could see the woman he had fallen in love with all those years ago quite clearly defined and sitting in front of him.

She said in a halting voice, "They said he didn't suffer."

"He didn't, Dana. It was over, well, it was over very quickly."

"And you were there?"

"Yes. We'd gone to check up on Curtis when Alan Grant showed up."

"Alan Grant. My husband's partner in crime," she added bitterly.

"I don't believe that Curtis knew what Grant was planning, Dana. He just got him some information on the mission in Afghanistan. Curtis just thought it was a robbery of government funds, and he was going to get his share."

"Still a criminal, Sean. I can't believe he would do that. I really can't."

"That much money makes for a lot of temptation. I'm not saying it wasn't wrong, because it was. But I can understand the temptation."

"I guess I should too, considering how often I've succumbed to temptation in my life," she said guiltily.

"But the fact is I wouldn't be here right now except for Curtis. He sacrificed his life for ours. Just like the soldier he was. He took Grant out and gave his life in doing it. So, yeah, he did some wrong things. Some really stupid things. But you have to give the man that. And I know that he wanted to kill Grant because Grant had hurt you, Dana. That's why Curtis attacked him. He was avenging you."

She nodded, and more tears swept down her cheeks. "I know," she said in a barely audible voice. "I know."

Sean held her for a while and let her cry, trying to absorb her body shudders, her grief, but he knew he really couldn't.

When Dana finally pulled back he said, "There was a reward posted for the capture of the people behind this. It's been decided that you should have it, as Curtis's widow."

She looked stunned. "But Sean, you and Michelle risked your lives to—"

He squeezed her hand more tightly. "And Curtis sacrificed his life for us. And it's more than enough money to take care of you for the rest of your days. You'll never have to worry about finances, okay?"

It had been difficult getting the appropriate parties to sign off on this. Many were reluctant to let Brown's widow get anything, since he had been in on the crime. But Sean had pulled the biggest chit he had—

a personal plea to President Cole. After he came on board, everyone else quickly followed.

She put a shaky hand to her face and whisked some tears away. "That is very kind. Very generous."

"That takes care of the money part. But what about you?"

She shrugged, her look one of bewilderment. "I don't know. It's hard to even think clearly right now."

"Of course it is. And you don't have to think about it right now. What you have to do is get yourself well. You'll be going to rehab soon. And I'm going to go there with you." He held up his injured hand. She had evidently not noticed it before.

"Oh my God, what happened?"

"Just being clumsy. But we can rehab together, how does that sound?"

"That sounds really good," she said a bit breathlessly.

"You're not alone, Dana. Okay? You're not alone."

She sat back in the bed. "You know, I always thought we'd have kids. A big family."

"Life doesn't always work out the way you'd like. In fact, it almost never does. I wanted to pitch in the major leagues. Ended up being a human shield in a suit instead."

She turned her head to look at him.

"I'm sorry."

"For what?"

"You know for what, Sean. You know."

"Blame is a two-way street."

"I wish it were so, but not in this case."

He patted her hand.

"You're way too good to me," she said.

"You're a good person."

"I've changed, you mean," she said, a weak smile crossing her lips.

"A good person," Sean said softly.

Later he walked back down the hall and left the hospital. The day was crisp and clear. He couldn't see a cloud in the sky, when for the last couple of weeks he couldn't remember not seeing them up there.

He climbed into the Land Cruiser where Michelle was waiting.

She said, "How did it go?"

"As well as could be expected."

She put the car in gear.

"You going to see her again?"

He glanced across at her. "I told her we'd rehab together. My hand, her body."

"You think that's wise?"

His brow creased. "Why wouldn't it be? She has nobody right now. She shouldn't be alone."

"Don't you think you might be giving her false hope?"

"False hope of what?"

"Of you two getting back together."

"Michelle, that is not going to happen."

"Does she know that?"

"Well, if you mean did I tell her there is no chance in hell we were reconciling, no I didn't. I thought the timing might be bad what with her husband just being blown up," he added in a harsh tone.

Michelle drove out of the parking lot. "Just saying is all. You might be setting her up for a greater hurt down the road."

"Is this female-speak that I'm somehow not understanding?"

"I thought it was pretty clear, actually."

"Okay, then let me be clear. Do you feel threatened by Dana?"

"Not unless she's going to join our firm as a partner."

"So just business then?"

She looked at him. "What else?"

"Fine. Then I can tell you unequivocally that she will never be joining King and Maxwell."

He looked away and thus didn't see Michelle bite her lip and inwardly groan.

"Look, I'm sorry, Sean. I didn't mean it like that. The words got jumbled up coming out of my stupid mouth."

"Wouldn't be the first time."

"Hey, I don't deserve—"

She stopped when she saw him turn and smile at her.

"Jealously is good for a relationship, business or otherwise," he said.

"You're a shit, you really are."

"I'll admit on the record that I am occasionally a shit."

"I'd punch you except you're injured."

"You've hit me before when I've been injured."

"Yeah, but you're older now. I don't want to do permanent damage."

He reached over and gripped her hand. "Do you know what I wished for when I was sitting next to your hospital bed waiting for you to wake up?"

Her gaze grew serious. "What?"

"That I would be the first person you'd see when you did wake up."

"And you were," she said, her voice suddenly cracking.

"Yeah, I was," he said.

"So your wish was answered."

"My wish was answered as soon as you opened your eyes."

"If we keep this up you're going to see me cry for the first time in your life."

"Not the first time."

She looked at him for a long moment. "I know."

Sean's phone rang. It was Edgar.

"Better take it," said Michelle. She turned away and wiped her eyes clear.

"Hello, Edgar." Sean listened. "Yeah, right, but... Well, I know that, only...Okay, I guess you didn't understand that it was only a—Hello?"

He put down the phone, looking disturbed.

"What is it?" Michelle asked. "Please don't tell me the Pentagon came and arrested Edgar."

"No, they didn't."

"Then what?"

"He accepted our job offer."

"What?" she exclaimed.

"Correction, to be precise he said he's 'accepting the job offer from *Ms. Maxwell*.'"

"That wasn't a job offer. That was a joke. You know that."

"Well, apparently he doesn't. He already gave Peter Bunting and the U.S. government his notice and he'll be at our office tomorrow to start work. Predictably, they were not happy with his decision since he's like the best intelligence analyst on the planet. And they will definitely not be happy with us. I think I see tax audits, congressional investigations, and random FBI wiretaps for the rest of our lives."

"Oh my God," Michelle said hopelessly.

"Yeah," said Sean, with a long sigh.

ACKNOWLEDGMENTS

To Michelle for always telling me how it really is.

To Mitch Hoffman for keeping me on my creative toes.

To Michael Pietsch, Jamie Raab, Lindsey Rose, Sonya Cheuse, Emi Battaglia, Tom Maciag, Martha Otis, Karen Torres, Anthony Goff, Bob Castillo, Michele McGonigle, Kallie Shimek, and everyone at Grand Central Publishing for doing your job so well. And special thanks to David Young; your reach extends across the pond, my friend.

To Aaron and Arleen Priest, Lucy Childs Baker, Lisa Erbach Vance, Nicole James, Frances Jalet-Miller, John Richmond, and Melissa Edwards for always having my back.

To Anthony Forbes Watson, Jeremy Trevathan, Maria Rejt, Trisha Jackson, Katie James, Natasha Harding, Aimee Roche, Lee Dibble, Sophie Portas, Stuart Dwyer, Stacey Hamilton, James Long, Anna Bond, Sarah Willcox, and Geoff Duffield at Pan Macmillan for leading me to number one in the UK and for a terrific visit this past spring.

To Praveen Naidoo and his team at Pan Macmillan in Australia, a special shout-out for leading me to #1 there. Three cheers!

To Arabella Stein, Sandy Violette, and Caspian Dennis for being so bloody brilliant.

To Ron McLarty and Orlagh Cassidy for your continually outstanding audio performances.

To Steven Maat, Joop Boezeman, and the Bruna team for keeping me at the top in Holland and for your wonderful hospitality this past spring.

To all my other publishers worldwide whom I met at the London Book Fair for doing such a terrific job for me in their respective markets. It's refreshing to know that not only are books not dead, they are flourishing.

To Bob Schule for always turning the pages.

To Chuck Betack for answering my military queries.

To Jim Haggar for the very timely magazine article. It got my imagination really going.

To Dick DeiTos and Todd Sheller for giving me the behind-the-scenes tour of mighty Dulles Airport.

To Tyler Wingo, I've always liked your name. Hope you enjoy the character.

To John Cole, I hope you enjoyed your promotion.

To MK Hesse, hope you liked seeing your name in the pages.

To Kristen, Natasha, and Lynette for keeping me on the straight and narrow.

And to Laura Jorstad for a great copyediting job. Your timeline was particularly impressive!

The Target
DAVID BALDACCI

ISBN: 978-1-4472-2529-4

When revenge gets personal, the stakes get higher . . .

Government operatives Will Robie and Jessica Reel are faced with a lethal mission. An attack from North Korea looks likely as US involvement in an attempted coup is revealed, and a bond of trust has been broken at the very highest level.

Chung-cha is a young woman who was raised in the infamous Yodok Camp. It's a place where honour, emotion and compassion don't exist. Cold, calculating and highly skilled, Chung-cha has been trained to kill. And the task she has been given is to destroy the enemy at all costs.

A dangerous and deadly operation of cat and mouse plays out between East and West. But who will fall prey at the ultimate showdown when the true quarry is finally revealed . . . ?

Read on for an extract of the next book in the Will Robie series, following on from *The Innocent* and *The Hit* . . .

The men could not have looked any more tense. It was as though the weight of the world was resting on each of their shoulders.

Actually, it was.

The president of the United States sat in the seat at the end of the small table. They were in the Situation Room complex in the basement of the West Wing of the White House. Sometimes referred to as the "Woodshed," the complex was first built during President Kennedy's term after the Bay of Pigs fiasco. Kennedy no longer thought he could trust the military and wanted his own intelligence overseers who would parse the reports coming in from the Pentagon. The Truman bowling alley had been sacrificed to build the complex, which had then undergone major renovations in 2006.

During Kennedy's era a single analyst from the CIA would man the Situation Room in an unbroken twenty-hour shift, sleeping there as well. Later, the place had been expanded to include the Department of Homeland Security and the White House Chief of

Staff's office. However, the National Security Council staff ran the complex. Five "Watch Teams" comprised of thirty or so carefully vetted personnel operated the Situation Room on a 24/7 basis. Its primary goal was to keep the president and his senior staff briefed each day on important issues by allowing for instant and secure communications anywhere in the world. It even had a secure link to Air Force One in the event the president was traveling.

The Situation Room itself was large, with space for thirty or more participants and a large video screen on the wall. Mahogany had been the wood surface of choice before the renovation. Now the walls were composed mainly of "whisper" materials that protected against electronic surveillance.

But tonight the men were not in the main conference room. Nor were they in the president's briefing room. They were in a small conference room that had two video screens on the wall and a row of world-time clocks above. There were chairs for six people.

Only three of them were occupied.

The president's seat allowed him to stare directly at the video screens. To his right was Josh Potter, the national security advisor. To his left was Evan Tucker, head of the CIA.

That was all. The circle of need-to-know was minuscule. But there would be a fourth person joining them in a moment by secure video link. The staff in the Situation Room would normally have been walled off from this meeting and the coming communication. There was only one person handling the transmission. And even that person would not be privy to what was said.

The VP would normally have been part of such a meeting. However, if what they were planning went awry, he might be taking over the top spot because the president could very well be impeached. Thus they had to keep him out of the loop. It would be terrible for the country if the president had to leave office. It would be catastrophic if the VP were forced out too. The Constitution dictated that the top spot would then go to the Speaker of the House of Representatives. And no one wanted the head of what could very well be the most dysfunctional group in Washington to be suddenly running the country.

The president cleared his throat and said, "This could be momentous or it could be Armageddon."

Potter nodded, as did Tucker. The president looked at the CIA chief.

"This is rock solid, Evan?"

"Rock solid, sir. In fact, not to toot our own horn, but this is the prize for nearly three years of intelligence work performed under the most difficult conditions imaginable. It has, frankly, never been done before."

The president nodded and looked at the clocks above the screens. He checked his own watch against them and made a small adjustment to his timepiece. It looked as though he had aged five years in the last five minutes. All American presidents had to make decisions that could shake the world. In numerous ways, the demands of the position were simply beyond the ability of a mere mortal to carry them out. But the Constitution required that the position be held by one person.

He let out a long breath and said, "This had better work."

Potter said, "Agreed, sir."

"It will work," insisted Tucker. "And the world will be much better off for it." He added, "I have a professional bucket list, sir, and this is number two on it, right behind Iran. And in some ways, it should be number one."

Potter said, "Because of the nukes."

"Of course," said Tucker. "Iran wants nukes. These assholes already have them. With delivery capabilities that are inching closer and closer to our mainland. Now, if we pull this off, believe me Tehran will sit up and take notice. Maybe we kill two birds with one stone."

The president put up a hand. "I know the story, Evan. I've read all the briefings. I know what hangs in the balance."

The screen flickered and a voice came over the speaker system embedded in the wall.

"Mr. President, the transmission is ready."

The president unscrewed the top of a water bottle sitting in front of him and took a long drink. He put the bottle back down. "Do it," he said curtly.

The Target

The screen flickered once more and then came fully to life. They were staring at a man short in stature, in his sixties, with a deeply lined and tanned face. There was a rim of white near his hairline where the cap he normally wore helped to block the sun. But he was not in uniform now. He was dressed in a gray tunic with a high, stiff collar.

He stared directly at them.

Evan Tucker said, "Thank you for agreeing to communicate with us tonight, General Pak."

Pak nodded and said, in halting but clearly enunciated English, "It is good to meet, face-to-face, as it were." He smiled, showing off highly polished veneers.

The president attempted to smile back, but his heart was not in it. He knew that Pak would lose his life if exposed. But the president had a lot to lose too.

"We appreciate the level of cooperation received," he said.

Pak nodded. "Our goals are the same, Mr. President. For too long we have been isolated. It is time for us to take our seat at the world's table. We owe it to our people."

Tucker said encouragingly, "We completely agree with that assessment, General Pak."

"Details are progressing nicely," said Pak. "Then you can commence your part in this. You must send your best operatives. Even with my help, the target is a very difficult one." Pak held up a single finger. "This will be the number of opportunities we will have. No more, no less."

The president glanced at Tucker and then back at Pak. "We would send nothing less than our very best for something of this magnitude."

Potter said, "And we are sure of both the intelligence and the support?"

Pak nodded. "Absolutely sure. We have shared that with your people and they have confirmed the same."

Potter glanced at Tucker, who nodded.

"If it is discovered," said Pak. They all became riveted to him. "If it becomes discovered, I will surely lose my life. And America, your loss will be far greater."

He looked the president directly in the eye and took a few moments seemingly to compose his words carefully.

"It is why I asked for this video conference, Mr. President. I will be sacrificing not only my life, but the lives of my family as well. That is the way here, you see. So, I need your complete and absolute assurance that if we move forward, we do so together and united, no matter what might happen. You must look me in the eye and tell me this is so."

The blood seemed to drain from the face of the president. He had made many important decisions during his term, but none so stressful or potentially momentous as this one.

He didn't look at either Potter or Tucker before

answering. He kept his gaze right on Pak. "You have my word," he said in a strong, clear voice.

Pak smiled, showing off the perfect teeth again. "That is what I needed to hear. Together, then." He saluted the president, who gave a crisp one in return.

Tucker hit a button on the console in front of him and the screen went black once more.

The president let out an audible breath and sat back against the leather of his chair. He was sweating though the room was cool. He wiped a drop of moisture off his forehead. What they were proposing to do was quite clearly illegal. An impeachable offense. And unlike the other presidents impeached before him, he had no doubt the Senate would convict him.

"Into the breach rode the five hundred," the president said in barely a whisper, but both Potter and Tucker heard it and nodded in agreement.

The president leaned forward and looked squarely at Tucker.

"There is no margin for error. None. And if there is the least hint of this coming out—"

"Sir, that will not happen. This is the first time we've ever had an asset placed that high over there. There was an attempt on the leadership last year, as you know. While he was traveling on the street in the capital. But it was botched. That was from low-level internal sources and had nothing to do with us. Our strike will be quick and clean. And it will succeed."

"And you have your team in place?"

"Being assembled, and then they'll be vetted."

The president looked sharply at him. "Vetted? Who the hell are you planning to use?"

"Will Robie and Jessica Reel."

Potter sputtered, "Robie and Reel?"

"They are the absolute best we have," said Tucker. "Look what they did with Ahmadi."

Potter eyed Tucker closely. He knew every detail of that mission. Thus he knew that neither Reel nor Robie were intended to survive it.

The president said slowly, "But with Reel's background. What you allege she did. The possibility of her going—"

Tucker broke in. Normally, this would be unheard of. You let the president speak. But tonight Evan Tucker seemed to see and hear only what he wanted to.

"They are the best, sir, and the best is what we need here. As I said, with your permission, they will be vetted to ensure that their performance will be at the highest level. However, if they fail the vetting I have another team, nearly as good, and certainly up to the task of performing the mission. But the clear preference is not the B Team."

Potter said, "Why not simply deploy the backup team? Then this vetting process becomes unnecessary."

Tucker looked at the president. "We really need to do it this way, sir, for a number of reasons. Reasons which I'm sure you can readily see."

The Target

Tucker had prepared for this exact moment for weeks. He had studied the president's history, his time as commander-in-chief, and even gotten his hands on an old psychological profile of the man done while he was running for Congress many years ago. The president was smart and accomplished, but not that smart, and not that accomplished. That meant he had a chip on his shoulder. Thus he was reluctant to acknowledge that he was not always the smartest, most informed person in the room. Some would see that attribute as a strength. Tucker knew it to be a serious vulnerability ripe for exploitation.

And he was exploiting it right now.

The president nodded. "Yes, yes, I can see that."

Tucker's face remained impassive but inwardly he breathed a sigh of relief.

The president leaned forward. "I respect Robie and Reel. But again, there is no margin for error here, Evan. So you vet the hell out of them and make damn sure they are absolutely ready for this. Or you use the B Team. Are we clear?"

"Crystal," said Tucker.

Will Robie, unable to sleep, stared at the ceiling of his bedroom while the rain pounded away outside. His head was pounding even more, and it would not be over when the rain stopped. He finally rose, dressed, put on a long slicker with a hood, and set out from his apartment in Dupont Circle in Washington, D.C.

He walked for nearly an hour through the darkness. There were few people about at this hour of the morning. Unlike other major cities, D.C. did sleep. At least the part you could see. The government side, the one that existed underground and behind concrete bunkers, and in innocuous-looking low-rise buildings, never slumbered. Those people were going as hard right now as they would during the daylight hours.

Three men in their early twenties approached from the other side of the street. Robie had already seen them, sized them up, and knew what they would demand of him. There were no cops around. No witnesses. He did not have time for this. He did not have the desire for this. He turned and walked directly at them.

The Target

"If I give you some money, will you leave?" he asked the tallest of the three. This one was his size, a six-footer packing about one hundred and eighty street-hardened pounds.

The man drew back his windbreaker, revealing a black Sig nine-mil in the waistband that hung low over his hips.

"Depends on how much."

"A hundred?"

The man looked at his two comrades. "Make it a deuce and you're on your way, dude."

"I don't have a deuce."

"So you say. Then you gonna get jacked right here."

He went to draw the gun, but Robie had already taken it from his waistband and pulled down his pants at the same time. The man tripped over his fallen trousers.

The man on the right pulled a knife and then watched in amazement as Robie first disarmed him and then laid him out with three quick punches, two to the right kidney, one to the jaw. Robie added a kick to the head after the man smacked the pavement.

The third man did not move.

The tall man exclaimed, "Shit, you a ninja?"

Robie glanced down at the Sig he held. "It's not balanced properly and it's rusted. You need to take care of your weapons better or they won't perform when you want them to." He flicked the weapon over them. "How many more guns?"

The third man's hand went to his pocket.

"Drop the jacket," ordered Robie.

"It's raining and cold," the man protested.

Robie put the Sig's muzzle directly against his forehead. "Not asking again."

The jacket came off and fell into a puddle. Robie picked it up, found the Glock.

"I see the throwaways at your ankles," he said. "Out."

The throwaways were handed over. Robie balled them all up in the jacket.

He eyed the first man. "See where greed gets you? Should have taken the Benny."

"We need our guns!"

"I need them more." Robie kicked some water from the puddle into the unconscious man's face and he awoke with a start, then rose on shaky legs. He did not seem to know what was going on, and probably had concussion.

Robie flicked the gun again. "Down that way. All of you. Turn right into the alley."

The tall man suddenly looked nervous. "Hey, dude, look, we're sorry, okay? But this is our turf here. We patrol it. It's our livelihood."

"You want a livelihood? Get a real job that doesn't involve putting a gun in people's faces and taking what doesn't belong to you. Now walk. Not asking again."

They turned and marched down the street. When one of the men turned to look back, Robie clipped him in the head with the butt of the Sig. "Eyes straight.

Turn around again you get a third one to look through in the back of your head."

Robie could hear the men's breathing accelerate. Their legs were jelly. They believed they were walking to their execution.

"Walk faster," barked Robie.

They picked up their pace.

"Faster. But don't run."

The three men looked idiotic trying to go faster while still walking.

"Now run!"

The three men broke into a sprint. They turned left at the next intersection and were gone.

Robie turned and headed in the opposite direction. He ducked down an alley, found a Dumpster, and heaved the jacket and guns into it after clearing out all of the ammo. He dropped the bullets down a sewer grate.

He did not get many opportunities for peaceful moments and he did not like it when they were interrupted.

Robie continued his walk and reached the Potomac River. This had not been an idle sojourn. He had come here with a purpose.

He drew the object from the pocket of his slicker and looked down at it, running his finger along the polished surface.

It was a medal. In fact, it was the highest award that

the Central Intelligence Agency gave out for heroism in the field. Robie had earned it, together with another agent, for a mission undertaken in Syria at great personal risk. They had barely made it back alive.

In fact, it was the wish of certain people at the agency that they not make it back alive. One of those persons was Evan Tucker, and it was unlikely he was going away, because he happened to head up the agency.

The other agent who had received the award was Jessica Reel. She was the real reason Evan Tucker had not wanted them back alive. Reel had killed members of her own agency. It had been for a very good reason, but some people didn't care about that. Certainly Evan Tucker hadn't.

Robie wondered where Reel was right now. They had parted on shaky ground. Robie had given her what he had believed was his unconditional support. Yet Reel did not seem to be capable of acknowledging such a gesture. Hence the shaky parting.

He gripped the chain like a slingshot and whirled the medal around and around. He eyed the dark surface of the Potomac. It was windy; there were a few small whitecaps. He wondered how far he could hurl the highest medal of the CIA into the depths of the river that formed one boundary of the nation's capital, separating it from the commonwealth of Virginia.

The chain twirled several times in the air. But in

the end Robie didn't fling it out into the river. He returned the medal to his pocket. He wasn't sure why.

He had just started back when his phone buzzed. He took it out, glanced at the screen, and grimaced.

"Robie," he said tersely.

It was a voice he didn't recognize. "Please hold for DD Amanda Marks."

Please hold? Since when does the world's most elite clandestine agency have its personnel say, "Please hold"?

"Robie?"

The voice was crisp, sharp as a new blade, and in its undertone Robie could detect both immense confidence and a desire to prove oneself. That was a potentially deadly combination for him, because Robie would be the one doing this woman's bidding in the field while she safely watched from a computer screen thousands of miles away.

"Yes?"

"We need you in here ASAP."

"You're the new DD?"

"That's what it says on my door."

"A mission?"

"We'll talk when you get in here. Langley," she added, quite necessarily because the CIA had numerous local facilities.

"You know what happened to the last two DDs?" Robie asked.

"Just get your butt in here, Robie."

extracts reading groups
competitions books new
books discounts extracts extracts
competitions discounts
books new
events books
new reading groups
extracts
new reading groups
interviews extracts
events extracts books
discounts events
new books events events
events new interviews books extracts
discounts extracts discounts books
www.panmacmillan.com
extracts events reading groups
competitions books extracts new